A NIGHT TO REMEMBER

"Adeline," Ben whispered, "don't hold yourself back from me. I won't hurt you."

"No . . . I shouldn't be letting you—"

"But you are," he said into the curve of her shoulder. "And I shouldn't want you. But I do."

"Ben," she gasped. "Please—"

"No one will ever know you like I'm going to, Addie. You can keep the rest of the world at bay, but you're going to let me inside. You understand what's happening between us. You know nothing is going to stop it, no matter what either of us do." She moaned as he found the tender spot he had been seeking, as he brought her to the fine edge between pleasure and madness. "I want you to remember this," he said, crushing the words against her mouth. "Remember every time you think of me."

LISA KLEYPAS is a 24-year-old graduate of Wellesley College who speaks French and Spanish as well as a smattering of Russian. She became the Massachusetts Junior Miss and National Kraft Hostess of 1982 and, in 1985, she won the title of Miss Massachusetts and competed in the Miss America pageant. *Where Passion Leads; Love, Come to Me;* and *Forever My Love* are available in Onyx editions.

LISA KLEYPAS

GIVE ME TONIGHT

AN ONYX BOOK

NEW AMERICAN LIBRARY

A DIVISION OF PENGUIN BOOKS USA INC.

NAL BOOKS ARE AVAILABLE AT QUANTITY DISCOUNTS WHEN USED TO
PROMOTE PRODUCTS OR SERVICES. FOR INFORMATION PLEASE WRITE TO
PREMIUM MARKETING DIVISION, NEW AMERICAN LIBRARY, 1633 BROAD-
WAY, NEW YORK, NEW YORK 10019.

ONYX TRADEMARK REG. U.S.PAT. OFF. AND FOREIGN COUNTRIES
REGISTERED TRADEMARK—MARCA REGISTRADA
HECHO EN DRESDEN, TN., U.S.A.

SIGNET, SIGNET CLASSIC, MENTOR, ONYX, PLUME, MERIDIAN
and NAL BOOKS are published by NAL PENGUIN INC.,
1633 Broadway, New York, New York 10019

First Printing, April, 1989

1 2 3 4 5 6 7 8 9

PRINTED IN THE UNITED STATES OF AMERICA

Dedicated with love

to

Patsy Kluck
LaVonne Hampton
Billie Jones

Lost, yesterday, somewhere between sunrise and sunset, two golden hours, each set with sixty diamond minutes. No reward is offered, for they are gone forever.

—Horace Mann

1

THE DREAM NEVER CHANGED, ONLY BECAME MORE vivid each time it happened. She could recall every detail even in her waking moments. The strangeness of the images never failed to alarm her. It wasn't like Addie to think of such things . . . no, she was practical and sensible, never given to the kinds of reckless adventures her friends tried to involve her in. What would they think if they knew about the dream that returned to plague her so many nights? She would never tell a soul about it. It was a moment of madness, too personal to confide in anyone.

Her body was relaxed in slumber. Gradually she seemed to awaken, realizing that someone else was in the room, circling the bed with quiet steps. She kept her eyes closed, but her heart started to beat fast and strong. Then there was no movement in the silence, and she held her breath as she waited for a touch, a sound, a whisper. Gently the mattress depressed with the heavy weight of a man's body—a phantom lover, faceless and nameless, bent on possessing her as no one ever had. She tried to roll away from him, but he stopped her, pressing her back into the pillows. A heady masculine scent filled her nostrils, and she was gathered in hard-muscled arms, pinned underneath him, filled with his warmth.

His hands swept over her skin, circling her breasts, slipping between her thighs, and as he touched her she writhed, burning with pleasure. She begged him to stop, but he laughed softly and kept tormenting her. His mouth was hot on her neck, her breasts, her stomach. Then blinding desire coursed through her, and she wrapped her arms around him, drawing him closer, wanting him desperately. No words were exchanged between them as he made love to her, his body surging over hers like a slow, pounding surf.

Then the dream changed. Suddenly she found herself on the front porch, and the sky was heavy with the ripe darkness of midnight, and someone was standing in the street, staring at her. It was an old man, his face concealed by the shadows. She didn't know who he was or what he wanted, but he knew her. He even knew her name.

"Adeline. Adeline, where have you been?"

She was frozen with fear. She wanted him to leave, but her throat was locked and she couldn't speak. It was then that Addie always woke up, perspiring and breathless. It was so vivid . . . it had seemed real. It always did. She didn't have the nightmare too often, but sometimes the dread of it was enough to make her afraid to sleep.

Sitting up slowly, Addie wiped her forehead with the corner of the sheet and swung her legs over the side of the bed. Her head was spinning. Although she was quiet, she must have awakened Leah, who was a light sleeper.

"Addie?" came a voice from the next room. "I need my medicine."

"Be right there." She stood up and took a deep breath, feeling as if she'd run a long distance. After she administered the medicine and Leah's pain began to fade, Addie sat down on the bed and looked at her aunt with a disturbed expression. "Leah, have you ever dreamed about people you've never met, things you've never done, but somehow it all seems familiar?"

10

"I can't say I have. I only dream about things I know." Leah yawned widely. "But I don't have your imagination, Addie."

"But when it seems like it's really happening—"

"Let's talk about it in the morning. I'm tired, honey."

Reluctantly Addie nodded, giving her a brief smile before going back to her own room, knowing they wouldn't talk about it tomorrow.

Addie walked into the bedroom and set down her purse, humming along with the radio as it played "I'd Be Lost Without You." Her arrival was a welcome relief to Leah, who was permanently confined to the bed, an invalid for the past five years. Aside from the radio in the corner and the woman they had hired to stay with her occasionally, Addie was her only connection to the world outside.

They made an odd pair, a maiden aunt and her twenty-year-old niece. There were few similarities between them. Leah was from a time when women had been fussed over, protected and sheltered, kept in ignorance about matters pertaining to the intimate relationship of a husband and wife. Addie was a modern young woman who could drive an automobile and bring home a paycheck. Unlike the Gibson girls of Leah's generation, she hadn't been sheltered from hardship or knowledge. Addie knew what it was like to work. And she knew, as her friends did, not to trust in the future. They had all been taught that only here and now mattered.

To wait, save, and hope for better things was naive. To believe in nothing was the only way to be safe from disillusionment. They overdosed on sex and sophistication, until the novelty of their outrageous behavior wore off and it was commonplace. Women smoked as much as they pleased in public, and passed around flasks of strong drink under the table. They kicked their legs high as they danced the Charleston, and used rough language that once would have caused any man to blush. It was fun to be young and frivolous, fun to go to movies, listen to jazz, park in their shiny black Fords and flirt and tease their boyfriends long past midnight.

They were a hard-bitten lot, but Leah took comfort in the fact that her niece was less brittle than the rest of her friends. Addie had an understanding of responsibility, and innate compassion for others. She hadn't always been that way. As a child Addie had been willful, intractably selfish, disrespectful of Leah's authority. But a hard life had taught Addie bitter lessons that had softened her pride and gentled her spirit, turning her willfulness into an inner core of steel. Now many others drew constantly from Addie's strength: the patients she nursed at the hospital, the friends who called for her help when they needed her, and most of all Leah herself. Leah needed her more than anyone else.

The tune on the radio changed to ''Blue Skies,'' and Addie sang along with the chorus.

''You're off-key,'' Leah observed, sitting up in bed, and Addie bent over to place a smacking kiss on her forehead.

''I'm always off-key.''

''How is everything in town?''

''The same,'' Addie said matter-of-factly, shrugging. ''No work. People standing on street corners with nothing to do except chin-wag. This afternoon the line at the unemployment relief station is all the way down to the barbershop.''

Leah clicked her tongue. ''Goodness gracious.''

''Nothing interesting to tell you today. No new gossip, nothing going on. Except there's the strangest old man wandering around town.'' Addie walked over to the nightstand and picked up a spoon, flipping the bowl of it against her palm as she spoke. "I saw him outside the apothecary shop after I picked up your medicine. He looks like one of those old drovers—heavy beard, long hair, and kind of a weather-beaten face."

A tired smile crossed Leah's face. She was paler than usual and strangely listless. During the past few months her perfectly white hair had lost its brilliance, her dark-eyed liveliness had all but vanished, leaving behind a mixture of resignation and peace.

"Lots of old cowboys wandering around nowadays. Nothing strange about that."

"Yes, but he was standing outside the shop as if he was waiting for me to come out. He looked at me so hard, just staring and staring, and he didn't stop until I reached the end of the street. It gave me the strangest feeling, all creepy inside. And he must have been around seventy or eighty years old!"

Leah chuckled. "Older men always like to look at a pretty girl, honey. You know that."

"The way he looked at me made my skin crawl." Addie grimaced and reached for a green glass bottle. It was one of a large assortment of medicines on the nightstand, medicines that could not cure the relentless spreading of cancer through Leah's body but eased the pain of it. Dr. Haskin had said it was all right for her to take a dose whenever necessary. Now every hour of her day was punctuated with a spoonful of opiated syrup. Carefully Addie held a spoon up to Leah's lips and used a handkerchief to dab at a stray drop which had fallen on her chin.

"There. You'll feel better in just a minute."

"I already feel better." Leah reached for her hand. "You should be visiting with your friends instead of fussing over me all the time."

"I like your company more." Addie smiled, her dark brown eyes gleaming impishly. For all its charm, her face was not spectacular. Her cheekbones were blunt and her jawline too pronounced. However, she gave the impression of striking beauty. She had an allure no one could precisely describe, a luminous warmth that shone through her skin, a ripe intensity in the color of her eyes and honey-brown hair. Jealous women could point out the flaws in her looks, but most men considered her to be nothing less than perfect.

Addie set the spoon down on the bedside table and eyed the high stack of sensational novels filled with stories of helpless maidens, daring deeds, and villains foiled by conquering heroes. "Reading these again?" she asked, and clicked her tongue at Leah. "Are you ever going to behave?"

The gentle teasing pleased Leah, who had always prided herself on having plenty of spunk. Until the cancer had struck she had been the most active and independent woman in Sunrise. The idea of marriage, or any other claim on her freedom, had never tempted her. But she admitted it had been a blessing in disguise when Addie had come to live with her.

The child and a nominal inheritance had been left to her at the unexpected death of her sister and brother-in-law. Raising a three-year-old girl had been a responsibility that changed Leah's life, making it richer than she had ever thought possible. Now at the age of sixty, Leah seemed happy as a spinster. Addie was the only family she needed.

Although Addie had been born to Sarah and Jason Peck and brought up in North Carolina for the first three years of her life, she couldn't remember any other parent but Leah, any other home but this little town in central Texas. She was a Texan down to the marrow of her bones, had inherited the Texans' lazy way of speaking and flat, stretched-out accent, their need for open sky, their hot temperament and deep-rotted sense of honor. She had inherited the strength and backbone of the Warner family, which had risen to greatness and fallen into decay long before Addie was born.

The Warners had founded the town of Sunrise near an overland trail that was eventually replaced by miles of railroad track. Texas cattle had stamped out that trail, tough, hardy longhorns with square faces and eyes that glittered with the fire and meanness of the Mexican fighting bulls they had descended from. Twice a year the longhorns were driven up north on long trail drives to Kansas, Missouri, and Montana.

It had taken tough men to run those cattle drives, men who couldn't afford to have families, men who were willing to live in the saddle for weeks on end, breathing thick dust and eating food that had been cooked over a fire made with dried buffalo dung or cattle chips. But in spite of the hardships, there was freedom in the life they had chosen, and an irresistible challenge in taming the longhorns and the land they rode. Leah often entertained Addie with endless stories about Russell Warner, her great-grandfather, who had owned one of the largest spreads in Texas.

Now the time of cattle barons and their huge cattle outfits was over. The range was no longer free and open, it was fenced into barbed-wire pens. Everyone had a little piece of Texas. The cowboys, the life and spirit of the old system, had drifted west, or turned into homesteaders, or even turned to rustling. The clumsily sprawling acres that had once been the Sunrise Ranch were now covered with oil workers, metal fences, and oil rigs. Addie felt sorry for the old cowboys that ocasionally wandered through town, so taciturn and resigned to the fact that the only kind of life they could ever belong to had been taken away from them. Old men with no place to rest.

"See this?" Addie held up the green glass bottle and turned it in the sunlight. "The man I was telling you about—his eyes were exactly this color. Real green, not just muddy hazel. I've never seen anything like it.''

Leah shifted against her pillow, looking at her with sudden interest. ''Who is he? Did anyone mention his name?''

''Well, yes. Everyone was whispering about him. I think someone said his name was Hunter.''

''Hunter.'' Leah put her hands up to her cheeks. ''Ben Hunter?''

''That sounds about right.''

Leah seemed aghast. ''Ben Hunter. After all this time. After fifty years. I wonder why he'd come back. I wonder what for.''

''He used to live here? Did you know him?''

''No wonder he was staring at you. No wonder. You're the spitting image of my Aunt Adeline. He must have thought she'd come back from the grave.'' Pale and upset, Leah reached out to the nightstand for a headache powder, and Addie rushed to the water pitcher to get her something to wash it down with. ''Ben Hunter, an old man,'' Leah muttered. ''An old man. And the Warner family all split up and moved away. Who would have dreamed it back then?''

''Here, drink this.'' Addie pressed the cool glass into one of Leah's hands and sat down next to her, patting the other hand with unconscious vigor. Leah downed the powder and a few sips of water, then clasped the glass with trembling hands. ''My goodness, why are you so upset?'' Addie chided quietly, hardly knowing what to say. ''What did this Ben Hunter ever do to you? How did you know him?''

''There are so many memories. Lord have mercy, I'd never have guessed he'd live this long. He's the one, Addie. The one who killed your great-grandfather Russell.''

Addie's mouth dropped open. ''The one who—''

"The man who ruined the family and the Sunrise Ranch, and killed Grampa Warner."

"He's a murderer, and he's just walking around free as a bird? Why isn't he locked up somewhere? Why didn't they hang him for killing Russell?"

"He was too slick. He hightailed it out of town as soon as people began to realize he was the one who'd done it. And if that old man you saw today really was Ben Hunter, then it seems he was never caught."

"I'll bet it was him. He looks like the kind of man who's capable of murder."

"Is he still handsome?"

"Well . . . I guess . . . for an old man. Maybe some old woman would want him. Why? Was he handsome when he was younger?"

The best-looking man in Texas. That's not a yarn, either. He was something else. And everyone liked him, even though there were rumors he'd been a mavericker and even a rustler. Charming when he wanted to be, smart as a whip. Why, he could read and write so well that some said he'd graduated from some fancy eastern college."

"And he was just a ranch hand?"

"Well, a little more than that. Russell made him foreman just a week or two after he came here. But after he arrived, things went sour."

"What kinds of things? Problems with the cattle?"

"Much worse than that. The first spring after Ben first appeared on the doorstep, my Aunt Adeline—the one you were named after—disappeared. She was only twenty years old. Ben took her and her brother Cade to town one day, and when it came time to leave, they couldn't find her. It was like she'd vanished into thin air. The whole county looked for day and night for weeks, but they never found a trace of her. At the time no one blamed Ben, but later on people began to suspect he'd had something to do with her disappearance.

There was never any love lost between the two of them.''

''That hardly proves he did anything to make her disappear.''

''Yes, but he was the most likely suspect. And then just after fall roundup Grampa Warner was found dead in his bed, strangled.''

Though she'd heard that part of the story before, Addie's face wrinkled with disgust. ''How awful. But how did you know for certain Ben Hunter did it?''

''The cord that was used to strangle Russell was a string from Ben's guitar. He was the only one on the ranch who played the guitar. Oh, he could make the most beautiful sounds with it. Music would just float out over the house at night.'' Leah shuddered delicately. ''I was just a little girl then. I would lie in bed and listen to that music, thinking it was just like angels' songs. And there was something else they found . . . oh, yes, a button off Ben's shirt, right there by the body.''

''Sounds to me like he was guilty.''

''Everyone thought so. And he had no alibi. So he sneaked out of town in a hurry and he's never been seen or heard from since. If he'd come back before now, he'd have been dry-gulched in a minute. But now I guess he figures he's too old for anyone to want to hang him.''

''I don't know about that. People around here have long memories. I think he's bought himself a whole lot of trouble by coming back. I wonder if it really is Ben Hunter. Do you think he's sorry about killing Russell?''

''I don't know.'' Leah shook her head doubtfully.

''I wonder why he did it.''

''He's the only one who really knows. Most people think he was paid to do it. Grampa Warner had a lot of enemies. Or maybe it was . . . something about a will . . . I never understood.'' Leah sank back into the pillow, suddenly exhausted. Addie gripped her slender hand tightly as she felt it go limp. "Don't you ever go near him," Leah said breathlessly. "Don't ever. Promise me.''

"I promise I won't.''

"Oh, Addie, you look so much like her. I'm afraid of what might happen if he gets near you again.''

"Nothing would happen," Addie said, unable to understand why Leah's eyes were so feverishly bright. "What could he do? He's the one who should be afraid, not us. I hope someone tells the police about him. No matter how old he is, justice is justice, and he should pay for what he did.''

"Just stay away from him, please.''

"Shhh. I won't go near him. Don't fret." Addie waited until Leah fell into a troubled sleep. Then she stood up and walked over to the window staring outside. She remembered a leathery face the color of tobacco, and startling emerald eyes. Had that old man stared at her like that because she resembled Adeline Warner? She wondered how close the likeness might be. Never having seen any pictures of her, Addie had only Leah's assurances that she looked like Adeline. There were no photographs, no keepsakes, nothing to prove that Adeline Warner had ever existed, save a carefully inscribed name in the family Bible.

Disappeared. How could someone disappear without a trace? Every time she'd heard mention of the missing Adeline, the mystery of it had fascinated her. Today was the first time she'd ever heard about Ben Hunter having something to do with it. Unable to contain her curiosity, she pressed Leah about it when she brought in her dinner tray that night.

"Just how much am I like Adeline?''

"I've always said you're the living image of her.''

"No, I don't mean looks. I mean the way she *was*.

Do I ever act like she did, or talk the way she did? Do I like some of the same things?''

"What strange questions to be asking, Addie. What does it matter how much like her you are?''

Addie stretched out at the foot of the bed, smiling lazily. "I don't really know. Just curious."

"I guess I can tell you a few things. You're very different from Adeline Warner, honey. There was something a little wild about her, something exciting, and it didn't sit well on a girl her age. She was spoiled by everybody.'' Leah paused and her eyes became soft and distant. "Adeline was sweet as sugar when she got her own way, and that was pretty often. But there were things about her that made me uneasy. I was fascinated by Aunt Adeline, thought she was the most beautiful woman alive, even more beautiful than my mother. But she was a schemer. And people never seemed to mean as much to her as money.''

"Did people like her?''

"Goodness, yes. All the Warners doted on her. Her father was just wild about her. She was Grampa Warner's favorite child, even though Cade was his only son. And every man in the county fell in love with her sooner or later. The men went crazy for her. And Ol' Man Johnson—when he was young, he lost his head over her, never did recover from her disappearing like that. She had him in her spell, just like she had everyone else.''

"Definitely not like me,'' Addie said ruefully, and chuckled. "Now, if only I looked like Mary Pickford, no man around here would stand a chance.''

"You don't give yourself the chance, honey. The only men you see are the ones in the hospital. Veterans of the war. Crippled and tired men—it's not good that you spend all your spare time nursing and taking care of them. You should be visiting with young men your own age. Going to dances and parties instead of hiding here with me.''

''Hiding?'' Addie repeated the word indignantly. ''I am not hiding from anything. I like to spend my time with you.''

''But there are times when you could call one of the neighbors to come and stay with me a few hours. You don't have to be here all the time.''

''You're talking like it's a terrible chore to be here with you. But you're the only family I have. I owe you everything.''

''I wish you wouldn't say that.'' Leah turned her attention to the dinner tray and salted everything on the plate with a heavy hand. ''I wish I could know I've done right by you. I don't want you to wind up an old maid, Addie. You should be married and have children.''

''If the Lord intends that, he'll send the right man along—''

''Yes, but you'll be so busy taking care of me, someone else'll get him.''

Addie laughed. ''One thing's for sure. If I do end up married, it won't be to anyone I've met so far. There's no one in Sunrise I'd have as a husband. And the only new man in town is Ben Hunter.''

''Don't tease about him. He worries me. Even if you hadn't told me he was here, I'd still know something was wrong. It's like a shadow's fallen over the town.''

''Isn't that strange? I feel like something's different in the air too. Like something's waiting to happen. Now that Ben Hunter's returned, wouldn't it be funny if the old Adeline suddenly appeared after fifty years of being missing?''

''She'll never come back,'' Leah said with utter certainty.

''Why not? Do you think he killed her?''

Leah was quiet for a long time, her gaze becoming

distant. "I've thought about it for years. I think her disappearing like that bothered me more than anyone except her daddy. I never stopped wondering what happened on that day she vanished. It's haunted me all my life. I think something strange happened to her, something different from being killed or kidnapped, or running away, like most folks said. People just don't disappear like that, not without some clue about what became of them."

"So you don't think Ben Hunter killed her?"

"I don't think he knew anything about what happened to her."

Addie felt a little chill chase down her spine. "It's like a ghost story."

"There's someone I always wanted to talk to about it—one of the old cowpunchers at the Sunrise Ranch, a man by the name of Diaz. A superstitious old Mexican who had his own ideas about such things. Everyone used to love to hear his stories. He'd talk for hours about stars, magic spells, and ghosts, just about anything you could think of. Sometimes he could predict the future, and more often than not it'd come true."

Addie grinned. "How? Did he look into a crystal ball or something?"

"I don't know how. Diaz was just odd. He could make the craziest things seem natural, and since he believed in them, he could almost make you believe too. But he left the ranch for good before I could work up enough nerve to ask him what he thought about Aunt Adeline disappearing."

"That's too bad," Addie said pensively. "It would be interesting to know what he would have said."

"It sure would."

Addie went out on Friday with Bernie Coleman to see the new all-talking feature at the movie house. Mr. Turner, the theater owner, had just installed sound equipment last year, and the whole town of Sunrise went enthusiastically to see the latest pictures. *Coquette* was Mary Pickford's first talkie, and Addie had been enchanted not only by the fine acting but also by Mary's new bobbed hairstyle.

"I think I'll get my hair cut short and curly," she mused as Bernie walked her home, and he laughed, leaning close and pretending to examine her straight honey-brown hair.

"You with her curls? That's the limit."

Addie smiled at him, wrinkling her nose. "I could get a permanent wave."

"Baby, compared to you, Mary Pickford's not so hot."

"You're sweet," she said, and laughed as she slipped her hand into his. On the outside, Bernie was slick and sophisticated. He tried to seem bored by everything, tried to view the world through jaded eyes, but Addie had long ago discovered the streak of kindness in him. No matter how well he hid it from others, Addie had seen on occasion that Bernie was tenderhearted, the kind of man that couldn't stand to see a hurt animal or an unhappy child. Because of his family's money and his blond good looks, he was considered to be a handsome catch, but Addie had no designs on him. That was, perhaps, why he was so interested in her. Men always seemed to want what they couldn't have.

Bernie's hand tightened around hers as they neared her house at the end of the street. Instead of leading her to the front doorstep, he took her into the shadows beyond the glow of the porch light. "Bernie, what are you doing?" Addie questioned, giggling. "This grass is wet, and my shoes—"

"Sign off for a minute, baby." He held a finger to her lips. "I want a few seconds alone with you."

Addie bit his finger playfully. "We could go in the house. Leah's upstairs, probably asleep."

"You're not the same in the house. You change into another girl as soon as you walk through the door."

"I do?" She stared at him quizzically, more than a little surprised.

"Yes, you do. You get all dull and serious. I like you when you're dizzy and fun. You should be like this all the time."

"I can't be dizzy and fun all the time," Addie said with an impish smile. "I've got to work sometimes. I've got to worry sometimes. It's part of being an adult."

"You're the only girl I know who talks like that."

She stepped closer and put her arms around his neck, brushing her lips against his smooth cheek. "That's why you like me, slicker. I'm a novelty for you."

"This is why I like you," he said, bending his head and kissing her. The feel of his mouth on hers was pleasant. To her, their kisses were friendly gestures, casual signs of affection. To Bernie, they were promises of better things to come.

Long ago Bernie had become aware that Addie didn't intend to let him go any further than this. But that didn't stop him from trying. In his mind there were two kinds of women, the ones he respected and the ones he didn't. In a way, he rather liked Addie the way she was. But if she ever did let him go as far as he wanted with her, it would be his dream-come-true to make her into the kind of woman he didn't respect.

"Addie," he said roughly, holding her tighter, "When are you going to say yes to me? When are you going to start living? Why don't you and I—"

"Because," she said, sighing ruefully. "Just because. Maybe I'm being a silly romantic, but I just think we should feel more for each other than this, if we were going to be closer."

"Things could be so good between us. I wouldn't ever hurt you." His voice dropped to a whisper as he pressed soft kisses on her lips. "I want to be the one to make you a woman. I know you haven't ever trusted anyone enough. But it'll be right for you and me, so damn natural and good. Addie . . ."

She twisted out of his arms with a choked laugh. "Bernie, stop. I'm not ready for that, not with anyone. I . . ." She looked around and chuckled nervously, lowering her voice. "I can't believe we're having this conversation on the front lawn. I'll bet all the neighbors are listening."

But he didn't share her amusement. He stared at her solemnly. "All I know is that something's wrong with a girl who locks herself away from life the way you do."

The accusation hurt. "I don't," she protested, more bewildered than angry. "Bernie, what's wrong? Just a minute ago, we were laughing—"

"Are you holding out for marriage?" he asked bluntly. "Is that why you won't make love with me?"

'I don't want to marry anyone. And I don't want to be anyone's . . . you know. I don't feel that way with you. I like you, Bernie, but there has to be more. That doesn't mean I'm locking myself away from life."

"It does." His faced reflected his frustration. "The only people you care about in the world are your aunt and yourself, and the rest of us can go to hell."

"That's not true!"

"You don't connect with people," Bernie continued relentlessly. "You're in your own private world, and the only one you let in is Leah. But when she's gone, there won't be anyone for you. You've cut us all out. You won't give and you won't take."

"Stop it!" Suddenly the things he said were unbearable. She hated him for telling her, even if he was right. "I don't want to hear any more. And I don't want to see you again."

"If this is all I'll ever get from you, the feeling is mutual, baby."

Addie backed away from him and fled up the steps, her eyes watering. In the morning, all she said to Leah about the date was that she and Bernie were finished. Leah was sensitive enough to keep from asking questions, seeming to understand what had happened without being told.

Over the next few days Addie didn't have time to think about Bernie. She was too busy taking care of Leah. There was no way to deny that time was catching up to Leah very quickly. It would not be held off much longer, not by medicine or prayers, not even by Leah's will to live. Daily the older woman was growing weaker and less interested in what was going on around her. Although this end was what Doc Haskin had led her to expect, Addie was moved by fear and helpless frustration to send for him.

The elderly doctor did nothing but sit by Leah's bed and talk to her quietly, his presence temporarily banishing her confusion and dullness of spirit. The sight of her aunt's feeble smile sent Addie's spirits soaring, which made it that much more difficult to bear what Doc Haskin said to her after he had left Leah's room.

"Not much more time, Addie."

"But . . . she's going to hold on a little longer. She's already looking better—"

"She's accepted what's going to happen," he said in his kindly way, his face as brown and wrinkled as a nutshell, creased with sympathy. A shock of silver hair fell over his brow as he looked down at her. "You'd better try to do the same. Help her go easy. Don't fight it."

"Don't fight it? Don't . . . God in heaven, what are

you saying? Don't you have anything that can help her? Some stronger medicine or—''

''I won't give you a lecture, my girl. I can't tell you anything about her you don't already know. All I can say is, it's going to be soon, and you should get ready for it.''

Stricken, she turned away from him and tried to stifle the choking feeling that had risen in her throat. It was panic she was holding back, a primitive panic that would not be eased with any words of kindness. She felt Doc's frail hand on her shoulder, and heard his words as if he were standing far away from her.

''We've each got our time to live out on this earth, child. Some have more than others, but we all know when it's over. Leah's led the best life she could, and the Lord knows that. There's nothing for her to be afraid of, and nothing for you to do but follow her example. You've got the rest of your time to get through.''

Addie struggled to explain the terrible suspicion lurking in her heart. ''Not without her. I'm afraid . . .''

''Afraid of her dying?''

''Y-yes. Oh, not about what'll happen to her . . . I know she's going to a better place, where there'll be no pain or . . . but without her, there's no reason for *me* to be here.''

''Nonsense. Absolute nonsense. You're an important part of Sunrise. You belong here just as much as everyone else does.''

''Yes,'' she whispered, biting back the burning words: *I don't feel that way. I don't belong.* She couldn't say it out loud. Ducking her head, she let herself cry, and Doc Haskin left her with a brief pat on the shoulder.

Addie could not fall asleep that night. Perhaps it was the pattering rain and claps of thunder, perhaps the gnawing worries about Leah, but she could barely keep her eyes closed. She jumped up and went to the next room to check on Leah every few minutes. There was an almost imperceptible shifting of her body, a restless twitching of her hands. Addie stared down at the white fingers plucking at the bedspread, and she put her hand over Leah's, hoping to calm it. *So cold. Her skin feels cold.*

Mechanically she straightened the covers and tucked them more tightly around Leah's shoulders. As she walked back to her room, Addie shivered. She felt strange tonight, light-headed, her heart beating rapidly, her very soul trembling with an unfamiliar emotion. She prayed feverishly, with words childlike in their simplicity. Please bless Leah. Please take her pain away. Help me to be brave. Help me to know what to do.

After minutes of kneeling by the bed with her hands clasped, Addie discovered the right side of her face was flattened against the mattress. She had nearly fallen asleep. One more check on Leah and she'd be able to nod off. Groggily she staggered up and went into the next room once more, standing by the bed. Leah was utterly still. The twitching had stopped.

"Leah? Are you all right?"

She touched Leah's hand. Waxen, still. Addie had seen that look before in the hospital. Her mind knew what it meant, but her heart denied it desperately. She needed Leah. Leah was her family, her responsibility, her comforter. With dreadful reluctance Addie circled her fingers around the boneless wrist, searching for a pulse. There was no throbbing there, nothing. She was dead.

"Oh, no. Oh, no." Slowly she backed away from the bed, unable to believe Leah was finally gone. The blow of it was worse than she had feared. Greater than the pain was the emptiness of knowing she would never talk to Leah again or be able to run to her for comfort.

The walls around her seemed to turn into the sides of a tomb. Panicking, Addie fled down the stairs and to the front door, fumbling with the knob and gulping back her sobs as it refused to turn. She tightened her grip on it and tried again, and then the door was opening and she was outside.

Holding on to one of the front-porch columns, she was drenched by sheets of cold rain. Her nightgown was heavy as it clung to her body. Since the house sat just on the edge of Sunrise, Addie could see the town stretched out before her, the outlines of buildings and automobiles, the shine of wet pavement and the tiny distant figures of couples crossing the street. She leaned against the scratchy wooden post, feeling the coldness of the rain on her face. "Leah," she said, and her eyes brimmed with salty tears. "Oh, Leah."

Then slowly Addie became aware that someone was near, watching her. She had felt that gaze on her before, she recognized the chilling touch of it. She opened her eyes to look at him. Old Ben Hunter. He was standing in the street about ten feet away, his iron-gray hair plastered to his head and dripping with water. In her shock, she didn't question how he had come to be there.

"Adeline. Adeline, where have you been?"

Addie shuddered. *The dream,* she thought. Standing with her arms wrapped around a post for support, she stared at the old man while the wind whipped against her face. The taste of grief was bitter in her mouth, the salt of tears fresh on her lips.

"There's no reason to come back." Her voice shook violently. "No Warners are left. What do you want?"

He seemed confused by her anger.

"Murderer," she whispered. "I hope you suffered

for what you did to the Warners. I would've made you pay back then, if I'd been around fifty years ago.''

It seemed that he tried to speak, but no words would escape. Suddenly Addie knew what he wanted to say, she could see the thought in his mind as if it were her thought too, and her face whitened with fear.

But you were around, Adeline. You were there.

Paralyzed, she gripped the post and tried to say a prayer. Far down the street she could see people rushing through the storm from one building to another, dark shadow figures that became so blurred she couldn't tell how many there were. Addie was disoriented. The ground tilted and came up to meet her, and she could hear her own cry as she fell. The sound echoed through the darkness, a gentle darkness that swept over her in an inexorable tide. There was no fear or pain, only confusion. She could feel the world slipping away from her, leaving her in a dark void. Thoughts she didn't understand raced through her mind, thoughts that were not her own.

What have I left behind?

I didn't die . . . Leah . . .

Adeline, where have you been?

''Adeline, where have you been?'' A boy's voice pierced through the darkness, waking her none too gently. ''We've been looking for you everywhere. This really gets me! You were supposed to meet us two hours ago in front of the general store, and instead you decide to disappear. You're lucky I found you before Ben did! He's hit the roof about this, no kidding.''

Addie raised a limp hand to her brow and opened her eyes. There appeared to be a small crowd of people standing over her. Bright sunlight seemed to bore right through her skull. Her temples were pounding with the worst headache she'd ever had, and the boy's impatient monologue wasn't helping. She wished someone would hush him up.

"What happened?" she mumbled.

"You fainted right outside the tobacco store," the boy said with disgust.

"I . . . I'm dizzy. I'm hot—"

"Don't use the sun as an excuse. If that isn't just like a girl. Faintin' all over the place whenever they're in trouble, and then everyone has to feel sorry for 'em. No use pretendin' with me. I know a real faint when I see one, and this didn't come up to scratch."

Addie opened her eyes wider and glared at him wearily. "You are the worst-mannered boy I've ever met. Your parents should be talked to about this. Where is your mother?"

"She's your mother too, and she's at home, block-head." The boy, who could not have been over thirteen or fourteen, took hold of her arm with a surprisingly strong grasp and tried to haul her to her feet.

"Just who do you think you are?" Addie demanded, resisting his efforts to pull her up and wondering why the gawking people around them did nothing to interfere with the boy's assault on her.

"Your brother, Cade. Remember?" he inquired in tones saturated with sarcasm, and tugged her arm until she struggled to her feet and looked at him with astonishment. What an insane thing to say. Was this a joke? Or was he crazy? He was a stranger. But the sight of him was curiously familiar. With a sense of amazement, Addie realized she had seen him somewhere before. He was taller than she was, sturdy-limbed, glowing with the pent-up energy of an adolescent boy. Cade, if that was his name, was a handsome youth with shiny gold-brown hair and rich brown eyes. The shape of his face, the curve of his mouth, the tilt of his head . . . she knew it all.

31

"Y—you look like me," she stammered, and he grunted.

"Yeah. My bad luck. Now, come on. We gotta leave."

"But Leah . . ." Addie started, and despite her bewilderment, she felt her eyes sting with remembered grief. "Leah—"

"What are you talking about? Leah's at home. What are you cryin' for?" Immediately the boy's voice softened. "Adeline, don't start leakin' all over the place. I'll handle Ben, if that's what you're worried about. He's got every right to be mad, but I won't let him yell atcha."

Only half-hearing his words, Addie turned to look at the end of the street, wondering how she had gotten from her front porch to the middle of town. And then her heart stopped, and her grief over Leah's death was swamped by a wave of shock. The house was gone. The house Leah had brought her up in had disappeared. There was only empty space where it had once been.

"What's happened?" She put her hands over her chest to slow down the violent thunder of her heart. Nightmare. She was still in a nightmare. Her eyes wandered swiftly over the scene, searching for familiar things, finding only a trace here and there of the Sunrise she had known. Even the air smelled different. The paved street was a dirt road now, gouged with deep holes and thousands of hoofprints. The shiny Ford automobiles had disappeared, and there were only horses and wagons lined up in front of the wooden-plank sidewalk.

The sedate little stores were gone, and . . . why, the whole street was practically nothing but saloons. Saloons! What about Prohibition? Had they just decided to ignore the law? No electric signs, no movie palace, no bakery, no strings of telephone wires along the street. Sunrise was nothing but gaudy painted signs and rickety storefronts . . . and the people . . . Good Lord, the people! It looked like they were all at a costume party.

The few women she could see had piled their hair on their head in heavy masses, and they wore long, cumbersome dresses with high necks and tight collars. There were cowboys everywhere, wearing sugar-loaf sombreros or low-crowned plainsman hats, soiled bandannas, heavy batwing chaps, spurs with filed-down rowels, boots with arches and pointed toes. Heavily bearded and mustached cowboys, weighted down with firearms and pouches of ammunition.

A half-circle of them stood right around Cade and Addie, hats held respectfully in their hands, staring at Addie with fascination, respect, and something approaching awe. The strangeness of the scene frightened her. She had lost her mind, or they were all playing a trick on her.

Let me wake up soon, oh, please let me wake up. I'll face anything rather than this. Just let me wake up so I know I'm not crazy.

Why are you lookin' around like that?'' Cade demanded, taking her elbow and pulling her off the plank sidewalk into the street. He had to shoulder through the group of cowboys, who muttered expressions of concern until he said impatiently, '' 'S all right. She didn't really faint. She's just fine.''

Numbly Addie allowed him to lead her down the street. ''We gotta find Ben,'' Cade said, sighing heavily. ''He's been lookin' for you at this end of town. God Almighty, he must be hoppin' mad by now.''

''Cade . . .'' There was only one Cade she had ever heard of, and that was Leah's uncle. But Leah's uncle was an elderly gentleman who lived in the Northeast, a respected lawyer. Surely he had no connection with this impudent boy. She spike the name that was on the tip of her tongue, deciding at this point that there was nothing to lose. "Cade Warner?"

"Yes, Adeline Warner?"

No. No! I'm Addie Peck. Adeline Warner was my great-aunt—she disappeared fifty years ago. Oh, yes, I'm dreaming. But was Ben Hunter a dream too? Was Leah's death a dream?

"Where are we going?" she managed to ask, stifling a distraught laugh as she realized that she, too, was dressed in the confining clothes she had seen on the other women. She was swathed in a pink dress that pinched tightly at the waist. It was hard to walk in such heavy skirts.

"We're going home as soon as we can find Ben. Why were you two hours late? Flirting again? I don't mind you kickin' up your heels, but don't do it on my time again. I had stuff to do today!"

"I wasn't flirting."

"Then what were you doing?"

"I don't know. I don't know what's going on." Her voice cracked. Cade looked at her sharply, seeming to notice for the first time how pale she was.

"You feelin' all right, Adeline?" But she had no time to reply, because they came to a halt in front of a cast-iron-and-wood buggy with wicker seats, fancier than the other vehicles on the street, and Cade was helping her into it. "Just sit here while I go look for him," he directed. The wicker seat creaked as she settled into it, and she gripped the side of the buggy, hanging her head and breathing deeply. "I'll be back in a minute," Cade said.

As he left, she concentrated on fighting the nausea that was building inside of her. There was a distinct possibility she was going to lose the battle. *Nightmare or not, I'm about to be sick.* She looked around, and it seemed that everyone was staring at her. *No, I can't. I can't let myself give in to it.* By sheer force of will,

Addie managed to conquer the waves that had started to rise from her stomach.

"Here she is." She heard Cade's purposely cheerful voice and lifted her head to look at him. Her heart stopped beating as she saw a dark figure swing into the buggy seat and take the reins in one hand. She couldn't move, she was frozen right in her place as the man turned back to pin her with cold green eyes.

Oh, God, it's him, she thought, terrified. *But it can't be. He's supposed to be an old man.*

"Have a nice time?" he asked softly, not seeming to expect an answer.

Her throat clenched with fear. He continued to give her that hard stare while the low brim of his hat shadowed part of his face, and she went cold all over as she realized that this was Ben Hunter. Ben Hunter, decades ago. She had seen those same green eyes in the face of an old man with long gray hair and a stringy frame. But this man had short-cropped black hair and eyebrows as dark as coal, and broad shoulders that strained the seams of his cotton shirt. He was clean-shaven, young, hard-faced.

Murderer.

"I think she feels kinda sick," Cade volunteered, hopping into the back beside Addie.

"Good."

Ben turned around and flicked the reins, and the buggy started forward with a jerk. Addie clung to her seat, her eyes dilated as she stared at him, just barely noticing they were heading out of town. Several minutes of strained silence followed, while Addie's shock increased with each rotation of the buggy wheels.

Questions flew through her mind too quickly to be cataloged. She watched the countryside roll by, land that was raw and fresh, unrefined. All the houses that should have been there were gone. Sunrise was a little outcrop in the middle of endless miles of land, prairie land that spread wide and unbroken toward the west, whispering quietly beneath the sound of the horse's hooves and the buggy wheels.

Where were the buildings, the roads, the automobiles, the people? She clasped her shaking hands together, wondering what was happening to her, and suddenly Cade took one of her hands. Startled, she let her fingers remain motionless in his, and she felt the warm clasp tighten.

Looking up quickly, she met his lively brown eyes, the same color as her own. There was casual affection in his expression, as if she truly were his sister. How could he look at her that way? He didn't even know her.

"Blockhead," Cade whispered, and smiled before giving her a poke in the ribs. She didn't even flinch, but continued to stare at him. Ben must have heard the whisper, for he turned around and looked at Addie in a way that sent a chill down her back.

"Not that it matters much to you, but I'd planned on being back at the ranch by now." Ben's voice was taut with exasperation.

"I'm sorry," she whispered, dry-mouthed.

"I figure looking for you for two hours entitles me to know what the hell you were doing."

"I . . . I don't know."

"You don't know," he repeated, his temper exploding. "Of course you don't know. God knows what possessed me to think you did."

"Ben, she's not feeling good," Cade protested, keeping Addie's hand securely in his. Although he was just a boy, she felt a surprising amount of comfort in his presence.

"It's all right," she said to Cade, keeping her voice steady with an effort. "I don't care what he says."

"Typical," Ben snapped, turning his attention back to the dirt road in front of them. "You don't care about what anyone says. In fact, I can list on one hand the things you do care about. Dances. Dresses. Men. That's fine, since in the whole scheme of things it doesn't matter what you choose to do with your time. But I draw the line at the point when you start to interfere with the running of the ranch, infringing on my time and causing delays for everyone else. Did it ever occur to you that your closets full of clothes and your other extravagances are related to the amount of work that gets done on the ranch?''

''Ben,'' Cade said, ''you know nobody can understand you when you get started with all those fancy words—''

''I understood everything he said,'' Addie interrupted, her terror lessening. Whether this was a dream or not, Ben Hunter was only a man. A dirty, cowardly man who had brutally killed her great-grandfather. She stared at him with loathing in her eyes. ''I also understand that he has no right to give me a lecture about anything, not after what he's done.''

''What are you talking about?'' Ben's sharp glance silenced her immediately. Her spurt of bravery dried up, and she was speechless for several minutes, cowed into silence.

As they came to the edge of Warner land, a line rider rode up to greet them, and Ben exchanged a curt nod with him. Despite his mustache, the rider appeared to be only a few years older than Cade, and utterly bored with his duty of chasing down strays and keeping neighbors' animals off Warner property. Sooner or later every cowboy had to take his turn at line riding.

''How's everything?'' Ben asked, tilting his hat back on his head and regarding the boy quizzically.

''Pretty good. Branded a calf today, one somebody missed durin' roundup.''

''One of ours?''

The boy shrugged. "Most likely it strayed from the Double Bar. But they took one of ours last fall." Respectfully he touched the brim of his hat as he looked at Addie. "Miss Adeline."

As the cowboy rode off, Addie stared at Cade with wide eyes. "But putting the Sunrise brand on someone else's calf is stealing."

"Aw, Addie, you know an unbranded calf is fair game. Besides, you heard him. They took one of ours last fall. Now everything's fair."

"It isn't right—" she persisted, and Ben cut her off tersely.

"At the very least, it'll teach the Double Bar to keep their strays off our home grass."

"I'd expect those kinds of standards from you," she replied stiffly. "But to teach a boy Cade's age that stealing is right . . . it's criminal."

Suddenly Ben smiled. There was a malicious glint in his eyes as he glanced at her over his shoulder. "Just how do you think your father got his start in the ranching business, Miss Adeline?"

"My father?" she repeated, and flushed with confusion.

But I don't have a father.

"Yes, your father. He started out by working for another rancher and collecting his own little herd of rustled strays. Ask him sometime. He'll admit it without a second thought."

Cade seemed unruffled by the information. Apparently he had heard it before. What kind of men were these? What kind of morality was this? Addie averted her eyes from both of them, wondering at the easy way in which Ben had cut her down. Apparently he had known her long enough to have developed a distinct dislike for her, enough to feel comfortable in mocking her. In his eyes there was no respect for her, nothing but coldness.

38

The buggy traveled parallel to a gentle stream, and it was miles before any buildings were in sight. The main house was a three-story structure that dominated the center of the Sunrise Ranch, an elegant building with fluttering white lace curtains and a wide porch. To the right there were a corral and a large bunkhouse, to the left a considerable number of buildings and sheds. It looked like a small town in itself. The scene was liberally dotted with hired hands, horses, and a frisky dog. The sounds of woodchopping and tuneless singing mingled with the shouts and noises that accompanied the busting of a pony in the corral.

The buggy stopped in front of the main house, and Addie was motionless, paralyzed with bewilderment. What now? What was expected of her? Cade hopped out and stood by the side of the vehicle to help her down.

"Come on and get out," he said, grinning at her encouragingly. "You know Daddy won't be mad for long. Not at you. Hurry up, I've got things to do."

"Stay with me," she said quickly, clinging to his arm after she had descended from the buggy. His was the only friendly face she saw, and she would rather have him near her than be alone.

Cade pulled his arm away from her, however, and started off toward the corral. "Let Ben take you in," he said over his shoulder. "I think that's what he plans to do anyway."

"Damn right it is," came Ben's hard voice behind her, and before Addie could flinch away, her upper arm was compressed in a steely grip. "Let's go have a talk with Daddy, Miss Adeline."

She shuddered at his touch, finding it repulsive, but he propelled her up the steps and across the porch with an easy twist of his hand. Addie could sense his considerable strength as he ignored her attempt to resist him. He opened the front door without knocking, and she caught a glimpse of walnut paneling and rich velvet-pile carpets before she was pulled to a room that appeared to be the library. There was a combination of masculine scents in the room, saddle oil and cigar smoke, leather and wood.

"Russ? Ben said, releasing Addie's arm as the man in the library turned to face them. "I thought you'd be here."

"You're back late," Russell Warner replied. He looked like an older version of Cade, though his honey-brown hair was frosted with silver and he had a thick, close-trimmed mustache. He was a robust man with healthy coloring and a well-groomed appearance. Some men wore their authority naturally, as if its weight made no impression on their shoulders. Russell was of that class. He was a man who had been born to lead others. As he looked at Addie fondly, his eyes twinkled. "Looks like my baby's led someone on a wild-goose chase again." There was a painful thumping in Addie's chest as she stared at him.

This is my great-grandfather. And he thinks I'm his daughter. They all think I'm Adeline Warner.

She heard nothing of the conversation between the two men, just stood there quietly, exhausted from emotional strain, sick of the nightmare, and wanting nothing more than for it to be over. Then she was aware that Russell was speaking to her.

"Adeline," he said gravely, "this time you went too far. This is serious, honey, and it's time to do some explainin'. Cade and Ben thought somethin' happened to you. What were you doing in town that made you so late?"

She stared at him dumbly, shaking her head. Should she make up something? Play along with this?

A new voice entered the conversation, a feminine voice. "What's going on, Russ?"

Addie spun around to see a woman in the doorway,

a slender woman in her late forties. From having seen old pictures of her before, Addie knew that it was May Warner, Russell's wife. She had cornflower-blue eyes and an oval-shaped face that wore a tender expression. Her smooth blond hair was braided in an intricate knot at the nape of her neck, and covered with an indoor cap of lace fastened with a coquettish spray of flowers at the side.

As the woman slipped an arm around her shoulders, Addie could detect the sweet fragrance of vanilla that clung to her, as well as the fresh starch in her linen morning-collar. The fanlike sweep of her skirts brushed against Addie's as she squeezed her shoulders affectionately.

"Why is everyone bein' so dreadfully serious?" May asked, and her laughing gaze seemed to soften Russell's countenance. Ben's expression didn't change.

"We're waiting for Adeline to explain why she was two hours late in town," Russell said, much more casual than before. "She cost us a lot of time and worry, May, and she's got to learn there's a time for games and a time for gettin' work done. But right now I want to know what she was doin' while Ben and Cade couldn't find her."

Three pairs of eyes rested on Addie's face. She could hear a nearby clock ticking in the silence. She felt like a cornered animal. "I don't know," she said, her voice wavering. "I can't tell you because I don't know. The last thing I remember is being with Leah." Her voice broke as she tried to continue. It was all too much. She was too tired to face this any longer. "Leah . . ." The tension inside her snapped and she jerked her hand up over her eyes and she burst into tears.

She was vaguely aware of Ben leaving the room in disgust, and Russell's anxious promises of pocket money and bonbons to keep her from crying, and above all, May's soothing.

"I'm sorry," Addie choked, wiping her wet nose against the lacy frill of her sleeve, taking a handkerchief as it was thrust into her hand. "I'm sorry. I don't know what's happened. What have I done? Do you understand any of it?"

"She's overwrought. She just needs to rest," Addie heard May say, and she seized gratefully on the idea.

"Yes. I need to be alone. I can't think—"

"Everything's fine, sugar. Mama's here. Come upstairs with me."

Submitting to the gentle coaxing, Addie started to follow her out of the room, her head downbent. She saw a calendar on the small desk by the door.

"Wait," she said, breathing in shallow gasps as she saw the black numbers printed on the ivory paper. "Wait, She was afraid to look. But she had to. Even if it was a dream, she had to find out. The year. What was the year?

May paused in the doorway, while Russell stood behind her, both of them plainly confused by her behavior. Addie moved closer to the desk and ripped the top sheet off the calendar, holding it with hands that trembled so badly she could hardly read.

1880

The room reeled around her for one dizzying moment. "Is this right?" she asked hoarsely, extending it to May, who took it and read the date in an interested manner that was clearly intended to humor her. Addie waited with tightly clasped hands.

"No, it isn't right, sugar," May finally said. "This was two days ago." She walked over to the calendar and ripped off another sheet, crumpling it neatly and dropping it into the basket next to the desk. "There," she said with satisfaction. "Now we're right back on schedule."

"Eighteen-eighty," Addie breathed. *Fifty years ago. That's impossible. I can't have gone back fifty years.*

"Last time I checked, it was," May said cheerfully. "Now, come on upstairs, Adeline. You have no idea how tired you look. I've never seen you like this."

1880. Oh, yes, this was a dream. It could be nothing else. Numbly Addie followed her to a bedroom with fringe-trimmed curtains and elaborate flowered wallpaper. A brass bed with embroidered sheets and downy pillows was positioned between two windows. On the nightstand was a small crystal vase filled with wildflowers.

"Take a little nap, sugar," May said, pushing her gently toward the bed. "You're just tired, that's all. You can have a nice rest for a couple of hours. I'll have Leah wake you up."

Addie's pulse quickened. Leah was here? That couldn't be true. "I'd like to see her now."

"Rest first."

In the face of May's gentle insistence there was nothing Addie could do but take off her shoes and lie down on the bed. Her head sank into the softness of a pillow, and she turned her face into it with a grateful sigh, closing her burning eyes.

"Thank you," she mumbled. "Thank you so much."

"Feel better now?"

"Yes. Yes, I feel better. I just want to fall asleep. And never wake up."

"I'll go downstairs and have a talk with your daddy. We won't talk about this afternoon anymore, not if it makes you upset. You know he'd never do anything to make you cry. Why, he'd get you the sun and moon if you wanted them."

"I don't want the sun and moon." Addie whispered, barely aware of the light hand that smoothed her hair repeatedly. "I want to be back where I belong."

"You are where you belong, sugar. You are."

* * *

"Adeline? Aunt Adeline, it's time to wake up." A loud whisper broke into her slumber.

Addie awakened with a start, sitting up and squinting through the room. The walls were tinged a peach color as the setting sun cast its light through the windows. "Who is it?" she asked thickly, pushing her disheveled hair away from her face.

There was the sound of a little girl's giggle. "It's me. Grandma told me to wake you."

Addie blinked to clear her vision. A child approached the bed, a skinny girl with gray eyes and long black braids.

"Leah," she said hoarsely. "Is that you?"

Another shy giggle. " 'Course it is."

"Come here. Come closer." The child hopped onto the bed beside her, and Addie touched one of her braids with a trembling hand. Her heart ached and her lips pulled at the corners with an unsteady smile. *Good Lord, it is her. Leah!* She had never been so stunned in her life. The woman who had raised her, disciplined her, fed and clothed her, given her pocket money, was standing right in front of her. But she was a little girl. She could see Leah in this child's face, could hear Leah in her voice. "Yes, it is you. I can see it. Tell me how old you are."

"I'm ten. My birthday was last month. Don't you remember?"

"No. I don't remember," Addie said huskily.

"Why are you crying, Aunt Adeline?"

For you. For me. Because you're here and still lost to me. "Because I love you s-so much." Giving in to a powerful urge, she put her arms around the little girl and held her tightly. It didn't make her feel any better. Uncomfortable and bashful, Leah tolerated the embrace for only a few seconds before making a move to

44

pull away. Immediately Addie let go and wiped her eyes.

"We're having fried chicken for dinner," Leah said. "Your dress is all dirty. Are you gonna change?"

Addie shook her head slowly, wondering when all of this would end.

"Aren't you even gonna fix your hair?"

"M-maybe I should." Sitting on the edge of the bed, Addie jerked on her shoes. There was an ivory-backed brush on the painted dresser, and she pulled it through her hair after plucking the pins from the tangled mass. Same face, she noted as she looked in the mirror. Same eyes, same hair. "Leah," she said desperately, turning to face the little girl, "do I look the same to you as I always have? Is there anything different about me? Anything at all?"

Leah seemed puzzled by the question. "No. Nothin' is different. Do you want something to be?"

"I'm not sure." Addie faced the mirror again and brushed until her hair was smooth. She couldn't manage any styles as elaborate as those she had seen that day. Using a few hairpins, she pulled the front locks away from her face and let the rest fall down her back. After smoothing her bangs, she set the brush down and squared her shoulders. "I'm ready to go down now."

"Like that?"

"Yes. Is there anything wrong?"

"I guess not."

As they went downstairs, Addie noticed how beautiful the house was. The furniture was polished and elegant, draped with lace table covers and embroidered tidies for all the chairs and sofas. The curtains were made of expensive coarse linen in shades of chocolate brown and Turkish red, while the carpets were boot-heel deep. The appetizing smells of food and coffee wafted through the air, awakening Addie's appetite and reminding her she hadn't eaten in a long time.

"There aren't going to be any leftovers when I get through with dinner," she said, aware that her stomach was beginning to growl insistently.

Leah wrinkled her forehead. "There aren't gonna be what?"

"Leftovers," Addie said, and as the girl continued to look confused, she realized the word wasn't familiar. "Extra food."

"Oh." Leah's brow cleared. They neared the dining room and the sound of easy conversation and clinking dishes. As they came to the doorway, all sound vanished. Everyone was staring at her. Even Cade had paused in mid-bite. The room was filled with people, most of whom seemed to be family members.

Addie's attention was drawn to a pair of icy green eyes, and she saw that Ben Hunter was seated at Russell's right hand. Ben was looking at her with subtly veiled contempt. His glance encompassed every detail of her appearance, the loose hair and flushed face, the warm and tumbled picture she presented, and a cynical smile touched his mouth. What was wrong? Why was everyone looking at her like that?

The silence deepened, and she stumbled forward to sit at the first empty chair she saw. "Don't you want to sit at your usual place, sugar?" came May's quiet voice. Addie stopped and went to the other side of the table, sinking gratefully into the chair beside May. Her appetite had vanished completely.

"Caroline, fix a plate for your sister, please," May directed, handing Addie's empty plate to a pretty blond woman across the table. Caroline . . . that was the name of Leah's mother. *Does that mean she's my sister?* Since she'd been cast in the part of Adeline Warner, it probably did. *You'll know you're really insane when all of this starts making sense to you Addie.*

"Heard you had quite a day today," Caroline said, giving Addie a teasing smile. "I also heard you're not tellin' a thing about it. Since when have you started to keep secrets from us? If it weren't for talkin' about your latest exploits, dinnertime conversations around here would be as dull as a Sunday stroll."

"It was quite a day," Addie said cautiously, her eyes darting to Ben Hunter's face. His mouth twisted sardonically before he picked up a roll and broke it apart.

She was relieved as everyone began eating again, and her tension faded a little. Her appetite came back with a vengeance as she received a plate heaped with fried chicken breasts, steaming potatoes, and string beans glistening with butter. It was difficult to eat slowly when she was this hungry, but Addie didn't want to attract any more attention to herself. As the conversation around the table resumed, May leaned over and whispered in her ear.

"You're too old to be wearin' your hair down, Adeline. It's too late to change it now, but tomorrow night I want it pinned up like always."

Addie looked at her with round eyes. Was that why everyone had acted as if she had walked in the room with her dress unbuttoned? Just because her hair was hanging down? "Was that why everyone was looking at me like that?" she whispered back, and May gave her a wry, reproving glance.

"You know the answer to that."

So that was why Ben had looked at her so contemptuously. He thought she was trying to attract attention to herself. A knot of embarrassment and resentment tightened in her chest. Addie kept her eyes on her plate for most of the meal, only looking up to risk short glances at the people around her. The heavyset man with the gentle face who was sitting next to Caroline had to be her husband. He was completely unassuming, the least dynamic of all the men. Cade was quieter around the family than he'd been with Addie. Russell liked to control the conversation, and the only one he would tolerate interruptions from was Ben. What kind of position had Adeline Warner taken in all of this? Silently Addie watched, listened, and wondered.

Since Ben Hunter was indifferent to her glances, she had the freedom of studying him unnoticed. He was not handsome in the way Leah had led her to imagine. "Handsome" was Douglas Fairbanks or John Gilbert, with their well-polished faces and aristocratic elegance, men who looked like the prince in a fairy tale. Ben was rougher-cut than that, too swarthy to be a fairy-tale hero. The lower half of his face was shadowed with dark stubble. He needed a good shave, and it would help his looks if he weren't tanned so dark. But she had to admit he was attractive in a distinctive way. Of course there were those green eyes. And the force of his personality was powerful. He had a talent for wry understatement, and a gift for cutting honesty, as well as an immeasurably high opinion of himself.

He had the muscular build of a man accustomed to long days in the saddle, exposed to physical danger and backbreaking work. But why, when it was obvious he was educated, was he working as a ranch foreman? She knew enough about cowboys to be aware that most of them were unqualified to do anything else. Where had he come from, and why had he decided to settle here? He was hiding from someone or something. She would have bet a fortune on it.

As Russell Warner spoke at length about the ranch, all heads were turned in his direction, but Addie stared at Ben's profile instead. For the first time she began to understand the situation she was in, and she felt all the blood drain out of her face. Russell was still alive. Ben Hunter hadn't killed him yet. And she was the only one who knew what was going to happen.

2

THE SOUND OF LEAH'S *ADDIE, I NEED MY MEDICINE*
started every morning, a signal for the day to begin.
Addie lay still with her eyes closed as she waited for
that call, yawning and keeping her face buried in the
pillow. Why hadn't Leah called yet? Why hadn't—

She sat up with a wide-eyed start as if a loud alarm
had just gone off, her heart thumping at a frantic pace.
Her eyes darted around the room. She was still here.
*Another world away. What's happened to me? What's
happened to everything?*

Her surroundings were entirely different from what
she was accustomed to. The ruffly little pink bedroom
was not hers. It didn't suit her taste at all. She wanted
her own blue-and-white bedroom at home, with Leah's
painstakingly stitched needlework on the walls and the
clutter of rouge pots and lipsticks on the dresser, the
posters over her dresser—Valentino as *The Sheik* and
Mary Pickford in *My Best Girl*. She missed all of it.
She missed the familiar shape of the radio in the corner.

"Radio," she said out loud, stunned by the realization that here there would be no radios, no electric
light bulbs, no Kodak cameras or ready-made clothes.
They didn't know anything about the Great War or
Model T's, Charlie Chaplin or jazz music. Dazedly
she pondered the possibilities. She might as well have

found herself in the Dark Ages. It was that different from the world she was used to.

Flying to her closet, she flung open the door and stared at the dresses that hung there. Nothing that looked familiar. No short, jaunty skirts, no little cloche hats. She saw only long dresses, frilly blouses, and flowing skirts. The closet was overstuffed with a rainbow of garments, of shining silk, patterned batiste and thin floral-striped lawn, clouds of netting and satin roses. Obviously Adeline Warner had worn the very best money could buy. It took a minute to realize that most of the clothes were pink, in shades varying from the brightest carmine to the palest coral. "Acres of it," she said out loud, stunned as she looked from dress to dress. "Acres of *pink.*" It was a nice color, but this . . . this was a nightmare.

On the right side hung cotton and cambric dresses, simpler in design, that must have been intended for everyday use. Beautiful to look at . . . but to wear? She had a feeling that everything in that closet would be just as uncomfortable as the dress she had peeled off her body last night. Addie turned to the plump chair by the dresser to regard the soiled dress and the pile of white undergarments, and her face wrinkled with distaste. It had taken forever to get out of that mess.

Skeleton hoops, with a ladder of tapes up the front. A corset, and a cover that extended far over the hips, to which a short underskirt was fastened. It was inconceivable that a woman's body could endure being bound and compressed for so long. There were stays made of bone or metal, or something equally as painful, stitched into the tight corset. It had made deep red marks on her skin. Could she manage to get into any of these clothes without first squeezing herself in that contraption? It was doubtful.

The plainest dress she could find was a pink-and-white-striped batiste trimmed with clusters of ribbon loops. It took several minutes of trial and error to get dressed. Surveying herself down to her kid shoes, fastened at the sides with straps and buttons, and finished with bows on the toes, she grimaced at the picture she made.

When she finally appeared downstairs, Addie was relieved to discover only Caroline and May were having breakfast. They were both prim and proper in high-necked cambric dresses similar to hers. Evidently a crowd had just left, and a maid was clearing the dirty dishes from the empty places at the table.

"Good morning, Caroline," she said hesitantly.

"Glad to see you slept late. Looks like the extra rest did you a lot of good."

Addie glanced at the clock on the wall. Slept late? It was only seven o'clock. "I appreciated the extra sleep," she said slowly, and looked at the other woman seated at the table. " 'Morning, May."

"May?" the older woman repeated with a mixture of amusement and annoyance. "When did you decide to start callin' me by my first name? Only your father does that, Adeline." She looked down at the toast she was buttering daintily, her brows knitting together in a slight frown. "Ever since you got home from the young ladies' academy, you've had some odd notions."

"I'm sorry." Addie was immediately flustered. "M-Mother."

"Poor Addie," Caroline said gently, giving her a smile and patting the chair next to her. "Come sit by me. You've just got a case of the fidgets, that's all. You're like this every spring."

"Just wait until you get married and have children, Adeline," May said. "You'll be too tired to have the fidgets."

Addie went around the long table and sat next to

Caroline, feeling an odd tingle as she noticed the pregnant swell of Caroline's stomach.

"H-how are you feeling?"

"Much better, Adeline. It's real sweet of you to ask. I'm not having problems keeping my food down anymore." Caroline smiled and patted her stomach. "I know Peter wants a boy this time, but I just have a feelin' it's going to be another girl. That'll be fine for Leah. I think she'll like having a sister."

I met you once before, when I was a little girl and you were an old woman, Addie wanted to blurt out. *You're my grandmother. And that baby you're carrying is my mother.* She could hardly keep her eyes off Caroline, and she stared until the other woman frowned curiously.

"Somethin' the matter?"

"I . . . No. I just wanted to know what . . . what you're going to name the baby."

"I'm not sure," Caroline said thoughtfully. "Somethin' from the Bible. I like Bible names. If it's a boy, David. If it's a girl, Rachel. Maybe Ruth."

Rachel or Ruth. But her mother's name had been Sarah. Addie chewed her lip pensively and listened to Caroline and May talk about other possible names until breakfast arrived. Her stomach turned at the sight before her. Ham, fried potatoes, fried eggs, and hotcakes topped with a lump of melting butter. She'd never seen such an overloaded plate, except for the one she had been served the night before. Could it be that they ate like this all the time? She and Leah had found it difficult to keep their tiny kitchen stocked with basics like butter, sugar, eggs, and coffee. They had eaten meagerly. They had saved the scraps.

"I can't eat all this."

"Ain't no more than you usually have, Miss Adeline," the maid remarked matter-of-factly, and set down a pitcher of corn syrup beside Addie's plate.

"I'd rather have black coffee."

"You need to have somethin' in your stomach," May said. "You're going to the Double Bar this mornin' to go riding with Jeff Johnson, aren't you?"

Who was Jeff Johnson? Addie frowned slightly. Something Leah had once told her about Adeline Warner ran through her mind. *The men went crazy for her. And Ol' Man Johnson—when he was young, he lost his head over her. . . .*

Ol' Man Johnson had been fat, unkempt, and very rich. Could that be the same Johnson they were talking about now?

"I don't remember making any plans to see him," Addie said uncomfortably. "I don't feel like going anywhere. I don't think he'd mind, do you? I don't feel well this morning, at least not well enough to go riding with anyone—"

"You told me yesterday you had promised him," May said, and although her voice was soft, there was no mistaking the unyielding note in it. "A lady doesn't go back on her promises, Adeline, and it's not right to change your mind this late. And you know you'll have a good time once you're with him, sugar."

"You and Daddy are just hoping a romance will start up between 'em," Caroline said, laughing.

"I happen to think Jeff might make a good husband. His mother is a well-bred woman who raised him to be a gentleman—"

"And Daddy likes the thought of a daughter of his married to the man who'll inherit the Double Bar someday."

"That may be," May admitted. "But all the same, Adeline promised him, and she's got to start honoring her promises."

"Did I really tell him yes, or did I just say I would consider his invitation?" Addie asked desperately, hoping to find some way, any way, out of the coming disaster. She was a terrible rider, close to incompetent.

"You jumped all over his invitation," Caroline said dryly. "And talked about it all yesterday mornin' until you went to town."

"I've been feeling differently about things since then."

"No more arguing about it." May was determined to be firm. "You'll leave as soon as you can change into your riding clothes and get Diaz to escort you to the Double Bar. That man ought to be good for somethin' around here besides sitting on the porch and tellin' stories."

"She could ride over with Ben," Caroline suggested. "I heard Ben say he had some business over there he was going to take care of this mornin'. I don't think he's left yet."

"No!" Addie felt herself turn pale. "No, I can't do that. I'm not going with him."

"Don't be difficult, sugar," May coaxed. "I know you aren't partial to him, but—"

"I don't know why she dislikes him so much." Caroline rolled her eyes and grinned. "If I ever saw a man worth chasin', it's Ben. With that black hair and those green eyes—and those shoulders—why, I dare you to find a thing wrong with him."

Addie was left speechless. There was nothing wrong with Ben, unless you considered strangling someone with a guitar string a small character flaw.

"Adeline has no need to chase after a ranch foreman," May said, giving Caroline a stern glance. "She's going to marry just as well as you have, Caro, and that means someone with better prospects than Ben."

"Ben's got an education," Caroline pointed out mildly, immediately rebuffed. "And he works hard, from can-see to can't-see. And everyone likes him—"

"Where did he get his education?" Addie interrupted.

"He's never said exactly where, but I suspect—"

"That's enough talking about Ben," May said shortly. "You know better than to encourage your sister in that direction, Caro. Ben's young, but he's a seasoned loner. Men like him constantly have to sleep on new ground. A cowhand's just a nomad, and nothin' can change that."

"Daddy seems to think he's settled here for a while," Caroline pointed out.

"Your father and I don't always agree on such things. Now Adeline, if you're not going to eat, then run up to change."

Addie nodded, standing up from the table. *I'm going to get away from all of this. I'm going to run as far as I can, just as soon as I get a chance to be alone.* Of all the things she didn't know, including who she was, how she had come to be here, where the real Adeline Warner was, and what had happened to Leah, she knew one thing for certain. Ben Hunter was a murderer, and she didn't want to be anywhere near him.

Going back upstairs to the pink bedroom, she hunted reluctantly for some appropriate clothes, finally locating a brown riding skirt with a looped-up train, a cream-colored blouse, well-worn boots, and a flat-topped hat. Right next to the boots were three pairs of spurs with star-shaped rowels, each pair made in a different style. Picking up one of the them by the heel bank, Addie examined it closely. It was like a finely worked piece of jewelry, silver engraved with flowers and elaborate scrolls. The points of the rowels were darkened with dried blood and horse hair. A spasm of disgust crossed her face, and she set the spur down by the others.

"Adeline," came May's muffled voice through the door.

"What, M-Mama?" Good Lord, how difficult it was to call someone that.

"I told Ben you'd be goin' with him. He's saddlin' up Jessie for you. Hurry, sugar, and don't make him wait."

"After yesterday, that's the last thing I plan to do."

"That's my good girl."

Addie's heart was heavy with dread as she changed her clothes and stuck several extra pins in her hair to keep her twisted chignon in place. Wild ideas of how to avoid being with Ben raced through her mind, but none of them were even remotely plausible. Suddenly she asked herself why she was afraid of him. He wouldn't dare do anything to hurt her now, in broad daylight, with everyone knowing where they were.

Ben's way was the coward's way. He would sneak up on someone if he was of a mind to hurt him. A spurt of hatred gave her courage. She would have to stick it out. She would have to survive whatever might happen. And there was no real danger for her. If history was following in the same course as before, Ben's intention was to kill Russell, not her.

Shoving her foot into a leather boot, Addie worked it on until it was firmly in place, then did the same with the other one. As she stood up and wiggled her toes, she realized how odd it was that they fit so perfectly. No two people's feet were alike, and yet the soles of these boots were worn in the same places that her own shoes had always been. They conformed perfectly to each arch, every line of her feet. Addie walked over to the mirror and looked at herself, surprised by her own reflection.

Where was that girl with the bright red lips and flesh-colored stockings, the girl who had worn dropped-waist dresses that showed off her legs and made her look so boyishly slender? The woman in the mirror looked fussy and old-fashioned, a feminine doll with protruding breasts and a nipped-in waist. Though the riding outfit was less confining than the other clothes in the closet, she still felt helpless, bound by the starched underclothes. What she wouldn't give for the silk knickers and short skirts she was used to wearing!

It was wrong for a woman to be forced into this image, this ripe and maternal appearance, this false voluptuousness. This kind of woman was passive and appealing, an exaggeration of femininity, an object for men to admire, desire, dominate. How long could she last like this? How long before she suffocated in corsets and crinolines?

Addie went out of the house and headed for the barn, her steps slowing as she saw Ben Hunter already seated on a horse and leading another by the reins. Similar to any other experienced cowboy, Ben looked natural on a horse, comfortable and supremely confident. The chestnut mare he was leading was an unusually light color, almost golden, a high-stepping animal with plenty of spirit evident in the toss of her head and the jaunty way she moved.

She was magnificent, and to Addie, terrifying. It had been so long since she had ridden, not that she had ever been good at it, and it would take hours of practice to reacquaint herself with all that was involved. And to have to get on that horse with Ben watching . . . Her heart was thumping so fast she could feel it in every part of her body.

"You forgot your can openers," Ben said, his insolent green eyes flickering down to her boots.

She had never seen a man as handsome as he was, with the brim of his hat shading his eyes and a crisp white shirt rolled up at the sleeves, and his lithe body clad in snug-fitting Levi's with buckskin patches on the knees.

"Can open . . . oh, you mean my spurs," Addie

stammered, hating herself for being so jittery around him. "I'm not wearing them anymore. They're cruel and . . . and unnecessary."

"You told me last week you couldn't ride a horse like Jessie without them."

"Jessie and I will get along just fine without them," she muttered, walking up to the chestnut and stroking her nose. The horse tossed her head away irritably. "Be nice, Jessie. Are you going to be a good girl for me today? Are you—"

"You two can carry on a conversation later. Let's get going."

Slowly Addie walked around to the left side of the horse. It was the left side you were supposed to mount on, wasn't it? She struggled to remember some of the things she had once been told about riding. Don't let the horse know you are afraid. Let Jessie know who is master. Jessie's ears perked up as she sensed Addie approaching.

"There's a sidesaddle on her," Addie said, her stomach clenching at the sight. She had no idea how to ride sidesaddle.

"That's the kind you always use. You've insisted on it ever since the academy."

"No, I can't today. Put another kind on her. Anything else."

Ben's face hardened. "I don't have time for your games this morning. I don't have time to pander to your whims, no matter how much you enjoy giving orders. If you don't like it, complain to Daddy later. But for now, get on that horse."

"I despise you," Addie said fervently.

"That fancy private school didn't teach you much in the way of manners, did it?"

"I don't owe you an ounce of courtesy. You don't show the least bit for me. As far as I can tell, you're more insolent than a man in your position has a right to be, Mr. Hunter.''

"Mr. Hunter," he repeated, and a jeering smile flashed across his face. "So we're on formal terms now."

She threw him a scornful glance. "Were we ever on anything else?"

"I seem to remember that we were, if only for the space of five minutes. That day in the barn . . . remember, Miss Adeline? I've never seen anyone get riled so quickly, and all because I wasn't tempted by the way you throw yourself at a man—"

"I never did anything like that!" she burst out, horrified. Was he actually saying that she had tried to seduce him? "I would never throw myself at you, of all people!"

"Deny it," he said, and shrugged carelessly. "It doesn't change what happened."

"That wasn't me!"

His speculative gaze lingered on her indignant face. "Same big brown eyes, same honey-colored hair, same cute little figure. Could have sworn it was you."

Her face was cold with distaste. What a liar he was. "And you say you refused me?"

"Hard for you to accept, hmmn?"

"Someone like you would have jumped at any offer from your employer's daughter."

"Like I told you then, I have no interest in spoiled, hard-hearted little girls."

"Well I have no interest in greedy, insolent ranch hands with swelled heads."

His eyes flashed dangerously. "You're hardly in a position to fault anyone for greed, Miss Adeline."

"Why do you say that?"

"You have to ask?" His brow arched. No doubt he was silently reminding her of some past incident.

"I have nothing on you," she said brashly. "You'd do anything for a piece of this ranch."

There was a harsh silence between them as his gaze locked with hers.

"Get on the damn horse," he said softly.

Her anger gave her the strength to swing up into the saddle and hook her knee into place before she had second thoughts about what she was doing. The ground seemed miles away. Nervously Jessie danced around while Addie tried to soothe her. A thousand prayers for mercy flashed through Addie's mind. The horse was nothing but a massive bulk of muscle and tension, ready to explode out of her rider's control, and both Addie and Jessie knew it. The sidesaddle offered only precarious balance. It would be a miracle if she managed to stay on the horse.

"Good Jessie, good girl. Easy, Jessie," she murmured through stiff lips, yanking on the reins in an effort to calm the animal.

"For God's sake, whatever your problem is, don't take it out on the horse. I've never seen you so heavy-handed with her before.

Ignoring him and pulling harder on the reins, Addie somehow managed to turn the horse around, and with a jerk that nearly unbalanced her rider, Jessie shot forward. As they galloped away from the stable in a mad, out-of-control flight, Addie was aware of Ben riding parallel to her.

"What's the matter with you?" he snapped. "Slow down. You're not in a race. At this race you'll wear her out before we're halfway there."

She strained her arms with all her might as she tightened the reins, relieved when Jessie, however reluctantly, obeyed the command. They slowed to a canter and Addie worked at catching her breath. If she could just get through this morning, she promised herself, she would never ride again.

GIVE ME TONIGHT

"Why the hurry?" Ben inquired sardonically. "Can't wait to see Jeff?"

"Why do you ask in that way? What do you think about Jeff Johnson?"

"You wouldn't be interested."

"I might be." Carrying on a conversation, no matter how unpleasant, might help take her mind of the predicament she was in. "What do you think of him?"

"He's a jackass with a hot temper and a big mouth."

"Because he might not always agree with your opinions?"

"Because he has the damnedest habit of flaunting his ignorance whenever he gets the chance. He's never known what it's like to work for anything in his life. Which is why you're perfect for each other."

His words stung. "You don't know anything about me or what I've done." She thought of the hours at the hospital she had spent nursing, the backbreaking hours of carrying buckets and changing beds. The strain of pretending she was unaffected by patients' wounds, their sickness and pain. She'd always been mild and gentle with them, no matter how tired or frustrated she was. And then there were the days she had spent at home, taking in extra sewing to supplement her income when Leah's medical bills began rising. Addie could remember hunching over the sewing machine until her back ached, plying needle and thread until her eyes were sore. She had done it all without indulging too often in self-pity, but now to be accused of never having worked was unbearable.

"I asked what you thought about Jeff Johnson, not me," she said coldly. "You're jealous of him, aren't you? You wish you had all that he has."

He gave her a measuring glance. "No, ma'am. There's nothing of his I'd have on a silver platter."

Including you, was the silent implication. She looked ahead, her grip tightening on the reins. Her

61

anger must have communicated itself to Jessie, for the rhythm of her hooves began to quicken until they were galloping. Instantly Addie knew she'd lost control of the horse, and she felt a stab of panic. She jerked on the reins, putting her weight into it, but Jessie ignored the frantic signal. Addie hissed every curse she knew through her teeth.

"What are you doing?" she heard Ben demand, but she couldn't answer. She yanked the straps of leather in her hands with all her strength, and suddenly the horse stopped and reared with an angry whinny. Desperately Addie tried to cling to the ridiculous little saddle. As soon as the horse's forelegs touched the ground, she was bucked off the animals' back. She was too stunned to make a sound. For a moment she was weightless, paralyzed in anticipation of hitting the ground. Then came the hard slam of her body as she landed. Pain seared through her in a burning streak, followed by the sickening sensation of having the wind knocked out of her. Curled in a fetal position, she lay motionless, her eyes closed as she tried to recover herself.

Addie felt herself being turned over carefully, and she choked on her first breath. Ben was beside her on the ground, murmuring something in a quiet voice. There was pain all through her body, and a terrible ache in her chest. In her struggle to breathe there was nothing left but fear and a terrible sense of aloneness. Nothing was worse than being alone with pain. Her eyes slitted open, and she saw Ben's dark face above her, but she couldn't have moved had her life depended on it.

"What kind of game are you playing?" he muttered. "You could have been hurt, you little idiot."

Her throat opened with a gasp, and she was finally able to fill her lungs with air. Rapid breaths scoured her throat, and she shuddered from the burn of it. The pressure of tears built up behind her eyes, but she couldn't let herself cry, not in front of him. Shakily she covered her eyes with her palms, aware of the masculine form bent over her. Oh, for Ben of all people to see her like this . . . he would laugh at her . . . perhaps even now he was silently laughing at her misery. Embarrassment and confusion swept over her. *No more. It's not going to work. I can't pretend anymore. I can't lie anymore.* Her lips trembled as she fought against a wave of anguish.

"For God's sake," she heard Ben say roughly. And suddenly it seemed that it was not Ben with her at all, but a stranger. A stranger who pulled her into his arms and stroked her back, whispering something low and harsh. There was no passion in the way he held her, nothing but the casual comfort he might have given a frightened child.

Revolted by his touch, she tried to push him away. But his arm was a strong bar around her back, pressing until she fell against him in a soft collapse. One of his hands slid up the back of her neck and he was rubbing it with the tips of his fingers, and it felt so surprisingly good that she went still. The unshed tears faded away magically, and the pain in her chest began to subside.

Slowly she uncovered her eyes and let her arms drop by her sides as she leaned on him. *You shouldn't let him touch you,* she told herself dazedly, knowing how wrong it was, but she didn't want to move away from him. Not yet. His hands were strong but sensitive as they worked down to her shoulders. There was a brief hesitation before he let his palm drift along her spine, stroking gently.

A strange, overwhelming silence settled over them. Addie wondered why he was holding her in such a way, and why she wasn't fighting him. Of course it meant nothing. When he let her go, she would hate him just as much as she had before. But for a few moments she let herself bask in the feeling of being safe and protected. Was it really Ben Hunter holding her? He was warm and living and vital. No ghost, no demon, no shadow of the past. His arms were warm around her, his body sinewy and hard.

There was no sign of what he was thinking or feeling. His breath touched her hair in light, even gusts, while his heart beat steadily underneath her ear. The silence went on for so long that Addie knew it had to be broken. She searched for something to say, but the more she tried, the more difficult it was to think of anything. The odd panic grew until she was completely tongue-tied. It was with relief that she heard him speak.

"Are you in pain?"

"N-no." She pulled away slightly and raised a hand to her hair self-consciously. He looked down at her with those unnerving green eyes, causing her cheeks to flame. "I'm s-sorry," she stuttered, having no idea what she was apologizing for. "I couldn't breathe—"

"I know." His arms loosened and withdrew from around her, and he made a pretense of straightening his shirt collar. "It was obvious you were a little shaken up," he said tonelessly, looking around and reaching for her hat, which lay just a few feet away.

It dawned on Addie that they were both making excuses for what had happened. She accepted her hat without a sound, bending her head over it while the hot green scent of sun-warmed grass rose to her nostrils. The sun blazed on her hair, striking off golden highlights. Ben watched her covertly as she refastened the hairpins of her chignon.

She looked up then, her brown eyes wary, and Ben was startled by her tumbled appearance. He'd never seen her look anything but cool and perfect. The beginnings of a new awareness of her stirred inside him, and all his senses were awakening. To his disgust, he realized that with the slightest encouragement he would have taken whatever she cared to offer. She'd had him right where she wanted him.

But unlike before, she made no move to seduce, taunt, or tease. There was a touch of fear in her eyes, and no end of anxiety. Was it all an act? There was no way of knowing.

Addie fumbled with her hat, trying to set it on her head at the right angle, while her mind raced with worry. *I can't pretend I'm Adeline Warner anymore. I'm no good at it.* But was there any choice? There didn't appear to be. She was trapped here, and it seemed there was no going back. This was a real world, just as real as the one she had come from, and she could either thrive in it or be eaten alive. She would have to continue as Adeline Warner. There was nothing else to do, nowhere to go.

And she couldn't let herself forget, ever again, that Ben Hunter was her enemy. Addie looked at him, experiencing a shock when she met his eyes, so keen and aware. Some part of her was finally able to grasp the danger of him. Of all the disasters that could happen, the very worst would be to find herself close to him again. She moved away from him, trying to get up, and he took her hand, pulling her to her feet. Addie jerked her hand away as soon as she was able, rubbing the back of it as if to erase the grip of his fingers.

Ben shook his head slightly, his eyes locked on her face. "What's happened to you?"

She stiffened, her insides going cold. "Nothing's happened. What do you mean?"

"You've been acting strange ever since Cade found you yesterday. Your face, your expressions . . . everything's different."

No one else noticed a difference in her, not even

Russell or May. Uneasily she wondered just how perceptive he was.

"I don't feel like humoring your whims, Mr. Hunter. Nothing about me has changed."

"Then tell me this—how is it in the space of twenty-four hours that you've forgotten how to ride? Why didn't you remember about what happened between us in the stable? Why are you walking around as if you're seeing everything for the first time?"

"My father doesn't pay you to pester me with stupid questions," she snapped, and he grinned, seeming more at ease.

"That sounds like the Adeline I'm used to. And for once you're right. I don't get paid for asking you questions. I get paid for taking care of business, and that's what I'm supposed to be doing. So if you're feeling better . . ."

"I . . ." Nervously she looked at Jessie, who now stood with the reins hanging down to the ground. "I need a few more minutes."

He stood up and resettled his hat. "I've got to be at the Double Bar. Right now."

"Then go! And take Jessie with you. I don't want anything more to do with her."

"Are you serious? How the hell are you planning to get back home?"

"I'll walk back."

"Don't be a fool. That'll take you hours. No—knowing you, it'll take days." As she met his eyes defiantly, he swore, and his hands flexed as if he longed to shake her. "Of all the mulish, unreasonable, troublesome females I've ever come across . . ." In the silence which followed, he noticed the trembling of her lower lip, the residue of her reaction to all she had just gone through, and his exasperation was tempered with an emotion she couldn't quite identify.

"Adeline." He reached out with one hand, and she

froze. His thumb brushed across her lower lip in a touch so light she thought she might have imagined it. A flutter went through the center of her body, lingering in the pit of her stomach. She jerked her head back.

"Don't touch me!"

He half-smiled, shaking his head at her behavior, which clearly struck him as ridiculous. "Of all the things about you I've ever taken exception to, the one thing I could never fault was your riding. Until today you've always had a good seat and light hands. What's wrong? Is it the horse?"

Her eyes fell before his. "I can't ride sidesaddle any more."

For some reason, he didn't press for a more explicit answer. "Then don't. After today. But for the rest of the morning you'll have to put up with it."

"I can't."

"You sure as hell don't expect me to switch with you, do you?" he asked, nudging her chin upward with the edge of his forefinger. This time she didn't protest, knowing it wouldn't do any good.

"It would m-make it easier for me."

"Adeline, just think of how it would look. Me, perched on that dainty little saddle, riding up to the Double Bar to do business with Big George Johnson. I'd planned to make a few threats to him—that's the only way to get through to him. Oh, I think Big George is gonna shake in his boots today, especially when he sees me prancing up on a sidesaddle with my knee hooked around the pommel."

"Stop it." Addie found herself smiling unwillingly at the picture he painted. "I just want to know what you're going to tell Rus—my father after I get thrown again and wind up with a broken neck."

"It sounds as if you're asking for a riding lesson." Ben's amusement disappeared all too quickly, replaced by a sneer. "Imagine that. Adeline Warner needing a few pointers from little ol' me."

"You're crazy if you think I'm trying to get attention from you!"

"Then why the attempt at femme fatale?" He cast a meaningful glance at the patch of ground where they had both been.

Addie swallowed back a sharp-tongued retort, wondering if it would be more in character for her to argue with him or pretend that her fall from Jessie had been a silly feminine ruse to get his attention. He seemed inclined to believe the worst of her—why not play on his ego? Besides, she had to come up with some explanation of why she'd handled the horse so ineptly. Ben might as well think she'd fallen on purpose.

"I should have known you wouldn't be enough of a gentleman to oblige me," she murmured, peeping up at him through her lashes. There. That sounded flirtatious, and perhaps it would throw him off-balance. Let him believe this entire episode was a ploy to attract him. He'd expect nothing less from Adeline Warner.

Instead of being disconcerted, Ben was frankly amused. "The merchandise doesn't appeal to me, honey." He gave her an assessing glance. "Not that it doesn't come in a pretty package."

Oh, she absolutely detested him! "You're too kind," she said stiffly.

Suddenly he grinned, the hint of malice leaving his expression. "Why the antics this morning? Just bored, hmmm? Am I the only man left in the county who isn't head over heels in love with you?"

"Probably," she said carelessly, causing him to laugh.

"Don't try again, Adeline. It's a dangerous game. I'm nothing like the boys you like to dangle by their heartstrings."

"I'm sure you like to think so," she said disdainfully. "But you're all alike. No matter what age, you're *all* just boys. You like to play the same ridiculous games over and over again, and . . ." She closed her mouth with a snap.

"And what?" he prompted. As she remained silent, his gaze seemed to burn through her. "What do you think the difference is between a boy and a man, Adeline?"

"I wouldn't know. I have yet to meet a real man."

He gave her a jeering smile, and when he spoke, his voice was smooth and drawling, sending tremors up and down her spine. "I don't think you could recognize one, darlin'."

"A man is someone who has *principles,*" she said, enunciating the word as if it would surely be unfamiliar to him. "And the strength to stand by them. Someone who wouldn't always put himself first, others second. And also—"

"Please." He held up a hand as if in self-defense. "I'm sure it's a long list, and very entertaining. But I don't have the time."

"You'd never measure up to it anyway."

Ben chuckled. "Darlin', you're hardly an authority on the subject."

His condescension rankled. She knew more about men than he thought! Although women back in these days were raised on silly Victorian principles, she had grown up in a time that was far less prudish. Her peers had prided themselves on being modern and sophisticated about sex. They had seen plays and read books about it until they ceased to become shocked by such openness and had merely been bored by it. Although Adele had never had an affair, she was part of a generation which had come to adulthood wondering what all the commotion was about.

"I'm not as sheltered as you seem to think," she said.

"I have an idea you're not as experienced as you seem to think."

"How do *you* know? I believe you said that you resisted my . . . er, advances in the stable."

"You still can't believe I turned down your offer, can you? I had no idea how much it bothered you."

"Don't look so smug. It didn't bother me at all! I'm *thrilled* nothing happened between us. You can't imagine how . . . What are you doing?"

He took her arm in a firm grip and pulled her over to Jessie.

"Don't," Addie said, her voice changing rapidly. "I can't manage her."

"You're too rough with her. Her mouth is sensitive, and you're fixing to tear it up. You're also bumping your heel against her side, which doesn't exactly set her straight about what you want her to do."

"I admit I'm not handling her well." Stubbornly Addie turned away from the horse as Ben urged her nearer to the animal. "But the rest of the problem is the fact that that animal is mean and bad-tempered, and that's nothing you can fix."

"She just needs the right handling. Like any female." Ben rested his hand on the saddle, preventing her from slipping by him. "Now, get on."

"Stop it. I've had enough of y-your orders." The rage she felt was directed more at herself than him. She had gotten herself in this mess by not putting her foot down this morning. She should have refused to go in the first place. Now there was nothing to do but get back on the horse.

"Enough," he said, turning her around and taking her by the waist. "I don't know what inspired you to play this game—"

She managed to knock his hat off as she struggled with him. "It's not a game!"

"—but if you want to pretend you don't remember how to ride, then I'll oblige you. You want a riding lesson? I'll give you one hell of a lesson, Adeline."

Before she could say a word, he handed her the ends of the reins and lifted her up into the saddle. Instinctively she scrabbled for a secure position on the horse's back, clutching at a coarse mane, and Jessie started to fidget. Addie closed her eyes and clung tighter, knowing she was going to be thrown again. Ben swung up behind her, his powerful thighs clamping down on the mare's sides.

"She's jumping around again," Addie gasped, drawing in the reins as tightly as she could.

"Stop yanking on those," he said, sounding irritated. "You're going to bruise her mouth."

"She's trying to kill me, and you're worried about—"

"Give me the reins." He took them in one hand and slid his other arm around her midriff, pulling her against him as Jessie tried to rear on her hind legs. Addie's breath caught in her throat, and she clung blindly to the arm around her, frozen with fear. Contrary to her expectations, she didn't fall off. Ben's hold on her was hard and secure, his body perfectly balanced as he accommodated Jessie's motion with no effort at all. The mare quieted soon, sensing the futility of opposing his commands. "Turn your heel out. You're kicking her again."

She was paralyzed. "I'm just trying to stay on."

"Turn your heel out."

As soon as she realized Jessie was going to stay still, Addie let out a taut sigh and obeyed, loosening her death grip on Ben's arm. Slowly his hand slid to the front of her midriff, settling in a place perilously close to her breasts. "Now, take the reins. And keep them loose."

"S-stop talking in my ear," she said, uncomfortably aware that his murmur had produced a tickling sensation in the tops of her thighs. "And take your hand off me."

"Isn't it what you wanted?" he asked, and his hand remained where it was.

"You are the most insulting—"

"Take her around the cottonwood and back.'

"Do you mean walk or run or—"

"That depends on how much time you intend us to spend together."

Addie had had enough of his ridicule. In a flash of anger she gave Jessie a heartfelt kick in the side, hoping the mare's jerk forward would dislodge Ben. He only laughed and settled one hand on her hip. Swift as the wind, they flew toward the cottonwood tree, and Addie's eyes half-closed as the warm spring air rushed against her face.

"We're going so f-fast," she protested, her lips stiff.

"Then make her go slower. She'll do what you tell her." He sighed impatiently. "You're a hell of an actress, Adeline. I'd almost swear you didn't know how to ride this damn horse. And we both know better, don't we?"

Tentatively she increased the tension on the reins, surprised to find that Jessie obeyed the signal. "Not so hard," Ben directed, his hand covering hers to adjust her grip. Instinctively she shifted her weight in the saddle, finding a more comfortable seat. And then an unexpected feeling of ease stole over her.

"Bring her around the tree." His voice grazed the hollow behind her ear and skimmed down her spine. "Gentle. Don't pull sharply." The body of the horse leaned into the turn, and Addie found it all too natural to relax against Ben's chest. He sounded mildly exasperated as he adjusted her hold on the reins. "She's getting away from you. Slow her down. Like this. Yes."

"She doesn't want to go that way—"

"It doesn't matter what she wants. You're in control."

"Should I just—"

"Gentle. Be easy on her."

Addie's face was drawn in concentration. The rhythm of the horse's gait seemed to echo in her head, pounding, pounding on a locked door, while an elusive memory struggled to break free. Staring at the horse's fluttering mane, the land around her, the blue sky with its white clouds yawning in the distance, she searched her mind and tried to remember. Then it happened. One moment there was nothing but blankness, and in the next, a bolt of understanding burned through her. All of a sudden she knew what she was doing, as if she had remembered something she had learned long ago. But that was impossible. She had never been able to ride.

"Take her around the other way and bring her to a walk," Ben directed, and Addie discovered that the mare obeyed with just the lightest pressure on the reins. Magic. Addie gave a breathless laugh, and she could sense Ben's wry smile.

"All coming back to you?" he inquired dryly, his hand sliding upward until his thumb rested in the valley between her breasts. The heat from his palm seared through her blouse. Swallowing hard, she said nothing, concentrating on bringing Jessie to a stop.

When the sound of the mare's hooves had gone and all was still, Addie was acutely conscious of that hand, the caress of his thumb in the hollow of her bosom. "And this was all for my benefit," Ben said softly. "I had no idea it would be such an enjoyable morning. Tell me, how far in advance did you plan this? Or have

I been treated to a spontaneous performance?'' One part of her mind demanded that she struggle away from him in outrage, but she was confused and strangely weak. Not a sound escaped her lips. Her heart was thrashing in her chest, her breathing shallow. His thumb stroked the undercurve of her breast as she sat there facing away from him, and Addie was tormented by shame and pleasure as she felt her nipples harden. *What am I doing?* she wondered frantically. *Stop him!*

Ben was silent, but Addie could feel his chest rising and falling at a slightly faster rate. With horror, she felt his hand begin to move upward, and she grabbed his wrist, making a strangled sound of protest. His arm dropped away from her, and he dismounted leisurely. Then he turned around to face her, bracing his hands on either side of the saddle.

They stared at each other in silent fascination. Addie waited for him to jeer at her for the way she had let him touch her. It had been disrespectful and insolent, something she should have demanded an apology for. Ben's eyes raked over her, and he swallowed hard, the only indication that he'd been affected by her. For different reasons, they each chose to pretend it hadn't happened.

''All right now?'' Ben asked quietly. For once, there was no mockery in his gaze.

''Yes,'' she answered, nearly inaudible. ''I think I can ride her now.''

''Sure?'' he pressed, and for the first time his tone was gentle.

''Yes.''

Almost reluctantly he pulled away and strode to his horse. Addie watched him with wide eyes. She actually missed the presence of him at her back, the hard arm around her, his voice close by her ear. He had meant to taunt her, had taken liberties in order to teach her a lesson, but his closeness had had a different effect than either of them expected. Something was terribly wrong with her, to find a man she knew to be a murderer so attractive.

She tried to find excuses for herself. *It's all because of the men I'm used to. He's different from them. He has things they'll never have.* The men she'd dated had been preoccupied with the defeat that faced them daily, the unemployment, the scarcity, the lack of control. Their lives had been robbed of the security their parents and grandparents had enjoyed. Sooner or later they were forced to move to the city for work. Their women were hard and sophisticated, scornful of love, eager for excitement.

And here was Ben Hunter, the exact opposite of those weary young men. Arrogantly he had made his own place in a rough world. Life was his to tame, or at least he thought so. It had been a long time since she had met a man with Ben's confidence, his vitality. He would never be bullied by a woman, never be crushed by her scorn. *He's not used to a woman who'll stand up to him,* she thought, and that realization made her more than a little intrigued. It would be soulsatisfying to force his respect for her, to make him acknowledge that he couldn't dominate her.

His face was inscrutable again as he mounted his horse. To look at him, she would never have guessed anything out of the ordinary had happened. Self-consciously she did what she could to fix her clothes, knowing she was disheveled.

"Let's go," Ben said dryly. "I think we've kept Jeff waiting long enough, don't you?"

She nodded and applied her heels lightly to Jessie's perspiring sides. When she was assured that the mare was going to give her no more trouble, Addie cleared her throat and tried to appear as unruffled as her companion.

"Why are you going to the Double Bar?" she asked.

"Business."

"Concerning what?"

"That unbranded calf we recently acquired."

Addie couldn't hold back a triumphant smile. "The one we branded that you said was fair game? The one we stole in order to teach them to keep their strays off our land?"

"Yeah, that one. And while you're looking so self-satisfied, you should know they moved their boundary line into our territory yesterday to pay us back for it. Ripped our fence clear out of the ground."

"You're joking!"

"No, ma'am. In some territories, that's enough of an excuse to reach for a shotgun."

"What are you going to do?"

"Work out some kind of compromise with Big George. It won't be difficult. Sunrise and the Double Bar are big enough outfits to handle a few range disputes. Besides, everyone's got their eyes on this little romance between you and Jeff. The only one who likes the idea of a possible marriage more than your father is George." Ben smiled sardonically. "Neither one of the doting papas is going to do anything to stand in the way of true love."

Addie was stunned. "I'm not getting married to anyone."

He arched a dark eyebrow and smiled skeptically. "You sure managed to get a lot of people excited about the possibility."

"What if I decide we're not right for each other? What if I break things off with Jeff?"

"You do like to buy trouble for yourself, don't you? I'd say you'd better tread lightly this time. The Johnsons don't like to be toyed with. And when it comes to his son, Big George is mighty sensitive."

Addie was silent with anxiety as they crossed the border between the Sunrise Ranch and the Double Bar.

A line rider from the Double Bar rode up to greet them, his gray roan stamping as the riders stopped and exchanged greetings.

" 'Mornin'," Ben said, and the cowboy nodded, meeting his eyes with cool challenge. When range disputes had occurred, it took several days before excited tempers were calmed down. Everyone was involved in the controversy, from the bosses on down to the ranch hands.

"Your business?"

"Paying a friendly call," Ben replied.

"Just being neighborly," Addie tacked on nervously, earning a killing glance from her companion.

The line rider's eyes were admiring as they flickered over her. " 'Mornin', Miss Warner. Fine day, ain't it?"

"Just fine," she replied with an appealing smile, one which he returned without hesitation.

"You two go right on along, Miss Warner."

When they were out of earshot of the cowboy, Ben scowled at her. "There isn't a man in Texas who's safe from you."

"I wasn't flirting!"

"The only men you don't flirt with are the ones you're related to."

She longed for a way to puncture his arrogance. "I guess you know everything about me. Isn't that right, Mr. Hunter?"

"There's one thing I don't know."

Addie pretended to be shocked. "Imagine that. What could it possibly be?"

"Where you were during those two hours yesterday."

"Why do you care about that? What difference could it make to you?"

"It's a small town. Hard to stay out of sight that long. Cade and I went over that town with a fine-tooth comb, and there was no trace of you."

"Did anyone say where they had seen me last?"

He gave a short laugh. "Old Charlie Kendrick said he saw you vanish into thin air. Of course, he'd been drinking deadshot for three days straight."

"Vanish," she repeated shakily, and managed to laugh. "How ridiculous."

"Look over there." Ben was staring at an approaching rider, his eyes narrowing. "Sugar-britches couldn't wait for you."

"Is that Jeff?"

"Can't you tell who it is?"

"The sun's in my eyes."

The rider stopped beside Addie, touching the brim of his hat and flashing her a smile. She was amazed to see a strong hint of Ol' Man Johnson in his face. So it was him! How handsome he had been when he was young! His hair was the color of mahogany, and his bright blue eyes were set in a tanned face. He was built along solid lines, but husky rather than fat. He looked like a gentleman, and a one-hundred-percent charmer, if his smile was anything to judge by. As Addie met his sunny blue eyes and felt the warmth of his grin, she couldn't help smiling back.

"You're a little late," he said, without taking his eyes off Addie. "Any problems?"

"Nothing serious," Ben replied lazily. "Tell me, what kind of disposition am I likely to find your father in?"

Jeff looked at him with obvious dislike. "Same as always."

"I was afraid of that." Ben glanced in the direction Jeff had just come from. "I trust you'll see Miss Adeline back home safely?"

"It's a guarantee," Jeff replied. "Come on, Adeline."

She hesitated, looking back at Ben uncertainly. "Ben . . ."

78

"Hmmm?" There was nothing but indifference in his face.

She wanted to thank him—for what, she wasn't certain. "I . . . I'll see you at dinner, I guess," she stammered, and the corners of his mouth deepened with the trace of a smile.

"Only if you don't forget how to ride Jessie on the way back."

She glared at him. Seeing her impotent anger, Ben chuckled, clicking to his horse and riding away.

"What did he mean?" Jeff demanded, looking nettled, and Addie stared ruefully after Ben's retreating figure.

"He's just being nasty," she said. "As usual."

There was a short silence before Jeff reached over and took her free hand, lifting it to his mouth. "I missed you," he said softly. She didn't know how to reply. To her he was a stranger, but he looked at her as if they had shared many private moments together. "Good Lord, you're beautiful. More beautiful than I've ever seen you. What is it about you that makes my heart ache so much?"

Addie stared at him in wonder. *He sounds as if he's in love with me,* she thought in alarm. *Just how close have I been with him? . . . I mean, how intimate have he and Adeline been? Oh, I wish he wouldn't look at me that way!*

"Let's go to our place," he said, his blue eyes seeming to swallow her whole, and she nodded slowly, drawing her hand away from his.

"Their place" turned out to be a secluded spot near a gently rushing stream that just bordered the Sunrise Ranch. While the horses drank downstream, Addie allowed Jeff to seat her in the shade of a hardy tree.

"I was afraid you wouldn't be here this morning," he said, sitting beside her and slipping his arm around her back. Her spine stiffened at the familiar gesture, but he seemed not to notice.

"What would you have done if I hadn't been?"

"I would have ridden to the ranch and gotten you myself." Jeff smiled crookedly. "I couldn't have let another day go by without seein' you."

"Exactly how long has it been?"

"An eternity. Seven days, two hours, thirty-seven minutes."

Addie laughed, and he bent to kiss the tip of her nose. Surprised, she jerked her head back. "Are you turnin' shy on me?" he asked tenderly. "You've never been shy with me before, sweetheart." As he bent over and pressed his lips against the side of her throat, she colored and pulled away from him. For heaven's sake, what was the matter with these men? She'd been manhandled more in the past twenty-four hours than she had ever been in her life! "I should've expected you to turn skittish on me," Jeff grumbled. "You know it only makes me want you more."

"Maybe I just want to talk a little."

Immediately his blue eyes were grave. " 'Bout what? The stuff I told you about the other night?"

"I . . . I don't remember what that was."

"You . . . Oh, God's sake, Adeline. Isn't there anything you won't tease me about? If you don't want to talk about it, there won't ever have to be another word. It's enough for me to know you won't stand in the way."

Addie frowned, staring at him curiously. Was he referring to a marriage proposal? Or some kind of plan they had hatched up?

"No, I won't stand in the way," she said, hoping that would encourage him to drop some more clues.

"You think Leah understood what she heard?"

"I . . . I don't know."

"Just keep an eye on her, that's all."

"I w-will—"

"Aw, honey, don't look so worried. It's all gonna work out fine. We'll get it done in time. You trust me, don't you?"

"Yes, I . . . Jeff!"

He had taken her by the shoulders and pulled her halfway across his lap. "Enough talkin', Adeline. I'm gonna die if I wait one more second."

His mouth covered hers in a kiss that lasted for a long time. After her initial surprise, Addie lay passively in his arms, answering the pressure of his lips. *My Lord, I never dreamed I'd be kissing Ol' Man Johnson,* she thought nervously, and suddenly it was hard not to giggle. His hand slid to her breast, cupping lightly, and she tensed at the intimate touch, finding it anything but arousing. They were supposed to be familiar with each other—but she didn't know him at all, and she couldn't pretend to enjoy his roving hands. It was difficult to hide a sigh of relief when his hand slid to her waist and stayed there. At last he lifted his head and smiled down at her, apparently satisfied with her response, lackluster though it had been.

"I love you," he whispered, causing her to cringe inside. She couldn't make herself say it back. She had never told any man that she loved him, and she didn't want the first time to be a lie. Feeling horribly guilty, she tried to look at him as he looked at her.

"Oh, Jeff," she said, her voice trembling, and he didn't notice that the betraying quiver was caused by agitation, not love.

He held her silently, clasping her against his chest, and she discovered with some surprise that it was rather soothing to be held by him. How different this was from the torment and excitement she had found in Ben's arms. The hair on the back of her neck rose as she remembered Ben's mouth so close to her ear, his hand resting lightly on her body . . . Oh, how could she have let him? Now he'd never allow her to forget it.

The rest of the morning was strangely relaxing. They were quiet for long stretches of time, curled up together as they watched the gurgling stream. Although Jeff seemed to feel she belonged to him, he didn't paw her, and he wasn't heavy-handed. He kissed her often, but he was gentle with her, as if he were afraid she might break. Many times Addie would turn her face to find him staring at her raptly, apparently mesmerized. What had Adeline Warner done to cause this obsession?

"Adeline Johnson," he murmured as he held her, and she jumped slightly.

"What?"

"That's who you'll be, pretty soon. Adeline Johnson. Sounds good, doesn't it?"

"It sounds different," she said cautiously.

He drew his knuckles down the side of her face. "Witch," he whispered. "You have the face of an angel. And the heart of a witch. I'll never be free of you—I couldn't be if I wanted to. You own my soul, Adeline."

"I don't want to own anyone."

"You're a mystery. I'll never understand you. I guess no one ever will. You get a grip on a man's heart, and every now and then you give it a little twist . . . but always so sweetly. And it's only because you're so beautiful that I let you tie me in knots the way you do."

The intensity of his stare made her uneasy. "Don't, you'll make me conceited," she said, and laughed in an effort to break the tension. Jeff followed her lead, breaking out into a low laugh.

"I've got to see you tomorrow," he said, watching her as she stood up to brush the leaves and dirt off her skirt.

GIVE ME TONIGHT

"I don't know." Addie smiled at him. "Something
tells me I'll be very busy."

"I miss you, Adeline. And I'm gettin' tired of the
way your father and his bulldog keep such a close eye
on you. I never get to visit you without them hangin'
over me like—"

"His bulldog?"

"Ben Hunter. Lord knows why your father has taken
to him, or why he trusts him. It's not safe for you to
be around him."

"Why do you say that?"

"He's up to no good, honey. Just think about it.
Stranger comes to Sunrise, talkin' like an easterner and
carryin' a forty-four. Has a reputation as a maverick
hunter and a gambler. Somehow finds his way to Sunrise Ranch and hornswoggles your daddy into hiring
him on. Anyone with eyes can see he's on dodge from
the law. You can always tell when a man's lyin' low."

"I guess you can." Addie stared into the stream and
frowned thoughtfully. Then she asked him to take her
home.

Russell decided to talk to Addie in the library before
dinner that night—for what reason, she couldn't guess.
As she sat down in a deep leather chair and watched
him puff on a cigar, she found it comforting to be near
him. Having been raised by a maiden aunt, she'd never
been accustomed to a masculine presence in a home.
She liked Russell's scratchy, deep voice, the scents of
horses, leather, and the trace of strong drink that clung
to him. He had the same vigor that she had admired
in Ben, the same robust appreciation of life, and his
roughness appealed to something inside her.

It was incredible to look in Russell's face and realize
she resembled him. Perhaps it was mere coincidence,
or her imagination, but it seemed to her that they even
shared some of the same mannerisms. He treated her

83

with a disconcerting mixture of directness and indulgence, one minute talking to her as frankly as if she were a man, the next spoiling her without limit.

"Lately I haven't talked to you much, Adeline."

"No, sir."

"You spent some time today with Jeff."

"Yes, we—"

"What goes on between you two durin' these visits?"

"I . . . He . . . Nothing much."

"He acts like a gentleman around you?"

"Yes. Absolutely."

He nodded, blowing out a ring of smoke. "That's good. Jeff is a good boy, for a Johnson. Soft, maybe, but he'd never dare treat you wrong. He say anything 'bout when he's plannin' to ask me for permission to marry you?"

"No."

"Then he ain't caught yet."

"No, sir."

"Well, he will be soon. But to catch him you got to hold him at the right distance. Understand?"

"I think so."

"Not too close, not too far. Hold him tight, but don't choke him. That's the way your mama caught me." Russell noticed Addie's sudden smile, and he chuckled, beaming with pride. "If you want him, we'll get him for you, honey. Just look at you. I got me the prettiest girl in Texas."

"And . . . I've got the most distinctive father."

"Distinctive?" Russell appeared to be pleased. "Distinctive. Five-dollar word. So you learned somethin' at that school 'sides watercolorin' and manners. Your mother might have been right about sendin' you there. But don't tell her I said so."

As he looked at her, his pride deepened until his chest was filled with it. Besides the Sunrise Ranch, he considered Adeline to be his greatest accomplishment. Any achievement of hers was a credit to him, while her faults . . . well, he preferred to ignore those, except to chastise her occasionally, just for show. Cade and Caroline were good children, but they were too much like their mother. Adeline understood things that most women, in his opinion, weren't capable of understanding. She thought with good, hard common sense, more like a man than a woman. And she belonged to Texas as he did. She had his nerve, she was cut from his mold.

Other men had well-behaved daughters, unassuming creatures who knew their places, women who would someday be obedient and pliable to the will of their husbands. But his daughter was wild, untamed, and beautiful. His disapproval of her independence warred with his pride in it. She thought for herself, she made decisions by herself, and there was almost no freedom he wouldn't get her.

"Let's go in to dinner," Russell said, holding out the crook of his arm, and Addie took it with a smile.

As soon as dinner was served and the edges were taken off everyone's appetite, the conversation began. Russell proved within five minutes that he was in fine fettle. "Well, Ben . . . I want to hear what that son-of-a-bitch fence cutter George Johnson had to say when you told him I want my fence back up!"

Caroline and her husband, Peter, winced at his loud voice and strong language, glancing at their ten-year-old daughter. Leah was staring raptly at her grandfather.

"Daddy," Caroline protested mildly, "the child—"

"Take the child up to bed," came the answering roar. "I want to hear what my son-of-a-bitch neighbor had t' say. He is what he is, and I won't call him anything else. Start talkin', Ben."

Addie glanced at Ben, whose face was perfectly inscrutable. There was, however, a betraying twinkle in his eye as he regarded Russell. You didn't have to know Russell long to understand that he thoroughly enjoyed working himself up into hearty bursts of temper. Leah was hurried upstairs by Caroline.

"We seem to have a few philosophical differences with Big George." Ben studied his table knife and turned it idly as he spoke. "Plainly speaking, he doesn't like your fence. He doesn't have one, and he doesn't see why you need one."

"I had that fence put up to protect *my* land," Russell said, his face reddening. "To protect Warner property from rustlers. And neighbors."

"Big George seems to think the range is open and belongs to everyone."

"He's got the wrong damned idea. What's inside my fence belongs to nobody but me!"

Ben looked at him and said nothing, a smile playing on his lips. Addie nearly caught her breath at the sight of him, with the soft evening light shining on his black hair and bronzed face. It was difficult not to stare like a foolish schoolgirl. And it was indeed foolish to be taken in by his looks. It didn't matter what a man was on the outside when he was capable of such betrayal, cruelty, and cunning. But he seemed so affectionate toward Russell. Could it be that even now he was looking at Russell with the idea of killing him uppermost in his mind? She turned her eyes away from him and forced her attention back on the conversation.

" . . . George said we'd built the fence too far into his property," Ben was saying.

"Hogwash!" Russell exploded.

"Oh, I don't know, Russ. You've always been one for cutting your slice of the pie a shade bigger than the others."

There was dead silence around the table as Russell

stared at him bug-eyed. Ben met his gaze without flinching, that same smile still lingering on his lips. Addie was amazed at his daring. Suddenly Russell laughed deeply, and relieved chuckles erupted from the rest of the group. "Don't know why some say you're dishonest," Russell remarked, still chortling. "You're so honest it offends me. All right. What does that son-of-a-bitch George want in the way of . . . of. . ."

"Remuneration?"

"If that means slickin' his ruffled feathers down, yes."

"He wants half of that watering hole on the border of the property. And he wants to be paid for that maverick calf we . . . adopted."

"Adopted," Addie repeated, unable to resist breaking in. "First we stole it, now we adopted it. It sounds better every time I hear it told. You sound positively paternal, Ben, talking about that poor little lonesome critter who needed to be taken in."

He grinned at her. "I have a soft spot in my heart for neglected animals."

Their eyes met in challenge. "How altruistic."

"No, just enterprising."

May decided to interrupt their exchange. "I wish the two of you would quit tradin' words no one else understands." The statement was heartily seconded by the rest of the gathering, and Addie laughed as she stood up from the table.

"I'll leave while you discuss the details, then. I'm going to take a short walk outside, now that the air is cool."

"Don't go too far," May cautioned.

"I won't, Mama." It startled Addie, to hear that word come so easily to her own lips, and her smile faded as she left the room.

The night air was cool and fresh. She inhaled the

scent of it and knew there was something missing. There was a difference between this Sunrise and the one she had left. Here there was no seasoned, mellow fragrances of corn growing and fruit ripening. The farmers would not plow this ground and coax their harvest from it for another twenty or thirty years.

Sunrise was still the ranchers' domain. They liked the land raw and uncultivated, they liked the town frayed and comfortable, worn down and full of saloons. This was more of a man's world than the Sunrise she had come from. Moodily she kicked at a dry clod of earth and went to lean against the wooden fence by the house. There were lights on at the bunkhouse, and the muted sound of cowboys' laughter. Scattered across the ground were flashes of light. Fireflies winking at each other.

What am I doing here? she wondered as she braced her forearms on the fence. Loneliness smote her all at once. She wanted Leah desperately, not the little-girl Leah but the woman who had been her only parent, the woman she had known all her life. She wanted someone who understood her, someone who *knew* her, not as the spoiled Adeline Warner but as the person she really was. Her throat was tight as she fought to control her longing. It wouldn't do to think about it, not when she had to turn all of her concentration to learning everything she could about her situation.

Sighing and closing her eyes, she leaned her head on her hands and tried to remember what Leah had told her about Adeline Warner's disappearance. It was all enshrouded in a haze of grief. Frowning deeply, she focused on the faint recollection of a name. *She said she'd wanted to talk to someone. Diaz. I've got to find him. I've got to ask him—*

Addie heard the sound of booted feet behind her, felt the touch of someone's fingertips on her arm.

"Adeline—"

88

"Don't!" She spun around, her heart leaping. "Don't touch me!"

Ben held his hands up as if she were wielding a revolver. "Okay. Okay. No one's touching you."

She put her hand up to her chest, taking an unsteady breath. "Don't walk up behind me like that again."

"From the way you were leaning, I thought you were sick."

"Well, I wasn't. But you nearly frightened me to death."

She could see the white flash of his smile in the darkness. "Sorry."

"An apology from you," she said, exhaustion robbing her voice of its intended tartness. "It's been one surprise after another today."

"Your mother asked me to bring you back in."

"I have a question or two to ask you first."

He inclined his head slightly. "About?"

"For starters, where did you get your education?"

He braced an arm on the fence and leaned against it comfortably, sliding a hand into his pocket. "Is it so obvious that I have one? I'm flattered."

"I'd like to know. Please."

" 'Please' from you. Now, that is a surprise. I'm almost tempted to tell you. But you wouldn't believe me."

"Did you go to college?"

"Harvard."

"You're lying."

"I said you wouldn't believe me. But it's true. I even graduated. After that, my father offered to pay me to stay away for good."

"Why?"

"Why? Obviously he didn't like my company," he murmured with a half-smile, and stood up from the fence. "Time to go in."

"Is your family from the Nor—"

"No more questions. I've bared my soul enough for one night." He reached to take her arm and stopped in mid-motion as she edged away from him. "Oh, yes. No touching. Come on, Adeline."

Everything he said and did was carefully cataloged in her mind. She would have to remember it all. Maybe that was why she had found herself here. Maybe she was intended to expose the other side of him, to interrupt the events that would lead up to Russell's death. *The fact that I'm here must change a lot of things. The fact that I'm here instead of Adeline Warner is just the beginning of it all. Everything will be different now. I'll make it different. I'll stop Russell's murder. I'll ruin Ben Hunter before it ever gets that far.*

After she retired for the night, she turned fitfully as questions burned through her mind. There were things she had to know. Things she had to find out tomorrow. Addie threw off the light sheet that covered her and rolled over onto her stomach, hot and frustrated . . . frightened.

Her thoughts stilled as the clear, lovely notes of a guitar floated through the windows from a distance. Haunting, sweet music. Was that Ben? She didn't know the melody, but it was the most beautiful thing she had ever heard, soothing and faultlessly played. She could sense the entire ranch settling down to listen. Soon Addie ceased to wonder at the source of the music and relaxed. How could someone like Ben play something so beautiful? she thought drowsily, and then she thought of Leah, sleeping only a few rooms away. She wondered if Leah was listening.

3

ADDIE WAS UP AT DAWN WITH THE OTHERS, UNABLE to stay in bed while the smell of breakfast crept stealthily through the air and the sound of quiet morning conversation floated up to her from the dining room. She washed and dressed quickly, feeling strangely at peace in spite of a long and restless night.

Was there any way to get back to the Sunrise she belonged in? She didn't know how to go back—she didn't know how she'd gotten here in the first place. What if she was stuck here forever? Addie shivered at the thought and pushed it aside. There was no use worrying about that. It didn't seem as if she could do anything about it. If it was all a dream, it would end sometime. And if she was crazy, it was better to pretend to herself and everyone else that she wasn't.

But there was something practical for her to think about. Russell Warner was still alive, and she might be the only one who could keep him that way. To the rest of the family and everyone in Sunrise, she would be Adeline. She would figure out how to be who they thought she was. From now on, no one would notice anything peculiar about her. And while he was fooling them all, she would find some way to expose Ben for what he was and stop him from killing Russell. As things stood now, Russell would be murdered just after fall roundup. She had until then to change everything.

Addie went downstairs with a light step. As she walked into the dining room, she painted on a bright smile. "Good morning," she said airily, seating herself by May.

"What in tarnation's got you so happy?" Russell demanded. His eyes twinkling.

"Nothing." She leaned to the side as the maid reached over to pour her coffee.

"I think it may have something to do with Jeff," May said, pleased by the thought. "Isn't that right, Adeline?"

"It might be," Addie conceded, stirring sugar into her coffee. "I have to admit, Jeff is super."

A blank silence greeted her statement.

"Super?"

Addie realized her mistake and covered it hastily. "New expression." *You'll hear it about fifty years from now.* "It means nice . . . wonderful."

Russell chuckled. "Don't know why young people have to go makin' up new words. We got all we need."

"Because young people always think they're feelin' things no one has ever felt before," Caroline said reasonably. "Thinkin' up new words only makes sense to 'em."

"Adeline, are you going to see Jeff again today?" May's face was warm with motherly interest.

"Well, we'd talked about it."

"I want Adeline to be out with me today," Russell interrupted brusquely.

There was a short silence around the table. Then May spoke with a frown etched on the corners of her mouth, displeasure knitting her brow. "Later you can take Cade—"

"Cade will be in school all day," Russell countered, his jaw set obstinately. "And Adeline and me haven't been ridin' in a long time. She wants to go. Don't you, punkin?"

Addie nodded eagerly. "Yes. It sounds like a fine idea."

"We'll look over the ranch, see things are bein' done right, won't we, honey?"

She grinned at him. "We sure will."

"Wait." Ben's eyes darkened with annoyance. "The men don't need to have her looking over their shoulders and putting in her two cents about what they're doing."

Addie sat up straighter in her chair, looking directly at him. "I won't say a thing to anyone."

"You don't have to," he replied curtly. "Just looking at you is going to distract them." He turned to Russell, his voice becoming softer, more persuasive. "We've got a lot of things to do today, and no time to put up with her antics. Most of them get to see a woman seldom enough, Russ, and they can't help staring. But to have one right there while they're trying to work, and one that looks like Adeline—it's asking a little much, isn't it?"

Addie frowned, wondering if there had been a compliment hidden in there. It was hard to tell. "I'm glad you've got a foreman smart enough to tell us what to do, Daddy," she said, her eyes round. If she'd had Mary Pickford curls, she would have twirled one around her finger.

Russ harrumphed irritably. "No one tells me what to do with my daughter, Ben. She's lookin' over the ranch with me today."

"By all means." Ben's face was smooth, wiped clean of all emotion.

By the time Addie and Russell arrived at the barn, Ben had already left to organize the ranch hands as they began the projects that would keep them busy all summer. The horses were saddled and ready to go. Russell exchanged a few words with one of the cowboys who had been assigned to do some of the necessary farmwork near the ranch. Someone had to take care of the chickens and gather eggs, harvest alfalfa hay and stack it.

Making hay was a difficult job. It took experience to know when the hay was well-cured, when the color was right, how long it should lie in the swath after being mowed, and when it was dry enough to be stacked. It was drying out in the fields right now, changing color under the bright, hot Texas sun. There was nothing like the sweet smell of well-cured hay. It had a perfume that seemed to saturate the air for miles around.

But the cowboys took little pleasure in such work. They felt it was beneath their dignity to perform such tasks—why, that was a job for sodbusters, not cowboys! And since they were merciless in their teasing of each other, the hands who had to do sodbuster work were artfully ridiculed by the other cowpunchers.

While Russell was talking with the ranch hand, Addie approached Jessie from the side. " 'Morning, Jessie. I see you're not wearing that nasty old sidesaddle today. What a pretty horse you are. Yes, you are.'' Jessie's head turned in her direction, ears twitching expectantly. ''We're not going to have any problems like we did yesterday,'' Addie continued, reaching a hand in her pocket and pulling out a lump of sugar. ''We're making a deal, Jessie—you know what it is— and this is evidence of my good faith. And believe me, if you live up to your end of the bargain, there's more where this came from.''

Jessie bent her head and took the sugar delicately between her lips, looking at her with wary brown eyes. Suddenly she gobbled it and pushed her nose strongly against Addie's midriff, nudging her for more. ''I can tell we're going to be good friends,'' Addie said conversationally, pulling out another lump and extending it to the horse. Jessie's nose was as soft as velvet as it brushed her palm in search of the sugar. She stroked the side of the mare's neck and showed her the spurless boots she wore. "See, Jessie? Slick-heeled, just for you."

Jessie offered not one twitch of protest as Addie slipped the tip of her boot into the stirrup and hoisted herself up into the saddle. After swinging a leg over the saddle, she arranged her divided skirt and looked at Russell expectantly. He had just finished his conversation.

"I'm ready."

"Looks like y'are." Russell mounted his horse, a large white gelding named General Cotton, and they rode away from the house, out into the range. "I guess you know your mama wasn't too happy 'bout this," he said, looking like a boy who had just gotten away with a prank.

"I don't understand why," she replied, sincerely puzzled. "What could be wrong with me looking over the ranch with you?"

"She's always had plans for you, Adeline. Plans about making you into somethin' you aren't meant to be. Sending you to that school in Virginia to learn about fancy manners and poetry books, hoping you'd find some eastern lawyer or businessman to hitch up with—well, I knew it wouldn't work. I knew you'd want to come back where you belong. Cade and Caroline favor your mama. She wasn't born to ranching. She's settled into this life pretty well, but in her heart she'll never stop hankerin' for her people in the East. But I think you favor me, Adeline. And you and I were born to this." He waved his hand at the land in front of them. "Look around you. Would you trade all this to live in a hotel or a town house with the kind of goody-goody May wants for you? You don't want a man decked out in city clothes, someone with soft hands and white skin, afraid of dirt and animals, and everything that's nat'ral. They city whips the manliness out of 'em. Our boys out here are rough-cut, Adeline, but they're men, and they got respect for a woman. Too much respect to let 'er wear the pants in the family and do their work. A man out here knows how to take care of a woman.''

Addie listened to him with growing alarm. She didn't want to wear the pants in the family or to bully any man. If or when her thoughts ever turned to marriage, she would need the kind of husband who would let her be his partner, his lover and friend. Was it useless to hope that someday she would find someone who would let her be his equal?

''Let's talk about something else,'' she said, her forehead creasing, and obligingly Russ started lecturing her on the running of the ranch. The horses' hooves splashed through a shallow stream, then thudded along the edge of an alfalfa field. A line of trees bordered the other side, having been planted there to act as a windbreak. On the other side of the field, the lush green of the land turned to the dry brown-green of true rangeland. Addie noticed that all the trees they passed by had clipped edge on the bottoms, like skirts that had been hemmed too short.

''Why have the lowest leaves of all the trees been clipped like that?''

Russell seemed pleased by her interest. ''That's the browse line, honey. That's about as high as the livestock can reach when they browse over the land and chomp on the trees. When you see that, you know the land is being overgrazed. That's why Ben moved the herd further out to richer land. If he didn't, the grass would be so thin the cows'd have to eat on a dead run to get enough.''

''But how long can you keep moving the herd around before you run out of good land?''

''Run outta land?'' Russell laughed uproariously.

GIVE ME TONIGHT

"We got half a million acres. We're not gonna run out anytime soon. And if we did, there'll always be more land in Texas."

"I don't know if Texas is as big as you think. Sooner or later the land—"

"Texas not big? It covers practically the whole country, 'cept for the little bit we let the other states divide amongst themselves."

They rode over miles of arid rangeland, past herds of longhorns whose heads were dipped low as they grazed lethargically. Russell's face was alight with an emotion beyond pride as he regarded the animals with their swishing tails and lethal horns. "Beautiful, ain't they?"

"There certainly are a lot of them."

"Not bad for a man who started out with nothin' but two dollars in cash and an empty belly. Feels good to a man, Adeline, to look over what he owns and know he's built somethin' that'll last forever. To know he'll go on forever. This'll never be anything but Warner land, and I was the one who took it for his own."

Addie stared at him and felt a rush of pity. *But when you were killed it all fell to pieces. There was no one to take over, no one to hold it together. The herds were rustled or sold off, the ranch was ruined. Cade was too young to take over. And I guess Caroline's husband was too weak, not the kind of man that others would follow. It didn't last forever.*

"This is all mine," Russell said, relishing the thought. His voice lowered a few notches. "And someday it'll be yours."

"Mine?" she repeated, startled.

"Now, honey, don't tell me you weren't listenin' when I explained it to you the other day."

Addie had no idea what he was talking about. Maybe

he'd explained something to Adeline Warner. But not to Addie Peck.

"I didn't really understand," she said carefully.

Russell sighed. "Aw, doesn't really matter. Wills are men's business anyway. You don't have to understand anything, honey. Just—"

"Explain it again," Addie interrupted gently, watching him like a hawk. "Please. I'll try very hard this time. What is this about a will?"

Russell seemed to puff up with self-importance. "No one around here has the kind of fancy will I'm gettin' drawed up. I had to send for a Philadelphia lawyer to come here and do it right. He'll get here in about a month."

"There aren't lawyers here who could draw up a good will for you?"

"Not like the young hustlers back east. When it comes to the law, they know every trick there is. And I don't want any chance of a mistake bein' made with this will."

"What's so special about it?"

"Well, I've been thinkin' a lot about what'll happen when I pass on. I don't aim to for a while, mind you. But I got to thinkin'—who's gonna carry on after me? Who's gonna look after Sunrise? Caro and Pete don't care nothin' about ranching. They're talking about movin' east after the baby's born."

"To North Carolina?" Addie guessed. It was where her mother, Sarah, had grown up, married, and eventually died.

"That's right. Guess you've heard 'em mention it." He snorted. "East. Pete would feel at home there, sure enough. He's not a cowman. I'd hoped we'd make something of him when he an' Caro came to live at Sunrise. But he couldn't rope a calf if it stood still for him."

"What about leaving the ranch to Cade?"

"Cade can do whatever he set his mind to, but his heart's not here. He already wants a taste of city life, and when he gets it, he won't want to leave it. Too much like your mama. And May will see to it that her son gets a college education and winds up in a fancy office with glasses settin' on his nose and a pile of books on his desk. I hate to say it, but Texas just ain't in him. So that leaves you. But you can't inherit Sunrise, honey. No matter how smart y'are, you're just a woman."

"And that's nothing I can change," she said wryly.

"So I was plannin' to do like everyone else around here, have the ranch sold off when I go, and divide the money between the ones I leave behind. You'd be a rich woman if I did that. You'd have enough money to do whatever you wanted for the rest of your life. I had it all settled in my own mind. But then Ben came along."

Addie looked at him sharply. "What does Ben have to do with it?"

Russell smiled. "He runs the ranch as good as me. No dust settlin' on that one. When he says he'll do something, it gets done, one way or another. I like that. Man you can depend on. So I figured I'd make him trustee. That just means I'll leave Sunrise to you in trust, and he'll manage everything."

"You can't be serious!" Addie exclaimed, bug-eyed. She was as outraged as if she were Russell's real daughter. "You're putting him in charge of your ranch, your money, and your *family?* He can do whatever he wants with us? Everything we have will be at his disposal? My Lord, he isn't even related to us!"

"I'm puttin' a few clauses in this will," Russell said, as if that was supposed to soothe her. "For one thing, Sunrise can't be sold off without the family's approval."

"What if Ben turns out to be a bad trustee? Can we fire him?"

"No, that's one thing y' can't change. He's trustee till he's dead and buried. But don't fret—he'll be damn good at it. I'll rest easy, knowin' I left things in his hands.

The very same hands that are going to strangle you!

Addie's mind raced. Ben had the perfect motive to kill Russell. After the will was signed, he would be in control of the entire ranch and a large fortune, just as soon as Russell Warner was dead.

"Daddy, I know you trust him," she said, her voice wavering. "I know you depend on him and care for him. But it would be a mistake to put him in that position after you've gone."

"Aw, honey," Russell said soothingly, "I know you're prob'ly a mite disappointed at gettin' Sunrise in trust instead of all that money. But this is the only way the ranch won't go to pieces. Ben's my only insurance against it. I don't want my ranch to die just 'cause I have to. It's as simple as that."

"Have you told Ben yet?"

"Not yet."

"It might be good to wait awhile," Addie murmured, and as she heard no reply from Russell, she fell silent. She tried to concentrate on the scene around them rather than go into a helpless tirade. That wouldn't do her cause any good. *Later,* she promised herself. There would be a chance to reason with Russell later, when she could pull some good arguments together.

The land was swarming with men and cattle, and the air was thick with dust and the smell of animals and sweat. Thousands of cattle were being treated for blowflies and screwworms, insects which settled in open wounds and fed on oozing flesh. The suffering longhorns were daubed with a mixture of grease and carbolic acid, which killed off the large maggots and relieved the animals' excruciating pain.

But the longhorns didn't know that the men were trying to help, and they reacted violently. Vicious curses sailed up the sky as the men danced out of the way of animals that had turned on them. There were clouds of dust curling, rising and settling around the moving figures, powdering the men's clothes, and sticking to their skin. All around them the cattle churned like a river of red-brown water.

Russell and Addie stopped to watch, keeping well out of the way.

"Hard work," Addie said, almost to herself. "Baking in the sun. Getting hurt so easily. No machines to help, no time to rest. Makes no sense for anyone to want to do this kind of work."

"Wait till the worst-tempered animals have to be dehorned," Russell said, and grinned.

"Why do they do this? What makes a man choose to be a cowboy?"

"Don't know that a man ever asks himself that. He either does or he doesn't, that's all."

"There's no glamour in it. It's nothing at all like the novels and magazines describe it. And they certainly don't get a lot of money for what they do—"

"The hell they don't! I pay my boys forty dollars a month. That's nearly ten more than they could get anywhere else in the country for the same job."

"I just don't understand what the attraction is for them."

Russell was not listening. "C'mon, honey. Ben's over there pullin' out a steer from a boghole."

She followed him reluctantly, riding further down the pasture to the site where two longhorns were stuck fast in a boghole, having tried to evade swarms of flies by wallowing in deep mud. One of the steers was making plaintive noises, while the other was silent and exhausted, making no protest as it was pulled out with ropes tied to the cowboys' saddle horns.

Addie's lips tightened with disdain as she looked at Ben, who had tied the ropes around the longhorn. His Levi's were black with mud all the way up to his knees and beyond. It looked like he'd been doing some wallowing right alongside the cattle. Sweat made streaks through the dirt on his face and the sides of his neck, and caused the ends of his black hair to curl damply against the back of his neck. That was where he belonged, in the dirt.

"Ben seems to have gotten the worst of it today," she commented with a trace of satisfaction.

"He's not afraid of work." Russell regarded his foreman fondly. "The men respect him for it. And they know he won't ask them to do somethin' he wouldn't do himself. Hardest thing in the world, Adeline, is to work for a man you know is lazier than you are, just like it's easy to work hard for someone you respect."

It didn't fit conveniently into her picture of Ben Hunter. After all, he would murder Russell for his own personal gain. Money the easy way. That kind of man didn't take to hard work . . . wasn't that true? She wasn't pleased by the discovery that Ben might have a few good qualities to complicate her vision of him as an unscrupulous criminal. She wanted it all to be cut-and-dried.

If only there were someone she could talk to about him, someone to help relieve her burden of silence! Everyone was so maddeningly pleased with Ben. They admired and respected him, not knowing what kind of man he really was.

As if he could feel her stare, Ben turned his head to look at her. She was amazed by the intense color of his eyes, emerald fringed with thick black lashes, set deeply in his dark face. For a second she couldn't move, trapped by his intent gaze. Despite the distance between them, it seemed as if he could read her mind, and she felt heat rising in her cheeks. She was relieved when he finally returned his attention to the steer struggling out of the boghole.

The animal stumbled forward on unsteady legs and collapsed at the edge, having lost the will to do anything but lie there and die. Swearing, the men went to the quivering longhorn and strained to lift it to its feet. After a long struggle the men succeeded in their task, and the longhorn staggered away to find a place to graze. Leaving the others to pull the second steer out, Ben walked over to Russell and Addie, wiping his hands on the back of his pants. Addie noticed the way his smile turned cool when he looked at her, and something inside her shifted uneasily.

"Miss Adeline. Hope you aren't offended by the cussing." He tilted his head back and squinted up at her. As he had intended, the remark served to remind her that she was out of her depth in this, a scene that belonged so utterly to the men. The language, the work, the clothes—every detail was a complete contrast to the feminine surroundings women were usually relegated to. According to the dictates of this world, she was supposed to be in the kitchen or bending over needlework, not riding around the range with her father.

"I've heard language worse than this," she said. "It's nothing less than what I'd expected."

Ben kept his thoughts well-hidden as he looked at her. He couldn't explain to himself why his feelings for her had started to change. They had disliked each other from the first moment they met, and with each of her visits home during vacations, their mutual intolerance had increased.

It had been a long-dreaded day when she'd returned from the girls' academy for good. He couldn't stand the games she liked to play, her capricious moods, her ability to shake everyone up and wrap anyone she wanted around her finger. She had always been haughty to him, until she became intrigued with his lack of interest in her, and that had resulted in the scene in the barn when she'd tried to seduce him. After he turned her down coldly, she decided to treat him with simple loathing, which had suited him just fine.

And then . . . it seemed incredible, but she had changed in the twinkling of an eye. There was no way of knowing whether it was permanent or temporary, but this new Adeline had a different effect on him than the old one. Ben had never noticed how beautiful she was, how vulnerable and disarming she could be. He almost wished he'd taken her up on her offer in the barn. At least that way he wouldn't be wondering now what it would be like to feel her body underneath his. Now he would never know, and although that was just as well, he was still unwillingly fascinated by her.

Addie looked around the pasture at the dirty, unshaven men, their clothes dark with perspiration, their faces adorned with unkempt mustaches or overlong sideburns. They kept on looking at her covertly. Without Russell nearby, she wouldn't have felt safe.

Ben noticed her uncertain expression and grinned. "Diamonds in the rough, every one of us. You'll never come across a group of gentlemen with higher regard for a lady. Some of them have ridden hundreds of miles just to catch a glimpse of a woman of good character."

"Including you, Mr. Hunter?" she asked, her voice soft and lethal.

"I've never been particularly interested in women of good character, Miss Adeline."

Addie fumed inwardly. Oh, how he loved to give just the right amount of disrespectful emphasis to her name! How could Russell just sit there without realizing Ben was subtly insulting her?

"It's a relief to know decent women are safe from your attentions, Mr. Hunter."

He grinned lazily, looking her up and down. "I should warn you, I make an exception every now and then."

Russell chuckled richly. "The key to my Adeline's heart is to give her compliments, Ben, lots of 'em. They do a lot to sweeten her disposition."

"Only if they're sincere," Addie corrected. She glanced meaningfully at Ben. "And I see through most people who are wearing false fronts."

"I never knew you put much store by sincerity, Miss Adeline."

"Then you don't know as much about me as you suppose, Mr. Hunter."

"Enough to have formed an accurate opinion."

"That's just fine. Form all the opinions about me you want, as long as I don't have to hear them. Your opinions bore me."

Ben's eyes narrowed.

Russell laughed in the silence that followed. "Don't you two ever quit?"

"I've got to get back to work," Ben said, looking at Addie and touching the brim of his hat in a gesture that contained only a modicum of politeness.

"He's het up, all right," Russell said with enjoyment, as Addie watched the foreman stride back to the boghole."

"Why do you seem so pleased about it?" she asked, tight-lipped. "And why do you let him say such things to your daughter?"

"For one thing, when it comes to Ben Hunter, you take up for yourself better than I could. For another, you'd turn on me like a tornado if I broke in. You like to trade words with him. Hell, I like to trade words with him too. Difference is, you can get him mad and I can't. I like to see him mad every once in a while.

Good for a man to have a flare-up every now and again. Not easy to get a rise outta him. Fact is, you're the only one who can do it right. He's as short as a pie crust around you.''

"I don't do it on purpose," she muttered. God knew there was no reason for her to provoke Ben. It didn't help her cause any. If only she could swallow the sharp words that came to the tip of her tongue when Ben spoke to her. How much of an advantage she would have if she could stay cool and calm while he was angry! But she couldn't keep silent or cool, not when his mere presence filled her with such tension. She couldn't control her feelings when Ben was near. She found herself saying things she couldn't hold in. He brought out the worst in her, and it seemed she brought out the worst in him.

Her thoughts were interrupted by an urgent shout from Russell, who had leaned forward in his saddle "Hey! That steer's turned on em—someone dump him!"

Addie's eyes widened with alarm as she saw what had happened. As soon as the steer had struggled out of the boghole, it angrily turned its horns against its rescuers, enraged and ready to do battle. The huge horns shook threateningly at the man closest by. Quickly the steer lunged, powerful muscles bunching under the mud-encrusted hide, and all Addie could see was a flurry of motion. There was a short scream from the cowboy as he was wounded. Ropes were swung to catch the steer and hold him fast, but in the dust and frenzy the lassos missed their mark. Addie cried out as she saw the red gleam of blood and the rag-doll limpness of the boy as he fell.

Maddened by the snap of whirling ropes, the steer twisted sideways. Ben dived at the crumpled figure on the ground, catching at the leg of his chaps and pulling him away from the animal. The steer followed the movement quickly, his head bent to plunge forward in pursuit of the body sliding through the dust.

"Dump him!" Ben shouted hoarsely, but another rope failed to catch one of the longhorn's legs. His voice pierced the air. "Oh, *shit.*" Someone threw Ben a rifle, which smacked heavily in to his palms. Holding it by the barrel, he raised it in the air. Addie's heart stopped as she understood what he intended.

"Daddy," she whispered, wondering why no one was going to shoot the steer. She heard no sound from Russell.

Ben's body arched as he raised the makeshift club higher, and with a sharp, vicious movement he brought it down on the longhorn's forehead. The animal dropped without a sound, crashing to the ground, momentum causing it to slide forward until Ben was forced to scuttle backward. The point of a horn came to rest near his booted foot. Then Ben was motionless, staring at the twitching longhorn. There was silence in the pasture. "Couldn't anyone around here manage a head catch?" Ben finally asked of no one in particular, sighing as he went to the boy on the ground.

"Did you kill him?" Russ asked, dismounting from General Cotton.

"No. Just stunned him a little. He won't be giving anyone trouble for a while."

"How's the boy?"

Addie was having trouble calming Jessie's attack of nerves. As soon as the horse's skittishness was under control, she dismounted and left the reins hanging.

"Not good," Ben said grimly. "A couple of punctures in his side, and a head wound that's going to need some stitches. Watts, get me a needle and thread. The rest of you get back to work. There's a considerable number of animals out there needing to be doctored."

"Daddy," Addie asked Russell quietly, "do you have any liquor on you?"

"Always." He pulled a monogrammed silver flask out of one of his many vest pockets and handed it to her with a grin. "Whiskey okay?"

"Perfect."

She shook the flask, trying to judge by the slosh how much liquor there was inside, and headed toward the men on the ground. Ben pressed a wad of cloth to the unconscious boy's side and scowled as he saw Addie walking toward him. "For God's sake, get back to your horse," he snapped. "And try not to faint."

"Fainting is the last thing I have in mind," she said shortly, coming over to the boy and kneeling beside him. For once she knew exactly how to handle the situation. Oh, how she longed to cut Ben down with the news that she had worked as a nurse for the past three years! "You didn't ask for an antiseptic. Whiskey'll do fine."

He took the flask from her with one hand while clamping a folded handkerchief on the wound with the other. "Good. Your help is appreciated. Now get out of the way."

Addie had to hold her ground. She remained where she was, suddenly desperate to help. Somehow, on the vast land encompassed by the borders of the Sunrise Ranch, in the midst of strangers and their confusing rituals, among the short-tempered men and the sea of animals, she had found something she knew how to do. She knew how to tend to a wound, she had been one of the best nurses in the hospital when it came to an emergency. No one could find fault with her bandaging and stitching. But Ben didn't know that, and he intended to stand in her way. Addie had to prove to someone, to herself, that she was useful. She could belong. She had to be given the chance to show it.

"I can help," she said. "I'm going to stay."

Ben dropped the flask and caught her wrist in a crushing grip. "I'll say this only once," he said through gritted teeth. "This isn't the time for you to play ministering angel. He doesn't need his hand held. He doesn't need you to coo over him and flutter your eyelashes. So move your sweet ass over there and stay out of the way, or I'll drag you away by the hair. And I don't care if Daddy sees or not."

"Take your hand off me," Addie hissed, her eyes gleaming with fury. "Are you planning to stitch up his wound with those dirty paws? I know more about this than you'll ever hope to know. Do you think I'd offer to do it if I didn't? *Let go!* And if you want to be of any help, open that flask and give me that bandanna around your neck."

His eyes were hard and searching as they met hers. She saw the flash of anger, and then the beginnings of curiosity. Slowly his hand uncurled from her wrist.

"Every stitch better be perfect," he said, his voice menacing in its quietness. "And if you aren't able to back up your words, you'll answer to me. Understand?"

She nodded shortly while a wash of relief loosened the tightness in her chest. "What kind of thread is Watts bringing?" She dampened the bandanna with whiskey and blotted the wound. "Cheap cotton, I'll bet."

"We can't all afford silk." Ben sneered.

"I can. Do you have a knife?"

"For what?"

"Do you have a knife?" she repeated impatiently. He reached down to his belt and unsheathed a gleaming bowie, giving it to her handle-first. She burrowed under the hem of her riding skirt, extended a leg, and cut one of the pink ribbons threaded through the lace border of her pantaloons. At the glimpse of the shapely calf that rose from the edge of her boot, several of the men who had lingered several yards away to watch began to mutter and exclaim among themselves.

"Jesus. That little display will be talked about in the bunkhouse for years to come," Ben muttered, sounding peculiarly strained.

"What do you mean?" she asked, flipping her hem back down and turning her attention to the ribbon. Expertly she stripped a thread from it. "Oh, you mean showing my leg." Her voice dripped with sarcasm. "Heavens, I didn't remember my modesty is much more important than helping a wounded man. Such unladylike behavior—but surely I haven't shocked *you,* Mr. Hunter." Her mocking smile faded as she saw the expression on his face. Why, he looked as if she had just done something dreadfully indecent, something that *had* shocked him.

Surely a quick glimpse of her leg couldn't have that effect on a man. She and her friends had walked down the streets of Sunrise wearing skirts that ended at the knees, and sometimes never received a second glance from the men who passed by them.

As she handed the knife back to him, his fingers curved slightly around the handle, and she felt a small shock at the sight of them. He had strong hands that showed signs of hard work. But how strangely sensitive they were. The hands of a murderer. Flushing, she tore her eyes away and turned her attention to the thread, grateful when Watts arrived with a paper of needles and a pair of scissors. She threaded the silk through the cleanest needle and soaked everything with whiskey. Carefully she pierced the first edge of ragged flesh with the needle, then the second, drawing them together with a neat ligature knot.

"Can't you do it a little faster?" Ben asked.

Calmly she took the second stitch. "I can do it so the scar will be practically invisible. See how it will fade into the frown line—"

"Yeah . . . real nice. But we don't have any need for a good-looking corpse. So hurry."

"There's no need to be so dramatic. He's not going to die, and you know it." Addie resisted the urge to say anything else. This was no time for an argument, no matter how tempting the prospect. As she was tying off the last knot, Ben wiped the last of the blood off the boy's forehead. "Kitchen surgery," Addie said, surveying her work with pride. "But he couldn't get better from a doctor."

"It'll do," Ben replied evenly.

She looked down a the cowboy's face then, pushing back a tendril of matted hair that had fallen on the temple. "Curly red hair. I'll bet he gets teased a lot for that."

Ben seemed to relax, his tension easing. "Who could resist?"

"And freckles too." Deep copper freckles that stood out in spite of the darkly tanned skin. The unconscious face was still round with the plumpness of youth. He didn't yet have the lean face of an adult. He looked so vulnerable and alone that her heart ached with compassion.

"Pink silk thread," Ben remarked, and Addie frowned a little.

"I hope it won't embarrass him."

"No, ma'am. He'll never want those stitches out. I guarantee he'll brag for days about where that pink silk came from." His mouth curled sardonically. "The envy of the bunkhouse."

"He's not much older than Cade," she said softly. "Poor boy." She felt sorry for someone so young having to live such a hard life. But it was a better life than many others would have. At least this boy would have the chance to keep his innocence. And these wounds would heal. She had tended veterans in the hospital who had once had young faces and innocent hearts. They had come back from the war crippled, blind, bitter. She had shared some of their bitterness, out of empathy, out of the emptiness of her own life. But that was in the future, she reminded herself. None of it had happened yet. Those veterans hadn't even been born yet. The war hadn't taken place.

As she looked down at the boy, she didn't know her eyes were dark with loneliness, her expression compassionate. Ben went still with surprise, his breath catching in his throat. Adeline Warner had always been a pretty girl, with too much spirit and not enough heart. Sassy, selfish, sharp-tongued—a girl like that was someone to avoid. But just now her face was soft and heart-stirring in a way it had never been before. What had happened to give her this new air of vulnerability? What magic had brought such mystifying sweetness to her face? Had it been there all the time? Was he just beginning to notice something everyone else had long been aware of?

Russell walked up behind Addie, looking over her handiwork. He seemed to be puzzled by what she had done. "Where did you learn to close up a wound like that?" he barked.

Ben watched as the question caused Addie's cheeks to color.

"It's not much different from regular needlework," she said with a half-smile. "Just messier. What about his side? Is it still bleeding?"

"Not much. The temporary dressing will do until we can get him back to the bunkhouse."

"Good." Addie glanced down at herself and saw the blood on both her sleeves, causing the material to cling stickily to her arms. The sweet, warm smell of it drifted to her nostrils, combining with the heat of the sun to overcome her with a wave of nausea. As she looked away, she caught sight of the steer and couldn't help remembering the thudding crack of the rifle against its skull. Afraid she might throw up, Addie grimaced shakily and struggled to her feet without asking for help. "Excuse me," she whispered, and walked away, breathing deeply and clenching her fists. She stopped when she reached Jessie, leaning against the horse's side and resting her forehead against the saddle. Concentrating on the musky scent of leather, she stayed very still. After a minute had passed, the contents of her stomach began to settle down.

She heard Ben's quiet voice behind her. "Here." He had gotten a clean handkerchief and a canteen of water from somewhere. She turned her face to watch him blankly as he dampened the cloth. She even suffered his touch without protest as he reached out to wipe her face, her eyes closing as she felt the cool cloth slide over her cheeks and eyebrows.

"Why are you doing that? Is there something on my face? What is it?"

"Just dust. Hold out your hands."

She stared down at the brownish bloodstains in the crevices between her fingers. "Oh, I—"

"Spread your fingers." The corner of the handkerchief erased every last spot on her hands. Why was he being so considerate?

"Thank you."

He offered the canteen to her. "Water?"

Gratefully she nodded, taking it in both hands and tilting her head back as the liquid slid down her throat. After handing it back, she looked at him uncertainly. "Thank you," she repeated, a question in her eyes.

He smiled at her, causing her heart to miss a beat. "You smell like a dance-hall hostess."

She chuckled a little breathlessly. "I spilled as much of that whiskey on you as I did on me."

"I'll give you your due. Your work was good. Although I'd have bet two bits beforehand that you wouldn't have been able to do it. I'm beginning to wonder how many more surprises I should expect from you, Adeline."

"Addie." The correction came out before she could stop herself.

"Addie," he repeated huskily. "That what you were called in school?"

"Kind of."

"You okay now?"

"Yes."

"You should go back to the house. It's too hot out here for you."

She didn't know what to do when he was being nice to her. "I guess I will."

His eyes moved over her face. He seemed to be on the verge of asking her a question, but something impelled him to keep silent, and he left her.

Addie dipped her bare toes in the stream, relishing the coolness of the rushing water. The hem of her skirt was getting damp, but prudently she tried to keep as much of her legs covered as possible. "Shame on you," she said, casting a wicked glance at Jeff. "I'd swear I just caught you looking at my ankles."

"You have beautiful ankles. The most beautiful I've ever seen." He slid his arm around her shoulders and turned her to face him. A hot kiss was pressed into the hollow of her throat, causing her to squirm in protest. "And the most beautiful toes, and heels—"

"Oh, stop it." Addie giggled and twisted away from him. "And don't hold me so tight. It's too hot."

Jeff loosened his arms, scowling in a way that made her want to laugh. She was fond of him, but at times he tried her patience sorely.

Addie had learned to treat Jeff with the same kind of affectionate mockery she used for Cade. She'd hoped to cool Jeff down, guessing that his feeling for her was not the love of a mature man for a woman but a boy's perverse love for something he knew was beyond his reach. Unfortunately her efforts to put distance between them were only making him want her more.

There were moments when she was charmed by him, moments when he was boyish and sweet, and almost embarrassed by his own gentleness with her. It was then that she was happiest in his company. She needed a friend, and he was the closest thing to a confidant she had.

As to the physical side of their relationship, it wasn't difficult to handle him. She had no desire to make love with him, and when he tried to coerce her into it, she set him back with a coolness that infuriated him. It wasn't that Jeff didn't attract her. But Addie didn't want real intimacy with him. Something warned her that it would be a terrible mistake, and an instinct that strong must be obeyed.

There was an arrogant side of Jeff that bothered Addie. He liked to boast about his family's money and his father's influence, and she believed a man should stand on his own two feet, not ride on someone else's coattails. And Jeff seemed so ridiculously young when he swaggered. Like a child, he was demanding and relentless about what he wanted, and he sulked if he didn't get his way.

It was amazing, the difference between Jeff and Ben Hunter. They were complete opposites. Jeff was boyish, outspoken, easy to understand. Ben was a man no woman could ever hope to understand, more complex than any man she'd ever met. In a subtle way he seemed removed from everyone, even while he was arguing with Russell, charming May and Caro, or exchanging tall tales with the ranch hands. He seemed to be fond of Russell, but it was clear Ben didn't need anyone. What had happened to make him so independent? Was there anyone he really cared about?

What a mystery he was, attractive and repellent, charming and cold, gentle and harsh. In her heart of hearts she was afraid of him, not merely because of what he would do to Russell, but for an even deeper reason. He made her aware of herself as a woman in a way no one had before. He could do it with a look, a gesture . . . he cast some kind of spell over her merely by being in the same room. And the strangest thing was, she knew he didn't do it consciously. There was some kind of invisible current between them, and she didn't know how to explain it. How could you fight something you didn't understand?

"Adeline . . ." Jeff's wheedling voice broke into her thoughts. "Why are you so far away? Did I do somethin' to get your dander up?"

"Of course you didn't." She looked at him and smiled. "I'd tell you if you did something to make me mad."

"No, you wouldn't. Women don't tell stuff like that. They like to turn all cold and quiet and make you guess what you did to get 'em mad."

"Most men have the most interesting theories about women. Women are helpless, women don't have much sense, women are neither honest nor straightforward, and really don't know their own minds anyway . . . honestly, I think one of you men should write a book."

"Why would anyone want to write a book about that?"

Addie grinned. "For future generations. So some girl can read it someday and understand how much better off she is than poor old Grandma at her age."

"No man'll ever understand women enough to write a book about 'em."

"You know, women have their own theories about men."

"Like . . . men are stronger, smarter, and make more sense—"

"No, those are men's theories about themselves. Erroneous, for the most part."

"Erro. . . ?"

"Wrong. Men don't know the first thing about themselves. They always manage to hide the things that are the most attractive about themselves, by thinking they have to act like Don Juan or Valentino."

"Like Valen. . . ?"

"But a woman doesn't want a man who's as slick as that. And she doesn't want someone who's going to treat her like she's a steer to be rounded up and roped and busted."

Jeff grinned at that. "How else you gonna treat a woman when she gets ornery?"

"With understanding," Addie said, and settled down on the ground, leaning on one elbow. "With tenderness. But most men aren't strong enough to be gentle. And they're not strong enough to love someone without breaking her spirit. A man likes to make his woman into a reflection of himself. Impossible here to find a man who would let his woman be a separate person as well as his wife."

"What's gotten into you?" Jeff looked at her with a puzzled frown. "You never used to make things so complicated before. Did you learn it at that school in Virginia? All this stuff about reflections and separate people. That has nothin' to do with a man and a woman. Man has a wife. She shares his bed, takes care of his house, has his children. That's all there is to think about."

"And what about a man's obligations to his wife?"

"Puts food on the table and a roof over her head. Protects his family, honors his promises."

Addie sighed, raising her eyes to his. "I wish things were that simple. I wish I didn't have to think about so many other things. It would be so much easier if I didn't."

"Adeline, half the time I don't know what the hell you're talkin' about."

"I know you don't," she said wistfully. "I'm sorry."

She thought about that conversation when she went to bed that night, wide-awake and vaguely anxious until she heard the sweet sound of guitar strings. Ben, and that strange, yearning song he played so often. It was her favorite now, and she knew nothing of the words or the name. *Who is he serenading with that music?* she wondered, staring through the darkness. Ben's serenade . . . played for no one? For all of them? For a woman he had once longed for, someone he had wanted desperately?

What would it be like to be wanted by him? She pictured herself and Jeff as they had relaxed today at the edge of their clearing by the stream leaning against each other and sharing long, slow kisses. What would it have been like with Ben instead of Jeff? Instead of auburn locks, her fingers would have sifted through coal-black hair. Uncomfortably Addie rolled over onto her stomach, trying to shake the thoughts. She was appalled by the direction her wonderings had taken. But perhaps it was normal, even natural, to be curious about Ben.

Pulling her into his lap . . .

Addie squeezed her eyes tightly.

His warm breath on the inside rim of her ear as he whispered . . .

She let out a short, embarrassed groan and buried her face in the pillow. How could she let herself imagine such things? *Go to sleep,* she ordered herself, trying to block out the soft guitar music and head-spinning thoughts. Gradually she relaxed, her body going limp as she escaped into sleep. But Ben Hunter was in her dreams as well, more vivid than any dream figure had a right to be.

She was in a bedroom, draped across the mattress, naked underneath a cool sheet. Her eyes were fixed on the doorway, where a shadow shifted and moved into the room. It was the dark figure of a man. As he walked to the side of the bed, the muscled slope of his bare chest and shoulders gleamed in the moonlight. Sitting up with a start, she clutched the sheet to her breasts. He looked at her as if she belonged to him, his eyes tender and mocking, and she was frozen in place as she stared back at him. *No, Ben,* she wanted to whisper, but her lips wouldn't form the denial.

Something inside her body began to clamor, a hunger too sharp to bear. Wanting to flee, she made a move to the side, and Ben caught her wrists in his hands. He bent his head to kiss her, his mouth scalding and sweet. His hands stripped away the sheet, drifted over her naked body, wandered from her breasts to her stomach. The moonlight seemed to dim, leaving them in darkness, and his kisses left hot imprints on her skin, his hard flesh fitted to hers, his bare back flexed under her hands. She arched up to him, wanting him, aching, moaning his name—

Addie woke up with a gasp, her hair falling in a tangled swath across her face. Her heart was beating wildly. Her skin was feverishly hot. What was the matter with her? It was the dream she had experienced so many times before. But this time Ben, not a stranger, had been making love to her.

She jumped out of bed and went to the window, clutching the sill and breathing deeply of the night air. There was nothing but silence outside. Nothing stirred in the darkness.

What is happening to me? she asked herself, tears of bewilderment coming to her eyes. She was in Adeline Warner's bedroom, wearing Adeline's nightgown. *I've taken her family, the man who loves her. I ride her horse, sit at her place at the table, use her hairbrush.* But she wasn't Adeline Warner, she was Addie Peck, and she wanted to go home. She wanted to be in a place where everything was familiar. She didn't want to bear the strain of worrying about Russell's murder. She didn't want to ruin Ben Hunter. She wanted no part of it anymore. *No escape.* The thought would drive her mad.

Although Addie could find humor in the differences between the life she had once led and the one she was leading now, some things were hard to bear. She had never once wished she were a man, or envied a man's freedom, until now. Trying hard to copy May and Caroline's example, she struggled to curb her natural impulses. Since she'd been brought up in a household without men, she'd come to take the freedom of speaking her mind and making decisions for granted. As head of the tiny household, she had earned a living and paid the bills. But here there were so many things she couldn't do and say, so much she was prevented or forbidden from doing.

Women had to be unassuming. Women had to be quiet. Addie had to be careful to take up no more than a small percentage of mealtime conversations. The men didn't like a woman's interruption into their business discussions, even if she had something important to say.

Men could be outspoken about what they wanted. Women had to maneuver skillfully and indirectly. Whispered conversations, closing the doors discreetly, correcting or reproving with affection in her voice—that was a woman's way. She could be straightforward when speaking to a child, servant, or another woman, but never with a man. With a man you had to hem and haw and simper. Addie found that even Russell was more approachable when she was coy and sweet to him, and he would send her away with a threat to lock her in her room if she didn't "stop actin' like she was wearin' breeches."

One thing she'd never expected was her own increasing hunger for male companionship. This world was sexually segregated, a fact which everyone—men and women alike—took for granted. But she had grown up in a different time, when men and women interacted constantly, as friends and partners, and sometimes as professional associates.

Not here. Not now. She was relegated to an existence inhabited mostly by women who filled their days with caring for their children, exchanging feminine secrets, and forming close female friendships. She was quickly tired of talks about childbirth, courting, children, and marriage. Men played minor roles here. They came in for dinner, patted the children, and answered the wives' questions in monosyllables.

When a neighbor's or a cousin's husband traveled, she would come to stay at the ranch for a week or even several weeks, to compare letters and gossip, do needlework and talk about her family. A woman had no status in the real world except as someone's wife. It was only in the company of other women that she became a person with authority and privilege. Daughters imitated their mothers and older sisters until they were able to reproduce the same manners, the same habits, the same kind of friendships.

Sometimes Addie sought out Ben just for the sheer pleasure of being able to argue and let out her frustration, and he always obliged her. He would debate anything with her, holding nothing back and talking to her without the polite condescension other men used when speaking to a woman. It was a relief to be treated like a human being, even if Ben was sarcastic and insulting. Their arguments had become private conspiracies, conducted behind the others' backs. Her battles with him would have been stopped, one way or another, had anyone else been aware of them, and Addie didn't want that. In a way, Ben had become her safety valve.

She still knew little about him, despite the amount of time they spent near each other. Ben escorted Addie and Caroline to town, found a few minutes to spend with Russell and Addie as they watched the busting of a horse, and brought the young cowboy with the pink silk stitches in his forehead up to the house in order to thank Addie personally for what she had done. Ben also escorted Addie to the Double Bar on the mornings that she went to meet with Jeff. Occasionally she was prompted by a sixth sense to turn around, and she would find Ben standing close by, watching her like a cat after a mouse, looking for God knew what.

Addie stood in the parlor, pushing aside the lace curtains just an inch and looking out at the steps of the veranda. Night had almost fallen. From the next room came the clatter of plates being cleared from the table and the murmur of voices. A bulky figure sat on one of the steps outside, his back to her, his hands busy with the task of rolling a cigarette with tobacco and a corn husk. The Mexican named Diaz. She wanted badly to go out and talk to him, but she had no idea of what she would say, what she would ask. Why was he just sitting there? It looked as if he were waiting for something.

As she stood there, he turned his head slowly and looked at her through the window, his wrinkled brown face illuminated by the last rays of sunset. Their eyes met, and Addie held her breath. She saw something in his eyes, an awareness that made her almost light-headed. He knew her. He looked at her as if he knew *her,* and about the fact that she wasn't Adeline Warner. She was almost certain he did. Agitation hummed through her veins.

"What are you looking at?"

She whirled around at the sound of Ben's voice. He was leaning against the doorframe, his long legs crossed.

"Nothing," she said sharply, dropping the window curtain. Ben smiled lazily and walked over to the window, glancing outside. Diaz was facing outward again, silhouetted against the darkening sky.

"Diaz—interesting old character," Ben mused. "Can't work worth a damn, but his stories are so good we had to hire him on. He's worth his weight in gold on a trail drive."

"I didn't ask for your opinion." Suddenly Addie made up her mind and walked out of the room, brushing past Ben on her way to the front door. He tucked his hands in his pockets and followed her.

When she walked across the veranda, Diaz turned his head and smiled slightly, nodding his head at her.

"Mr. Diaz," she said nervously, clasping her hands and wringing them together. His eyes were so bleak she could see her reflection in them. "Mind if I sit with you for a minute?"

"Of course. Please." As he gestured for her to do as she wished, she saw that his face was kind. He was a grizzled old cowboy, his skin darkened by years of working in the sun, his gray hair flattened from having worn a hat all day. His body was squat and solid, slightly paunched, but undeniably hardy. Hands that were rough and strong from hard work rested on his knee as he sat with his feet propped on the steps.

Silently she sat down beside him, locking her arms around her knees, heedless of the damage the rough steps might be doing to the fabric of her dress. Ben went to lounge near the bottom of the stairs, pretending not to notice Addie's obvious desire for him to leave.

"There's something I'd like to discuss with you," she said to Diaz, and stopped in confusion. She didn't know how to continue. What exactly did she hope to learn from him? What was it that Leah had said about him? *He had his own ideas about such things. Everyone used to love to hear his stories. He could predict the future . . . he could make the craziest things seem natural. . . .*

Diaz smiled as if he could read her thoughts, picking up a short hemp rope near his feet and coiling it carefully. "Look at that sky," he said, gesturing with the tail of the rope. "So clear you can see every star. Nights like this get me to thinkin'. Folks looked at those same stars a hundred years ago, prob'ly thought the same things 'bout 'em as we do. And a hundred years from now, they'll still be lookin' at 'em. The stars never change."

"You sound kind of superstitious," Addie said hesitantly.

"Superstitious? Yes, ma'am. I've seen and heard of things that'd make any man in his right mind superstitious." His voice was heavily flavored with a Texas drawl.

As she looked at him, there was an awakening of hope inside her heart that wouldn't be quelled. The understanding she sensed in him was not the result of wishful thinking. If there was such a thing as intuition, then hers was prompting her to ask some questions. He had some answers. She would stake her life on it.

"So you believe that things can happen that don't make any sense? Things that sound like they belong in a storybook?"

"Of course. I've seen a lotta miracles in my lifetime. Trouble is, most people don't see 'em for what they are." Noticing the cynical twist of Ben's mouth, the older man smiled. "That one, there," he said, pointing to Ben, "he's one of those. He'll try to explain away miracles if he can't figger 'em out."

"But that doesn't mean miracles don't happen," Addie said, and Diaz smiled at her.

"Well, y'see—"

He was interrupted by Ben's jeering laugh. "Whatever it means, I know one thing. It doesn't do anyone any good to believe in hocus-pocus like miracles and little elves—"

"We're not talking about elves," Addie said, irritated by his interruption. "And if you want to talk about them with Mr. Diaz, come back later, but for now *I'm* having a private conversation with him, and if you're not going to leave, you can at least keep quiet."

Ben grinned, standing up and dusting off the seat of his Levi's. Clearly he thought she was indulging in a flight of fancy, and he was far from interested in hearing about it. "All right. I'll leave you two to discuss your hocus-pocus. I've got a guitar to restring."

Addie watched him stride away, her gaze troubled, and then she sighed. "I have a question. It sounds too silly to talk about with *him* listening. It's a question about time."

"Time? That's somethin' I don't pretend to know much about, Miss Adeline." He smiled. " 'Cept it goes too fast, an' I sure do like to waste it."

"I've been thinking about things that happen to people in the past and whether or not it would be possible to . . . well, to go back and change things."

"That'd be a miracle, all right. A big one."

"Do you think time could work that way?" She flushed as she realized how silly she must sound.

Diaz did not seem to be surprised by the question. "Do *you* think it works that way, Miss Adeline?"

"I'm not sure. Time is just hours and minutes. That's how I've always thought of it. Now is now, and yesterday was yesterday, and there's no going back. That's how everyone thinks of it."

LISA KLEYPAS

"Not everyone."

"But I'm beginning to think of it in a different way, as if it's a distance that could be traveled. As if there could be a road between now and yesterday. What do you think?"

His black eyes gleamed. "Let me see if we can make sense outta this. We're all movin' forward through time right now. But if you c'n go forward, don't you think you c'n go backward too?"

"Yes. Yes, I do. Then you think someone could go back in time? You really think it could happen?"

"Yes, ma'am. That it could ain't a question t' me— but then, I like to believe in such things."

"So do I," she said softly.

"Don't bet it happens a lot, though. Couldn't be many who deserve a second chance."

"What do you mean, a second chance?"

"Well, that's all goin' back in time is, ain't it? A second chance. Why would someone get to go back for any other reason?"

"To change things other people did."

Diaz shrugged. "Maybe. But I think we each gotta worry 'bout our own business." He paused and looked at her shiftily. "Now, let's say someone could go back in time. Someone like you, maybe. Why would you be there to change anything, 'cept if it was to change somethin' y' once did?"

"But what if I went back to a time before I was ever born?"

Diaz tilted his head thoughtfully. "Don't know if that could happen."

"You don't think I could go back earlier than the time I was born? Then you're saying a person could only move around in her own lifetime?"

He smiled and shrugged. "This is all gettin' too tangled up fer me."

"Me too," Addie said with a defeated sigh. Tiredly

she stood up. "But thank you. You've given me something to think about. Oh, and . . . please don't tell
anyone what we were talking about. Especially not
Ben."

"No, Miss Adeline," he said with a grave smile.

Troubled, she turned and walked toward the corral.
*I don't believe anything he said was right. I know I
don't belong in this time. I was born in 1910. Adeline
Warner was born first, not me. Unless . . . unless I
really am Adeline Warner.*

Impossible. She shrank from the idea. It was crazy.
But everything that had happened to her was crazy.
Suddenly her heart was pounding roughly, pounding
so hard her chest hurt.

She couldn't be Adeline Warner. What about Addie
Peck? What about her life with Leah and the years
she'd spent living in the house on the edge of Sunrise?
Shivering, she thought about the two hours during the
afternoon when Adeline Warner had disappeared.

"What happened that afternoon?" she whispered.
"What happened to her? Where did she go?"

Frightening thoughts flew through her mind. Maybe
she went to the future. Maybe she lived twenty years
in the space of that two hours and then came back
here. Maybe Addie Peck had just been a misplaced
Adeline Warner.

"No," she gasped, and leaned against the gatepost
of the corral, her head spinning. "I don't have Adeline's memories. I have my own. I'm not her. I don't
want to be her. Oh, God, why am I in her place?"

Addie wanted to cry, but no tears came to her eyes.
She was dry and numb. She remembered the peaceful,
orderly life she had led with Leah as her companion.
It had been difficult and lonely, but she'd always been
secure in the knowledge that each new day would be
the same as the one before. Why had that been taken
away from her? Why was she here in the place of a

girl who'd been wild and temperamental, selfish and spoiled? *That's not me,* she thought desperately. *I'm not Adeline.*

A cold feeling swept over her, and she swayed against the wooden post. A picture emerged behind her eyes. It was an image of Sunrise, the sides of the unpaved main street lined with wagons and old-fashioned contraptions pulled by tough-bodied horses. Everything was slightly askew, like in a dream, but the details were startlingly clear. She could feel the wooden boards of the sidewalk under her feet, smell the dust stirred up by wagon wheels.

As she walked down the street, it seemed as if a stranger had taken over her body and was walking in her shoes. The town drunk, Charlie Kendricks, careened against the side of a storefront and paused to watch her pass by. She saw her hands flick her skirts to the side in a contemptuous gesture, as if she would be soiled by walking near him.

A breeze blew a trendril of hair across her face, and she stopped to pin it back, looking at her reflection in a small store window. Then the image of her face disappeared, although she could still see the street and buildings beyond. Startled, she raised her hand to the pane of glass, but it wasn't reflected back at her. Suddenly the brightness of the sun struck off the window, blinding her. Covering her eyes, she gave a cry of pain, but she couldn't hear her own voice. Heat surrounded her, burning with the intensity of a thousand suns, and she felt her body shriveling, dissolving, hurtling down into an endless well of time and space. She heard the sigh of an old woman's last breath . . . and a baby's cry.

Addie opened her eyes, and the vision disappeared. Breathing through flared nostrils, she tried to gather her wits, and clung to the gatepost for support. That was what had happened to Adeline Warner the day she disappeared.

"That was what happened to *me*," she whispered. "It was me."

Adeline Warner and Addie Peck were one and the same. One woman, two different lifetimes. She'd been born twice, once in 1860 and once in 1910 . . . both lives were combined in her, and she remembered parts of each.

Terrified, Addie pushed herself away from the corral and began to run. It didn't matter that there was nowhere to run to. She had to find a place to hide, long enough to be away from everyone and think. She couldn't go back into the house. She couldn't face anyone.

"Addie?"

The soft inquiry stopped her in her tracks. She looked at the bunkhouse steps where Ben sat with a guitar resting across his knees, slender steel strings trailing from the neck of it. He set the guitar to the side and stood up, his eyes narrowed. "Addie, what's wrong?" She couldn't move, just stared mutely as he walked over to her. "What happened?"

"N-nothing—"

"Did Diaz say something to upset you?"

"No. Please don't touch me. Don't." She quivered as his hands closed over her arms, his thumbs fitting in the hollows of her inner elbows. The touch of his hands was warm. He peered into her pale face and slid his arm around her shoulders, urging her toward the house.

"Come with me. I'll take you back."

"No," Addie said, trying to pull away from him.

"Okay . . . okay. Don't get all worked up. Come here." He pulled her to one of the sheds next to the corral, hidden from view, and turned her to face him. The outline of his shoulders was crisp against the night sky. He was strong enough to do anything he wished, strong enough to kill. But his hands were gentle as they clasped her arms. She knew he could feel her trembling. "We're going to talk, Addie."

"I . . . I can't."

"What did Diaz say to you? Just tell me. I'll take care of it."

"No, don't talk to him," she managed to say. "Don't."

"I will if you don't tell me what's wrong."

She shook her head helplessly. "Everything's wrong, especially me. Everything's wrong." Unconsciously she gripped his forearms, her face tinted white in the early-evening light. "Ben, I'm different than before, aren't I? Don't you see a difference? You said I'd changed since that afternoon. You said it yourself."

A frown inserted itself between his slanting brows. "You mean the afternoon when Cade and I couldn't find you in town?"

"Yes. I've been different since then. Like another woman."

"Not that different."

"Yes, I am," she insisted, her nails digging into his forearms. Ben didn't seem to notice the pain of it as he stared down at her. "You said even my face was different."

"So I did," he said lightly. "Yes, I've noticed a few changes in you." A teasing note entered his voice. "Welcome ones."

"I know things I didn't know before. And I can't ride as well as I used to. I'm not that Adeline Warner anymore."

"Why is it so important to be different from the way you were before? I wouldn't disclaim everything about the old Adeline if I were you." His cool, sensible manner made her feel a little better. She envied his control, his lack of fear. How wonderful it would be to look at the world as he did and believe that everything was rational and in perfect order. "There were a few things about you I'd come to admire."

"How am I *different?*"

"There are thing about you I didn't notice before, I guess." Ben paused and let go of her arms, bracing them on the wall behind her, forming a circle that enclosed her securely. "You're softer, somehow. You have more compassion. And you have the sweetest smile I've . . ." Their eyes met in the darkness, and Addie felt every bone in her body dissolve. Weakly she leaned back against the wall, her breath shortening. "You've always seemed pretty callous for a woman," Ben continued. "On the outside as innocent as a baby, on the inside as hard-hearted and cash-minded as any painted cat in Abilene—"

"What's a painted cat?" she whispered, and he laughed quietly.

"Ever hear of a bawdy house, honey?" The word "honey" was a casual endearment that everyone used. But when Ben said it, it was an audible caress.

"Oh," she said, her face coloring. "How can you be so rude when—"

"We seem to have a problem understanding each other, Adeline. How did you manage to learn so many new words and forget so many old ones?"

"I . . . I don't know."

"The way you look right now is different from before. As if you need someone to take care of you. You've leaned on Russ in the past, haven't you? He's solved your problems, shouldered your burdens. But for some reason, you haven't been leaning on him lately. Why not? Have you two had a falling-out? Is that the problem?"

"No. Don't ask questions, I'm tired of questions, and I don't need someone to take care of me—"

"Yes, you do. There's been a hungry look in your

eyes for days. A look of needing a man. Isn't Jeff fulfilling his role as your nearly-betrothed?''

Flinching, she turned away and tried to leave, but he wouldn't let her. His hands rested on her shoulders, and the hint of strength in his grip promised to increase if she didn't hold still. The protective walls around her heart seemed to crumble. The more she tried to steel herself against him, the more helpless she was. There was a dreamlike stillness between them, as each tried to see into the mystery of the other.

"No, he isn't," Ben said huskily, breaking the silence. "And you're looking for something better. So you're beginning to see him for what he is, hmmn?''

"No, I'm not! I mean, yes, I know what he is, and I like him just fine!''

"You like him for his looks and his money, and of course, his amiable personality. And at the same time you despise him for being a weak fool. No woman can stand a man who'll let her control him.''

She glared at him, the line of her jaw showing through the delicate roundness of her cheek as she clenched her teeth. "You're making me sound awful. I'm not like that.''

"I've had you figured from the first moment we met. Oh, there've been some revisions along the way, but I've still got you down right.''

"You couldn't begin to understand me," she said, her voice locked high in her throat.

"You know what a mavericker is, Addie?''

"A cattle thief.''

"An entrepreneur. He doesn't let anyone stand between him and what he wants. I'm that way by nature, Addie, and so are you. And neither of us has respect for any folk who'll let us take advantage of them. I have a feeling it won't be long before Jeff's charms are going to pall, and you'll start looking for someone who won't let you manipulate him. Don't look so offended. You know it's the truth."

"It is not," she said swiftly. "You don't know the first thing about me, or about what's between me and Jeff."

His smile was taunting. "Don't I?"

"No," she said coolly. "Jeff is more than man enough to take care of me. And I don't manipulate him!"

Ben grinned, noting that her paleness had been replaced by a healthy flush of indignation. "Be honest. You lead him around by the nose."

"I don't!"

He smiled mockingly. "Such impressive loyalty to a man who doesn't know the first thing about you. I'd bet my last cent your conversations with him aren't worth a good cuss. But maybe it isn't his mind you're interested in. Possibly he provides a good roll in the grass. Admittedly his looks are passable, and then there's that mighty attractive ranch his father owns—"

"My relationship with Jeff is none of your beeswax!"

"None of my *what?*"

"You know what I mean!"

His eyes twinkled, and she realized he was laughing at her. "Yes, I know what you mean."

She was struck by the thought that he was Russell's mortal enemy. She desperately wanted it not to be true. "Ben . . . you would never hurt my father, would you?"

"Hurt Russ?" He looked startled. "God Almighty, no. Of course not. What gave you that idea?"

"He trusts you more than he trusts anyone else. You're closer to him than anyone. You're in a good position to hurt him."

Ben's face went blank, as if a mask had slipped into

place. All his warmth fled in an instant. "I owe him my loyalty. He gave me a new start when I needed one, a chance to work hard and get paid well for it. And honor aside, I have practical reasons to justify his trust in me. Why should I bite the hand that feeds me? I'd be crazy to hurt him." He straightened away from her and tilted his head toward the house. "Come on. I'll walk you back." His lips curved in a humorless smile. "Did anyone ever tell you that you have a talent for spoiling a mood, Addie?"

"What kind of mood?"

Ben laughed, shaking his head, and he took her arm. "Sometimes—not often—Jeff Johnson has my sympathy. Come on."

4

THE BUGGY PULLED AWAY FROM THE MAIN HOUSE AS Watts clicked to the horse, and Caroline settled more comfortably in the wicker seat. "Caro, is this going to jolt you too much?" Adeline asked worriedly, fussing with the pillows and sliding another one behind her back. "If it's at all dangerous for you to be going to town with me, I'll—"

"No, I'm not *that* far along yet. And I just have to get away from the ranch for a little while or I'll scream. Don't you remember how I was with Leah? I could go anywhere and do practically anything up to the last week. No, maybe you don't remember too well. You were just ten years old. Isn't it funny, that Mama had us ten years apart and I'm havin' this one ten years after Leah? She'll probably be a second mother to this baby just like I was to you."

The two women spoke in near-whispers to keep from embarrassing Watts, the ranch hand who was driving them to town. Babies and childbirth were women's matters, ones that men liked to hear about as little as possible. If Watts heard anything they said, he didn't let on. He was a quiet man, a few years older than Addie, a little less than average height, but stocky and broad-shouldered. His dark blue eyes were often filled with equal parts of mischief and malice. Though he'd been perfectly polite, Addie was vaguely uncomfortable whenever she spoke to him directly. He treated

135

her with such overdone respect it almost smacked of contempt, and she had no idea why.

"Have you decided on the names for the baby yet?" she asked Caroline.

"If it's a boy, Russell. And if it's a girl, Sarah. After our great-grandmother."

"Yes," Addie said, feeling a lump of pleasure-pain in her throat. "That's a pretty name." That was the right name. Her mother's name. *But she won't be my mother anymore. Not if I'm already here. Not if I'm Adeline Warner.* What an intriguing thought. Maybe she would be around to see Sarah grow up, come to know her as she never had been able to before.

Every now and then Addie wondered still if she were in the middle of a dream. In this moment, as she looked into Caroline's pretty flushed face, she knew it was real. The sun on her back was real. The jostling of the buggy and the mounted figures of cowboys in the distance weren't the products of a dream. She couldn't deny what was in front of her eyes. But could she ever stop grieving for the loss of the life she had known?

It was difficult to know how she felt about the Warners. She liked them, she felt a casual sort of affection for them all, but she certainly didn't have the kind of love for May and Russell that a daughter should have for her parents. Cade and Caroline were both likable, but she felt no strong attachment to either of them. She didn't know them.

"As soon as I have the baby, Peter and I are going to move our little family to North Carolina," Caroline said. "And I can hardly wait."

"Do you have to?" Addie protested. "North Carolina's so far away."

"Mama's people already have a job lined up for him, and we'll get a real nice welcome from them. And I know Leah will love it there."

She won't. She'll come back to Texas someday.

"Couldn't Peter do something in Dallas, or some-place closer? I know he doesn't like ranching, but there are other things in Texas he could—"

"It's Texas we want to move away from, Adeline. Oh, you look like Daddy did when I told him that! I'm just not a Texan at heart. I don't see the same things in it that the rest of y'all do, and neither does Peter. This land looks barren to me. It's desolate . . . lonely . . . and sometimes it's so boring I could die for want of something to do. Don't you think of it as a mournful place?"

Addie looked out over the endless plains of summer grass and tried to see it that way. But the sky was brilliant with sunshine, and her eye kept moving from red-orange clusters of Indian paintbrush to cotton-wood and mesquite trees. Further out were fields of yellow-eyed bluebonnets, rippling like a violet ocean when the wind blew. The men were working hard on the land, tending the cattle. This land, this life, held an irresistible attraction for them. Addie hadn't under-stood it before, but she was beginning to.

Any other place in the world would have been too crowded. Here the men had a huge expanse of range to ride, where they worked until they were bone-weary, and when their day was over they came back to the mess-house and the appetizing smells of sourdough bread and meat smoked over mesquite wood. If the night was warm, they brought their bedrolls and mat-tresses outside and slept under the open sky. The cow-boys didn't find this life unbearably lonely. It was as civilized as they could stand. And for the family there were weddings, picnics, barbecues, quiltings, dances, and shooting tournaments, almost no end of excuses to see people and call on neighbors if you got lonely for company.

"No, I never think of it as a mournful place," she

said thoughtfully. "Or boring. There's always something to do and something happening. I'd rather be in Texas than anywhere."

"Even after you went to school for two years in Virginia? I don't understand you, Adeline. How could you choose this dusty old ranch over a civilized place to live in, with lots of people around and modern conveniences . . ."

Addie stopped listening as Caroline continued to talk about the wonders of city living. She could picture Sunrise as it would be fifty years from now, replete with modern conveniences Caroline couldn't even imagine. Had that Sunrise she had known been preferable to this? Maybe not. You could be just as lonely with lots of people around. Being happy was more than that, more than having stores and automobiles and movie theaters close by. Being happy was something that had always eluded her, and would continue to, until she found the answers to questions she had only begun to ask herself. *I think I'd be happy if I had someone to share things with. Someone who needed me.* And then maybe she wouldn't care where or when she was living.

". . . there's no future for Peter here," Caroline was saying. "He's not the kind of man who'll be happy on a ranch. He needs a nice job in an office somewhere, where he can earn a living with his mind, not his hands. He's not interested in a bunch of mangy old cows, and there's no point in him trying to be. The only man capable of filling Daddy's shoes is Ben, and everyone knows it."

Confusion again. Always that first clutching sensation of confusion when she thought of Ben and Russell. Why was she cursed with the knowledge of their destinies? She wished she didn't know. Knowing was a terrible responsibility, the responsibility of preserving Russell's life and maintaining her guard against

Ben at all times. But how, *how* could Ben have done it? There must be two men living in his skin.

"Look over there," Caroline said, and Addie saw a rider approaching them at an easy canter. Even before she saw his face, she knew it was Ben by the familiar tilt of his low-crowned felt hat. The front of the brim was angled low over his forehead in a way that meant business. Only a tenderfoot or a dandy wore his hat on the back of his head.

Ben rode his horse parallel to the buggy and slowed to a walk, touching the brim of his hat in a respectful gesture as he nodded to Addie and Caroline. "Well, if it isn't the two prettiest women in Texas."

"Hello," Caroline said, smiling sunnily, while Addie pretended interest in the scenery on the other side of the buggy. "What are you up and about this mornin', Ben?"

"Work as usual." He smiled raffishly. "But if I had the time, I'd take you to town myself and buy you the tallest glasses of lemonade you've ever seen."

A full-blown simper appeared on Caroline's face in less than five seconds. "Oh, you slick-tongued rascal. Isn't he a honey, Adeline?"

Addie turned her head to regard Ben impassively. He looked impossibly virile, clad in the standard uniform of Levi's, boots, and a worn shirt. The sunlight glowed in his eyes and along the edges of his cheekbones. He was one of the few men on the ranch who shaved every day, but his beard was so dark there was always a shadow of bristle on the lower half of his face. She wondered how his jaw would feel against her fingertips—smooth in one direction, sandpapery in the other. It was part of what made him so dangerous, his vibrant attractiveness. Why couldn't he have been ugly?

"Aren't you supposed to be working?" she asked curtly.

"Adeline, how rude," Caroline said in protest.

"Well, around this time he's usually roping, de-horning, or debogging something. Are you taking a rest today, Mr. Hunter?"

Ben smiled and reached in his shirt pocket to pull out a white slip of paper. He handed it to the cowboy at the front of the buggy. "Watts, this is a list of supplies for you to pick up in town. Just charge them to the General Store account."

"Alrighty." Watts pocketed the list.

"Mrs. Ward," Ben said to Caroline, "it's going to be a hot day. Are you sure you're up to it?" Which was a tactful way of referring to her pregnancy. As he addressed Caroline, his manner was so friendly and concerned that Addie was surprised and perhaps even a little resentful. *He never behaves that way with me.* He was always mocking her. *Just once I'd like him to ask me something in that tone of voice!*

"I'm just fine, thank you," Caroline replied, daintily twirling the silk-wrapped handle of her sage-green parasol. "Just eager for a change of scenery. Don't worry 'bout me."

"In that case, I'll be getting back to work. But I have to leave you with a warning, Mrs. Ward."

"Oh?"

"Keep a close eye on your sister. She's mighty hard to keep track of in town. She'll disappear before you can blink twice."

"Sometimes I do, sometimes I don't," Addie said. "It depends on the people I'm with."

Ben smiled sardonically while his eyes made a thorough study of her. He noticed the hat perched on top of her piled-up hair, a frilly little hat decorated with artificial strawberries and pale pink netting. Slowly his gaze wandered from the little white collar of her dusty-rose princess dress to the rows of tiny folds that demurely emphasized the fullness of her breasts.

There was a spark of challenge in her eyes and disdain in her expression. Did she know when she looked at a man like that, it made him want to tame her? If the two of them had been alone together that very minute, he might have shown her a remedy for her haughtiness.

Knowing herself to be the object of such an overt inspection made Addie indignant and strangely warm. She forced herself to stare right back at him, her eyes dark and velvety above her pinkening cheeks. A lock of hair, the glistening color of brown sugar, blew across her face, and slowly she reached up to pull it aside. It was a purely feminine gesture, unconsciously alluring. And Ben was aware of that, as he was aware of everything about her. Every move she made set something alight in him, like flame and dry tinder. It filled him with powerful consternation.

Women had never been a mystery to him. He was the kind of man who instinctively understood a woman's needs, and he'd always made good use of that knowledge. An impudent girl just out of her teens shouldn't be able to have this effect on him. But Adeline was a mystery, and he was drawn to her even as he resented her hold on him.

"I'll see you later," he said abruptly. "Behave yourselves."

"We'll try," Addie replied, her voice withering, and she and Ben exchanged an unsmiling glance before he touched his hat and rode off.

"He's quite a man," Caroline murmured, watching Ben's departure with admiring eyes. "If I weren't married, I just might have given the women of Falls County a run for their money."

"I don't think he'd want a respectable woman."

"I've heard he visits a woman in Blue Ridge pretty regular."

"A lonesome widow?" Addie asked sarcastically.

"I don't know. That's a good question. Do you suppose—"

"I don't care to suppose anything about him. We've got better things to talk about."

They changed the subject and began to discuss other things, and their animated conversation lasted throughout the day. They had a pleasant time in town, shopping and talking to people they passed on the sidewalk. After her initial shyness, Addie discovered she and Caroline had a similar sense of humor, as well as a similar way of looking at things. It became much easier to think of Caroline as her sister.

They could talk comfortably about almost anything, even the most private matters. With each minute they spent together, Addie felt herself confiding more and more. When they arrived back at the ranch, they were still deep in conversation, and they decided to sit in the front-porch swing, unwilling to go inside just yet.

"I don't see Ben anywhere around here," Caroline said, her eyes twinkling. "Guess it's safe to stay around you a little longer."

"What do you mean?" Addie rested her feet on the porch while the swing rocked and creaked gently.

"Only that my nerves are frazzled whenever you're near each other."

"Why?"

"Why? Because I'm always ready for an explosion between you and Ben. You were terribly rude to him this mornin', Adeline. And the way he looked at you— why, I'm surprised your hat didn't catch on fire!"

Addie laughed. "He was just trying to intimidate me by glaring."

"No, that wasn't glaring." Cautiously Caroline glanced around and lowered her voice. "That was *looking.* Peter used to look at me like that before we were married. Believe me, there's no doubt about it. Ben's taken with you."

"Don't be silly. I'll admit he likes to argue with me, but—"

"He'd like to do more than argue with you. I tell you, Adeline, if you tried bein' nice to him once in a while, you'd have him eatin' out of your hand."

"I don't want him eating out of my hand. I don't want him anywhere near me."

"This isn't the first time I've noticed him lookin' at you like that, either. I've seen it before today."

Addie's nonchalance dissolved rapidly. "You have?"

"Mmmn-hmmn."

Suddenly Addie was intensely curious. Underneath his sarcasm and coolness, did Ben really harbor some kind of romantic interest in her? The thought should have appalled her, but somehow she was foolishly pleased by it. She was embarrassed to hear her own sheepish snicker.

"When?"

"I can't believe you haven't noticed! During dinner the other night, I asked him to pass the salt, and he was so busy watchin' you I got the pepper instead. I didn't say anything, of course—just took it like it was what I asked for—"

"Watching me? What was I doing?"

"Just talkin'. He pays attention whenever you start talkin'. And he listens to everything you say. Peter was trying to ask him some questions, and Ben just kept turnin' his head to listen to you, and finally Peter gave up. If you sweet-talked Ben a little, Adeline, you'd have him on the hook, and you could reel him in just as easy as—"

"Why would I want to reel *him* in? I've got Jeff Johnson. I thought you all wanted me to marry him."

"Wellll . . . you and Jeff make a good pair," Caroline conceded. "I've always thought so. But between the two of 'em, I'd choose Ben Hunter in a minute."

"Choose him for what? To be my beau? That's a

ridiculous idea. And even if I didn't think so, Ben would laugh his head off at the notion. You heard Mama the other morning. Ben's a loner. He wouldn't want a relationship with a respectable woman.''

"I don't know 'bout that. Mama likes to exaggerate sometimes. She's just tryin' to steer you clear of Ben because she doesn't want you to wind up married to that kind of man. She thinks he's too much like Daddy.''

"What's wrong with that?''

"Mama told me once that even though she loved Daddy, it would've been easier if she'd married one of the beaus she'd had back east and stayed there. She's never really liked livin' out here, y'know. She won't ever feel like she really belongs. She comes from different stock.''

"Daddy said something like that to me the other day,'' Addie said absently.

"Daddy's a strong-willed man. I guess Mama never realized how much, until it was too late. She always thought she could kind of bend him to her way of thinkin'. But she never could. So she wanted it to be easier for us than it was for her, which is why she encouraged me to marry Peter. And for the same reason, Mama's tryin' to marry you off to Jeff. They're both nice men, but kind of . . . soft. Do you know what I mean?''

"Soft? But Caro . . . you love Peter, don't you?''

Caroline hesitated almost imperceptibly. "Of course I do. He's a good man, a good husband and father. He's steady and loyal, and sweet-natured. But there's no vinegar between us.''

Despite the serious nature of the conversation, Addie couldn't help smiling. "Vinegar?''

"You know that trick Mama taught us, about putting a little vinegar in when you're making pecan pie, to keep it from bein' too candy-sweet? That's what I'm talkin' about. Adeline, this is private talk, just between two sisters. I just don't want you to make a mistake. The kind of mistake that I . . .'' She stopped and shrugged helplessly.

"I'm listening," Addie said, afraid Caroline wouldn't finish what she was trying to say. And she wanted very much to know what it was. She and Leah had never had this kind of talk. Leah had never known much about marriage, and Addie hadn't been especially interested in the subject until now.

"Well, I don't want you to get the wrong impression. I'm very happy, Adeline. Very happy. I'm just sayin' you need to be careful when you choose the man you're going to be with for the rest of your life. Don't pick someone you can manage too easy. You—especially you—need a little vinegar in your marriage."

"Are you saying you don't think I should marry Jeff?''

Caroline sighed and laughed a little. "You're so direct sometimes! Just as blunt as Daddy. No, I'm not sayin' anything about Jeff in particular. I'm telling you to marry someone who makes your heart pitter-patter. Mama and Daddy always taught us marriage is somethin' you have to calculate and plan. I . . . sometimes I wish I hadn't taken it to heart quite so well. No woman should be cheated of marryin' the man she loves, Adeline. There's no compensation for it later, no matter what they tell you."

"Caro, you look so sad."

"Sometimes I am, when I think about the mistakes I've made."

"Was there ever someone you . . . still think about?''

"Maybe there was. A long time ago."

"And you felt special about him?''

"Oh, yes. I felt special about him." Caroline smiled

reminiscently, all at once looking younger and terribly wistful. "He and I were at each other all the time, like cats and dogs. Like you and Ben. Seeing you two reminds me a little of what it was like. He was Daddy's trail boss. He was the kind of man that Daddy and Ben are. Very charming, but he liked to get his own way. Very stubborn. I thought I hated him at first. I felt so nervous around him. He always thought he knew everything." She slipped one foot out of her shoe and wiggled her toes with a sigh. "Lord, my feet are tired."

"What happened between the two of you? You have to tell me the rest," Addie said eagerly, intrigued by the thought that Caroline, with her wholesome face and picture-perfect manners, had been romantically involved with Russell's trail boss. What an odd pair they must have made!

"You can't talk about this to anyone else, ever. You have to promise."

"I swear I won't. On the Bible. On anything you want me to."

"All right," Caroline interrupted, smiling slightly. "The rest of the family knows about it—exceptin' Cade—so you'd most likely hear about it sooner or later."

"I didn't know you'd ever been interested in anyone but Peter."

"I met Peter durin' my two years at the academy in Virginia. He was going to military school, and we noticed each other at a dance. He looked *very* good in a uniform—what man doesn't? We struck up an acquaintance, and began to write each other, and he took me to meet his parents durin' one of our last vacations. He was so kind and sweet-natured, and everything just fell into place. We got engaged. Then I came home for a spell, and that was when I met Raif Colton. You were just a little girl. Do you remember him?"

"A little," Addie lied. "I guess I was too young to notice much about him."

"As soon as we met each other, Raif set his sights on me—wouldn't leave me alone—which made me furious and sent Mama into a tailspin." Caroline shook her head and made a wistful sound. "Raif was so . . . so . . . I can't describe him. I felt like a different woman around him. I'd always been the quiet one. Russell Warner's oldest daughter, so well-behaved, so proper. No man had ever tried anything with me— y'know? But Raif cornered me in the house one day when no one was around, and . . ." Caroline looked at Addie's expectant face and blushed hotly. "He let me know how he felt about me. He was so tender, and frightening, and exciting. And after everything was said and done, I knew he loved me. But I was all set on marryin' Peter—the smart thing to do, the sensible thing. Mama knew about Raif, and she did everything in her power to keep us apart. All summer Peter and I stayed engaged, and plans for the wedding were made, and Raif did his best to convince me to marry him instead."

"Did you love him?"

"I loved both of them. I loved Peter with my mind. I was safe with him. But I loved Raif with my heart. I loved his passion, his wildness. It was impossible to choose."

"But you ended up marrying Peter."

"Yes. I was afraid to take a chance on Raif."

"What happened to him?"

"After the marriage, he stayed on at the ranch for several months. I begged him to leave, but he wouldn't give up, even after he found out I was going to have a baby. It was hell—you can't know . . . Lord, you can't imagine. I had no peace, not for one minute. I found out the difference between loving a man with your mind and your heart. I came to realize the mistake I'd made, and I wanted to die of misery. I made a decision, that I'd run away with Raif. Nothin' was as important as he was, not money, family, honor. Not even Peter. We were goin' to leave together, after he came back from drivin' a thousand head of cattle up to Dodge. But one night on the trail, the longhorns got spooked. Crazy animals—they'll stampede at anything, even a sneeze. And Raif was killed.''

Addie was flooded with sympathy. "Caro . . . I'm sorry . . ."

"That was ten years ago. Enough time has passed by to make it tolerable. I couldn't bear it at first. But I had Peter, and I've always loved him in a certain way. That gave me enough strength to live through the grief. I'm married to a special man.''

"I think you're special," Addie said softly, and meant it.

"Me? Why?"

"Because of the way you've survived."

"Oh, there's no trick in that. You might be surprised by the things a person's able to survive through. There's always somethin' to hold on to. There's always someone that needs you, somethin' that needs your attention. It takes your mind off feelin' sorry for yourself.''

"But it makes me afraid of loving someone, the thought that I might lose him.''

"You can't let yourself worry 'bout that. It's better to have love for a little while than not at all, isn't it?''

Addie laughed huskily. "I guess. I'm not sure."

Caroline regarded her for a long moment. "Right now I like you more than I ever have, Adeline. For a little while I thought Daddy had finally done it—spoiled you rotten to the core. But he hasn't. You're a sweet girl.''

"Thank you," Addie said, her eyes suddenly bright. For the first time she felt as if the two of them were family. She realized that she did care about Caroline. She felt a bond between them, of trust and affection, so strong that it seemed it had always been there. She felt as if they were sisters. It had happened all at once, like the flip of a coin. How short a distance it was from indifference to love.

Caroline leaned closer. "I'll tell you somethin' only Mama and Peter know," she whispered.

"You don't have to tell me any of your secrets."

"I want to. I want you to remember what I've told you. Don't ever be afraid of lovin' someone, or you'll make the mistake I did. I don't let myself think of the might've-beens. It would hurt too much. But I have something very special to remember Raif by. More than memories. The greatest treasure he could've given me."

Addie went very still. "Leah?" she asked inaudibly, her mouth barely framing the name.

Caroline nodded and smiled tremulously. "You've been so sweet to her lately, spendin' time with her. You have a special feelin' for her, don't you?"

"Yes. Oh, yes, I do." Addie leaned over and hugged her tightly.

"Before I was married to Peter, Raif and I had a few days together," Caroline whispered. "He never knew it was his baby. I promised Peter I wouldn't tell him. But just lookin' at her reminds me how much Raif loved me. Every woman should be loved like that, Adeline, at least once."

"Sometimes I wish for that," Addie said humbly, while she burned inside with longing and hope, and relentless doubt. Involuntarily she thought of Ben, his sensual smile and threatening charm. "And sometimes I want to be unattached forever." Like Leah had been. Leah had had a fulfilling life in spite of being unmarried . . . she'd been happy . . . hadn't she?

Not always, a small voice whispered inside. Leah

had worried that Addie would turn out to be a spinster too. And she had been so wistful sometimes. There had been many lonely, quiet hours for her. Yes, there had been a part of Leah that must have wished for a husband and a real family.

"Unattached forever?" Caroline repeated. "I wouldn't want that for you, Adeline. Think of all you'd miss out on."

"But what if I fell in love with the wrong man?"

"Wrong by whose reckonin'? Mama's? You'd most likely be best off with the kind of man she doesn't want for you. Someone like . . . well, like Ben."

"Why do you mention him?" Addie asked, suddenly irritated. "What do you see in him that I don't? If you're hoping that something will develop between Ben and me, you're going to be disappointed. I just plain don't trust him. How do you and everyone else know that he won't go bad? How do we know he won't turn mean, or turn on Daddy, or something else just as awful? He's attractive on the surface, but inside . . . why, there's no telling what he's really like."

"Is that what you think about him?" Caroline looked surprised. "Well, I s'pose he might be different on the inside than he seems. I just always took him at face value. But I'll tell you somethin'. The only way to find out what he's really like is to get closer to him." She peered at Addie quizzically. "There a chance you might be interested in him?"

"Maybe," Addie admitted reluctantly. She thought of Russell, and her mouth tightened. "For certain reasons."

"Then take a chance on him! Spend some time with him! You might be surprised how much you and Ben have in common. He'd be so nice to you, if you'd just let him. I'm sure of it."

As Addie thought over the idea, she began to see the sense of it. Spend some time with Ben, get to know him, try to gain his friendship. If she could make him like her, that would make him a little vulnerable to her, wouldn't it? Wouldn't it be easier to outsmart him if he trusted her? It made no sense to make him think of her as an enemy. Then he would always be on his guard when she was near. And she was the only thing that was going to stand between him and his plan to kill Russell. But how plausible was her attempt to befriend him going to seem?

"He wouldn't be nice to me," she said doubtfully. "He'd only laugh at me if he thought I was interested."

Caroline smiled with satisfaction. "Now, that's one thing you'll never get me to believe."

Addie received her first opportunity to be nice to Ben much sooner than she'd expected. Late in the afternoon he and two line riders were entangled in the first serious confrontation between Double Bar and Sunrise men. Ben came to the main house with a battered face and a tersely worded report for Russell. Russell's roar could be heard across three counties. The fight between the cowboys had been about his "bob-wahhr" fence, and he was livid at the suggestion that he didn't have the right to fence in his own land. Why, how was he going to keep control over his cattle and stop them from drifting where they shouldn't? How could he protect his property from thieves and rustlers?

"Now, Russ, hold on," came Ben's voice from behind the door as he and Russell talked in the office. The rest of the family stood in the hallway and eavesdropped unabashedly. "I know how you feel, but you can't blame them for being angry when one of their horses was killed by that damn fence. The animal was cut to pieces. It was the worst godawful mess I've seen in a long time."

Russell was not disposed to see their side of it. "I don't care what made 'em mad. They attacked three of my men, including my foreman, and cut up my fence! Well, it's goin' back up, with five strands instead of four. If Big George wants a war with me, he'll find out quick that he's bitten off too much this time!"

There was a short silence. Then Ben spoke, and although he sounded casual, there was an undertone in his voice that commanded attention. "We fenced in some public land along with our own, Russ, not to mention a considerable amount of water. That makes us unpopular with just about everyone. There's a lot of sympathy out there for Big George. They all need water and grass for their cattle, and some figure we've got more than our share."

"Is that what you think, boy?" Russel demanded furiously. "You think we've got more than our share?"

"I think you know when it's time to be diplomatic. I've seen you slick down a lot of ruffled feathers when too many tempers were high. We're the biggest outfit around here, and that makes us an easy target. It's going to get worse, Russ. Fence-cutting is just the beginning."

"We're not some greasy-sack outfit they can push around. We can take whatever they're fixin' to dish out!"

"Possibly. But do we want to? We've got enough on our hands just taking care of our own business." Ben's voice softened as he spoke persuasively. "The system's always worked without fences. We all depend on each other. You can't turn us into an island. We can't survive alone. I say we start putting that money we've been spending for reels of barbed wire and kegs of staples into hiring more line riders. We can't afford the trouble those fences are going to earn us."

Addie could almost see the bullheaded expression on Russell's face as he replied, "I say I'm the top man around here, and I decide where to put my money. Tomorrow I want those cedar posts stuck back in the ground and strung with five strands of wire.''

Ben swore softly, and then there was the sound of his booted feet as he walked toward the door. The family scattered, all darting out of the hallway and finding various tasks to busy themselves with. Addie met Ben at the front door as he started to leave the house. She felt a reluctant twinge of pity as she saw the bruise on his jaw and the faint shadow underneath one eye.

Ben looked at her stonily. ''I've had about enough of the Warners for one afternoon. So if you'll excuse me—''

''You're going to have a black eye.''

He pulled the handkerchief from around his neck and dabbed at the bloody corner of his mouth. ''Lady, that's the least of my problems.''

''I know.'' She risked a smile and inclined her head toward the kitchen. ''Come with me. I'll get you something cold for that.'' As he followed her into the kitchen, she picked up a clean dishrag and threw a glance over her shoulder. ''Stay. I'll be back in a minute.''

While he waited in the kitchen, staring after her restlessly, she went downstairs to the stone-floored ice cellar, where the perishable food was packed tightly with ice, straw, and sawdust. It was dark and blessedly cool down there. Addie wasted no time in filling the dishrag with ice and hurrying back upstairs. Ben took it from her, hesitating before applying it to his face.

''Put it on your eye,'' she said impatiently, and indicated a nearby chair. ''And sit down. I want to see to your jaw, and you're too tall.'' She wet another cloth at the sink. ''How are the other two men?''

''About the same.'' Ben sank down in the chair with a sigh, while the aches and pains in is body began to make themselves known. "They visited Cook and had him see to them as soon as we got back. I didn't have time." He turned his face into the ice, relishing its coldness. "We were lucky it didn't turn into gunfire. Ow!" He winced as Addie pressed the cloth to the corner of his cut lip. "Careful with that thing!"

"I'm sorry. I know it must hurt."

"Damn right it does."

She smiled into his baleful green eyes and took care to be even more gentle in her ministrations. She knew from her nursing experience that men were stoic and silent about their wounds until they were assured of a woman's attention. Then they started complaining and demanding to be fussed over.

"Would you like something to drink?"

"I had a drink when I came in to talk to Russ."

"I . . . we . . . couldn't help overhearing some of your conversation."

He smiled sardonically. "With your ears pressed to the keyhole, I guess you couldn't."

"When he calms down and thinks about things, he might change his mind. A little common sense will make him see that—"

Ben snorted at the suggestion. "You know him better than that. This isn't a matter of common sense to him. It's a matter of pride. He won't back down."

"What are you going to?"

He shrugged, looking away from her. "Put the fence back up."

"Even though you don't believe in it?"

"I've told Russ what I think. That's my job. He's made the decision. That's his job. Whether or not I like his decision, I'm going to live by it. The alternative is to leave, and I'm not ready to."

"Why not? There are other ranches that would hire you in a minute."

"I get the feeling you're hoping I'll go." Ben didn't

miss the way she blushed and looked away. His eyes were cool and watchful as he continued, "Why won't I? Because I like Sunrise. And I gave my word to Russ that I'd stay as long as he needed me."

"You're very loyal to him, aren't you?" Addie asked. There was a fine edge to her voice that must have been unfathomable to him.

'He's one of the best men I've ever known. And one of the few I've ever met who deserves complete honesty. It would be easier just to tell him what he wants to hear. But I respect him too much for that."

"He thinks of you as an adopted son." The way she spoke made it sound far from a compliment. "What about your own family? What about your own father?"

"I've got a nice family in Illinois. And a respectable father, who's worked at a bank for the past twenty-five years." Ben grinned, his mood lightening. "Every time I'm anywhere near my father, he goes into the early stages of apoplexy. We don't have much in common, he and I."

"With a Harvard education—if you really got one— you could have gotten a job back east. Why did you decide on Texas?"

"The only place I'm not wanted by the law . . . yet." His deadpan assertion was so close to what she had been thinking that Addie started. Then she saw the dance of mischief in his eyes. He was taunting her. She scowled at him, unamused, forgetting her intention to be sweet to him.

"I never know when to believe anything you say!"

"Poor Addie. And here you are, dispensing your charity and goodwill to a wounded man—"

"Oh, stop it," she said, thoroughly disconcerted by his sarcasm. "I don't know why I tried being nice to you. And you're not *wounded*, either. You're just a little beat-up."

"A real angel of mercy, aren't you?" He reached

up experimentally to touch the corner of his mouth, which had stopped bleeding. She bent closer to peer at it.

"It doesn't look too bad to me."

"Only because you're not the one wearing it." His mouth tilted roguishly at the corners. "Don't I get a kiss to make it better?"

She snorted at the question, knowing he didn't really mean it. "You'd probably die of shock if I did."

Slowly he set the ice down on the table. He decided to take a gamble. "Try it and see," he invited softly.

Addie stared at him in amazement. Her heart jerked as if it danced on the end of a string. Surely his last words had been the ultimate mockery. She knew she was staring at him, but she couldn't help it. He didn't mean it . . . oh, he couldn't mean it. But . . . he looked as if he did.

I can't. I just couldn't. He'd make fun of me if I took him up on it. He'll make fun of me if I don't, too. He'll say I was afraid . . . he has too much of an ego to accept that I just didn't want to kiss him.

But she did want to.

Look at him sitting there, just daring me to make a move. He looks good even when he's dirty and messed up. Leah always said she figured the Devil would be a mighty handsome man.

Why is he so tempting? It's the bad in me. The bad in him appeals to the worst part of me.

What would it feel like?

Ben appeared to be relaxed, but she knew he was as alert as a cat. She wished he didn't look so predatory. He had issued the challenge; now he was waiting for her response. She forced herself to smile carelessly. Bending quickly, she brushed her lips across his in the lightest of touches, too fast for him to respond.

"Feel better?" she asked in a sugar-coated voice,

and he eyed her sardonically, the moment of tension almost broken. But not quite.

"Hardly."

"Well, what were you expecting?"

Now the challenge was thrown to him. He accepted it without hesitation. Standing up in a swift movement, he caught her waist in his hands and backed her up until the edge of the table pressed into her buttocks. She didn't know what to do or where to put her hands. Her palms came to rest on his upper arms, on the hard swell of muscle that tightened at her touch. And she looked up at him, confused and excited, and curious. Just this once it wouldn't hurt. She would let it happen, and she didn't care what he said or thought afterward. He lowered his dark head and nuzzled her ear, and the touch of his hot breath in the hollow behind her earlobe made her shiver.

"That's a good question," he said. "What should I expect from a woman like you?" He heard her swallow convulsively, felt her body tense as he drew closer. She wasn't trying to move away, although they both knew he would have let her go easily had she made a move to be free. The skin of her arms was soft underneath his fingers.

Suddenly she seemed very fragile to Ben, someone to be handled gently and treated with tenderness. He'd never felt that for anyone in his life, or held a woman who trembled at his touch. He was accustomed to women who were comfortable with men, well-versed in the ways a man liked to be pleased. But there was a vast gulf between their knowledge and this woman's. Despite her attempts at sophistication, she didn't have much actual experience, of that he was fairly certain. There was no way her shyness, her uncertainty, could be manufactured. Why did it arouse him so?

"Addie," he murmured, and her breath caught as

his mouth began to wander to the edge of her jaw. "Don't pretend with me. Not ever."

"Wh-what?"

"I hope I'm not imagining you. Am I, Addie?"

"No—"

"It doesn't matter if I am." His hands urged her upward, gently forcing her to rise on her toes. "Don't pull away, Adeline."

She wanted to pull away, but her body was thrilling with exhilaration, guilt, and fear. Her face turned that necessary half-inch, to an angle that aligned with his. She was lost in the deep green sea of his eyes. His arm slid around her back, trapping her, keeping her close, and suddenly both of them were aware of her breasts pressed snugly into his chest.

As he bent his head to kiss her, she held her breath and her eyes closed. Just as their lips met, there was the sound of footsteps outside the kitchen door, and Russell's imperious voice.

"Addie? Addie, where are you?"

They broke apart in a startled movement. Addie flushed and spun away from Ben, touching her mouth with her fingertips as if he'd left a brand. There had been no time to feel anything but a delicious hint of warmth . . . but that was more than she ever should have known of Ben Hunter.

"We're both in the kitchen," Ben replied, swiping up the dripping cloth full of ice and holding it to his face as he sat down abruptly. He and Addie stared at each other for one burning moment until Russell strode into the kitchen.

"I see she's got you fixed up good," he said, seeming not to notice Addie's discomposure. "Adeline, there's a thing or two we got to talk about."

"Oh?"

"That Johnson boy—well, things hafta change between you and him."

"What do you mean?" she asked warily. "The quarrel is between you and Big George. That doesn't have to affect my friendship with Jeff."

'The quarrel's between the Warners and the Johnsons. Which means there's no more friendship between you and Jeff. You're not goin' to see him anymore, or even talk to him. Understand?"

If he had approached her in a different way, she might have tried to understand his viewpoint. But the way he said it, as an order for her to follow, a command for her to obey, fired her temper as quickly as if he'd set a match to gunpowder.

"It looks like we have a few things to discuss," she said evenly, trying to keep calm."

"There's nothin' to talk about."

Ben cleared his throat. "Looks like it's time for me to leave."

"Stay," Russ commanded without looking at him. "This won't take long."

"But then again, it might," Addie said tersely. "Because you seem to think that all you have to do is dictate orders and watch me rush to obey. But I'm an adult, and I have some say in this."

"Now, Addie, don't be stubborn, or—"

"Or you'll send me to bed early? Or give me less pocket money? I'm not a child to be disciplined. I'm an adult."

"You're my daughter."

"I have the right to take part in the decisions that affect me."

"You sure as hell don't!" Russell exploded. "Because I'm the one who makes the decisions, and I'm damn well not going to come to you for advice about my business—"

"This is *my* business too! You and Mama have been pushing Jeff at me for weeks. Half the time I've gone to see him only because I wanted to please you. Now suddenly I'm supposed to turn my feelings off and give him the freeze because of some arbitrary whim of yours. But I can't do that.''

''Dammit, why are you so all-fired anxious to cross me?'' Their eyes met in challenge, and Addie saw his anger increase as he realized she wasn't going to bow down easily. But he was canny, and he decided to change tactics. ''Honey,'' he said in a conciliatory voice, ''we'll get someone a lot better than Jeff for you. Any man in Texas would give his left . . . would give a lot to have you. Ain't that right, Ben?''

''Don't drag him into this!'' Addie snapped, saving Ben the necessity of replying. ''And I won't be pacified by having the prospect of some other man dangled in front of me like a new toy.''

''Then what the hell *do* you want?''

''For you to stop treating me like I'm something to be moved around and managed and maneuvered, just like your cattle. Just like Mama and Caroline.''

His face turned purple. ''As long as you live under my roof, eat at my table, and live off my money, you'll do what I say. Just like they do.''

Addie felt tears of fury spring to her eyes. ''And talk to whom you tell me to? And marry the man you choose for me?''

''That's right.''

''It's not right,'' she said huskily, thinking in a split second of Caroline and the man she had lost. ''It's not right at all. *You* wouldn't let someone run your life like that. Why do you expect it of me?''

Russell's face was hard. ''Because you're a woman. Smart, yes. Too smart for your own good, and damned spoiled. But you're still just a woman, and there's no gettin' around it. I'll give you rein when I can, Adeline, but not this time.''

''But—''

''You want a woman's privileges and a man's rights

too. But you can't have both. Look at you. Tears ready to fall. You can't hold 'em back—that's because you're a woman. Do you think a man would do that? You stick to your female weapons, honey, and let me make the decisions. You got your place and I got mine.''

''Don't you think I have a sense of honor? Of pride?'' she demanded hoarsely, struggling to hold back the humiliating tears. It was a sign of weakness, one he had taken good advantage of. ''Being a woman doesn't mean I don't have sense and intelligence. It doesn't mean I don't need freedom.'' There was a terrible pressure behind her eyes. She wadded the back of her sleeve against her nose, needing a handkerchief. Although Ben was silent, she was afraid she would see mockery in his eyes. She didn't look at him. As she stared fixedly at Russell, her heart burned with resentment. 'I'll see Jeff if I want to,'' she said in a muffled voice.

''You do that, little girl, and I'll bring you to heel so damn quick you won't believe it.''

Addie was too angry and humiliated to say anything. She felt trapped as she stood there, cornered, and she had to break free or choke on her own helplessness. Striding through the kitchen, she yanked open the door and fled down the back steps. It was dark outside, and the shadows offered refuge.

Ben looked at Russell, his green eyes expressionless.

''What are you gonna say?'' Russell demanded hotly. ''She's my daughter, damn you. You think I wasn't fair to her?''

''You already know,'' Ben said, turning to leave.

''You stay away from her. Let her lick her wounds in private. I won't have you two commiseratin' behind my back. And I just might be tempted to fire you if you take her side against me!''

Ben arched an eyebrow, turning his head slowly and

staring at him. They both knew he was completely indifferent to Russell's blustering. "I'll leave whenever you give the word, Russ."

Russell cursed under his breath as the other man went to follow Addie.

She stopped in the shelter of a storage shed, leaning against the rough wooden planks and crying wretchedly. She had never felt so lonely or helpless. If only there was some sanctuary she could find, even a temporary one! If only she could go to sleep, and wake up to hear Leah calling to her . . . *her* Leah, not that little girl!

It was an intolerable idea to be sentenced to stay here forever. But it was intolerable, also, to think of going back to a place where she had no one at all. *What am I going to do?* she thought, and pressed her wet cheek against the shed as she began to cry even harder.

She heard a voice right behind her ear, a voice laced with sympathy. "It's not that bad, darlin'."

Turning around, she looked at Ben while the moonlight silvered the watery trails down her cheeks. *You don't know how bad it is,* she wanted to say, but she couldn't. He was so close they were almost touching, his powerful body casting a large shadow. The earth seemed to shake under her feet as she reached out for him blindly, and then he pulled her close into the protection of his body. Her head fell against his shoulder, and she wept at the infinite relief of it. Senseless, to feel safe and warm in his arms, but the sweetness of it flowed through her veins like strong wine. Illusion or not, every moment of it was something to treasure—the heat of his body, the smell of him, the abrasion of his unshaven jaw against her temple. After a while she tried to explain herself, feeling somehow that he would understand.

"I can't stand being t-told what to do all the time. I want to run . . . but th-there's nowhere . . .''

"I know. I know." He stroked her hair, his fingers trailing through the warmth of it.

A wild impulse came to Addie, to tell him some of the secrets that swelled so painfully in her heart. If only she could. She wanted to be close to him, but that couldn't be reconciled with what she knew about him. She should be terrified of him. Why was the wanting becoming so much stronger than the fear? How tired she was of questions that had no answers. Wearily she pushed all of it out of her mind and let herself be held a little bit longer.

"For a few minutes I hated him," she said after a minute, her voice catching.

"You and the rest of the county," Ben said quietly. "He's not making himself too popular these days."

"He wants me to be like Caro and Mama."

"No. He doesn't want you to change, no matter what he said back there. He's so damned proud of you, Addie. You're the only one around here who won't let him bully you."

"Except you."

"That's because I don't like the alternative."

She sighed shortly. "I felt about a foot tall in that kitchen. Especially when he—"

"He's just on a rampage. You know better than to wave a red flag at him when he's in a contrary mood."

"I shouldn't have cried in front of him," Addie whispered, and her eyes smarted at the memory. "I hate myself more than him for that."

"Don't."

"I proved him right, acting like a child—"

"Addie . . ." He pried her face from his neck and looked into her reddened eyes. "Stop it. It didn't prove anything. No one likes to have his pride stomped on like that, especially not in front of someone else. Some men would have cried too.''

He paused for a long moment, his thumb moving in a caress from her cheek to her temple. "I did the last time I saw my father.''

"You?'' she asked, bewildered. "Why? An argument, or—''

"Always. I never had a civil conversation with him. We always used to argue. It was our way of showing we gave a damn about each other. But the last year at the university I didn't see him even once. I was told to stay away from him. I was bad for his health. I went to visit him after I graduated, to set things right between us and tell him I was going to Texas. And I realized after I told him that he didn't care. Indifference . . . well, that hurts worse than hatred. That was why I cried. In front of him. And I hate myself for it.''

"Do you still?''

"No. But God knows I'll never forget. And neither will he.'' He smiled down at her, his teeth gleaming white in the darkness. He looked so invulnerable, it was impossible to imagine him caring about what anyone said or did to him. She couldn't imagine him crying. Why had he entrusted her with such a revelation? Merely to bolster her up? To help ease her own shame?

"Ben,'' she said tentatively, her heart beating a little faster, "sometimes you're very nice.''

"Never without a reason, honey.'' All at once he changed, his tenderness melting away to reveal a mocking smile. His eyes seemed to burn right through her clothing.

"I didn't think so,'' she said, suddenly nervous. They were going to pick up what they had started before Russell had interrupted them in the kitchen. The taste of anticipation was sweet on her lips. "What was your reason for being so nice tonight?''

GIVE ME TONIGHT

"Maybe I want something from you."

"Too bad you won't get it."

"Oh, I will eventually."

"Not if I can help it," she parried, wondering why he wasn't trying to take advantage of her.

His smile widened as he saw that her lips had parted. "Liar. You're dying for me to kiss you."

She tore herself away from him and gave him a shove. "If you ever try to kiss me, the only thing you'll get is a swift kick, you self-important jackass—"

"What a temper," he said, and laughed, catching her loosely in the circle of his arms. "Don't fly away just yet, Addie. I'm still planning to finish what we started back there."

"You leave me alone!" She wedged her arms between them, preventing him from drawing her closer. "If you feel the urge to be with someone, go visit your woman in Blue Ridge."

There was ruthless amusement in Ben's smile. Addie could have bitten her tongue off as she realized she had sounded jealous.

"What makes you think I have a woman in Blue Ridge?"

"Caroline said you did."

"How would she know?"

"She listens to gossip—"

"Seems to be a family habit."

"*Do* you visit a woman in Blue Ridge?"

His voice was silky. "Now, why would I want to do that, when I've got you here?"

Addie twisted away from him with an infuriated sound. Ben laughed and blew her a kiss as she stomped off to the house, his eyes following her alertly until she disappeared from sight.

5

"ADELINE, YOU DON'T KNOW HOW HARD DADDY'S takin' this. You said hardly a word to him yesterday, or the day before. Why don't you talk to him? You don't know how much you're hurtin' him."

She looked at Cade mutinously while the two of them walked by the smokehouse and kicked at chips of wood. "You don't know how much he hurt *me*, Cade. What would you do if he ordered you not to see any of your friends? What about that little brown-haired girl you like to call on, Jeannie something-or-other—"

"Janie."

"Yes, her. What if he told you not to visit her anymore?"

Cade was forever a diplomat. "I guess I'd agree, 'f I believed in his reasons."

"Ha! You wouldn't either. You'd want to see her, and you'd be mad at Daddy for acting so high-handed."

He grinned. "Yeah, but I couldn't stay mad as long as you. You and Daddy, you're ones for holdin' grudges. Me? . . . I don't see the sense in bein' mad about somethin' you can't change."

"There isn't any sense in it," Addie agreed grimly. "But I've never pretended to be as nice as you, Cade, and I can't help being mad."

Since her falling-out with Russell, she'd kept out of

his way, finding an unexpected hardness in herself every time she thought about forgiving him. Until now he'd let her do and say almost anything she wanted. But for him to turn around and curtail that freedom, treating her like an object to be put back in its place, had been too unexpected. You couldn't allow someone free rein and then pull it in too suddenly, too tightly.

Like any daughter on bad terms with one parent, she sought out the affection and support of the other. May wisely refrained from criticizing either Addie or Russell, or taking one side against the other. Instead she offered sympathy to both of them privately, knowing that each was too hardheaded to be induced to see the other's viewpoint. Addie and Russell were barely on speaking terms.

Though her problem with Russell disturbed her a great deal, Addie didn't talk much about it, especially not to Ben. She felt acutely embarrassed whenever she looked at him and remembered how she had sobbed in his arms. What did he think of her now? Ben didn't mention the episode. His tenderness of that night had disappeared, and he was his usual mocking self toward her. But sometimes he looked at her as if he were silently laughing at her newfound shyness, and all it took was that one look to set her teeth on edge. Then she would wait for a jeer that never came . . . ah, how *detestable* he was!

She sought consolation for her bruised ego in May's company. May was always calm and gentle. There was quiet grace in everything she did, a grace that was not learned but came from an inner source. Caroline was like that too. They were the kind of women who would never allow the world to change them. Addie knew herself to be a complete contrast to them. She was always struggling and changing, always wanting things and being resentful when she couldn't get them. She understood what Russell had been trying to tell her before. *None of the family would be able to survive Russell's murder,* she thought moodily. *No wonder it went to pieces after he was gone. They'll all do well enough if everything's secure and organized and comfortable for them. But when disaster happens, they need someone else to do the struggling for them. It's good to be gentle and nice, but there are times when you just can't be, or the world will walk right over you.*

A week after Addie had been forbidden to see Jeff, the family prepared to travel nearly fifty miles to attend the wedding of Jeff's younger brother Harlan to Ruth Fanin, the daughter of a wealthy rancher. Sunrise and the Double Bar tacitly agreed to put aside their differences for a few days. They all loved a wedding. It gave them a chance to see old acquaintances, trade stories, drink freely, and dance until the soles of their feet were bruised. The cowboys from different ranches ate meals together, talked about wages and work, enjoyed the free liquor and took as much advantage as possible of the host's hospitality. And every rancher in Texas liked to show off what he considered to be his own legendary hospitality.

The women at these affairs were always outnumbered by men, which meant the favor and attention of every available female was constantly sought after. Addie was apprehensive about attending the wedding. What would she do when people she didn't know expected her to recognize them? But at the same time, she was excited. She hadn't been dancing in a long time. She wanted to listen to music and be among crowds of festive people.

The day before they were to leave, May came upstairs to help Addie pack, finding her in the middle of a heap of dresses. Addie had been trying on dresses for an hour, none of which she wanted to wear, and she had the urge to take a match to her entire wardrobe.

"I'd cry," Addie said in frustration, "if it would help anything."

May's face softened with concern. "Sugar, your face is all red. What's got you so upset?"

"These." With a sweep of her hand, Addie indicated the pile of clothes around her. "I'm trying to find something to wear for the dance after the wedding, but I don't have anything to wear that's not pink. I hate it. It's practically all I wear from morning till night, and I'm sick of it."

"I tried to talk you into some different colors when we were having them made. But you insisted on it. Remember how stubborn you were?"

"I must have been dead from the neck up," Addie said feelingly. "Can you tell me *why* I decided on all-pink?"

"I believe Jeff said it was his favorite color on you," May replied placidly.

"That's just wonderful. Now I can't even see him anymore, and I'm stuck with a closet full of pink dresses."

May couldn't hold back a smile, though she tried. "Adeline, it is a pretty color on you—"

"No, don't even try," Addie said, beginning to smile reluctantly despite her exasperation. "I'm inconsolable."

May clucked her tongue sympathetically and busied herself around the room, picking up dresses and piling them on the bed. "We'll fix everything, sugar. Just give me a minute to think."

Addie felt her temper subsiding as she and May worked to put things back in order. There was something almost magical about May's effect on her, something soothing and wonderful about the scent of vanilla, the gleam of her tidy blond hair, the graceful efficiency of her slim white hands. It was May's self-appointed role to comfort and soothe, arrange and organize, to keep the house and all its occupants in perfect harmony. Addie knew she wasn't as forbearing as May, and she wasn't certain she wanted to be. But she appreciated that quality in May just the same.

"Let's see if we can find something for you in my closet."

"Are you sure?" Addie looked at her in surprise. "Well, we're pretty much the same size. But your waist is smaller."

"I've noticed you haven't been lacing as tightly as you used to. I've been meanin' to speak to you about that, Adeline."

Addie frowned. She'd always had a figure. But that had been in a time when young women didn't use corsets. In 1930, an old woman would wear whalebone coutils, a middle-aged woman wore the lighter version, called a corselette, and someone Addie's age would wear only a brassiere and a lightweight foundation garment. Now she was being measured by different standards, and in 1880 a twenty-four-inch waist was decidedly large. Every woman, young and old, wore strong whalebone corsets fortified with flat lead weights and laced as tightly as they could bear.

"I can't breathe when it's tighter than this."

"Of course you can," May said. "You have in the past."

"I've changed, Mama. Really, I have."

"It might be uncomfortable at times, but it's just not elegant to let your waist get that big, sugar. And besides, it's not good for your back to go without support."

"I'll try to lace tighter," Addie muttered, knowing she'd faint if she did.

May beamed at her. "That's my good girl. I just want you to be the prettiest girl at the dance. And you will be. I'm going to give you that blue-green dress I've never even worn."

"Oh, I couldn't take something you've never—"

"I've decided it's too young for me. It'll be the perfect thing for you. Come try it on."

Addie followed her down the hall to her bedroom. May and Russell slept in separate bedrooms in order to keep from having more children. After becoming aware of that, Addie had questioned Caroline about it, unable to imagine a man as robust as Russell going without a woman for the rest of his life. Caroline had blushed slightly. "I suppose there must be someone he visits occasionally," she had said.

Addie had been disturbed by the thought. "But how strange. It seems as if he and Mama still love each other."

"Of course they do. Even though Daddy might go to bed with another woman, he loves Mama as much as he always has."

"But for them not to share a bed together—"

"It doesn't mean anything, really. He can love Mama with his heart even though he might love another woman in a physical way."

"No he can't," Addie said, her brows knitting together. Fidelity wasn't something to be compromised on.

"Why not?"

"Because he just can't!"

Thinking about that conversation now, Addie peered at May's pristine yellow-and-white bedroom, and then watched her sort through the dresses in the closet. "Mama," she asked carefully, "if two people are going to get married, do you think it's important for them to feel passion for each other?"

May turned around, looking surprised, and then she smiled. "My goodness, sometimes you're even more outspoken than your daddy. What brought on that question?''

"I was just thinking about marriage, and love."

"The two should go hand in hand. It's important to love the man you marry. But it's even more important to have interests that are compatible with his. As for passion, that's not as necessary as you might think. Passion fades. Love will always be there, and so will compatibility. Does that answer your question?''

"Partly," Addie said thoughtfully. "You don't think passion is a *bad* thing, do you?''

"In some ways, yes. It blinds people to what's really in their hearts. They're more easily swayed by passion than reason, and that's a bad thing. It's an empty emotion.''

Addie didn't agree at all, but she held her tongue rather than argue. In the silence, May turned back to the closet and located the dress she'd been looking for. "Here it is, Adeline." She laid it on the bed with a flourish, and Addie went to look at it.

"It's the most beautiful dress I've ever seen," she said, touching a fold of it reverently. The turquoise dress shimmered and glistened in the daylight. It had a heart-shaped neckline, elbow-length sleeves trimmed with ruffles, and an elaborately draped skirt ornamented with gauze and moss roses. She could hardly wait to try it on.

"If you like it, it's yours."

"I love it," Addie exclaimed animatedly, and they both chuckled as she scooped it up and went over to the mirror to hold it against herself.

"It'll be beautiful on you, with that honey-colored hair and those pretty brown eyes," May observed, her face glowing with pleasure.

"Why do you look so happy?" Addie demanded with a laugh. "I'm the one who's getting the dress."

May came up to her and gave her a quick hug from

behind. "I'm your mama. I'm always happy when you are, sugar. Haven't I told you that before?"

A queer sensation went through Addie as she saw their two faces in the mirror. For a split second she saw a child posing in front of that same mirror in finery borrowed from May's closet, and then the image disappeared, leaving her shaken. "Yes, you have," she whispered.

"Adeline, what's wrong?"

Slowly Addie turned to look at her, and something inside clicked into place, like the missing piece of a puzzle. Suddenly May looked familiar to her, in a different way from before. Addie was stunned by the dearness of that face, the ache of love that had taken hold of her heart in just an instant. The sight of May's concerned expression brought forth another image, much clearer than the first. Addie could see herself as a little girl, tearful and guilt-ridden, seeking May's forgiveness. *Mama, I'm sorry. I'm so sorry . . .*

"I just remembered something," Addie said huskily, her gaze becoming distant. "A long time ago I borrowed something of yours without asking. A gold bracelet, wasn't it? And . . . I lost it, didn't I?"

"That's all forgotten."

"But it did happen," Addie pressed.

"Yes, but it's not important now."

But it had happened.

Remembering that was enough to make Addie believe. *I've just got to be her daughter. May is my mother. I know she is.* Her eyes stung, and she wiped at them fiercely. Her throat ached as she tried to speak.

For so many years I've wanted you . . . never even hoped . . . no reason to hope.

May held her arms out and gathered her close, her expression clouded with confusion. "What? What's wrong?"

Addie rested her head on that soft shoulder, trembling with emotion. "Nothing. Nothing at all, Mama."

The land surrounding the Fanins' main house swarmed with people, animals, and vehicles. The house seemed more like a hotel than a home, large enough to accommodate countless guests and visitors. After the barbecue this afternoon and parties tonight, the wedding would be held tomorrow morning, followed by a dance and two days of festivities.

"I didn't expect there'd be this many people," Addie whispered to Caroline, who laughed dryly.

"Looks like Mrs. Fanin invited a few hundred of her closest friends. I suppose she thought a turnout smaller than this would've made her look stingy. Look—over there on the veranda. She's makin' a point of receivin' everyone. How would you like to coo over five hundred people in a row? That's what I call hospitality."

Peter and Russell helped the women out of the carriage, while Cade caught sight of a friend and ran off to join him. Addie averted her gaze from Russell's as she took his hand and stepped down to the ground. Before she could turn away, he stopped her with a quiet warning.

"I'll have my eye on you most of the time. Don't let me catch you anywhere near that Johnson boy. And I mean that, Adeline."

"I thought a cease-fire had been called."

"It has. But that doesn't mean the war's ended. And I don't want you to give any one of those fence-cutters so much as a howdy-do. Got that?"

"It's not my war."

"Yes it is. You're a Warner."

She nodded shortly and turned away from him, joining May and Caroline as they went to greet Mrs. Fanin.

"Mah goodness, how long it's been!" Mrs. Fanin exclaimed in a syrupy drawl, her dark eyes almost disappearing as she bestowed a brilliant, crinkling smile on them. "Oh, Adeline, how beautiful you are! I 'spect we'll be at your weddin' next, won't we?"

Adeline smiled uncomfortably. "I don't know about that—"

"And, Carolahnn . . . you, in this heat . . . we'll have to sit you down with a cool drink right away. May, Ah just cain't believe how sweet your two girls ah. Y'all must let me show off some of the gifts Ruthie has received."

"What did we give her?" Addie whispered to Caroline as they followed Mrs. Fanin into the house.

"Crystal artichoke plates."

Addie couldn't smother a grin. "Nice to know we gave her something really useful."

Caroline, who had helped May pick out the plates, lifted her nose in the air. "Ruth already has everything she needs. Most important, Jeff's younger brother for a husband."

Immediately Addie's smile disappeared. "Caro, if you see Jeff around, tell me. I've got to explain some things to him."

"You're askin' for trouble, little sister. And you don't need to explain anything to him. He already knows why you haven't returned his notes or gone to meet him."

"Just tell me if you see him," Addie said impatiently.

After admiring and exclaiming over the tables loaded down with Ruth's wedding gifts, Addie and Caroline managed to escape to their rooms in order to take brief naps and freshen up before the barbecue. May remained by Mrs. Fanin's side to help her receive the rest of the guests.

A cool breeze drifted into the room, easing the heat

of the day, but Addie couldn't sleep. She went to the window and watched the activity outside. Hundreds of names were being called back and forth as old friends renewed their acquaintances. Busily she repeated the names to herself, hoping she'd remember enough of them to avoid offending anyone or causing embarrassment to herself.

The scene quieted as afternoon approached, while people retired to their rooms to prepare for the night ahead. Addie's stomach began to growl as tantalizing smells floated through the air. It wasn't difficult to envision the pork that was roasting and crackling over the fire at this very moment. There would be smoked sausage, brisket, and potatoes, not to mention all the different kinds of pies and cakes for dessert. Surreptitiously Addie loosened her corset strings, letting her waist expand a good inch and a half, sighing in relief. No one would notice. Elegance be damned. She was hungry.

"I think everyone looks just wonderful," Caroline said, clinging to Peter's arm as the Warners went down the stairs in a small group. They all moved slowly out of consideration for Caroline's awkward gait. May and Addie were on either side of Russell, the hems of their dresses brushing the edges of the steps as they descended.

Addie was fascinated by the people walking in and out of the house. Caro was right. Everyone did look wonderful. It could have been a scene right out of the movies. She marveled at the fact that it was real. The women wore beautiful, frothy dresses trimmed with profusions of flowers and lace. Tiny waists were cinched in with fringed sashes or large bows, hair was curled into masses of ringlets and pinned in large puffs.

The men were even more remarkable in their finery than the women. After seeing men dressed in nothing but rough denims and cotton workshirts for so long, it was a pleasure to behold them all turned out in their best. Many wore light-colored shirts, bright silk scarves, and exquisite made-to-order boots, while the more affluent were attired in fashionable city clothes, striped trousers, light summer suits, and satin vests. Addie wanted to giggle as she saw how many of them had patent-leather hair, slicked down and shiny with Macassar oil, flat on top, with all the wave and curl combed out.

"Adeline, you're a picture tonight," Russell said gruffly, glancing down at her.

The rich melon-pink of her dress brought out the peach tones of her skin, and made her brown eyes darker. The neckline of her dress was moderately low and the sleeves short, leaving her neck and shoulders bare. The two ruffled skirts of her dress were trimmed with plaited ribbons that rustled as she moved.

Addie smiled reluctantly. "Thank you, Daddy."

"There's just one thing. Don't let me catch you sneakin' off with that Johnson boy."

"You won't," she said sweetly. She was going to find Jeff, but she would certainly make sure Russell didn't catch her.

Outside, music was provided by several fiddles, a guitar, and a banjo, and there were wreaths and streamers of colored tissue everywhere. People moved down the long tables, filling their plates with generous helpings of everything from crisp pork to raspberry pie. As she approached the tables, Addie was suddenly besieged by offers of help—"Miss Adeline, let me get some of this for you" . . . "Miss Adeline, could I hold your plate for you whilst you decide what you're gonna have?"

It didn't take long to realize most of the men around her were from the Sunrise Ranch. As Caroline explained it later, every cowboy from Sunrise considered it his special duty and privilege to watch over the Warner women. Addie found herself with a small crowd of men, each of whom had appointed himself as her guardian and protector, and she was both amused and touched by their antics as they vied for her attention. They were rough-cut in many ways, but their sense of chivalry couldn't be faulted. Recklessly she promised to dance with each and every one of them tomorrow night, and she laughed as they pretended to quarrel over what order they would be in.

"If I were you, there's someone in particular I'd save a dance for," Caroline murmured below the general noise, and Addie grinned cheekily, popping a tender morsel of chicken into her mouth.

"Who?"

"Look over there. The one talkin' with Mr. Fanin."

Addie followed Caroline's gaze and stopped chewing in mid-bite as she saw a slim, attractive man standing by Mr. Fanin, holding a drink in one hand and gesturing with the other. He wore beige trousers, a white shirt, and a patterned vest that emphasized his broad shoulders. She couldn't see his face, but she noticed he had black hair trimmed closely at the back of the neck. Tanned skin contrasted sharply with the snowy whiteness of his turned-down collar. His very posture, confident and straight-backed, seemed to proclaim he was a dangerous man to trifle with.

Addie kept her eyes on him while she resumed chewing. "Interesting," she commented. "Who is he?"

"It's Ben, silly!"

She nearly choked on her food. "It is not!"

"Are you blind? Take another look."

"It isn't," Addie said stubbornly, swallowing with difficulty. "Ben isn't as tall as that, or as . . ." Her voice withered away as he turned his head in response to someone's greeting, and she recognized his profile. "It is Ben," she said, stunned.

"I told you."

She had never seen Ben in anything but Levi's, work clothes, and a dusty hat. How had he managed to turn into that stylish, well-tailored stranger? He looked the same and yet so different she was afraid to trust her eyes. "Look at him, all dandied up," she said almost under her breath, trying to ignore the tumult in her breast.

"One handsome man, isn't he?"

"Any man looks better after bathing and putting on clean clothes."

Caroline snorted. "Oh, tell the truth, Adeline."

But Addie couldn't reply. Having sensed her amazed stare, Ben turned and looked at her, and his eyes filled with an insolent appreciation that made her pulse quicken. Then he smiled lazily and returned his attention to Mr. Fanin, as if Addie held little interest for him.

She couldn't help being tense during the rest of the barbecue, half-expecting Ben's touch on her arm or his voice in her ear. Surely he'd have to come by and say hello, if only for the sake of politeness. And when he did approach her, she would set him back on his heels in no time at all. No matter how handsome he was, she'd let him see how indifferent she was to him! But as the afternoon wore on, he made no move toward her. Addie was oddly deflated at not having the chance to talk to him. *His time is his own—the Lord knows I don't care how he spends it,* she thought, trying to work up some healthy disdain. Let him talk to every woman there but her. She didn't care a bit.

After the crowd had eaten its fill and the food began to settle down to overfilled stomachs, the afternoon was lazy and quiet. Voices that had previously been animated became languid, chairs tipped back, eyelids half-lowered with contentment.

"Look who's coming over," Caroline said, cleaning her plate with one last bite of ham. Two young women were approaching, both of them wearing Indienne dresses made of striped cambric and cotton, the bodices cut low to reveal white muslin chemisettes underneath. The women looked vaguely familiar, but Addie had no idea what their names were. Looking down hurriedly, she lifted a hand to one of her eyes. "I can't see who it is—have something in my eye," she muttered. "Who is it?"

"It's Ruthie, and your old playmate Melissa Merrigold," Caroline said. "Melissa's going to be Ruthie's maid of honor. Are you all right?"

"Just a twisted eyelash." Addie looked up and blinked rapidly, pretending instant relief. "There. All better. Oh, Ruthie and Melissa, how are you?"

Ruthie, a pretty black-haired girl with a long, narrow face, gave her a many-toothed smile. "Just fine. Thought we'd come see how y'all liked dinner."

"I had to get a better look at Adeline's dress," Melissa chimed in, leaning over and hugging Addie lightly, in the manner of an old friend. Melissa was tall and slender, with round blue eyes, sharp cheekbones, and long, aristocratic hands. "It's the most darlin' thing I've ever seen!"

"Thank you," Addie said, smiling at the artless flattery. She felt obligated to return the compliment. "I like your dress too, especially those little ribbons." The chemisette and the sleeves of her dress were adorned with colored bows.

Melissa fingered one of the bits of ribbon on her left sleeve, adjusting it to a perfect angle. Just then Addie saw that her pinkie was crooked at an artificial angle, as if it had once been broken and not set properly. She stared at the long white hand, her eyes widening. In a flash, she saw two little girls tossing a ball back and forth. One of them tossed it especially high in the air . . . *"Try to catch that, Missy!"* The unfortunate

Melissa had caught it the wrong way, and her pinkie was broken.

"Missy . . ." Addie asked in a strange voice, "does that finger ever hurt you?"

Melissa grinned at her, displaying her hand in a practiced pose. "This finger? . . . Mah one flaw. Don't tell me you were just thinkin' of that afternoon."

"Missy?" Ruth repeated, wrinkling her brow. "I've never heard you called that before."

"Adeline's the only one who's ever called me that," Melissa replied, smiling fondly at Addie. "She has since we were little. And no, the finger never hurts at all, it's just a little crooked. You haven't mentioned it in years, Ad."

"But I was the cause of it when I threw that ball so high—"

"No, it was me. I've always been such a clumsy thing. Never have known how to catch anything 'cept men." She looked over at Caroline, who was shifting uncomfortably in her chair. "Caro, when's the baby due? Pretty soon, huh?"

While Caroline and Missy talked, Ruth perched on the chair by Addie's and leaned over to whisper to her, "Harlan says your daddy won't let you see his brother."

"No. Tell me, how is Jeff? I haven't seen him in days."

"He's about ready to die from loneliness," Ruth said, her eyes twinkling. "Don't know what you've done to him. That boy, he doesn't want to even look at any girl but you."

"I haven't seen him anywhere—"

"He and his friends are busy plannin' some of the stuff for later on tonight." Ruth giggled. "It bein' Harlan's last night and all, they got to liquor up and have their fun. But Jeff's around here somewhere. And if Harlan can be believed, Jeff's goin' to try to see you right after dinner's finished.''

"Thanks, Ruthie.''

After that, Addie listened with only half an ear on the conversation around her, her attention absorbed by the Johnson clan, which was gathered on the other side of the crowd.

In the center of the family sat a heavyset man with huge hands and massive jowls, his eyes bright blue, his hair dark red, and his complexion ruddy. Though he had already finished dinner, a full plate reclined on his lap, from which he picked choice bits of food. He possessed a kingly air to match his considerable proportions. It had to be Big George. She saw some of his children gathered around him, including the soon-to-be-wedded Harlan, but there was still no sign of Jeff.

The crowd dispersed as the sun began to set. For the rest of the evening the men and women would be separated. The men would celebrate Harlan's last few hours of bachelorhood with liquor and ribald advice, while the women would give Ruth more presents to open, talk and giggle about men and their eccentricities, and then retire early so they would all look fresh in the morning.

Addie walked to the main house with Caroline, feeling lost, out of place. Just before they reached the steps, she saw Jeff around the corner of the house, his face urgent as he stared at her.

"Adeline,'' he said softly, wanting her to slip away to talk with him. She stopped and looked around quickly, wondering if anyone would notice her absence. Surely not. People's minds were on the evening ahead.

"Adeline, don't,'' Caroline said, laying a hand on her arm, not looking at Jeff. "It's not worth it. Daddy's gonna find out.''

"Not if you don't tell him."

Caroline's voice sharpened with irritation. "I won't, but he'll find out anyway. Don't be a fool."

"I can make my own decisions." Addie drew her arm away. "I won't be long, Caro."

"I could just shake you," Caroline muttered, walking up the steps without looking back, while Addie sneaked away with Jeff in search of privacy.

The best they could do was the blacksmith shop, a tiny shed located near the tin shop and storage buildings. It was stocked with branding irons, horseshoes, hammers, pliers and other tools, and two anvils. The air inside smelled of oil and iron. As soon as the little door was closed, Jeff pulled Addie into his arms and held her so tightly she could hardly breathe. "I've missed you," he said over and over again, raining kisses over her face, his hands biting as he pulled her against his body. His violence was unexpected. Addie was passive in his arms for a few seconds. Then she tried to push him away, squirming uncomfortably.

"Jeff," she said with a half-laugh, turning her face to avoid his mouth, "you're going to crush me." She wrinkled her nose as she caught a whiff of his sour breath. "What have you been drinking? I think you've had a little too much, slicker."

"I was gonna go crazy if I didn't see you soon," he muttered against her neck, his arms wrapped around her. "I was gonna do something . . . kidnap you, or—"

"Jeff, you're holding me too tight."

"I haven't held you for so long. Your father's got a hell of a lot to answer for."

"What do you mean? For keeping us apart?"

"Yes, and for buildin' that damn fence. He's bargaining for trouble, and he's gonna get what he's asking for."

"Now, wait a minute." Addie rose quickly to Russell's defense. "I don't like the fence either, but—"

"No one does. He's ridin' too high these days, honey. He has no right to hide you away from me. Don't you worry, it won't be for long."

"But he has a right to be angry. What about your men attacking three of ours, including our foreman—"

"We're not gonna argue now," Jeff said, his lips moving along the side of her neck. "Holy Moses, you like to argue just for the sake of arguin'."

"But you seem to think—"

"I need you. Be sweet for me, Adeline. Oh, I've needed you for weeks. Be sweet." His hand closed over her breast, causing her to jump.

"Stop it!" She pushed his hand away, feeling the heat rise in her face. Suddenly everything had gone wrong. All of her gladness to see him disappeared. "I came out here to talk with you and find out how you've been."

"You came out here 'cause you want me," Jeff said thickly. "And I want you too. It doesn't matter what your father does. I'm gonna have you, Adeline. I always wanted you more than anyone else. And no one's gonna stand in our way. My daddy'll make sure of it." He reached for her bodice again, trying to smother her protests with his mouth. Addie was infuriated by his clumsy groping.

"You sound like a little boy," she said, trying to twist away from him, "bragging about what his daddy's going to do for him . . . stop that, Jeff! I'm sorry I came out here with you, if this is . . . Ow!" Her head bumped against the wall as she struggled, and her scalp burned. His arms drew around her tightly. "You're hurting me," she gasped, lunging toward the door, almost toppling both of them over.

"I love you," he muttered, searching roughly for the fastenings of her dress. "Adeline . . . I need you."

"Don't!" Her anger mixed with fear as she realized he was out of control. The back of her head was forced against the wall by the pressure of his kiss. How far was he going to push her? She could call for help, but oh, what humiliation it might cause her and the family, and the trouble it would stir up! Why was he forcing her to make the choice?

"Please," she choked, turning her face as his lips slid across her cheek. His groping fingers popped some of the buttons on her dress. "Jeff . . . listen to me . . ."

She felt something hard press against her forehead, something metallic that swung gently. A horseshoe, hanging from a nail. Addie focused on the scrap of metal, straining to pull her wrists out of Jeff's grasp. It wouldn't be difficult to hit him with it as soon as she could get her hands free. But how hard? How much was enough to stop him without killing him?

"Jeff, what's the *matter* with you?" She pushed at him, infuriated as she felt his knee thrust between her legs. "Don't make me hurt you. I will, Jeff—don't force me." He seemed not to hear her, his mouth hot on her skin as he covered her throat with kisses. Then his grip on her wrists loosened, and she reached for the horseshoe. Simultaneously the door swung open and a fast-moving shadow slipped into the shed.

Jeff was grabbed by the scruff of the neck and hauled away from her. Addie stumbled forward until his grip on her was broken. She retreated to the wall, her eyes dilating as she tried to see through the darkness. There was the sound of a brief skirmish, a man's heavy grunt of pain, the sound of a body hitting the ground.

"Who is it?" Addie asked tremulously, gripping the horseshoe so hard the tips of her fingers were numb. "Jeff? Jeff . . ."

She heard his pained gasps as he sat up, and Ben's voice, so cold and soft that it sent chills down her spine. "Horny little son of a bitch. If you lay a finger on her again, I'll kill you."

"You have no right," Jeff muttered.

"I have every right. It's my job to protect all Warner property, including her. Now, get out, or I'll finish this here and now."

"I'll fix your hash real good for this, Hunter."

Ben snorted in disgust. "I hope you try."

Frozen, Addie watched the doorway as Jeff left. She sighed shakily. Ben closed the door with his foot and walked over to her, stopping a few inches away. She could just make out the outline of his head and shoulders. Although he was ominously quiet, she sensed the dark fury that consumed him. She dared not breathe a word. Without warning he took hold of her wrist, squeezing until she gasped in surprise and dropped the horseshoe. Pulling her arm away, she rubbed her sore wrist, bewildered.

"If y-you hadn't come in here," she stammered, "he might have—"

"There was a time," he said icily, "when I wouldn't have bothered."

"Ben . . . th-thank you for . . ." She shrank against the wall as he came closer. The familiar scent and shape of him did nothing to reassure her. Why was he so quiet? Why was she starting to sense that the real danger was just beginning? "Jeff acted so strange," she said, swallowing hard. "He was too liquored up to hear me. I think he was trying to—"

"And what if he had? What if he had raped you?"

"I wouldn't have let him."

"Do you think anyone would have heard you scream with all the music and drinking going on?"

"I was going to hit him with—"

"That horseshoe? Did you happen to notice how

easy it was for me to take it away from you? Do you think it would've been any different for him?''

''Maybe.''

''Or maybe not,'' he said savagely. ''And if he'd succeeded in getting what he wanted, you would have run to Daddy with the news, and then all hell would have broken loose. You little fool. Don't you realize we're on the brink of a range war as it is? You almost provided everyone with the perfect excuse to start it. They're all waiting for the first opportunity, your father included.'' His hands closed around her upper arms, tightening as she gave a cry of pain.

''Ben, let go of me!''

''Do you like the idea of causing all that bloodshed?'' he snarled. ''Men dying over you, blood being spilled . . . does that appeal to your vanity?''

She flinched and shook her head wildly. ''No. I didn't think about any of that. I just wanted to—''

''You wanted to prove to Russ that you're a big girl. And to hell with what he asked of you. Jesus, you think the world revolves around you, and you've got everyone else convinced of it! What have you done to make us all insane over you? Are you worth all the trouble you're trying to cause, Addie? Damn you, I've had enough of wondering!''

Her heart jumped with fear, and she made a move to escape. He caught her rigid body against his, easily holding her prisoner. Jeff had been strong, but not like this. Trying to fight Ben was useless. His muscles were as hard as steel, his body as tough as rawhide. ''Now that you've gotten rid of Jeff,'' she gasped, ''are you planning to take his place?''

''There's a big difference between him and me, darlin'.'' He sneered. ''The consequences if he takes you are a lot different than if I do. If you need a man so badly you have to sneak out here with him, I'm more than willing to satisfy you. We're all better off if I'm the one who does it.''

''I *hate* you.'' Wedging her hands against his chest, she shoved as hard as she could, managing to knock them both off balance. As they fell to the ground, Ben twisted to take the shock of the fall for both of them. Then Addie gave a muffled cry as he rolled on top of her. She tried to strike him, but he was too quick, catching her wrists and pinning them over her head. Outraged, she continued to struggle, stretched out underneath him while the ravaged neckline of her bodice sagged.

''Stop it, Ben! I've had to put up with enough of this for one night! If you don't let me go, I'm going to have you fired first thing tomorrow m—''

''Shut up.''

''I will not! You let me go, you stinking bully—''

''I said shut up!'' His tone was so vicious that Addie was startled into silence. ''Count yourself lucky I'm trying to remember your father right now. It's only out of respect for him that I'm not going to give you what you deserve. Dammit, stop wiggling!'

Her eyes had become accustomed to the darkness, and she glared at him furiously. ''If you're not going to give me what I *deserve,* then get off me!'' His response was to straddle her and dig his lips into hers. Even through her skirts she could feel the hard, protruding shape of him wedged between her thighs. The feel of him there, pressed against her so hard that their bodies seemed meshed together, made her tremble. Warm weakness seeped outward and upward from her loins, irrepressible, relentless.

No. She couldn't feel such a thing, not for Ben Hunter . . . her enemy . . . he was deadly . . . he was forbidden. In a sharp move she brought her knee up, trying to disarm him. Deftly he shifted so her knee struck the inside of this thigh, which was as solid and unyielding as a tree trunk. He pulled up the billows of her skirts and used his knees to spread her pantalet-encased legs wide.

"Is this what you're so anxious to avoid?" he demanded, lowering his hips to hers, and she gasped. He was startlingly turgid and hot as he pressed against her. "Because *this*," he continued, grinding his loins harder into hers, sending shock waves through her body, "is the result of all your little smiles and schemes, Addie—"

"I've never tried to arouse you on purpose—"

"You can do it to a man just by looking at him, and you know it. Hell, I don't blame Jeff for wanting you. It's the little game you play, making a man crazy with need for you and then freezing him out."

"No! I don't!" Addie stared up at him through the darkness, shaking with unfamiliar emotions. She was stunned by his violent anger. What had she done to make him so furious?

Ben's face loomed above her. His eyes gleamed like a cat's as he took note of the labored hiss of her breath and the curving of her fingers into claws. "You'd scratch my eyes out if you could," he muttered.

"Worse than that," she said, aware he was toying with her, hating him for it. "I'm going to make you *pay* for treating me like—"

His mouth slammed down on hers. It was a kiss of anger, not passion, meant to show her who was master. She groaned and fought him with all her strength. After nearly a minute had passed by, she realized how useless it was and went limp, surrendering. Finally Ben stopped and lifted his head, the harsh puffs of his breath striking her cheek. She knew his lips had to feel as bruised as hers did, but the thought gave her little comfort.

"Are you finished now?" she gasped. "You proved you're a big strong man. I'm sure you're satisfied. You won. There's just one thing I want to make clear. I heard what you said to Jeff a few minutes ago. Don't you *ever* call me property again. I'm not anyone's property, not my father's, and not yours. So remove your paws and get the hell off me!''

He glared down at her, unimpressed by her fury. ''When I'm ready.''

''What do you want me to do?'' she exploded. ''Pretend I enjoy this?''

''Maybe. Yeah, let's try that.''

''Go to hell! The only thing I feel for you is disgust.''

He was silent for a few seconds, looking over her and then shaking his head as if to clear his mind. ''I guess you do. But tonight I haven't exactly been enchanted by you, either.''

He shifted his weight off her, letting go of her wrists and fitting his thigh over her hips to keep her pinned down. Suddenly she could breathe again. Her arms fell by her sides, tingling as the blood began to circulate through them. She lay still, waiting for him to release her, trying to gather her wits.

Ben's eyes flickered over her chest as it rose and fell rapidly. Even bound in stays and tangled up in skirts as Addie was, there was no mistaking the enticing shape of her body. He couldn't help but recall the feel of her breasts crushed against his chest, the soft cradle of her hips. His anger vanished just as quickly as it had been roused, replaced by a purely masculine interest. He should be fired on the spot for what he'd just done to her, for the way he was lying over her right now with his thigh slung over her. Russell would string him up by the balls if he knew.

And yet, somehow he was certain Russell wasn't going to find out. Not if Ben's instincts concerning Addie were right. If she felt anything similar to what he was feeling, she wasn't altogether sorry she was in here alone with him. Of course, she'd never admit it. Ben looked down at her, debating his next move. Let her up and apologize? It would probably be best . . . but something inside rebelled at the thought of letting her go just yet. As long as he had her at his mercy, why not take advantage of it? She wouldn't hate him any less. And to hell with his scruples. He wanted her so badly he was about to burst into flames.

"You're sure disgust is all you feel, Addie?"

"Yes," she said sullenly.

"Not meaning to contradict you, darlin', but a little while ago I could have sworn you felt something very different from disgust. Just for a few seconds, you—"

"I don't care what you like to imagine, I didn't feel anything!" By now Addie was thoroughly humiliated, longing for the entire episode to be over. To compound her confusion, Ben bent over her and kissed the tip of her nose, as if they'd just had a friendly argument. Addie was utterly bewildered. There was never any way to predict what he might do.

"I'm sorry for calling you property," he murmured. "I didn't mean it."

"You did, or you wouldn't have said it. You're like all the other men around here. I can't abide the attitude you have toward women."

His lips smoothed over her eyebrow, then touched her eyelid in a butterfly caress. "Then help me change."

"I . . . I don't c-care if you change or not. I just want . . ." Her heart began to hammer in her chest as he kissed her chin. What was he doing to her?

"You want what?" he prompted, sliding his arm underneath her neck. She tried to push him away. But now that he had her in his grasp, he wasn't about to let her go.

"I want you to l-leave me alone."

"Are you sure?"

"Yes," she said faintly.

"Think I could change your mind?" His voice was as raspy as a cat's tongue, the sound of it sending shivers down her spine. She blinked, forgetting what he'd asked until he repeated the question.

Shaking her head jerkily, Addie made a move to get up. "You didn't say you were s-sorry for k-kissing me."

"I'm not."

"It hurt."

"That I'm sorry for." He picked up one of her hands and brought it to his jaw, stroking the back of her knuckles against it. The gentle scrape sent an electric shock down to her toes. "Your hand is so small." As she tried to pull it away he held it more firmly and pretended to examine the rest of her. Slowly he smiled. "Why, you're no bigger than a minute, Adeline Warner."

"Big enough to handle you," she snapped, and went scarlet as he chuckled.

"You might be at that."

"Oh, let me go, you crude, overbearing . . . I'll never forgive you for . . . No, Ben—"

"No what?"

"Don't do that.'

"Don't do what?"

"Ben—"

Her words were smothered as his mouth possessed hers, insistent and skillful, kissing her as she had never been kissed before. Feebly she tried to turn her face away, but he cradled the side of her cheek in his hand, his thumb tracing over her temple in a delicately drawn circle. He kissed her as thoroughly as he'd wanted to for weeks, exploring the inside of her mouth, savoring the texture of her inner cheeks, the ticklish spot at the roof of her mouth, stroking her tongue with his. She trembled, no longer trying to fight him, and her lips parted as she began to drown in a sea of fire. They kissed frantically, delving, tasting, consuming.

A low purr vibrated in Ben's throat, making the hairs on the back of Addie's neck rise. Her body went liquid inside. Oh, the pleasure was more than she could stand. Sensations surged together, and still she wanted more. What was she doing, here on the floor with Ben Hunter? She'd lost her mind.

"I can't think—"

"Hush. Be quiet for once." He followed the curve of her neck down to the upper rise of her breasts. Her heartbeat was rapid beneath his hand. Before she could stop him, his fingers slid underneath her dress until his hand was cupped around her breast. The friction between his palm and her bare flesh made them both gasp. His fingers flexed into the warm softness, his hand rotating until her nipple hardened and pressed into his palm. Addie moaned helplessly. She had never trusted any man with such intimacy, and it was frightening, and very good. Her mind screamed for her to stop, but the night was filled with madness, and the voice of reason had diminished into a whisper. She couldn't pull back.

His palm skimmed her ribs carefully, as if he were afraid she might break, and she arched up to him like a wanton. Her guilty, pleasured sigh filled his mouth as his hand returned to her breast, and his thumb made a slow excursion around her nipple. The sweet ache of it rippled all through her being. Writhing closer to him, she tangled her fingers in his hair and pulled his mouth harder on hers. Their tongues slid together and mated in delicious thrusts, their lips clung until they were completely sealed.

After a long time Ben lifted his head and took a deep breath in an effort to master the powerful urgings of his body. The need to take her, here and now, was almost impossible to contain. She was his obsession.

He wanted to know her most private secrets, explore her until he knew her body and soul as intimately as his own. With all his experience he'd never felt so drawn to another human being, or craved to know and be known so completely. He tugged briefly at her hair, his agile fingers hunting for pins and pulling them out. The locks that had been bound up and pinned away from others' sight and touch were now his, freed and loose.

Addie wound her arms around his neck as she felt his body move over hers, settling until they were molded together. The layers of clothing that separated them did nothing to disguise his desire and her softness, the hardness of him and the yielding woman's shape of her.

Trembling, she felt him ease her gown down, lifting her breast out of its confines, his hot mouth descending to her nipple, covering, pulling, sending streaks of lightning down to the pit of her stomach. Blindly she reached for his shoulders, gripping his hard-muscled flesh as she sought to tell him without words how it felt . . . *don't stop . . . don't ever stop*. His tongue feathered over her lightly, learned the tender-hard texture of her.

"Adeline," he whispered, moving back up to her lips and kissing her without restraint. "Don't hold yourself back from me. I won't hurt you." She shivered in his arms, her breath rapid and hot against his neck. His hand wandered down her body, beyond her waist, underneath her pantalets. She tensed as his fingertips searched her gently.

"No . . . I shouldn't be letting you—"

"But you are," he said into the curve of her shoulder. "And I shouldn't want you. But I do."

"Ben," she gasped, "Please—"

"No one will ever know you like I'm going to, Addie. You can keep the rest of the world at bay, but you're going to let me inside. You understand what's happening between us. You know nothing is going to stop it, no matter what either of us may do." She moaned as he found the tender spot he had been seeking, as he brought her to the fine edge between pleasure and madness. "I want you to remember this," he said, crushing the words against her mouth. "Remember every time you think of me."

She clung to him tightly, her hips arching upward.

"Much as I'd like to, I'm not going to take you here," he muttered, burying his face in her hair. "If for no other reason than because *he* would have." Sighing tautly, Ben withdrew his hand from between her thighs, bestowing a longing caress on her abdomen before pulling her skirts back into place. He looked around the shadowy little building as if noticing their surroundings for the first time. His lip curled with disgust. "A blacksmith shop."

Aching and frustrated, Addie shifted underneath him, her breath ragged. Ben smiled, pulling her into his arms and pressing her head against his shoulder, holding her until her quivering had stopped. The unsatisfied wanting was just as painful for him.

"I have to go back to Sunrise tomorrow after the wedding," he said, trying to sound casual. "Someone has to look after the ranch, and right now I don't trust it out of my hands more than a day or two. If you don't want to undergo a repeat of Jeff's performance tonight, then stay close to your father and your family."

"What if . . ." She paused and gulped hard before continuing, "What if I don't want a repeat of *your* performance?"

"What if you don't?" He sounded interested by the idea, and he nibbled lightly at the juncture of her neck and shoulder as he gave it due consideration. "I guess we'll find the answer to that when we're both back at Sunrise.''

He was humoring her. She knew he had no doubt she'd still want him later. Even now she had to fight against the urge to nestle against him. Instead she wriggled in protest, pulling her shoulder away until he stopped nibbling.

''And don't be surprised to find some of the Sunrise hands keeping an eye on you. Before I leave, I'm going to make sure they understand there'll be hell to pay if he comes within a hundred feet of you. If I find out he's done so much as look at you, I'll make him regret it sorely.''

''Even at the risk of starting a range war?'' she asked in a muffled voice, and he smiled grimly, amused by her feeble attempt at sarcasm.

''That's right. And if it has to start over you, darlin', you're looking at the man who'll fire the first shot.''

After Addie had restored her appearance as best she could, she spoke to May privately and pleaded a headache in order to avoid the rest of the evening. She couldn't face anyone right now, not when her thoughts were in a whirl and her head aching with confusion. Having gone to bed early, she lay in bed on her stomach with her arms clenched around a pillow, staring blindly at the wall. The Fanins' house was comfortable but hardly as elegant as the ranch house at Sunrise. The rooms here were small and plainly furnished, the beds lumpy and even a little musty. Leah was asleep in the bed against the opposite wall. They were sharing the room next to the one Caroline and Peter occupied.

Addie didn't want to think about what had happened that night, but she couldn't wish it away, and she couldn't forget about it. She kept hearing Jeff's voice, and what he'd said about Russell. *''He's riding too high*

*these days, honey. He has no right to hide you away
from me . . . don't you worry, it won't be long . . ."*

What had he meant by that?

"A little-boy threat," she whispered. "A frustrated
little boy who wasn't getting his way. It couldn't have
been more than that."

She sighed and rubbed her forehead, moving down
to the corners of her eyes and pressing the pads of her
fingers there. She closed her eyes and her mind continued to wander. Slowly the darkness behind her eyes
became endlessly deep, and the echo of a husky voice
came back to torment her.

*"Addie, don't hold yourself back from me. I won't
hurt you."* A warm mouth sliding over her skin, a hard
body promising ecstasy as it fitted close against hers.
*"No one will ever know you like I'm going to. You can
keep the rest of the world at bay, but you're going to
let me inside."*

Addie writhed and sat up with an indrawn breath,
her heart thumping. "Stop it," she whispered tightly.
"Stop it."

Ben was her enemy. She wouldn't let him kill Russell. She couldn't let him tear her defenses down. Russell was her father, her real father, and his life was her
responsibility. It was time to start doing something
about it.

She would have to warn Russell. Somehow she'd
have to find a way. Addie stood up and paced back and
forth across the room, her nightgown billowing out
behind her. She tried to imagine Ben plotting to kill
Russell, waiting until the new will was signed, and
then creeping up to Russell's room and committing the
murder. It was almost too logical and obvious a plan,
and it bothered Addie. Ben would have to know he'd
be the first one everyone suspected. Surely he'd be
more subtle than that.

And then there were the Johnsons, who hated Russell. A lot of outfits would like to get their hands on the Sunrise Ranch, tear down its fences, and take possession of its livestock and water rights. Just about everyone around, in fact. But more than anyone else, the Double Bar did. Maybe the Johnsons were in on the murder.

She stopped in her tracks as she remembered Jeff's words again. *"He's riding too high these days, honey . . . don't you worry, it won't be long . . ."*

That was a threat, plain and simple. There was little doubt in her mind that Jeff and Big George wanted Russell out of the way just as much as Ben did. Were they all planning it together?

"No." She shook her downbent head in confusion. "Ben hates the Johnsons. He'd never plan anything with them. And he loves Russell. He wouldn't kill him. I can't believe he would." She didn't want to believe it.

But Russell would have to be killed by an insider, someone who knew about his sleeping habits and which room was his, and how to get through the house. Someone who didn't have to get past the line riders that protected the property around the clock. It had to be Ben, especially since—according to history—he would leave town after the murder and never come back.

"Oh, Ben, that's not you. It's not you." She leaned against the wall and bit her lip.

Strong hands, touching her gently, coaxing purest fire to blossom inside her. *"I want you to remember this. Remember every time you think of me."*

Why is this happening to me?" she whispered in agony. "What have I done to be put through this? I'm still Addie Peck . . . but I'm Adeline Warner too. I'm remembering things from two different lifetimes, and I don't know which *me* is real." She fell silent as she saw the small figure stirring on the other bed, looking like a lump under the sheets. Leah had awakened.

"Aunt Adeline?" she said sleepily.

"Yes, Leah?" Slowly Addie walked over to her, trying to compose herself.

In 1930, Leah said that Aunt Adeline had been a schemer, materialistic and selfish. The memory of Aunt Adeline had made Leah uneasy. Why? What had Leah seen or heard to make her feel that way?

The child yawned and rolled over, staring at her with heavy-lidded eyes. "What are you walkin' around for?"

"I'm sorry I bothered you. I couldn't sleep. I was thinking about a hundred things, and I just had to get up."

"What were you thinkin' about?"

"Someone."

"I saw you go off with Jeff Johnson today," Leah said, those dark eyes losing all traces of sleepiness. "You're thinkin' about him, aren't you?"

"You saw me with . . . but . . . I thought all the children were playing by the corral."

"I came back early. I was followin' you and Mama into the house, and then you stopped an' sneaked off with Jeff Johnson. Mama said I shouldn't tell anyone, or you'd get it from Grampa."

"Yes, I would," Addie said ruefully. "I'd rather you didn't tell anyone. Why are you wrinkling your nose like that?"

"Why'd you sneak off with *him?*"

"I had to talk with him, Leah."

The girl wrinkled her nose again, as if she had smelled something unpleasant. "Oh."

"What's the matter? You don't like Jeff? Why not?"

"You told me not to say why."

"Oh . . . I . . ." Addie paused and looked down at

her, while curiosity leapt inside her. "I don't remember telling you that, Leah."

"You said it was our secret."

It took all of Addie's strength to swallow down her sudden raging impatience and keep from shaking the secret out of the child. She smiled and sat down on the bed, keeping her tone light. "Well, if you don't refresh my memory, I really won't be able to get to sleep. Why would I forget such a thing? Tell me what our secret is."

"Aunt Adeline, I'm tired—"

"Tell me, and then we'll both be able to go to sleep."

"Don't you remember? I was hidin' under the veranda, and you and Jeff were in the porch swing, talkin'."

"Was it in the morning or evening?"

"Evenin'."

"Was it a long time ago, or a short time?"

"Short time," Leah said solemnly.

"What were we saying?"

"You were talkin', real quiet, tellin' Jeff things about Grampa and Ben . . . and . . ."

"And what?"

"And a will. Grampa's will. And I made a noise, and you got real mad when you saw I was there. Don't you remember?"

"I . . . maybe a little." Addie closed her eyes, feeling dizzy. Russell's will.

Rushing down the porch steps, grabbing the frozen, dumbstruck child by the shoulders, hearing her own voice, soft and terrible in its icy rage. *What did you hear? What did you hear?* And then, gentle and cajoling and cunning: *Don't cry, Leah. I've decided you're a big girl now, old enough to share a grown-up secret. What you heard is our secret, Leah . . . and you can't tell anybody . . . .*

That was all she could remember.

"What was I saying about Grampa and Ben?"

Leah turned her face to the wall. "I don't want to talk about it."

Slowly Addie leaned over and kissed Leah's forehead. "I'm sorry if I scared you when I got mad then."

"It's okay, Aunt Adeline. Is it still our secret?"

"Yes, please, Leah," she replied, her voice thin, insubstantial. "You have sweet dreams, you hear?"

The child turned over and flopped onto her own pillow, sighing.

Her knees weak, Addie walked to her own bed and sat down.

Why would I be telling Jeff about the will? There was no reason to. Unless . . . unless I was plotting something with Jeff. Oh, but I couldn't have been. Not about the will. Why, that would mean . . .

Suspicion spread through her like poison. Wilfully she tried to deny it.

I was—am—Russell's daughter. I wouldn't do anything to hurt him, no matter what I was like before. I know I wouldn't.

"My God, what's going on?" she said through dry lips.

What kind of a person had she been before she had returned to Sunrise?

A schemer. And maybe something far worse.

6

THE WEDDING WAS HELD OUTSIDE IN THE COOL MORN-
ing air. Addie sat through the entire ceremony without
hearing a word of it, her mind feverishly occupied with
questions. Until now she had been certain about Ben's
guilt and her own innocence. It had been so easy to
picture him as the villain, and herself as the heroine
who would save the day. But nothing was black or
white anymore. Ben wasn't all good or bad, just as she
wasn't. And the most horrifying thing of all was that
if he wasn't guilty of plotting to kill Russell, *she* might
be. She couldn't forget what Russell had said to her
about the will.

*"Aw, honey . . . I know you're prob'ly a mite dis-
appointed at gettin' Sunrise in trust instead of all that
money . . . you'd be a rich woman if I did that . . .
you'd have enough money to do whatever you wanted
for the rest of your life . . .*

A rich woman.

How badly had she wanted to be a rich woman? If
only she could remember more about the things she
might have done in the past. If only there weren't so
many shadows crowded in her mind.

She cast her eyes over the congregation until she saw
Jeff's hatless head, his mahogany hair shining in the
morning light. He hadn't even looked at her this morning. Boyish, blue-eyed Jeff. Had he really been that
clumsy drunken stranger in the blacksmith shop last

202

night? She could hardly believe it. It seemed like a dream.

Ben was just a few seats away from her. She was astounded by the strange part he had played in all of it. He was the last one she would have cast as her rescuer. His head turned in her direction, and she looked away before their eyes met. She couldn't look at him, not after what had happened between them.

Wincing, Addie couldn't dispel the picture that flashed through her mind, the two of them writhing on the floor of the blacksmith shop. She could feel her cheeks burning with embarrassment as she bent her head to hide her face. The way she had let him touch her, the way she'd encouraged him . . . no, she could never bear to meet his eyes again.

In the last twenty-four hours she'd become a stranger to herself. Addie smiled bitterly as she recalled how this unwanted nightmare had begun. How full of fire and conceit she had been, so eager to convict Ben, so certain she would be Russell Warner's savior. But last night she had found herself clinging to Ben like a wanton, drunk with desire for him, with no thought of Russell or anything else to sober her. It had never been like that before, not with anyone. After her first resistance she had made no effort to push Ben away. So much for her self-righteous intentions.

And what Leah had said later that night in the privacy of their room was more disturbing than anything else so far. Addie hadn't forgotten a word of it. It made her more than a little afraid. What had Leah overheard her planning with Jeff? What had she and Jeff been conspiring to do?

No, I wouldn't have planned anything that would have hurt Russell, she thought frantically. *Not my own father. I may have been different then, but I would never have done something that horrible.*

Addie was alerted by the burst of happy cries from

the congregation when the ceremony was over. Blinking as if newly awakened, she raised her head and looked at the people standing up around her. Caroline tapped her on the shoulder after Peter helped her to rise.

"What are you daydreamin' about?"

"Nothing," Addie said quietly, rising from her seat and fussing with the sleeves of her dress.

Caroline was in a mood to tease. "Maybe you were thinkin' about the wedding you'll have someday."

Ben, who was standing just behind Caroline, happened to overhear. "A wedding?" he repeated, looking over Caro's blond head and making Addie the target of a polite, faintly curious glance. "You fixing to marry someone soon, Miss Adeline?"

As she looked at him and flushed, his green eyes flickered with a subtle light she couldn't mistake. Suddenly the whole world was filled with nothing but the two of them and the private memory of those sweltering minutes in the blacksmith shop. Addie felt trapped, as surely as if she'd been chained to him. Ben caught her look of alarm, and he smiled, allowing just a touch of smugness to shine through.

Addie longed to spit out some words that would wipe the masculine smirk off his face. "At the moment there's not a man in the world I'd agree to marry," she said sharply.

"Glad to hear it," he commented lazily, appreciating the way the sun struck off her honey-colored hair. She was unbearably tempting, all bristled up and uncertain, her mouth pursed and her brows drawing together. ,

Caroline eyed the pair thoughtfully and then turned to her husband with a smile. "Peter, take me into the house, please. If I don't have a glass of water in the next minute, I'll die of thirst."

Ben gave them an absentminded nod as they left,

and returned his attention to Addie, while the excited crowd milled around Ruthie and Harlan. He noticed the shadow of a bruise on Addie's wrist and frowned, reaching out to catch her forearm in his hand. She made no move to pull it away as he looked down at her delicately veined wrist.

"From him or me?" he asked gruffly.

"I don't know." She sounded much calmer than she felt. "Does it matter?"

"Yes, it matters." Though his voice was laced with irritation, his thumb was gentle as it stroked over the bruise. "I didn't intend to hurt you."

Her breath shortened. The movement of his fingers on her skin, there in the middle of hundreds of people, caused her heart to drive crazily against the wall of her chest. This couldn't continue. She had to make certain things clear, about what she would and wouldn't tolerate from him.

"Ben, what happened last n-night can't . . . You and I . . . just *can't*—"

"Yes we can," he returned softly. "And will as soon as I get half a chance."

"No, Ben—"

"You look a little tired, darlin'." His eyes caressed her strained face.

"That's your fault. I couldn't sleep after we . . . after you . . . I spent the whole night tossing and turning."

"I wish I'd been there to join you."

"Hush up! Someone will hear, and *please* don't touch me like that!"

He released her wrist with deliberate care, and Addie knew the wisest thing to do would be to turn around and leave as quickly as possible. But something rooted her feet to the ground, keeping her there, close to him but not quite touching.

"When are you leaving?"

"Soon." Ben laughed quietly. "You're not anxious for me to go, are you?"

"Yes. Oh, stop looking at me like that. I think Mama just noticed us talking together—"

"So?"

"She doesn't want me to associate with someone like you."

"I know that. But what do you want?"

She took a deep breath and looked at him directly. "I want us to forget about last night. It was a terrible misunderstanding."

"Not at all," he countered. "I think we understood each other quite well."

"Do whatever you want. I'm going to forget it ever happened."

"Do you actually think you can?" Ben raised his eyebrows and folded his arms across his chest as he peered down at her. "No. It's going to be there between us from now on. Every time I look at you I'll remember the taste of your lips, the feel of your—"

"Damn you," she whispered, now more worried than before about the mess she was in. She could manage him when they were fighting, when he was angry, but not when he was gentle and teasing. Not when he was looking at her with a gaze that seemed to burn through her clothes. She could remember the taste of him, too, and the devastating touch of his hands on her body. She was shaken by the urge to wrap her arms around his neck and press her face against his throat and simply breathe in the smell of him.

"I want you to stay away from me from now on."

"Don't tell me you don't want me to hold you ever again. Or kiss you, or—"

"Never again!"

"You want it right now," he said, smiling at her appalled expression. "Just as much as I do."

"Ben, stop it," she hissed, aware that people were

beginning to turn around and look at them. Picking up her skirts, she brushed by the rows of chairs and headed toward the house, discarding her pride in order to beat a quick retreat. Ben was right on her heels. Aware of his presence behind her, the long, measured strides that carried him so much farther than hers, she turned to face him as soon as they reached the veranda.

"You don't make any sense at all, Ben Hunter! All of a sudden you've decided you want me, when you wouldn't have me on a silver platter that day in the barn. What changed your mind?"

"Damned if I know. I haven't bothered to analyze it."

"Of course not. Like any man, you chase after the nearest female whenever the urge to rut strikes you. I seem like a good prospect this week, is that it? Well, you won't be welcomed in my bed, not *ever*, so set your sights on someone else."

"If the urge to bed someone was all that concerned me, Addie, I wouldn't look to you to satisfy it. Knowing who you are, do you think I'd be fool enough to wait at your heels, hoping for a quick tumble? I haven't been deprived of a woman's company in a long time. If I wanted to sleep in a woman's arms tonight, I could find one easily. Someone a hell of a lot more experienced than you, and not half as much trouble."

"Then what do you want from me?" she whispered.

His smile was designed to annoy her. "Haven't I made it clear?"

"No," she groaned miserably. "Ben, you've got to stop. You're turning everything upside down. You're making me miserable out of pure meanness. You know any kind of relationship between us is impossible."

"Why?"

She couldn't tell him why. Hastily she racked her brains. "I d-don't know what kind of person you are.

I don't know you. I don't think anyone around here does."

"I could say the same about you. But that's something we can change. We don't have to be strangers. Unless you're afraid of what'll happen if you let me get closer. Is that it?"

She stared at him in confusion, her heart turning over at the soft sound of his voice. "I don't know what to do, or what to tell you—"

"Nothing, for now. Nothing at all." A movement to the left of them caught Ben's eyes, and he glanced at the approaching figure before turning back to Addie with a wry smile. "It looks like we'll have to continue this later."

"Why?"

"Take a look."

May was wearing a distinct frown as she walked toward them. There was no mistaking the perturbation in her voice and on her face. She didn't even look at Ben, but addressed Addie instead, her blue eyes cool and unnerving. "Adeline, I don't like you runnin' off without sayin' a word to me about where you are going. There are people askin' after you, people we haven't seen in a long time."

"I'm sorry, Mama—"

"My apologies," Ben interrupted. "I shouldn't have taken her aside. Please don't hold Miss Adeline accountable for my selfishness."

"I know what to hold my daughter accountable for," May replied, looking at him with displeasure. "And she knows she's keepin' you from the things you should be doing. You were planning on returnin' to the ranch as soon as the wedding was over, weren't you?"

"Yes, ma'am."

"Then don't let us detain you."

Ben nodded respectfully to her and glanced at Addie with gleaming eyes.

"Good-bye," she said in a hushed voice, her pulse racing.

After Ben strode away, May fixed Addie with a suspicious stare. "Why is he lookin' at you that way? Something's happened. Has he made any advances to you? Surely you haven't allowed him to take any liberties, Adeline.'

"I . . . why . . . of course not," Addie stuttered. "We were just talking. Why do you seem so set against him all of a sudden?"

"Because I know what kind of man he is. And if you let him, he'll take advantage of you, of your innocence, your trust, and especially your vanity."

"Mama—"

"I'm going to speak frankly, out of concern for you. I wondered how long it would take before this conversation would be necessary. I knew it would come sooner or later. Ben is a handsome man, and he has a way about him. I understand what an impression he must make on a girl your age. And you're attractive to him for many reasons—your looks, your money, but most of all because you're Russell Warner's daughter. I know Russ likes to fancy Ben as another son, and Ben does his best to take full advantage of that."

Addie found herself in the unexpected position of having to defend Ben—she, who should have gratefully welcomed any censure of him! "I don't agree. He doesn't need to chase after me or anyone else for money. He's well-educated, and too proud to take advantage of—"

"For all his education, he was a mavericker before he came to Sunrise."

"So was Daddy, once."

"I want better for you than that. And I won't allow a man like Ben Hunter, a man just like your Daddy, to have my daughter."

Addie stared at her in amazement. There was an

undertone of steel in May's voice, a strength in her face Addie had never noticed before. Underneath her blond prettiness, there was more purpose and tenacity in May than she'd suspected.

"There's no chance of anything happening between Ben and me," Addie said slowly. "But why don't you want me to marry someone like Daddy?"

"I promised myself I'd do everything in my power to see that my girls had a better life than I did, that you wouldn't repeat my mistakes. Why do you think I insisted on both of you being sent to the academy? Why do you think I've tried so hard to make sure you have manners and fashionable clothes, and an education? Finally my dream for Caro has come true. She and Peter are movin' out of Texas. But if you're going to be buried here for the rest of your life, away from decent people and civilized places, I refuse to give you away to a man who won't treat you half as well as the cattle he owns. And that's what will happen if you settle for some ranch hand."

"But I don't want a different life from this. I don't want to be pampered and spoiled. I won't care if it's a little bit rougher than folks have it back east—"

"A little bit rougher," May said, her voice catching. "You don't know anything about the kind of life you could have. I was brought up in a beautiful home, among people with gentle manners, in a house with servants. I had my choice of beaus. And I came out here ignorant of the filth, the roughness of these people, the men wearing guns all the time, even at the dinner table. There are times when I still have to work harder than some of the servants in my mother's home."

"Mama—"

"The men out here won't shelter you from things no woman back east would ever have to tolerate, the crudity and the work, the county swarming with criminals and Indians—"

"It's not exactly *swarming* with them. Aren't you exaggerating a little?"

"Don't you use that tone with me, Adeline! I've been through horrors you know nothin' about. Just after I had Caroline, I begged your father to hire a nurse to help me look after her. I had to work all the time, cleaning, washing, and cooking, and I couldn't care for a baby every minute of the day. And he certainly did get a nurse—a Tonkawa girl to take care of my firstborn—an *Indian*. Imagine, after all I'd heard of them stealing white children, and then to walk into the nursery and see one of them holding my baby! A woman of one of the most cruel and merciless tribes—"

"They're not all like that. Caro told me that some of the women in the county have some friends among the women of the Indian settlement near here. They talk and share meals—"

"Is that what you would like to do? Visit with those . . . creatures . . . rather than be among your own kind of people? I insisted you go to the academy in Virginia because I wanted you to see what it was like there, how much better than here."

"I don't see what's wrong with having friendships with them, or living here, or marrying a cowman. I like it better here than anywhere else. I'm not like you and Caro. I'll probably never move out of Texas. And I don't want to be sheltered."

May's eyes glimmered with unhappiness. "You've always chosen to learn things the hard way. I know how useless it is to talk to you when you've decided to be stubborn. But for your own sake, you must think about what I'm tellin' you."

"I will," Addie said uncomfortably, ducking her head and looking away, unable to repress a short sigh.

"I don't understand why you married Daddy, if he wasn't the kind of man you wanted."

May's expression was infused with bitterness. "Your father went east to find a wife and bring her back to Texas. He courted me in North Carolina. I didn't know what kind of life he'd be takin' me to, and didn't much care at the time. I thought love alone would be enough to make me happy. A woman in love makes foolish choices, Adeline. And I don't imagine you'll be any different from me in that respect."

As was common for any large social function, the crowd was served plenty of good liquor, which helped to fuel the general carefree spirit. Some of the men conglomerated in small groups and proceeded to slap each other on the back heartily, talking about their land and businesses with seeming carelessness. Others freely admired the women, who were beautiful in their brightly colored dresses and masses of ruffles.

The younger people, who had eagerly awaited the night of music and dancing, busied themselves making new acquaintances and behaving as they thought grown men and women should. The steps they knew were not fancy or intricate, and the music provided by the cowboy band was not exactly elegant, but it was played with enthusiasm.

Addie found to her annoyance that she was keenly aware of Ben's absence, in spite of being claimed for every dance by a different person. What was wrong with her, that she couldn't keep herself from comparing Ben to every man she met and finding them all wanting? The most handsome ones here were unremarkable when compared to the memory of a man with black hair and vivid green eyes. No one else could stop her heart with his flashing smile, no one else dared to contradict and tease, and taunt as boldly as he did. She thought about him more while he was gone then she would have had he been there.

Occasionally Addie saw Jeff's face in the crowd among the lanterns and shadows, and she stayed as far away from him as possible. Occasionally he would ask someone to dance, but he kept his eyes on Addie as she was whirled around in time to the music. Her blue-green dress emphasized the whiteness of her skin and the rich dark blond of her hair, attracting many a masculine eye.

When Addie wasn't dancing, she stayed close to Russell, finding comfort in the fact that a silent truce seemed to have developed between them. She had no intention of apologizing for the argument they'd had, and neither did Russell, but they'd made an unspoken decision to go on as if it hadn't happened. So far they'd managed to recapture some of their former easiness with each other.

Well into the evening Addie's feet were aching from the fast round-dancing, and she was relieved when the music slowed down to a pace that the less spry members of the gathering could enjoy. She managed to wheedle Russell into a dance, pestering him with questions as they moved around the floor.

"As far as I can tell, no one's mentioned anything about the fences to you," she said, and Russell chuckled, both annoyed and admiring of her daring in bringing up the subject.

"Not at a weddin' dance, honey."

"But that's just for tonight. What about after the wedding's over and we're all back home again?"

Russell shrugged, deciding not to answer. Addie took it to mean he expected trouble later on, and a chill of premonition stole over her. "Daddy, I've been thinking about some of the things Ben had to say about that barbed wire."

"What kinda things?" Although his voice was quiet,

there was a menacing note in it. "Ben been talkin' against me behind my back, talkin' against my decisions?"

"No, no," she said hastily. "Just explaining to me. I didn't understand why everyone's so stirred up about your fences. It's because you've enclosed the water supply, isn't it? All the nearby grassland that the Double Bar owns isn't worth anything without the water rights. I didn't realize that before."

"It's my water. I was here long before Big George Johnson and all the rest of them. Before the war started, 'bout twenty-five years ago. I couldn't get a town job, so I came out west and claimed the land on both sides of it—which means all the range around it is mine. It always has been. But folks like the Johnsons started movin' in, pushin' in the boundaries of my ranch, expectin' half the water rights, when the river was always mine to begin with."

"I've heard you started out as a mavericker," she said, and he chuckled.

"Nearly everyone got his start that way, with a runnin' iron and a reata. Everyone did a little rustling, even the first sheriff of these parts. It was more respectable then. They didn't hold it against a man like they do now. But the price of cattle's gone up, and now a lot of folk think mavericking should be punished same as horse stealin'."

"They say that Ben—"

"Yeah, he was a mavericker. Almost got himself strung up for it by a vigilante committee before I hired him."

"Really?" Addie's eyes widened in fascination. "I don't remember that."

"You were away at the academy."

"What made you decide to off him a job?"

"Ben came ridin' up to the main house with a hot-tempered crowd not ten minutes away, all of 'em bent on stretchin' his neck as soon as they caught up to him. I gave him two minutes to speak his piece. I'll bet he's never talked so fast before or since.''

Addie grinned. ''I wish I could have seen it. He must have been sweating bullets.''

''Little cat. Don't you have any kindly feelin' for him a-tall?'' Russell demanded, laughing richly.

''Yes, but he's always so in control of everything. I just like the idea of seeing him a little shaken up.''

''He is every time you're around, punkin. I reckon you're the only woman who . . .'' Russell stopped suddenly and looked at her as if a brand new idea had occurred to him. He opened his mouth and closed it, as if he wanted to ask something but didn't know how.

''What?'' she prompted.

''Oh, nothin'.'' He shrugged with elaborate carelessness. ''Just wonderin' . . . what do you think about Ben, honey?''

Startled, she stared at him with a sagging jaw. He'd never had that particular gleam in his eye when mentioning Ben to her before. Hurriedly she collected herself. ''I think he's a good foreman—''

''As a man. You ever think about him that way?''

She shook her head hastily. ''Daddy, what a silly question. And don't you dare think about asking him what he thinks about me. There's absolutely no chance of *that* kind of feeling developing between us.''

''Don't see why not. Less you don't like his looks?''

Addie turned even redder. ''There's nothing wrong with his looks.''

''Nice-mannered and smart too.''

''Y-yes—''

''And he's the kind women take to.''

''Yes, but . . . Daddy, stop this. I don't want to talk about him.''

''S' all right with me. Just askin'.'' Russell appeared to be satisfied now that the subject had been brought to her attention. The music ended, and he walked her back to where they'd been standing before. Addie couldn't help noticing Jeff watching from several feet away, his eyes locked on her, catching her every movement and expression. Russell noticed too. "That Johnson boy's eyes are gonna fall outta his head," he remarked grimly.

Addie surprised him by laughing lightly. "He's the kind who never wants something badly until he knows for certain he can't have it."

"You still sweet on him?"

"I never was, in *that* way. He's never been anything but a friend to me."

"Then why the hell did you get so mad when I told you not to see him anymore?"

"Because I don't like to be ordered around, by you or anyone else."

Russell stood still and looked down at her, shaking his head and sighing with rueful pride. "Damned if you aren't me all over again. Don't see why you weren't born a boy."

Coming from him, that was a sizable compliment. Addie smiled pertly. "I like being a woman just fine, thank you. And getting back to the subject of Jeff, when are you going to change your mind about letting me see him?"

His good mood evaporated. "When it's safe. Which might be a long time from now."

"Safe," she repeated slowly. "Do you suspect we're in some kind of danger from the Johnsons?"

"We are from everyone." He seemed to forget she was his daughter as he talked to her with the frankness of one man to another. "We always have been, always will be. Not one man here who doesn't hate our big profits, not one who wouldn't try to tap into them if he thought of a good way to do it. I fenced in what I own in order to keep what's mine. No one likes that, 'specially not the Double Bar. Until lately I hoped we'd be able to git along with the Johnsons. When you're as big as we are, 'f a man's not your friend, he's your enemy. But now they've made the choice, and it's gonna get a lot worse than this.''

"You sound as if you're getting ready for war," Addie said, thinking of the danger that was in store for him. "I guess it's not a bad thing to be prepared. You're going to be careful, aren't you? I don't want anything to happen to you.''

"Don't want anything to happen to any of us, honey.''

"But people are mad at *you,*" she said, and suddenly she wanted to throw her arms around him, protect him from the world. He was her father. And in spite of his roughness, explosive temper, and the overbearing manner that seldom failed to set her teeth on edge, she loved him. "You're the one who's got to be careful. Daddy, are you listening?''

Although he nodded, she could see he wasn't listening, not as she wanted him to. There was no way she could confess what she knew and what she feared. Her chest felt tight as she realized the number of enemies he had. *All* of the ranchers around here, not just the Johnsons, hated Russell's power, his wealth, and most of all, his fences. She was inadequate to protect him. She wasn't strong enough to do it alone. She wished she could run to Ben for help, even though she knew the thought was pure insanity. No amount of wishful thinking would change what he was.

Ben was there to help unload the carriage the day the Warner family returned to the ranch. They were all relieved to arrive. Caroline was exhausted from traveling, Cade was fidgety and eager to stretch his legs, Russell was anxious to get back to work, and the rest were merely happy to be where there was privacy and the comfort of well-established routines. Addie was the last to emerge, having been squashed in the corner of the seat for the entire journey. She avoided Ben's gaze as he helped her down, disconcerted by her own crushed and rumpled appearance. They were unseen by the others, who were heading toward the front door of the main house.

"How was it?" he asked quietly, his hands lingering on her waist after her feet had touched the ground.

"The trip back home? Terrible."

"No, I was referring to the dance, the parties . . . the two days you spent out of my sight. Jeff give you any problems?"

She looked up at him then, undone by the note of concern in his voice, and saw no censure or mockery in his green eyes, nothing but warmth. Silken ribbons seemed to tighten around her heart. It was good to see him. She felt as if it had been weeks rather than days since she'd been near him.

"Jeff didn't bother me at all," she said, making an effort to sound nonchalant. "He didn't say a word to me the entire time. Of course, he stared a lot—"

"You should be used to that by now."

"I haven't been around him in a while."

"But he's not the only one who likes to stare at you."

Addie set her mouth sternly in order to prevent a smile. "I'm getting tired of this game. It's ridiculous. You're even causing Daddy to have strange ideas about the two of us."

"I've got a few in mind myself."

"I don't want to hear them."

His hands tightened on her waist when she would have moved away. "There's no way you can get out of it."

"Don't bet on it, slicker," she said in the tart manner of a flapper, and he grinned at the change in her voice.

"Every now and then you sound like . . ." He paused and shrugged. "I don't know what it is. But I have a suspicion there's more behind those big brown eyes than anyone else imagines."

"You'll never find out."

"Not for lack of trying," he assured her.

"Ben!" came Russell's voice from the house, and immediately Addie was released.

"He wants a report on everything that happened while he was gone." Ben's mouth twitched in amusement as he looked toward the window of the room Russell used as an office. "We'll talk later."

"*Did* anything happen?" she asked, touching his arm in an unconscious gesture, her eyes dark with concern. "Any trouble?"

The muscle underneath her fingertips tensed as if he'd received a small shock at her touch. Ben went very still, looking down at her with an intensity that weakened her knees. "No trouble," he said carefully. "Only when you're around, darlin'." Her hand trembled, but she didn't let go of him, overwhelmed by the yearning that had swept over her. Did Ben feel the ache of it too? He stared at her for what seemed to be hours, his face hard. All the forbidden longing in her heart was released in a torrent.

I could love him, she thought dazedly, *if I let myself.* And she already would, if he were anyone else in the world.

Lord, what am I going to do?

There was another roar from the house. "Ben, did you hear me or is somethin' blockin' your ears?"

"I'll be there in a minute," Ben called back with an impudence no one else in Texas would have dreamed of showing to Russell Warner.

"Go," Addie said thickly, releasing her grip on his arm, and he hesitated.

She would have expected him to make some sardonic remark. But there was nothing playful about his manner as he spoke to her huskily.

"I want to hold you, Addie."

She couldn't deny him, or deny that she felt the same. "Please go," she whispered. He nodded slightly, his eyes moving over her face. There was no need for further words. They both understood all that was left unsaid.

It was a fundamental part of the ranchers' code that when cowboys came to visit, they were welcome to a free meal, lodging, and whatever else the host's hospitality might include. Although the half-dozen men who appeared at the Sunrise Ranch were strangers, it was obvious by their appearance and smell that they'd lived in the saddle all summer long. The women of the household were busy all afternoon, distributing towels and soap for the men to have much-needed shaves and baths. Then there were piles of soiled clothes to wash and mend, so many that the air was pungent with the scent of lye and hot water.

By the time the visitors were seated at the table, May and Caroline were almost too exhausted to enjoy their own dinners. Although Addie had worked just as hard as they had, she wasn't tired at all. She was filled with a nervous energy that wouldn't subside. Methodically she ate everything on her plate, hardly tasting anything, listening while Russell involved himself in a conversation with the cowboys.

She and Ben tried to ignore each other. But a steady flame of awareness burned inside her. She was conscious of every movement he made, every word he spoke. And when she looked up from the intent perusal of her plate and caught a wayward glance of his, she was filled with a surge of delight.

When the meal was over and they were all replete, the men remained at the table and talked while the women discreetly cleared away the dishes. After most of the work was done in the kitchen, Caroline put a hand to her lower back and sighed wearily.

"I'm too tired to wiggle. Mama, would you come upstairs with me and help me out of these things? Peter won't go to bed for a good long while, but I've got to have some rest."

"Would you like me to help you?" Addie offered.

"That's all right," May said, patting her shoulder gently. "I will. After all you've done today, you should get to bed early."

"Yes, Mama."

Feeling strangely lost, Addie wandered out of the kitchen and into the hallway. The sounds of the men's voices, the flap-flap of cards and the clinking of bottles and glasses were clearly audible. For them, the evening was just beginning. Addie glanced at the stairs. The thought of going up to her room and closing herself inside four walls was unbearable. She looked at the front door, craving the freedom beyond it, and slipped outside before she had second thoughts.

The air was soft and sweet, the sky like black velvet. Hesitantly Addie walked down the front steps with no destination in mind, wandering alongside the house. On nights like this she and Leah used to sit with the windows open to catch the breeze, and they would listen to the radio for hours.

The ghost of a song went through her mind. *I never knew . . . a heart could ache like this . . . I never knew . . . I'd miss your sweet embrace . . .* Straining to remember the rest of it, she stopped walking and stood still. *I know I won't forget you, can't accept*

*we're through . . . Until the day you left me, dear, I
never knew. . . .*

Something stirred in her heart, the memories of sitting cross-legged in front of the radio and daydream-
ing . . . walking into Leah's room and sharing gossip
. . . tinting her mouth with sassy red lipstick before
going on a date with Bernie . . . making Leah laugh
by doing a modified Charleston in the middle of her
bedroom. Strange, how difficult it was to picture Bernie's face, or Leah's face. How faded the image of the
house at the end of Main Street was, and the rooms
inside, and the hospital where she'd worked.

Absently she hummed the rest of the song. *Now
every night . . . I close my eyes and dream of you . . .
I never knew . . . how sweet a dream could be . . . I
know I can't expect you to regret we're through . . .
Until the day you left me, dear, I never knew. . . .*

Addie folded her arms around her middle and
sighed. It was impossible to believe that the house she
had grown up in was gone. Leah was gone, and Addie
would never be able to go back to the Sunrise she had
known. And what did she have instead? That was an
interesting question. Thoughtfully Addie considered
her newfound circumstances. She had a brother and a
sister, a mother, a closet of pink dresses and a bad-
tempered horse, a reputation as a breaker of hearts,
an ex-boyfriend, a father who loved her, and a man
who wanted her. A man she wanted in return.

*Don't you understand what you're doing? Stop
thinking about him, stop dreaming about him, for Russell's sake if not your own. You don't belong with each
other.*

There was the sound of booted feet on the stairs,
moving with incredible quietness, and Addie froze.
Her pulse drummed as the footsteps drew closer and
she saw it was Ben. He stopped right next to her, his

eyes translucent in the darkness. She knew what he wanted.

Don't let it happen, she thought in panic, but there was a sense of inevitability about it all. Their coming-together was as natural as the sun rising and falling.

Ben didn't move or speak. There was a hollow sensation in his stomach, a feeling he'd experienced only a few times before. He'd been aware of it as he went home to face his father the day after graduation, and once again while being chased through the county by a noose-brandishing mob. He'd never been nervous because of a woman, not even his first one. But Addie wasn't just any woman, and he wanted her as he'd never wanted anyone else. He needed her too much for his own good—he knew that, but there wasn't a damn thing he could do to stop himself.

No man could withstand the temptation of her sleek body and silky hair, and a face that was at once wholesome and sensual. And there were other things that attracted him to her just as forcefully. She was strong-willed, forthright in expressing her opinions, a woman who would stand by a man in times of trouble. Sometimes she was vulnerable, wearing an expression of loneliness that started an ache in his own heart. He wanted her to trust him, give him the right to comfort and protect her.

"How did you know I'd be here?" she asked.

"Because I wanted you to be."

"The others—"

"Are concentrating on a bottle of deadshot and a deck of cards. The game didn't interest me."

Addie made an effort to sound flippant. "I'm sure they'll miss you."

"Not as much as you would have."

"You're so conceited. I w-wouldn't have missed you."

"Just the same, I couldn't let you stay out here alone underneath all these stars."

"I wouldn't have minded being alone," she said, her breath catching as his hands slid behind her neck. "I've never minded it."

His palms traveled up to the hollow beneath her jaw, coming to rest on either side of her face. He couldn't keep from touching her any longer. "Then say you want me to leave. Go on. Say it."

She closed her eyes, fiercely willing herself to say the words, but they wouldn't come out. "I can't," she whispered in despair.

"Because you belong to me."

"No, not to anyone. I . . . I don't know why I want you. I don't even *like* you."

He smiled and brushed a kiss on her lips, so light she could hardly feel it. The hint of warmth was enough to make her gasp. Then he waited patiently, waited while seconds dragged by, silently daring her to make the next move. Finally her face nudged past the frame of his hands and her mouth came in search of his. Her lips were soft and seeking, and Ben made a low sound in his throat, tightening his arms until she was forced to stand on her toes. Hungrily she answered the pressure of his kiss, the movements of his tongue, knowing she would never get enough of the taste of him.

He slid one hand up to the back of her neck and pushed his fingertips into her hair, wanting to bury himself in the softness of her. Addie touched him as she had dreamed so many times, moving her palms in circles across his back, straining her fingers through his hair, rubbing the pads of her fingers across his face and savoring the rough-smooth surface of his jaw.

"Finally," he breathed when their lips had parted, and she nodded, understanding his infinite relief . . . she felt it too.

"Don't look at me like that," she said, her fingers drifting across the back of his neck.

"I can't help it." One corner of his mouth lifted in a half-smile, and she smiled back at him unsteadily.

"It makes me nervous. You look like you're about to swallow me whole."

He pressed his mouth to her forehead and then strung kisses from her hairline down to the tip of her nose. "I've got better things in mind, darlin'."

She was overwhelmed by the pleasure of being close to him. "This is . . . just awful," she said, her voice catching. "What am I going to do?"

Nothing could stop Ben from kissing her again, with a need that had built up in him for weeks. Her mouth shifted under his, alternately playful and demanding. Their passion burned hotter than before, and he lost all awareness of everything but her. A shudder escaped him, and he fitted his hands over her hips, clamping their bodies together.

Addie wrapped her arms across his broad back. Wrong or right, she couldn't deny him, when her entire being begged to be filled with him. She could feel his hands skimming over her back and waist, but the sensation was blurred by her thick corset. Never had she resented the prison of laces and stays so much. All she wanted was to be naked in bed with him, learning the secrets that lovers shared.

Suddenly she realized how far she had traveled, the distance between what she'd once been and what she was now. With a shiver she pulled her mouth away, resting her forehead against his shoulder to keep him from finding her lips again.

"Addie?" he breathed, and she shook her head, gasping. He hooked an arm around her slender neck. "Tell me," he said, his mouth close to her ear. "Tell me."

"This isn't right."

"Oh, yes it is. It was meant to be like this between us."

"I sh-shouldn't. Not with you."

"Why not?"

"Something tells me I should be afraid," she said in a stricken whisper.

"Of me?" he asked, becoming so gentle she hardly recognized him. "Why darlin'?"

"B-because wanting each other this way isn't enough. Once the desire is satisfied, there'll be nothing to keep us from tearing each other apart. And I won't survive it. Don't you understand?"

"No, I don't. Do you think I'd turn on you someday? Is that it? I'd never hurt you, Addie—I couldn't if I tried. You have to believe that."

She looked up at him and nodded, her eyes glittering in the moonlight. The sight took Ben's breath away. "God, you're beautiful."

"I'm not." Self-consciously she tried to turn away, but he caught her chin and stared into her eyes.

"You are. Sometimes I can't take my eyes off you. I can't sleep without dreaming about you."

"I dream about you too."

"And about this?" He cupped her breast in his palm and lowered his mouth to her neck. She sighed and nuzzled her face into his shirt, pressing her cheek against the hard muscles underneath. Shivery delight raced through every nerve as he bit gently at a sensitive place on her throat. His thumb rushed over the peak of her breast, teasing, drawing pleasure from her body with every stroke.

"Does that feel good?" He caught her more firmly against him, continuing to fondle her lightly. "Does it?"

"Yes," she choked, knowing the admission was an invitation for him to do more. Ben kissed her again, his heart thundering. He was drunk on the taste and feel of her. Her scent seemed to follow a pathway from his nose to his loins. Now that he'd had a taste of her, he'd never be satisfied with anyone else. There was a natural combustion between them, the kind of affinity some people never found despite a lifetime of searching.

Addie molded against him, thigh to thigh, chest to chest, and still it wasn't enough. Wanting to climb inside him, she slid her arms around his waist and clung fiercely. Suddenly he broke their kiss with a low sound, pressing his mouth against her temple.

"Wait. Shhh . . . be quiet."

"What—"

"Hush darlin'."

She realized he was listening for something, that he'd heard something, and she went still. There was a shuffling sound in the darkness, the scrape of unsteady footsteps across the well-packed dirt, the hum of a muffled monologue. Ben looked toward the noise intently, willing his mind and body to cool down.

Addie sensed him drawing away from her, and she couldn't help making a sound of distress. "Hush," Ben whispered, stroking her back in a soothing motion, staring in the direction of the darkness beyond the corral. After a minute she let herself rest against his chest, her ear pressed to his heartbeat. She heard him sigh in exasperation.

"What is it?" Addie asked thickly.

"It's one of the boys walking a few feet off the ground. Watts."

"You mean he's had too much to drink?"

Ben grinned in spite of his frustration. "Give or take a quart."

Reluctantly he reached behind his neck to disentangle her arms.

"What are you doing?"

"I've got to see to him."

"He can't see us," she persisted as he unlocked her hands with gentle insistence. "He'll go away if we just ignore him."

He laughed and bent his head to kiss her swiftly. "I can't let him wander around the ranch like that, honey. He needs help."

Addie realized how shameless she had sounded, and how selfish, and she colored. "I'm sorry—"

"Don't start that or I'll be another ten minutes. Just go on inside." Ben loosened his arms from around her and started to leave her, swore softly and stole one more kiss.

Addie stood still, watching him stride off to the staggering cowboy. The night seemed cooler now, the blackness of the sky overwhelming. Instead of going into the house, she drew deeper in the shadows, her eyes dilating as she stared after Ben. He reached Watts and laid a hand on his shoulder to stop his pacing. Watts stumbled.

"Whoa, boy," she heard Ben say. "I see you had a good night in town." She couldn't make out the other man's mumbled reply, but it looked as if he would fall without the support of a steady arm. "Why don't you head in the direction of your bunk?" Ben turned Watts to face the bunkhouse. "You're gonna have a hell of a morning tomorrow. Might as well get a little sleep."

Another slurred remark from the cowhand, louder than the first.

"Jis . . . bin doin' little sshelebratin' . . ."

Ben laughed quietly. "Yeah, I can see that. Come on, pardner. No more celebrating tonight."

Suddenly Watts tore away from him and swiveled in a drunken lurch, cursing as he tried to stagger away.

Addie frowned in disgust, having a low opinion of men who liked to drink until they couldn't see straight.

Having no further interest in the scene, she headed toward the front steps. But a new note of concern in Ben's voice stopped her. "What in the hell's gotten into you tonight? I've never seen you this soaked."

Abruptly the cowhand's muttering disintegrated in a long groan of pain. Addie gripped the railing on the side of the steps as his mournful wail sent chills down her spine.

"Aw, Bennn . . . why'd she hafta do it . . . why . . ."

Ben gripped him by the shoulders and shook him slightly. "Who? A lady-friend? What happened?"

But Watts merely buried his face in his hands, and Addie realized with surprise and a sense of embarrassment that he was crying. She wished she had gone into the house, wished she hadn't been a witness to his private grief. Slowly she crept up the stairs, wondering what could have made him break down like that. She couldn't make sense out of his sobbing, but Ben seemed to understand it. She heard the compassion in his voice as he murmured to Watts.

"It's not your fault. Dammit, you should've talked to someone about it before filling your guts with forty-rod. No, there was nothing you could have done to stop her . . ."

Addie reached the front door and turned the handle. She glanced back and saw Ben's arm slung over the other man's shoulder. It struck her then, how unafraid he was of other people's weakness, how ready he was to share his strength with someone who needed it. Most men would have shrunk from such a scene. But Ben wasn't afraid of emotion, or of being needed.

Her eyes stung as she stared at him. For the first time she saw him as the man he was, not as she had feared or dreaded him to be. Ben looked up then, becoming aware of her presence on the steps, and his brows drew together in a gathering scowl. He hadn't expected her to be there. Knowing he wanted her to leave before Watts saw her, she slipped guiltily inside the house and went upstairs to her room.

7

ADDIE PACED BACK AND FORTH ACROSS THE FLOOR OF her bedroom, high-strung and restless. When she was tired of pacing, she flung back the light covers on her bed and lay down, her body rigid as she stared at the ceiling. She could still feel Ben's hands on her . . . *you belong to me* . . . She could hear the rasp of his voice in her ear . . . *I'd never hurt you* . . .

Addie flopped onto her stomach, burying her face in her pillow. The hours crept by as she lay there, but sleep wasn't something you could force. Downstairs the sounds of the men's voices faltered and tapered off, and gradually there was silence. They had all retired for the evening. Sighing heavily, Addie sat up and combed her hair away from her face with her fingers. Her thin white nightgown was twisted around her from hours of restless turning, and she stood up to straighten it out. Then she heard a sound on the stairs, and her heart stopped with a jolt of fear. Her first thought was for Russell.

"Daddy," she whispered, and fumbled blindly for her robe, throwing it on hastily before opening her door. Since her room was close to the stairs, she had an immediate view of whoever was approaching. Her shoulders sagged with relief as she saw Russell climbing the steps, leaning heavily on Ben. Her expression was tinged with reluctant amusement. Russell was thoroughly drunk. With the slow progress they were making, it would take a long time for them to reach the top.

"I tellya we're gonna make . . . lotta money this year," he was saying to Ben, waggling his finger to emphasize the point. "Betcha it'll go up to eight or nine dollars a hunnred on the hoof—"

"If you say so," Ben muttered, nearly losing his balance as Russell stumbled on the next step.

"Thas' right . . . this year . . . cow's jumpin' over the moon . . ."

"Only if you start thinking about breeding some better animals with your damn stringy longhorns."

"Thas' right . . . I'm thinkin' 'bout that . . . Smart boy—"

"Thank you."

"But . . . you ain' been smart 'nuff t' go after my daughter. My Adeline. Don' you know she's the pretties' girl in Texas?"

Ben dragged him up another step. "Yes, sir."

Addie raised her eyes heavenward. Russell was bound and determined to play matchmaker in his uniquely heavy-handed way.

"Then why haventcha . . . ?" Russ demanded, gesturing with his hand and nearly sending them toppling down the steps. "She's sweet-tempered—"

"When she wants to be."

"Got everythin' a man could want—"

Addie couldn't keep from interrupting any longer. "Do you need some help?" she asked crisply, and both men looked up at her, Russell with foggy surprise, Ben with a familiar narrow-eyed glance. "You're going to wake the whole house up," she said.

Ben shrugged. "Russ just tipped the bottle one time too many. Thought I'd help him upstairs."

"You've done a lot of that sort of thing tonight, haven't you?" she remarked, going halfway down the stairs and taking her father's other arm.

Russell squinted down at her. "You're up late, honey," he said mildly.

"So are you."

With a great deal of sweat and effort, they managed to get him up the steps and into his bedroom, a small miracle considering Russell's condition.

"Thanks," Ben said as they helped Russell to the bed, where he promptly collapsed.

"What possessed you to think you could get him up here alone?" Addie asked, arranging a pillow underneath the slumbering man's head.

Ben grinned, going to the foot of the bed and pulling off Russell's boots. "Optimism."

"Simplemindedness," she corrected, peering at him suspiciously, as if questioning his judgment. "And just how much have *you* had to drink?"

"Why? Are you offering to tuck me in too?"

Disconcerted, she turned and left the room, aware of his footsteps as he followed her and closed the door. Slowly she walked down the hall, refusing to look at him. Her heart began to beat faster as Ben passed the stairs and continued to follow her. "I'm perfectly sober," he remarked.

"I have no interest in your condition."

"Why are you up at two-thirty in the morning?"

"That's no concern of yours."

"So you couldn't sleep. I wonder why."

They reached her door and Addie stopped, afraid he was going to ask to be invited in, afraid of what she might say. She fortified her determination before whirling around to face him. He was unbelievably handsome with his black hair disheveled and his rumpled white shirt rolled up at the sleeves. Rapidly she tried to think of something, anything to say to forestall the question she knew he would ask.

"Ben, I wondered . . ."

"What?" He braced a hand on the doorframe be-

hind her and rested his weight on it. She shrank back
a little.

"What was the matter with that cowhand you talked
to tonight?"

"Watts?" Ben hesitated, as if debating whether or
not to tell her. "He went over to the next county to
hunt down the truth about a rumor he'd heard about
his sister."

"Oh?"

"He's been supporting his mother and sister on the
pay he earns, does odd jobs on the side to get extra
money. Apparently from what he found out tonight,
he couldn't provide enough for them."

"What did he find out?"

"His sister's working in a dance hall."

"As a dancer?"

"As a . . . fancy woman." That was a delicate way
of putting it. There were a hundred more colorful
words that were more commonly used to describe a
whore, all of which would have offended a lady's sen-
sibilities. He wasn't sure if Addie would have taken
exception or not.

"Oh, Ben." Addie's voice was soft with pity. "How
old is she?"

He shrugged. "Sixteen, seventeen."

"What if she had more money? How much would
it take so she wouldn't have to work there anymore? I
can find some way to get some from Daddy. You know
how tenderhearted he is inside—"

"I've already offered to help. Watts refused to take
a cent. At the moment he's not thinking too straight.
I'll try again tomorrow when his head is clearer." As
Addie continued to frown, Ben reached out to touch a
lock of hair that was trailing over her shoulder. He
tugged it gently. "Don't look so worried. It'll be all
right."

"I hope so." She looked down at the floor. "Sometimes I can't believe how much unhappiness there is in the world.''

"What are you unhappy about?'' Ben nudged her chin up with the tip of his forefinger and smiled into her eyes. "Tell me and I'll fix it.''

"You couldn't begin to,'' she said shortly, jerking away from him. "Just leave, please. I'm going to bed now.''

"Leave? But this is my favorite part of the evening.''

"Good night,'' she said firmly.

"I hope so.'' He smiled into her startled face, reaching past her to the doorknob, turning it with a deft twist. The door swung open as if eager to welcome him. Addie was speechless as Ben pushed her into the room and closed the door behind him with a nudge of his elbow. He hadn't asked to be invited. Typical of him.

"B-Ben . . .'' she stuttered.

"Hmmn?'' He arched an eyebrow in casual inquiry, rolling down his sleeves.

"Ben, get out of here. I . . . What are you doing?''

"What I've been wanting to do ever since we were interrupted earlier.'' He was starting on the front of his shirt now, freeing the buttons one by one. Stunned, Addie watched with her jaw hanging as the firm, tanned flesh of his torso was revealed by the gaping shirt. Then she glanced at the door, unable to believe Ben had come in here and started to strip his clothes off. Was this another one of her nonsensical dreams? It had to be.

She heard the rustle of his shirt dropping to the floor, and looked back with a start. He was bare to the waist. He seemed much larger without the shirt on, his shoulders broad, his arms and chest heavily muscled. The expanse of abdomen revealed by low-riding jeans was etched with washboard muscles, sun-bronzed except for the half-inch of paler skin that gleamed just above the top of his Levi's.

Addie pointed at his discarded shirt with a finger that trembled slightly. ''I told you to get out . . . I . . . Put that back on!''

Ben smiled slowly, walked over to her bed, and sat down. And held her eyes while he yanked at a boot. That calm, anticipatory stare was too much to bear. She found her tongue and began to babble, certain that any minute someone in the house was going to find out what was going on in her room.

''Ben . . . Ben, stop that and listen to me. I'm sorry for the things I did tonight that might have made you think I'm interested in doing this with you, because I'm not, I'm not ready to do this with anyone, especially not you, and if Daddy knew you were in here right now, he'd kill you, either that or tomorrow morning you'd find yourself on the wrong end of shotgun until you promised to m-m . . .'' Her voice stuck on the last word.

''Marry you?'' Ben finished for her helpfully. He pushed his boots aside with one bare foot and stood up. There was an enigmatic softness in his voice. ''Interesting idea, isn't it?''

''Not very,'' she quavered, knowing she had no control over the situation, searching for some retreat. ''Although I'm certain you like the idea of marrying someone with my money. And you know my father would give you everything he has if we got married, including the ranch, with no strings attached. Oh, I'll bet the prospect of being my husband holds no end of appeal for you.''

As Ben saw her distress, the hint of ruthless amusement faded. ''To hell with your father's money and the ranch. I don't need to be given anything. I have my own resources, including enough money to do whatever the hell I want.''

"H-how can that be?"

"Mavericking is a highly profitable venture, if done well. And I had a particular talent for it. So I don't need your money. But you're damn right—the idea of being your husband appeals to me. And in the next few hours I'm going to show you why."

She was shaken by a chill and then a flash of heat as she watched him unfasten the top button of his Levi's.

"Come here," he said, his stare direct and compelling.

Before she could stop herself, her eyes flickered down to the shadowy opening of his unfastened jeans, where the lean stretch of his abdomen continued downward into a furring of dark hair. In the course of her work at the hospital she had seen men unclothed before, but never anyone so uninhibited about it. People were always embarrassed without the protection of their clothes. Ben seemed to be entirely comfortable without them.

Her instinct to bolt was overpowering. Leave. All she had to do was leave the room. He certainly wouldn't chase her through the house while he was half-naked. She would head for the kitchen and stay there until he'd had enough time to cool down. She'd sit there all night if she had to.

Cautiously Addie took a step backward, trying to gauge the distance to the door, her nerves screaming for action. She started to move, and in the next second found herself hauled back against his body. She went still, her chest heaving, aware of his sinewy midriff against her back.

"I told you once before not to be afraid." Ben said, lowering his mouth to her ear. She stiffened as she felt his hand slide inside her robe and claim her breast, seeking to find its shape through the folds of her nightgown.

"Let me go," she whispered.

He rested his thumb in the valley between her breasts and rubbed gently before allowing his hand to wander down to her stomach and the pliant warmth between her thighs. The veil of her nightgown did nothing to disguise her response.

Ben nuzzled into the crook of her neck and inhaled the tantalizing fragrance of her skin. "I won't hurt you," he muttered. "You know that. The things we did before gave you pleasure, didn't they? It won't be any different now."

She gulped and shook her head, trying to suppress the anticipation that rushed out from the very core of her. There was no sound in the room but her labored gasps. Slowly his fingers moved further between her legs, and she groaned his name in protest, leaning her head back against his shoulder.

"It's not fair to take advantage of me this way."

"I'll take advantage of everything I can to get you. What's wrong with that?"

"Everything. You know I don't want to feel this way about you."

"That doesn't matter. I won't go away, and neither will your feelings. And I won't stop forcing you to face them until you accept the truth about you and me."

The truth, she thought wildly. *What is the truth?* Was she in the arms of a murderer? If he was capable of that, then everything he had said to her was a lie. She couldn't accept that. In her heart she had to believe in him, or never trust in anything again, especially her own instincts. The conflict, the doubt, tore at her with icy claws.

"Please," she wheezed, prying at his hands, and she stumbled away as he let her go. Spinning around, she looked at him in panic, his face branded permanently in her memory. Image after image blazed through her mind: Ben, kneeling by her after she'd

been thrown from her horse . . . risking his life for a
wounded man . . . laughing at her temper . . . fighting
Jeff for her . . . comforting Watts when he cried . . .
helping a drunken Russell to bed . . . holding her with
passion.

Ben—comforter, protector . . . lover.

He was no murderer.

*He didn't do it. He isn't capable of cold-blooded
murder.* That was the only truth she found inside. She
couldn't doubt it, no matter what price she might have
to pay for her faith in him. There was nothing else to
choose. With the decision made, Addie knew an overwhelming relief.

"What do you want?" she asked unsteadily.

Ben looked at her with a consuming gaze. "To be
part of you . . . part of your life. But I'll be damned
if I can stand not having your trust. I'm worthy of it."

"I know."

"Then I deserve the chance to prove it. Trust me.
Give me tonight. I swear you won't be sorry." As he
waited for an answer and she remained silent, he
wound her hair around his hand and pulled her head
back, forcing her to look at him. "Dammit, Addie,
I'm in love with you. And I'm through with games.
Do you understand? *I love you.*"

An ache of sweetness swept over her. She couldn't
speak. Her eyes filled with tears, and her arms crept
around his neck. Ben's impatience subsided as he felt
her quiver.

"Give me tonight," he said, knowing he had won,
and she pulled his head down to hers. He crushed her
against his body. The heat of his skin seared through
her nightgown, raising goose bumps of pleasure, causing the peaks of her breasts to tighten.

His mouth was savage, his arms bruising in their
strength. They were so close their heartbeats mingled,
and though Addie's pulse was pounding madly, Ben's

was like violent thunder. Their kisses lengthened, deepened, lingered.

His body was bronze and silver in the faltering light from the window. Addie splayed her hands over his back, explored down to the loosened waist of his Levi's, then stopped in sudden shyness. Ben murmured something indistinguishable and spread the edges of her robe, easing it down her arms. It dropped to the floor with a soft rustle.

She stood motionless, her fingers resting at his waist as he undid the tiny button at the top of her high-necked gown, then the next, following the trail of fastenings down to a spot just beneath her breasts. His lips brushed against her cheek, catching the last glimmer of a forgotten tear.

Unhurriedly he peeled the nightgown off her shoulders and let it drop in a circle around her feet. Their fingers tangled together as he took her hands and led them to his shoulders. She left them there and let him look at her, shivering slightly as his eyes traveled over her slender body. Impossible to look at his face, for fear of what she might see written there. She wanted to be everything for him. She wanted to be perfect for him. His gaze moved down her, returned slowly to her face, and his eyes darkened with passion.

"I knew you'd be beautiful," he whispered. "I knew I'd want you. But nothing close to this." He picked her up and carried her to the bed, his feet making no sound on the floor. Helplessly she clung to him, her feet dangling as his arm hooked under her knees. The whole world seemed to tilt as he settled her on the bed. He stripped off his jeans and bent over her. Biting her lower lip to hold in a moan, she closed her eyes as his mouth descended to her breasts.

Restlessly she twisted underneath him, craving the weight of his body on hers, and he slid his hand down to her stomach, pressing her against the mattress.

"Slow," he murmured, his fingers skimming the curve of her hip. "Slow and patient . . . Addie . . . love . . ."

"I want to be yours—"

"You are."

"I want you inside me."

"Not yet." His tongue feathered along the indentation of her midriff, causing her to quiver. "Not yet . . . we have time."

She stroked his hair, loving the feel of him, the freedom of touching him. In this moment he belonged to her . . . he was hers. Slowly her thoughts were drowned out by his gentle hands and his whispering. Random whispers, praising her, encouraging her to respond, heightening her pleasure.

"Your hips fit my hands . . . you're so smooth here . . . and here. Move closer . . . let me touch . . . don't be shy with me. I love the smell of your skin . . . like flowers . . . what do you want? . . . take my hand and show me . . . yes, like that . . ."

He was intent on knowing her better than she did herself. All secrets were stripped away from her in the darkness, everything that was private and intimate revealed. She refused him nothing, answering silent questions she had never dreamed he would want to ask. The need to know him in the same way, to understand his body, was a scourging fire.

Ben caught his breath as her hands moved down to his hips. Her fingertips grazed the edge of the coarse hair that feathered low across his abdomen. She hesitated, her fingers hovering near the pulsing, aroused length of him, and he knew she was uncertain. He ached for the feel of her hands on him, small, feminine hands that needed to be taught how to touch a man.

"Addie . . ." His hand slid to the back of hers, and she pulled away as if touched by fire. "No, no . . .

let me show you,'' he said, and it was difficult to keep his voice gentle when his body was shaking with eagerness. ''Make me ready for you,'' he urged, taking her hand in a stronger grip and shaping her palm to his aroused flesh, showing her how to pleasure him. She blushed in the darkness and followed the intimate lesson awkwardly, spurred on by the tremor of his fingers, the racing of his heart. Up and down her hand traveled, clasping loosely, pausing to test the silky texture of his skin. His breath rushed in her hair as she became bolder, and he let go of her, allowing her to touch him without guidance. She dared to whisper the same questions that he'd asked her, about what felt good, what he liked, and she was rewarded by his soft laugh.

''You're an angel,'' Ben murmured, kissing her possessively, lifting her hands up to his face and pressing her palms against his cheeks. ''. . . angel . . .'' His fingers searched through the damp tangle of hair between her legs as he continued to kiss her. Slowly, slowly, she felt the intrusion of his finger into her body, and she started, her thighs tensing.

''Don't tighten,'' he said huskily. ''Relax. Let me inside, darlin'.'' And she tried to release the inner clenching as she felt his finger slip even deeper. His touch was agile and sensitive, sliding and stroking until she arched up to him and froze with a faint sound, gripped in a surge of pleasure. The heel of his hand ground gently against the softness between her thighs, drawing out her ecstasy as long as possible.

Exhausted, Addie lay trembling in his arms, not knowing if minutes or hours passed before she lifted her lashes. He rose to his elbows above her, staring down at her face with burning green eyes. Languidly, greedily, she wrapped her arms around his neck and urged him closer, and he spread her legs with his knees, pressing into her.

The long, invasive thrust caused her to flinch in pain, but she surrendered to it instead of fighting, striving to accept the fullness of him inside her. Ben stroked the hair away from her forehead, kissed the salt-scented dampness of her skin. His lungs expanded with corrugated breaths as the depths of her body held him in a velvet grip. He moved in a careful, steady rhythm. Before he could teach her more, she lifted her hips in response.

Her eyes gleamed smokily as they searched his. "What does it feel like to you?"

His dark hair fell over his forehead as he looked down at her, momentarily silent as he tried to find the words. Then he swallowed hard and shook his head. "I can't describe it," he said huskily. "What about you?"

"I feel like you're part of me," she whispered. "We're one person. And I don't want to be separate from you again."

Suddenly fierce, he pulled her hips up with his hands and drove into her. Driven by the rhythm he had set, they sought a deeper joining, loved, enchanted, until the world was shredded around them. He found her mouth with his and buried his final groan in her throat, finding the same burst of fulfillment that had just contracted her flesh around his. And then they lay together in exhaustion, suffused with wonder.

Addie was the first to move. Sleepily she threw her arm across his shoulders and pulled herself on top of him until she was lying across his chest. With her bright eyes and ruffled hair, she looked so much like a curious kitten that Ben's mouth twitched in amusement. He trailed his fingers down the curve of her back.

"Ben?"

"What?"

"Do you still visit that woman in Blue Ridge?"

He smiled ruefully and framed her face in his hands. "God knows why I should be surprised by anything you ask."

"Well?"

"I haven't seen her in a long time. I haven't been with anyone since I first realized I wanted you." Absently he played with her hair, winding it through his fingers, brushing the ends across his face, enjoying the softness of it. "You've absorbed all my interest and desire for weeks. There wasn't enough left for anyone else."

Addie hated the thought of his being with another woman. In spite of his reassurance, she couldn't help feeling jealous. She didn't want him to have memories of other women and the pleasures they had given him. Did he think of her in a different way than he thought of them? Had making love with her been the same? Her thoughts wandered back to the woman in Blue Ridge.

"Did you care about her?"

"I didn't know her enough to care about her."

"But you and she—"

"We enjoyed each other's company in bed. But there's more to knowing a person than being familiar with her body."

She'd never pondered deeply what it must be like to make love with someone you didn't care for. "Did you even like her?"

"I guess you could say we were friends. But neither of us wanted anything more than that. I didn't want to know what was in her heart, and she felt the same about me." He was silent then, allowing her to think over what he'd said, and he resisted the urge to pull her closer.

"How cold." Her expression was a cross between distaste and confusion.

"In some ways it was."

"In what ways?" she asked, increasingly nettled.

"After the time in bed was spent, there was always silence between us. There was nothing to talk about, nothing to share. The satisfaction from our encounters was shallow. It didn't linger."

"Shallow or not, she obviously had something that made you come back for more. You went to her more than one time, didn't you?"

Ben paused and considered what lay at the heart of Addie's questioning. Perhaps it was uncertainty that had flared up in the form of a waspish temper. Was she afraid he would make comparisons between her and the women he'd had before her?

"Why aren't you saying anything?" Addie demanded peevishly. "Too busy counting?"

For a brief moment Ben wavered between sympathy and a strange kind of resentment. He was no knight in shining armor, nor could he ever be. He heard the disillusionment in her voice as she began to realize it. But she had to accept him for all that he was, including the imperfections.

"I've never pretended to have led a perfect life, Addie. I'm a man with all the needs any other man has. I've done my share of living, and that includes having been with a certain number of women."

"How many? Am I the third or fourth? The twentieth? The fiftieth?"

"I don't carve notches on my belt. I've never taken a woman for the sake of adding to the number that have passed beneath me. Only when I needed to be with someone. Sometimes I knew the women, sometimes I didn't. It never made a difference. But you're the only one I've ever been in love with."

She was silent for a long time, and he couldn't begin to guess at her thoughts. Finally she spoke in a small voice, all trace of combativeness gone.

"Do you ever think about any of them?"

"No. The truth is, I don't remember much about the time I spent with them."

She frowned as she traced the line of his collarbone. "If you never saw me again after tonight, how much of this would you remember?"

"Every detail," he said gravely. "Every second. Everything you said, every touch and sound, until my dying day."

Addie flushed and laid her cheek against his chest. "Ben, do you mind that I don't have experience? I didn't know what you wanted from—"

He rolled her onto her back and silenced her with a long kiss. When he lifted his head, his voice was ragged at the edges. "What happened between us a few minutes ago makes everything I've felt before pale in comparison." He paused, entranced by the sheepish smile that had begun to curve her lips. "As a mere novice, you nearly did me in. I don't know how I'll survive when you have a little more experience."

"You'll just have to grin and bear it," she said, and he chuckled as he lowered his mouth to hers again.

The hours raced by, slipping away until Addie began to dread the moment when Ben would leave her. All they had were precious minutes, mere parings and shavings of time, when they craved so much more. They talked drowsily and drifted in and out of slumber, and always when Addie awoke, she rediscovered the bliss of being nestled against his body, his arms securely around her. There were moments in which she felt as if he could see through to her soul. Whether they were locked together in frantic desire or peaceful exhaustion, the sense of oneness remained the same.

"I'll have to go soon," he said as early morning ripened, and she stirred in protest, wrapping her arms around him.

"Don't go. I won't let you."

"I could stay until we're discovered by the family,"

Ben mused, kissing the top of her head. "But in the name of fairness, we'll have to find some other way to break it to them."

If he had intended to jolt her awake, he had chosen his words well. The mention of the family was the one thing that could have done it. She stared at him wide-eyed. "Oh, Ben, how are we . . . what are we—"

"Well, we know one thing for sure. Russ won't mind."

"Well, of course he won't! But Mama will die."

"The effect on her won't be quite that drastic."

"Oh, yes it will. It's going to be a terrible shock for her. You don't know her like I do. She talked to me about what she wanted for me and Caro, and about her marriage to Daddy, and she was so bitter about everything, you just wouldn't believe . . . Ben, if we want her on our side, we've got to ease her into it or she'll just throw a fit and *never* approve, and I can't tell you how much it means to me to have her happy—"

"Shhh. I understand that."

"Good. I'm glad—"

"Wait. I said understand, not agree."

"What don't you agree with?"

"I want to know what you mean by easing her into it."

"I think we should get her used to the idea first instead of forcing it down her throat."

"If she were as frail as you seem to believe, she'd never have survived thirty years of marriage to Russ. And as I told you before, I'm through with games."

"Ben, please. It'll be so much easier on me this way. I'm already dreading the arguments and the tears. And she's not going to fuss at you, only me." She hesitated before adding, *"I* need the time as much as she does. I need to get used to the idea of marrying you. A few weeks of courting wouldn't hurt either of us.''

He scowled impatiently.

"Please," she said softly.

"If that's what you want, I'll give you time. But I'm going to set two conditions on your little plan. First of all, I'll give you two weeks . . . that's as long as my patience will hold out. Do whatever you can to prepare your mother and settle everything in your own mind, but in a fortnight we're breaking the news so wedding plans can be made.''

"And the other condition?"

He drew a finger from the base of her throat to the curve of her breast. "The days are yours. If you want to spend them playing courting charades, so be it. But the nights are mine.''

Her eyes twinkled with mischief. "Ben, we're not even engaged yet, and you think I'm going to let you—''

"We damn well are engaged. And I expect all the rights any other engaged man has.''

"Haven't you ever heard of waiting until the wedding night?"

His hand moved possessively over her body. "Tell me you won't deny me your bed until then, Addie. Or I'll have to make you say it.''

The delight of his touch almost caused her to forget what she'd intended to say. But she couldn't let him hand out orders so casually, not if this was to be a partnership.

"Of course I wouldn't deny you," she said, putting her hand over his and arresting its movement. "But I have a condition for you.''

His brows lifted in a sardonic quirk. "Oh?"

"I don't want you to tell Daddy about our engagement.''

"Why not?" he demanded, sounding annoyed.

"Because he can't keep a secret. Oh, I know what you're going to say—when business is involved, he can. But this isn't business, and when a secret has to do with anyone's personal life, it goes in his ear one minute and straight out his mouth the next. And he's not the most tactful man in the world as you well know—"

"All right, all right. I won't tell him. But if I find out you've gone behind my back and told someone— Caroline, for example . . ." He paused as Addie began to giggle softly at his grumbling. "Would you care to explain why you're so amused, ma'am?"

"A few weeks ago I'd never have dreamed we'd be having an argument over something like this. But I have to believe in all of this, because it's happening. What have you done to me, Ben?"

"I've fallen in love with you," he replied. There was nothing uncertain about his love, nothing held back or hidden.

Tremulously she smiled and placed a kiss on his lips. "Being this happy makes me worried."

He leaned over her, his expression utterly serious. "There's nothing to worry about."

She looked past him to the closed door. "People, events, the future . . . what if all it comes between us? What if we're separated by something we can't control?" Nameless threats waited beyond the four walls, threats that would test their newly forged bond. Her hand crept over his chest until she could feel the vital pulse of his heartbeat. Ben covered her hand and pressed it more firmly against his heart.

"Believe in me," he said huskily. "Believe in my strength. I won't let anything separate us. Not even you could drive me away now. No one in the world could fill the place in me that you do. If I'd never met you I'd spend a lifetime waiting for you to appear. Do you believe that?"

She thought of an old man, ragged and alone, standing in the rain. "Yes," she whispered, and reached for him, needing to remove all distance between them. She struggled to free the last inner stronghold. The words *I love you* were caught in her throat, begging to be released. She wanted to tell him, wanted to show him that she, too, loved him with the same sureness he had displayed. And yet that last bit of her heart could not be given. He didn't seem to notice her failure, but Addie was all too aware, and she tried to make up for it with the generous response of her body.

His mouth crushed hers in a kiss that sent excitement crashing through her, and all rational thought dissolved in a deluge of ecstasy. He took her with devouring passion, allowing no respite, no relief, thrusting into her as if his hunger would never be sated. His mouth played ceaselessly on hers, smothering her gasps into barely audible sounds. She relinquished herself to his possession, finally understanding how incomplete she was without him. Deliberately he urged her into a new plane of sensation, where self-consciousness was stripped away and she was left undisguised from him. With an incoherent murmur she twined her arms around him and matched his fire with her own.

Addie stirred only a little when he left her, too exhausted to take notice of the last kiss, the last caress, before she was alone again. It seemed like only a few minutes had passed before she heard voices downstairs. Daybreak arrived and light splashed through the windows of her room. She buried her head underneath a pillow, groping for a few minutes of sleep, and her body went limp.

She awoke with a strange sense of dread, noticing the light in the room had changed, darker now, tinged instead with smoky blue. Lazily she rolled back, blinking the drowsiness away, stifling a yawn. The sounds of women's voices downstairs had disappeared, as well as the sounds of men working and dogs barking outside. Everything was still. And then she heard the muted chug-chug of an automobile, and tires skimming a paved street.

Addie scrambled out from under the sheets and sat on the edge of the bed, her eyes wide. The bedroom was blue and white. There was an electric lamp in the corner. She stared at the poster on the wall, at Rudolph Valentino's slicked-black hair and smoldering eyes. She felt as if she would suffocate.

"No. No, don't let this be happening to me." Standing up unsteadily, Addie went to the door and tried to turn the knob. It was locked. "Let me out," she said, although there was no one to hear her, and she pulled harder at the doorknob. "Let me out!" Her voice was shrill with panic. *"Ben, where are you? Ben! Ben—"*

She jerked awake with a muffled sound, her heart pounding high in her throat. Trembling, she looked around at the pink-and-white bedroom and stumbled out of bed, going to the middle of the floor and turning around. It was all here. Her shoulders and spine relaxed. She went to the mirror and looked at her own chalk-white face, at the naked fear that still lingered there. It had only been a dream.

"I belong here," she said out loud, her voice shaking. "I belong here and I won't go back. I *won't.*" The brown eyes that stared back at her were full of desperation and doubt.

"Ahh . . . here comes the sleepyhead," Caroline said affectionately as soon as Addie came downstairs. Addie smiled wanly, sitting in her chair at the table. May poured her coffee and fussed over her, and a sense of comfort and ease began to steal over her.

"You did sleep late this mornin'," May said with a smile. "Did you have a good night?"

"I . . . I . . . What do you mean?" Addie asked nervously.

"Well, we've spent the last few days at the Fanins'. It certainly is nice to be back in your own bed, isn't it?"

"It's wonderful to be back in mine," Caroline remarked, putting a hand to her back. "Those beds at the Fanins' were so hard. These days I can hardly find a comfortable position to sleep in."

Addie regarded her sympathetically. "Poor Caro. But I almost envy you, looking forward to having a baby to take care of and love."

"They're somethin' to envy when they belong to someone else," came the wry response. "It's only when you have one of your own that you understand what trouble they are. And this one is givin' me more trouble than Leah did. Or maybe it's just that I'm older."

"Thirty isn't old at all."

"Tell that to Peter." Caroline smiled faintly. "I think he's gettin' ready to put me out to pasture."

"What do you mean?"

Caroline's smile disappeared. "Oh, nothin'. Just makin' noise."

"I don't understand—"

"You'll understand many things when you get married," May interrupted gently. "Includin' some of the little discomforts and worries a woman has to face."

"But it would be wonderful with the right person," Addie said dreamily, resisting the temptation of looking to see May's reaction as she spoke. "I can't wait to be married."

"And just who is it you're plannin' on marryin'?"

"Oh . . . no one right now." Addie interjected just the right amount of confusion in her voice. The subject was dropped, but May's eyes remained on her, watching her warily all morning.

8

RUSSELL LIKED TO GRUMBLE LOUDLY ON THE EVE-
nings when he worked in his office. The sounds of his
counting and frustrated exclamations penetrated the
walls and wafted down the hallway, clearly audible in
the parlor where May, Caroline, and Addie did needlework. May and Caroline mended clothes while Addie embroidered the border of a pillowcase.

They had been sewing a long time, long enough for
Addie to have grown sore from sitting. She shifted in
her chair and contemplated the scene around her. Cade
had finished his homework and gone upstairs for the
night, while the rest of the household was already
sound asleep. It was quiet in the parlor, too quiet for
Addie's peace of mind. She bent her attention to the
half-formed flower on the pillowcase in her lap, but
her thoughts wandered restlessly. May and Caro's
blond heads were bent over their work. It amazed Addie, how remarkably alike they were in their outward
serenity.

She wondered how they could look so tranquil, when
they really weren't any more peaceful than she was.
Inside they were restless too. Addie had seen and heard
May's bitterness as she had talked about the life she
could have chosen so long ago, a life very different
from this one. And Caroline was more complex than
any outsider would guess. Addie shook her head

slightly, staring at May and Caro. Why were they so much better at hiding their real feelings than she was?

At least I dare to say what I really think most of the time. But they almost never do. None of the women around here do. Who had made up the rule that women were never supposed to get angry, that they were always supposed to be tolerant and calm and forbearing? Men had decided that. Men liked their women to be just short of saintly, while they themselves never bothered to control their tempers or choose their words carefully. They could stomp all over other people and be as rude and coarse as they wanted, and then the women had to smooth things over afterward and make everything right again. May and Caroline were perfect examples of nineteenth-century womanhood. Caretakers, peacemakers.

I won't be like them, Addie thought moodily. *I couldn't even if I wanted to. It would mean playing a part all the time. And I'm not that good an actress.*

Caroline, however, played the part to perfection. Addie moved her attention exclusively to her sister. How different Caro's inward and outward selves were. She looked as if she'd never done or said anything improper in her life. Blond, serene, passionless . . . it seemed Caro had inherited little of her father's lusty nature. She appeared to be perfectly content to have a husband who didn't share her bed. A few weeks ago Peter and Caro had moved into separate bedrooms, using Caro's pregnancy as an excuse. At this very moment Peter was sleeping upstairs, with no expectation of seeing his wife until tomorrow morning at the breakfast table.

Addie had been astounded by the Warner family's lack of surprise at the situation. They had all taken it for granted that Caroline had no need to be intimate with a man unless it was for the purpose of conceiving children. But Addie knew about Caro's affair with Raif

Colton. Caroline was a woman of flesh and blood, not marble, and she had a need to give and receive love.

Addie felt sorry for Caroline. Was that all her sister intended to have for the rest of her life, a lifeless marriage and a few memories of passion? Addie had the feeling that inside Caro there still burned a love for the hot-tempered cowboy who had been her lover, the father of her firstborn, a man who'd been killed as violently as he had lived. As she sat there sewing placidly, did Caro ever think about him and what they'd shared? Maybe she couldn't let herself.

I could never make the kind of mistake she did, Addie thought in wonder. *I could never give Ben up for someone else, no matter how right or wrong it seemed. I guess I don't have the strength.*

Addie had never been so conscious of the differences between herself and the other two women as she was at this moment. Long ago they had accepted the role that women were supposed to assume. Sacrifice, submit, put your own needs behind everyone else's. Tolerate the things that bring you pain, bend like a reed in the wind. That took a different kind of strength from what Addie had. She had been raised to respect her own needs just as men respected theirs. She wouldn't last long as a martyr. She didn't have the quiet, steely patience it took to suffer uncomplaining day after day.

The days of her childhood were gone, but they were still a part of her. Living with Leah during those years after the war, she had learned to work and scratch for pennies, had discovered she could carry the weight of many burdens on her shoulders, just as long as she had the freedom to make her own decisions. That freedom of making choices must never be taken away.

And I'll never go through life without feeling and belonging, never again. I won't spend my days hoping they'll go by quickly, feeling numb about everything.

She jumped slightly as she felt the sting of her own needle. "Ouch!"

"Stuck yourself?" May inquired.

"Yes, Mama. I just can't concentrate on this."

"Why don't you find a book to read?"

Addie didn't feel like reading, but she nodded half-heartedly, setting her work aside. She grimaced as she saw she'd left a little spot of blood on the cloth, one that would have to be camouflaged with more embroidery. Then she heard the light, seductive plucking of guitar strings drifting in from outside, and her pulse quickened. Ben was playing his guitar on the steps of the small two-room ranch building he lived in, as was his habit when dinner was finished early. The melody was soft and coaxing.

"What a pretty song," Caroline commented, and Addie stood up hastily. It was impossible to resist the lure of that music.

"I'm going for a walk," she muttered, and left the room. They all knew where she was headed.

May called out after her, her voice low and compressed, "Don't be long, you hear me?"

Then Caro's voice, softer, cajoling, as she spoke to May. "Mama, you know whatever you say against him will only make her more determined. It might be wiser to say nothing."

"Good old Caro," Addie whispered, grinning to herself. Why had so many of the friends she had once known complained about their older sisters?

She went outside and skipped down the steps like a child, suddenly lighthearted. Her heart seemed to expand with gladness as she saw Ben. The moonlight cast silvery-blue highlights in his dark hair and illuminated the long stretch of his legs as he sat in the doorway of the little building. One of his feet was propped on a step, the other resting on the ground, while the guitar was saddled on his bent knee.

He smiled as he saw her and continued picking out a melody, his eyes never leaving her slender form. Addie hooked her fingers into a handful of material on either side of her skirt and swished it with each step she took, feigning nonchalance.

Their gazes met as she came nearer, exchanging wordless promises.

"Do they know you're out here?" Ben asked, nodding toward the house.

"I told Mama and Caro I was taking a walk."

"That's all? You didn't mention me?"

"They knew I was coming out here to see you."

Ben grinned. "Then it's a little coy to say you're just taking a walk, isn't it?"

She pretended to pout, turning to go back where she'd come from, pausing to throw him a glance over her shoulder. "If you don't want my company, just say so."

"I'd never say that, darlin'." He moved over a few inches and indicated the space next to him with the neck of the guitar. "Have a seat."

"It's too narrow. I wouldn't be able to fit in there."

His smile was devilish. "Give it a try."

Addie managed to squeeze next to him and fill the remaining space in the narrow doorway. "Oh, I can't even breathe—"

"I'm not complaining." He leaned over and slanted his mouth over hers. Her tongue met his, warmth against warmth, offering and tasting, until Ben's blood stirred with increasing vigor. He made a deeply appreciative sound before pulling his mouth away, mindful of the need to keep up appearances. Clumsily he reset his fingers on the strings and regarded the guitar as if he'd never seen it before.

"Did I used to know how to play one of these things?"

She chuckled and then nuzzled deeper into his neck,

loving the scent of his skin. "Yes. Play something beautiful for me, Ben."

He bent his head to the guitar and obliged. The haunting melody she had heard so many nights while alone in her bed seemed to curl around them. She pressed her cheek against his shoulder, her eyes half-closing with bliss. "That sounds so sad."

"Does it?" He continued playing, looking down at her thoughtfully. "It reminds me of you a little."

"I'm not sad."

"But not quite happy."

His perception was unnerving, and Addie couldn't deny it. She would be happy if she weren't afraid for Russell, and if there weren't such animosity between Sunrise and the Double Bar, and if her relationship with Ben wouldn't cause May such distress, and if her worries about her own past could be resolved . . . well, there was a list of such things to be taken care of.

"No, I'm not completely happy," she admitted. "Are you?"

"Sometimes."

She made a disgruntled face. "It's easier for men to be happy than women."

Ben laughed outright. "I've never heard that before. What makes you think it's easier for us?"

"You can do anything you want to do. And your needs are so simple. A good meal, an occasional night of drinking with the boys, a woman to share your bed, and you're in ecstasy."

"Hold on," he said, his eyes gleaming with wicked amusement as he set the guitar down and turned to face her, his hands coming to rest at her hips. They were surrounded by night music, the sound of the crickets and the rustling of the breeze through the hay. "There are a few points you've neglected."

"Oh? What do you need beyond the things I just mentioned?"

"A family, for one thing."

"Big or small?"

"Big, of course."

"Of course," she echoed wryly. "You wouldn't say that if you were the woman who had to bear the children."

"Probably not," he conceded, and smiled. "But speaking as a man, I like the idea of at least half a dozen."

It was difficult to picture him as a father. He was too well suited to the role of amorous bachelor. "Somehow I can't see you tolerating a house swarming with children, a baby spitting up on your shirt and another tugging at your pants leg."

"I happen to like children."

"Even messy ones?"

"Didn't know there was another kind."

"How do you know you like them?" she demanded.

"I have a niece and nephew, and they—"

"That's only two," she said triumphantly. "Two's a lot different than six."

"What are you getting at?"

"I'd just like to point out that you have no idea how much time, attention and worry half a dozen children would take."

"So you don't plan on having six?"

"Not a chance! Two or three's enough."

"Fine with me. As long as one of them's a boy."

"Chauvinist," she grumbled. "You get three chances, and if they're all girls, that's too bad. Having too many children makes a woman old before her time. And besides, I'd be so busy with six I'd never have time for *you*, and I'd always be too tired to make love, and—"

"You have a point," he said hastily. "Alright, we'll make it three."

"Ben, now that we're talking about our future, there's something I've been wondering about—"

"Later," he said, his breath ruffling the fragile tendrils of hair at the nape of her neck. She jumped as she felt the gentle nip of his teeth.

"But it's important. It's about our marriage, and—"

"Addie, I'm not going to sit here and go through a list." His hands wandered upward, passing her cinched-in waist and hovering underneath her breasts. "Not now. This is the first time I've been alone with you since last night."

A slight ache settled in her breasts, a sensation that demanded the soothing touch of his hands. "I missed you today," he murmured.

She wriggled back and pushed at him. "It's important to talk about this. There are things we should understand about each other. That's what courting is all about."

Ben sighed, letting go of her and bracing his arms on his bent knees. He sent her a sideways glance filled with sarcasm. "What is it you don't understand that can't wait to be explained later?"

"It's what you don't understand about *me.*"

Suddenly his green eyes were alert. "Go on."

"There are things that I need . . . this can't be the usual kind of marriage. I'm different from . . . other women around here."

"I won't argue with that."

"I'm worried about how a marriage between two people like us will work. We're both strong-willed, and we each have our own ideas about things."

"I agree. We'll have to make a lot of compromises."

"But there are some things I won't—can't—compromise on." She looked up and flushed as she met his eyes. "I'm sorry I brought this up. I don't really know what I meant to say—"

"I think you do."

"Maybe I shouldn't . . . it's too soon—"

"What are you planning to ask for? A trip around the world? The biggest ranch in Texas? Shares in the Northern Pacific?"

Addie couldn't help chuckling. "Oh, stop it."

He took hold of her wrists and pulled them around his neck until her hands locked in back. "Tell me," he said, kissing her forehead. "I'm running out of guesses."

"I want you to listen to me in twenty years the same way you do now. As if my opinions matter to you."

"They do. They always will. Anything else?" His lips traveled to her temple, lingering on the pulse he found there.

"Yes. I don't want to turn into a belonging of yours, an attachment like an extra arm or leg, someone who's expected to agree with everything you say. I won't be silent during the dinner conversations at our table." Now that she had started to open up to him, it was much easier to continue. "I need to be respected but not sheltered. I want your honesty, always, about everything, and to be given a chance to show I can do more for you than the cooking, the washing, and the sewing. All of that can be done by any woman. I want to have a place in your life no one else can take, and I don't mean a pedestal."

"I wouldn't try to put you up on one."

"You wouldn't? You wouldn't want me to change after we're married, and do everything you say, and never argue with you?"

"Hell, no. Why would I change the things that attract me to you the most?" He stroked the side of her waist and smiled lazily. "Let other men's wives play mindless fools if it pleases them. I'd rather have a woman who has some common sense. And why should I want you to agree with me all the time? It would bore the hell out of me to be with someone who parroted everything I said. Put your mind at ease, darlin'. I'm not marrying you in order to change you."

She looked at him with amazement. How different he was from the other men she had known. Bernie and his friends had been wild and reckless, the kind you shook your head over in private and wondered if they respected anyone or anything, even themselves. Most of the war veterans she had cared for had been bitter and strangely lost, unable to understand themselves or the world around them. And the men around here were a curious mixture of innocence and chauvinism. Grown-up boys, all of them.

But Ben was not a boy. He was a man at ease with himself, assured of his place in the world, strong and yet sensitive to others' needs. He wasn't innocent by any means, but he wasn't cynical either, possessing a sly sense of humor and a healthy amount of shrewdness. Addie put her hand on his arm, wishing she could tell him how much she appreciated his openmindedness with her. "Most men back in . . . I mean nowadays . . . wouldn't want their marriage to be the kind of partnership that I'm suggesting—"

"I won't hand out orders for you to follow. But on the other hand, don't get uppity about it. I'll be damned if anyone but me wears the pants in the family. Understand?"

Addie smiled and bit playfully at his shoulder through his shirt. She did understand. He would be manageable. "You always like to have your own way," she accused.

He bent his head to hers and growled near her ear. "You're getting to know my faults, Miss Adeline."

"I'm trying," she said, turning her mouth to his and offering him a feather-soft kiss. He took it without hesitation, ending it with a smack. "Where on earth did you get such an attitude about women?" she asked when their lips parted. "I'm surprised at how liberal you are. It's because of someone in your past, isn't it. Did you mother teach you to be so open-minded, or was it some other woman?"

He hesitated, his gaze almost predatory as he looked for something in her face. Whatever it was, he didn't seem to find it. "Maybe I'll tell you someday." The combination of his careless tone and piercing eyes made her uneasy.

"You could tell me now if you wanted. You can trust me with anything. Everything."

"Just like you trust me, hmmn?"

Addie's smile faded as she heard the light, jeering lash in his voice. "What do you mean? I do trust you."

He didn't answer for a second. Then to her relief, he changed with bewildering swiftness, picking up the guitar and strumming in an exaggerated cowboy style that made her laugh. The twangy tune reminded Addie of the western pictures she had seen at the movie house, pictures that had featured slickly handsome cowboys in ten-gallon hats.

"What are you playing? It sounds familiar."

"Something we sing on the trail."

The tune was "My Bonnie Lies Over the Ocean." As she recognized it, she fixed him with an accusatory look. "I know that, and it isn't a cowboy song at all."

"Yes it is."

"It's a song for sailors. I even know the words," she said, and demonstrated a line or two in a tuneless voice that made him wince: " '... bring back, bring back my Bonnie to me, to me—' "

"That's the part when we sing 'Roll on little doggies, roll on.' "

"Couldn't you have bothered to make up your own song instead of stealing one?"

"It wasn't stolen, just improved. Texas-style." He was so unrepentant that Addie giggled.

"You're shameless. And you need reforming." She smoothed her palm over his shoulder and glanced in the direction of the main house. "But I guess it'll have to wait. I have to leave, slicker."

The mischief left his eyes, and he put the guitar aside. His hand came to rest at her waist, staying her attempt to get up. She almost jumped at the unexpected tightness of his grip. "Why did you call me that?"

"Slicker? Why, it's just an expression." It had been a casual endearment she'd used for Bernie and some of the veterans at the hospital. "I've said it to you before and you never—"

"Where the hell did you get it from?" There were things about her, odd expressions included, that struck him wrong. He didn't like the inner awareness that she guarded part of herself from him, even now when she was in his arms. Sometimes he could sense the edge of fear in her, but it was impossible to know who or what she was afraid of. Was it him?

"I h-heard it in Virginia," she stuttered, damning herself for being a clumsy liar. "I won't call you that anymore if you don't like it."

"I don't."

She looked at him, confused by the faint sneer that had touched his lips. "I'm sorry," she muttered and made a move to leave. He jerked her back down on the step, his arm hooked around her waist. Their eyes met in an electrically charged glance. Addie was aware of his tension but couldn't understand it. "What's the matter?"

He looked exasperated enough to shake her. Wrapping his hand behind her neck, he forced her head back with a hard kiss. Addie wriggled in protest at his roughness, bracing her arms against him and trying to push him away. His chest was as hard as a brick wall, defeating her efforts to dislodge him. The strong hand gripping the back of her neck rendered her helpless, and Ben tightened his hold on her until she submitted with a small, angry sound. The kiss amounted to nothing more than a contest of physical strength. There was no use in fighting him.

His tongue demanded access to the inside of her mouth, and Addie clenched her hands into fists, her body rigid in his arms. Brutal, arrogant creatures—men thought force was the way to solve everything—and how *dare* he do this to her after all they had talked about earlier! Long after the hurtful kiss should have ended, he raised his head and glared at her, angry and aroused, and unsatisfied.

"What are you trying to do?" Addie asked coldly, touching her tongue to her puffy lips in cautious exploration. "You . . . you . . ." She tried to think of a word Russell would have used. ". . . son-of-a-bitch! You hurt me."

He showed not one bit of regret for the pain he'd caused her. "Then we're even."

"The hell we are! What have I said or done to hurt you?"

"It's what you haven't said, Addie. It's what you haven't done." And before she had any time to mull that over, he kissed her again. Bristling, she reached up and tangled her fingers in the hair at the back of his head, pulling hard until he stopped. "Damn you," he muttered, his eyes blazing. "I didn't want to love you. I knew you'd drive me crazy. Try to keep me at a distance. I'll be damned if I'll let you. I'll hammer away until I get inside you, and hang on no matter how hard you try to shake me off."

Heedless of her clutch on his hair, he slammed his mouth on hers, and this time Addie couldn't fight off the heat that raced through her body. She released her grip on his hair, her hands fluttering down to his shoulders. It was impossible to ignore the warmth of his steel-muscled body, the unsteady pounding of his heart. Her arms slid around his neck, and her breasts thrust against his chest. She matched her softness to his roughness, offered freely what he sought to take, met his violence with surrender. Silently her body communicated what she hadn't been able to say out loud.

Yes, I need you . . . love . . . yes, I'm yours . . .

As he felt her response, Ben groaned and released the nape of her neck. His arms wrapped tightly around her.

Their bodies burned underneath their clothes, hungry to be free of all that separated them. Ben's violence disappeared, and in its stead grew the sweet ache of desire. Intoxicated with a potent mixture of lust and love, he tried to fill himself with the taste and feel of her. His tongue plunged deep in a frenzy of hunger, and she moaned as she writhed against him.

They sought to be closer, but he encountered the hard ridges of corset stays as he searched for the shape of her. Her skirts were a mass of petticoats and protective layers of cloth. The only thing accessible to him was her mouth, and he devoured her wildly, kissing, kissing. Panting as if he had run for miles, Ben ran a shaking hand over her hair, remembering how it had trailed over his body last night. He was starving for the feel of her naked and unbound beneath him.

The impulse to take down the tight braids pinned to her head was too powerful to resist. Although he knew it would anger her, he found the end of a hairpin with his thumb and forefinger and pulled it out. Immediately Addie gasped and wrenched away from him as a lock of hair fell to her shoulder.

"Give that back to me," she snapped, flustered as she held her hand out for the pin. "What are they going to think if I walk in the front door with my hair falling . . . Give it back!''

He was tempted to refuse. Let her walk in like this. Let them see her all flushed and disheveled, and everyone would know for certain how things stood between the two of them. But Addie's imperious little hand was shoved further into his face, demanding the return of what he'd stolen, and despite the urgings of the demon riding on his shoulder, he placed the hairpin in her palm. She accepted it without a word of thanks, winding up her hair and fastening it securely in back of her head. Her breath came gustily between her lips, proof of the turmoil he'd caused within her.

''I didn't do anything to provoke that . . . that display. If you're going to behave like that, then stay away from me until you can find some self-control!'' She shot up and went down the two steps to the ground. This time he didn't prevent her, merely watched her with brooding eyes. ''You're perfectly capable of being a gentleman when it suits you, and from now on I demand—''

''You want me to be a gentleman? That's a far cry from what you wanted last night. Or is your demand only good up until bedtime?''

''Ohhh!'' She was too incensed to answer. Turning on her heel, she left to go back to the house, muttering curses against him and men in general.

Addie groaned softly in her sleep, twisting against the clinging sheet, floating in a netherworld of dreams . . . or was it memories? . . . watching herself in familiar scenes. She saw her own face, the same and yet so terribly different. The voice, the body, even the hair . . . it was all hers, but the shading, the resonation, the texture of the picture was different . . . twisted . . . off-key. Why were her eyes so cold? Why was her face so empty?

She and Jeff sat on the porch swing, talking in conspiratorial whispers, touching discreetly, absorbed in each other. The evening sky threw concealing shadows over them, and they sat close to each other, comfortable in the darkness. They had been there for a long time, drawn deeper and deeper into a secretive communion, until they broke past the barrier of forbidden subjects. And they discussed what should never have been planned.

"It's got to be done soon," Adeline whispered. She curled up closer to him, her eyes dark and feline as she concentrated on him. "He's waiting for his lawyer to get here from the East."

"You won't have to do anything. I'll take care of it. I just need a name from you."

"I'll have to think about it," she said, silently calculating. She would have to pick the right man, someone smart, someone without a conscience.

"Adeline, if you're worried about the rest of your family—"

"We'll all be better off this way." A hard smile curved her lips.

"But about how you're gonna feel after it's done—"

"I won't care. Why should I? If he cared about me, he wouldn't want to change his will. After it's changed, it'll be in trust for years, and I won't get anything till I'm an old woman." Adeline noticed the amazement in his expression, perhaps even a touch of fear at her callousness. She sought to soothe him. "He only cares about Ben Hunter. He doesn't want me to be happy. I never have been. But it'll be different with you, won't it, Jeff?" She stroked her finger down the front of his shirt, hooking it into the waist of his pants. Slowly she rubbed the back of her knuckle against his tightening abdomen. "We'll be happy together," she said, and Jeff sighed hungrily.

"Oh, yes. Yes. Just help me with the name. Someone from here. It's the best way. I'll do the rest."

She looked up at him narrow-eyed, considering, and then she leaned over to him. And whispered in his ear.

Oh, God, what was the name?

What had she told him?

Addie's eyes flew open, and she passed a hand over her damp forehead. She had broken out in a cold sweat. She lay there stiffly, trying not to think, closing her eyes, and feeling her eyelids trembling. For a long time she was still, covered with a chilling film of perspiration.

She knew now. *I've betrayed them all. I helped set it up.* She had once wanted Russell dead . . . she had conspired with the Johnsons to have him killed. After he died, she would have her money, and the Johnsons would take over the ranch, take down the fences, break up the family, and tear Russell Warner's legacy to pieces. She had to find a way to undo it. But how? Thoughts plucked at her brain with hot pincers until her head ached. She wanted a drink, a good stiff shot of something that would take the edge off her torment. But did she want it enough to sneak downstairs and get it? Addie couldn't make a decision one way or another, and just lay there waiting for some impulse to take hold of her.

Much later she heard the door open and close softly, but the sound was vaguely unreal. She kept her eyes closed, afraid to find out if it was another dream or not. Quiet footsteps. A movement in the darkness. The rustle of cotton. The slither of jeans. Then all was still except for the abraded sound of her breath. The mattress gave way beneath the weight of a man's body, the sliding of muscled legs along hers, the heat of his flesh as he lowered himself to her. A sob caught in her throat, and Addie lifted her arms, pulling him down to her. Welcoming the plundering of his mouth, she responded frantically to his kiss, needing him, craving him.

The warm fragrance of him surrounded her, and she breathed it in voraciously, tangling her hands in his hair, urging him to kiss her harder. His hands moved over her breasts, teasing her nipples, squeezing until she moaned. Biting her lip, she molded against him, her breasts flattening into his chest.

Ben shuddered and rolled over, taking her with him. Everywhere, everywhere her hair trailed and streamed in long strands of silk, lashing his neck and face and shoulders. Their lips blended in endless kisses, tenderly aggressive. As Ben gently hunted for the deepest taste of her, Addie thought she would die of pleasure.

Drawing her palms down his body, she marveled at the flexing breadth of his shoulders, the lean sides of his waist, the powerful muscles of his thighs. Her fingertips crossed the soft, taut skin of his hips, and she heard the quality of his breathing change, becoming raspy, stopping in that instant when she filled her palm and fingers with the throbbing hardness of him. She stroked him in the ways she remembered from the night before, her touch gentle but firm, and he gasped. His hands plowed into her hair as he held her head to his, capturing her mouth with a fervent kiss.

Clasping her buttocks in his hands, he urged her upward, dragging her along the length of his body. His lips found the peak of her breast and claimed it, drawing her into the recess of his mouth. Each tiny nerve was probed by the fine-grained surface of his tongue. Sliding her arms underneath his neck, she ducked her head and rubbed her cheek against his hair.

His whisper scalded her ears as he took hold of her hips and pulled her up until she was straddling him. "Take me inside you."

Unfamiliar with taking the lead, she hesitated before helping to guide him home, closing her eyes as he slid into her. The merging of their bodies was a slow drawing-together, a blending of softness and strength, sensitive and precise. Addie braced her hands on his chest, her hair hanging in a silken curtain as she bent her head. His fingers dug into her hips as he moved her back and forth, and his pelvis arched rhythmically up to hers. It was some wild, improbable fantasy, the pleasure so sweet it was almost like pain. Oh, she had heard about the things men and women sometimes dared to do together, but she had never imagined herself loving a man so wantonly.

She was caught in a fire too hot to bear, a storm that beat within and without, until she crumpled from the intensity and held on to Ben with a desperate grip. Her legs were trembling and tired. Sensitive to her every movement and rhythm, he understood immediately. Without a word he turned her over, smothering her whimper with his lips, driving into her again and again, and her body thrilled with an agonizing chord of ecstasy that pierced through every nerve. When it was over she continued to cling to him, aware of his eruption of pleasure.

The descent from such dizzying heights was slow. They relaxed together degree by degree, washed in the scent and taste of each other. Addie lay still as he massaged her back, his fingers pressing the base of her spine and working upward. He whispered as he caressed her, words of intimate praise that made her blush, and the moment was so blissful that she stretched like a contented cat. The darkness was no longer cold, but warm and alive, vibrant with sensations that rippled outward from their sated flesh. There were no nightmares hovering in this darkness, nothing but peace.

Try as she might to get used to it, the contrast between the nights and the days was startling to Addie.

It was brought home to her each time she met Ben's eyes, for she couldn't exchange the most casual of greetings with him at breakfast without remembering what the two of them had been doing only a few hours before. As the family left the table and scattered, each one of them concentrating on his or her plans for the day, Addie accompanied Ben out of the house and managed to have a few private words with him.

"Ben, w-wait," she stammered, touching his arm, and he stopped at the bottom of the steps, looking up at her as she stood a step above him. "There's something I have to talk to you about."

"Now?" He'd been wearing a mask all during breakfast, of courtesy so perfect it was almost a mockery, an attitude of endless politeness. Now he was looking at her as he had last night, his smile full of masculine arrogance.

"No, not now," she said, glancing around to see if they were being observed. "And don't look at me like that!"

"Like what?"

"As if . . . you . . . as if—"

"As if I'd spent the night in your bed?"

"Yes, and you don't have to act so smug about it."

"You do seem to have that effect on me," he said lazily. "It was all I could do to keep my . . . er . . . smugness under control this morning."

"Be quiet," she commanded, wanting to clap her hand over his mouth. "Someone's going to hear you."

She looked anxious and rosy-cheeked this morning, and there were faint smudges under her eyes from lack of sleep. A button near the top of her dress wasn't fastened, as if she'd dressed too hastily. Ben had never seen anything as charming as Addie Warner standing there and trying to scold him discreetly. If there hadn't been so many people around, he would have stepped up to her and kissed her.

"What do you want to talk to me about?" he asked instead. She sighed shortly, picking up her skirts and retreating up the steps. Now was not the time to discuss Russell.

"It can wait."

Hearing the tense note in her voice, Ben followed and stopped her with a touch on her arm. "Addie. Are you all right?"

She lifted her shoulders in an uncertain shrug. Gently he stroked the hollow on the inside of her elbow with his thumb.

"Do you need something, honey?" No one but Ben could ask a simple question in a way that sent a shiver down her spine.

"I need to talk to you privately."

"Tonight after dinner soon enough? . . . Good. Then give me a smile so I won't worry today. And fasten your top button, darlin'."

That night she would talk to him about Russell and the danger he was in. Knowing Ben's affection for Russell, it wouldn't be difficult to appeal to the more protective side of his nature. Surely she could convince Ben they needed to watch over him more, especially now that the conflicts between Sunrise and the Double Bar were growing in frequency and intensity.

Addie could hardly believe that someone would sneak in the house and kill Russell Warner in his own bed. But it had happened once, and succeeded because it was so unexpected. It couldn't happen again. Addie knew she'd already changed part of the Warner family history. She hadn't disappeared. She'd been here for weeks, a different woman than before, and she'd made choices the former Adeline Warner would never have made. She'd turned against Jeff and fallen in love with Ben. For the first time in her life she was part of a family. She'd found a place where she belonged. Addie would fight to keep all of that, and every last bit of strength she had would be devoted to saving Russell.

Russell was puffed up with pleasure when Ben casually left the table after dinner to accompany Addie on a walk outside. By now it was obvious to everyone that a full-fledged romance was in the making. Russell was even more gratified than Caroline. Of course May still had reservations about the match between her daughter and the ranch foreman, but strangely, she offered no objections when she saw them leaving together. Maybe she was beginning to see that opposing the relationship wouldn't do any good.

"My goodness," Addie breathed as soon as they were outside alone, "this is all going to be so much easier than I'd expected. Mama didn't say a thing. Oh, she looked very frosty, but she didn't say one word."

"Maybe the thought of me as a son-in-law isn't as hard on her as we anticipated," Ben mused, sliding an arm around her back, taking care to match his stride to her much shorter steps.

"Or maybe she thinks you're a temporary fling. You're just the kind I'd choose for that."

Ben feigned a scowl at her careless remark. "Me, a fling? That does it."

Addie laughed breathlessly as he scooped her up and headed toward the pasture in back of the house. "It was a compliment," she protested, giggling and squirming in his arms.

"Oh?" He arched his dark brows as he looked down at her. "It didn't sound like one to me."

"It was, it was. Where are you taking me?"

"To a place where I can take revenge in private."

"I meant what I said. Any woman would want to have a fling with you." She ran the tip of her finger down the part of his throat exposed by the open collar of his shirt, coquettishly tracing a pattern on the well-tanned skin. "You're very handsome. And you look like the kind who's good at . . . well . . ."

"Good at what?"

"Stop teasing. You know what I mean. I always wondered what it would be like with you. Even when I didn't like you, I still wondered."

He smiled, shifting her higher in his arms as he walked. "Has your curiosity been satisfied, ma'am?"

"Not yet," she said, fingering the buttons of his shirt. "But I know one thing for certain."

"What is that?"

She looped her arms around his neck and whispered in his ear, "You're every bit as good as you look."

He dropped a kiss on her throat, his eyes flickering, and he stopped walking as they reached a stack of dry, freshly piled alfalfa hay. His original intention had been to drop her in it and kiss her until she begged for mercy. But now all he wanted to do was give her pleasure. Her clasp on him tightened as he lowered her into the sweet-scented hay.

"Oh! No, we can't." She laughed and pushed at his chest. "Not now. Not *here*—"

"Give me a good reason."

"They're going to know exactly what we've been doing." Her pulse pounded madly as he straddled her and pulled up her skirts. "There'll be hay in my hair and on my clothes and—"

"We'll take care of it later. Every speck."

"Impossible." A disbelieving chuckle escaped her. "You're not really planning to . . . are you . . ." Her voice died away as he reached underneath her underwear to the bare skin of her stomach, stroking with the backs of his knuckles. "Ben," she said, and he smiled as he saw how fast her breathing was. Slowly he peeled her drawers down her thighs.

"It's a struggle, isn't it?" he asked, bending over her, his fingers trailing over her abdomen. "Your sense

She protested and tried to rise, then fell back as his fingers found her and began moving ceaselessly. With a long moan she turned her face into his shoulder, silently begging him to not to stop. He seemed to know exactly what her body craved, circling and teasing her sensitive flesh with the pad of his thumb, plunging his fingers deep within her, sometimes fast, sometimes slow. All the while he murmured in her ear, deliberately earthy, saying things that aroused her even more.

". . . anyone could see us right now, Addie . . . someone could walk by . . . one of the hands on the way to the bunkhouse . . . what if you knew someone was watching? Would you tell me to stop then?'' His stroking paused, as if his continuing depended on her answer.

"No,'' she groaned, lifting her hips, pressing his hand harder against her dampening flesh, and he resumed the excruciating torment.

"They're going to know what we're doing anyway,'' he whispered relentlessly. "I'm going to make you scream, and they'll all hear you.''

"I won't,'' she choked, and his smile was merciless.

"You're afraid you will.''

"No!''

And finally the pleasure was so intense that she did cry out, but he smothered the sound with his mouth, and in the aftershocks his tongue caught the throaty vibrations of her groaning. He kissed her for a long time, savoring her languid response. When she had recovered, she pulled free of his hands and mouth. Mortified by what had happened, she sat up and fumbled to rearrange her clothing. Ben helped her, suppressing a smile as he saw how worried she was.

"H-how long have we been out here?'' she asked, not looking at him.

"About ten minutes.''

"Oh." Addie's distress lessened. It had seemed much longer to her. But she continued to frown, brushing helplessly at the wisps of hay clinging to her dress until Ben lifted her chin with his fingers and smiled down at her.

"No one heard anything," he said flatly. "Or saw. I kept an eye open, just in case."

Addie blushed. "Then what you said . . ."

"All for your benefit."

She was too relieved by his answer to scold him for his arrogance. "I wasn't loud?" she asked, and he pulled her close, bewitched by her curious mixture of modesty and abandon.

"I kept you very quiet," he whispered conspiratorially, and her shoulders sagged.

"I should be mad at you."

"For what? Didn't it feel good?"

"I . . . Yes, it felt . . . But that's not the point."

"Forgive my lack of understanding, but what is the point?" Though he sounded grave, she knew he was laughing at her silently.

"It was different from before. It wasn't romantic, or serious, or—"

"It doesn't always have to be serious between us." His lips wandered across her cheek. "Sometimes it can just be fun."

"But that's not how I think of it," she said, her brow wrinkling. Fun? Lovemaking between two people who cared for each other wasn't supposed to be fun. It was supposed to be tender, loving, emotional. If they loved each other, it should mean something more than fun, shouldn't it?

"How can you think of it just one way?" Ben countered. "It's going to be different all the time. Sometimes it'll be romantic . . . gentle . . . and sometimes a little . . ." He paused and searched for a tactful word. ". . . earthier. Sometimes we'll be tender. And sometimes we'll play. What's wrong with that?"

As he saw she still was uncertain, he cradled her face in his hands and smiled down at her. "I understand. You like candlelight and romance, and God knows there's nothing wrong with that. But you'd get tired of that if you had it all the time." He grinned and pulled a few wisps of hay out of her hair. "You have to admit, moonlit nights and haystacks have their own particular charm."

"I guess they do."

"You guess?" His eyes twinkled. "What would it take to make you absolutely sure?"

Addie stared at him, relishing the warmth of his hands on her cheeks, the sheen of moonlight on his hair. He looked handsome and pagan in the darkness, mysterious and untamable. Her lover. Someday her husband. She wanted a lifetime with him. She wanted to hold him to her with every bond and word, every intimacy that two people could exchange. Her feelings for him were stronger, more terrifying than she had ever imagined they could be. Her hands came up to cover the backs of his, clasping tightly.

"I love you, Ben."

She felt the tremor in his hands. It took a moment for him to understand. Then his eyes traveled over her face, as if he were trying to assure himself she had spoken the truth.

"God, I've wanted you to say that." He lowered his head and kissed her roughly, unable to restrain his passion.

9

DURING THE NIGHT THE FENCING AROUND THE southeast pasture was destroyed and the line riders near the area attacked by a band of men they couldn't identify. Every strand of wire was cut in several places, every fencepost ripped clear out of the ground. The sound of gunshots was faint but distinct, and the crackling noise awakened Addie and the rest of the Warners. Addie fumbled in her room for a nightgown and robe, sleepy but profoundly grateful that Ben had left her a little while ago. Had he stayed with her just a half-hour longer, he would have been caught in her room. That wasn't something she wanted to explain her way through just yet.

There were exclamations and rapid footsteps up and down the hallway. Addie opened her door cautiously, rubbing her eyes. Russell had already gotten dressed and was heading down the stairs, while Cade emerged from his room with his shirt buttons fastened in the wrong places.

"What's happening?" Addie asked, and Russell ignored her as he went down the stairs hollering for Ben in a voice that must have carried halfway across the ranch. Cade raked a hand through his hair, causing it to stand up in a light brown shock. He shrugged as he met her eyes.

"Those were gunshots," she said, biting her lower lip. "Weren't they?"

Cade looked eager and worried at the same time. "Betcha it's about the fence." He followed Russell in leaps and bounds, his feet thumping noisily on the stairs. Peter, always a slow riser, appeared at his doorway and followed, while Caroline regarded him with a frown.

"Be careful," she said to her husband, but he seemed not to hear her. After he disappeared through the front door Caro and Addie exchanged a bemused glance. Unspoken thoughts hung in the air as they wondered how serious the trouble was, and what would happen next.

"What time is it?" Caro asked.

"I guess about two or three."

"Mama's already in the kitchen making coffee. Help me downstairs, Adeline."

Caro leaned heavily on her arm as they went down the steps, less out of physical necessity than a need for emotional support. Neither of them could think of a thing to say. There was no need to state the obvious. Most probably the trouble involved the Double Bar. The gunshots hadn't been far away, and the family had been expecting an attack of this kind. Men were banding together and cutting fences in a wide sweep through central Texas, either on their own initiative or because they were hired by belligerent ranches. War hadn't been formally declared, but there was no other way to describe the state of affairs between the Warners and the Johnsons.

"I hope it's over," Addie said grimly as Caro made her way down the last two or three steps.

"You hope what's over?"

"The gunfire. Right now they're heading straight for it, Daddy and the rest of them. Men are so foolhardy with guns in their hands. I just hope no one's been hurt. I can't stand the thought of . . ." She bit her lip and gripped Caro's hand tightly.

"You're thinkin' about Ben, aren't you?"

Addie was too distracted to hide her feelings. "They always depend on him to do everything," she burst out. "Even Daddy—whenever there's any trouble or danger, 'have Ben do it, have Ben take care of it.' Ben has to watch out for everyone else, but who watches out for him? He's only human, he's not indestructible, and I . . ." She sighed with frustration. "Oh, I don't know—"

"He can take care of himself. Don't worry 'bout him."

"He'll be the first one to arrive on the scene, riding straight into whatever hornet's nest has been stirred up. Oh, Daddy likes to think of himself as the one in charge, but we all know Ben'll be the one who has to pick up the pieces or make the next move."

"That's the kind of man he is. Cade and Peter are the kind who have to be guided and prompted. But Ben is someone that others just naturally follow. You wouldn't want him to be any different, would you?"

No. But I don't want to lose him. And there was a fear in Addie's heart that she couldn't explain to anyone. A fear that she had a large price to pay for her past mistakes. Time had given her a chance to atone for the kind of person she had once been. But what if more was going to be demanded of her? What if she was denied the life with Ben she wanted so desperately?

They went to the kitchen and sat at the table with May, who looked calm but fatigued, while outside the house came the sounds of abrupt, sleepy-voiced conversations. The bunkhouse had awakened. Minutes ticked away, then an hour had passed, and as Addie paced around the silent kitchen, tension clawed at her nerves.

"How long do you think they'll be?" she asked curtly, knowing neither of them could answer the question any better than sne could. Still, she had to talk about something or go crazy.

"There's no way of tellin'," May replied, methodically stirring her tea. "Why don't you sit and have somethin' to drink, sugar?"

"It's the Double Bar," Addie muttered, circling the table once again. "Daddy's been expecting them to make a move. Oh, why does he insist on fencing in all the water? It's pure contrariness on his part—"

"Your daddy has the right to do whatever he wants with his own land."

"But he's leaving them with no choice, and I think—"

"It's not up to us to think anything about it, just support your daddy's decisions."

Addie grumbled underneath her breath and darted a glance at Caroline, wondering if she agreed with May. Caro was concentrating intently on her coffee, clearly wanting no part of the debate. There was no way of knowing what her opinion was. Sighing, Addie decided to keep quiet and leave well enough alone. She only hoped that whatever had happened, Russell would control his temper long enough to listen to Ben. Ben didn't like the idea of the fencing any more than she did, and there was no doubt he'd try to soften Russell's reaction to the damage that had been done tonight.

Another half-hour crawled by, and then Addie heard the thud-thud of a horse's hooves. Without a word she darted to the back door of the kitchen and threw it open. Cade had been sent back to tell them what had happened.

"Shootin'," he said, bursting into the kitchen, his eyes brilliant with excitement. "It was the fence all right." He paused and gulped in a few deep breaths. "Hacked to pieces. And our line riders were shot at."

"By whom?" Addie demanded.

"No one they could recognize."

"The Double Bar. It had to be."

"Yeah, we think they were behind it. But they didn't use their own men. Hired 'em, most likely. We pegged one of 'em, too. Only it was in the back, which don't make us look too good—"

"What do you mean? Someone was shot?"

"It was before Ben and Daddy and us got there. Our line riders had already chased the attackers off, and shot one of 'em in the back. Ben and Peter are takin' the body over to the sheriff."

Addie felt herself turn pale. "But that's dangerous. The men could be hiding near the road somewhere. They might try to shoot Ben for revenge . . . or . . ." She glanced at Caroline. "Or Peter . . ."

"Ben'll keep a sharp eye out," Cade said.

"But it's dark. He . . ." She bit her lip and kept in words of panic, aware of May's reproving eyes on her. May was far from pleased over her daughter's untoward concern for the foreman.

"Daddy's assigning more of our hands to watch over our property," Cade continued glibly. "Tomorrow they'll start puttin' the fence back up again. 'Course, it'll take away from the other chores that need t' be done around here, 'specially gettin' ready for roundup." He nearly did a dance of glee right in the center of the kitchen. "Daddy says I gotta take off school for a few weeks and help around here. He says there's too much t' be done on the ranch to fool around with books—"

"That's fine," May said evenly. "You'll help your daddy in the daytime and study your books in the evenin'. Adeline and I will help you do your lessons so you won't fall behind."

Cade's grin collapsed. "Aw, Ma—"

"It'll be a long day tomorrow. Go upstairs now and get some sleep."

"*Sleep?*" he repeated, as if the concept was foreign to him. "After what happened tonight?"

May nodded implacably, and the boy trudged out of the room, his exuberance deflating fast. "You can do the same, Adeline," she said, turning her eyes to her younger daughter. "You won't help anyone by stayin' up."

"I . . . I can't go to bed." Addie sat down slowly, gripping the sides of her chair as if expecting to be pried forcibly from it. "I'll wait for them to get back." Her anxiousness wore down into numbness as time dragged by. The cup of steaming coffee in front of her gradually turned stone-cold, and she took no notice as Caroline replaced it with a new cup. Then that was cold too, and they still hadn't returned.

There was a sickening plunge in her stomach every time she heard a noise outside, each time she heard a man's voice and knew it wasn't Ben's. Her head dropped to her folded arms on the table and she closed her eyes, waiting, waiting for the footsteps that were different from anyone else's, for the voice that could ease her tension and calm her fears. She felt Caroline's hand on her shoulder.

"I'm going to pour more coffee. I think they're back."

Addie's head jerked up, her eyes fastening on the doorway in a blank stare. Wearily Peter walked into the kitchen and settled his large frame in a chair, accepting the mug Caro handed to him. Russell burst into the kitchen in much the same way Cade had, breathing fire as he started to tell May his version of what had happened. And then Ben closed the door behind him, quiet and calm, his green eyes clear despite the lateness of the hour.

He met Addie's hungry stare with a faint nod, understanding all that she wanted to say but could not. It was the hardest thing she had ever done to sit at the

and not knowin', Adeline. And there are things that need to be said between us.''

"It's hard to tell you how I feel about him when I know how *you* feel.''

"It's not a personal dislike. Lord knows he could charm the birds out of the trees. I just know he's not good for you.''

"But he is.'' Addie leaned forward and spoke swiftly, eagerly. "You don't really know him, Mama, not as he really is.''

"He'll be difficult to handle.''

"Not for me.''

"If you marry him you'll never get away from here.''

"I don't want to.''

"The two of you are like fire and powder. The explosions might be exciting for now, but you'll never have a moment's peace. Later you'll regret—''

"I'd die if I married a man who wouldn't let me argue with him. We're both strong-willed, but we're learning how to accommodate each other. And he listens to me, Mama, really listens, and respects what I have to say.''

"I know. I've heard the two of you. He talks to you as if you're a man. You might enjoy the novelty of that at first, but it's not right for him to treat you as if—''

"Why not? Why not talk to me as if I have a head on my shoulders?''

"He should treat you more gently, instead of tellin' you about men's business and worryin' you with things that don't concern you. You're a woman, Adeline, with your own place and your own concerns—''

"And I tell him about those too.''

"Oh, good Lord.'' May leaned her forehead on her palm.

"I know it sounds a little radical, but why do there have to be lines between a husband and wife they aren't allowed to cross? Why the separation and the distance between them? There are things you and Caro and all our women friends tell each other but wouldn't dream of mentioning to your husbands. But a man has a right to know his wife's personal feelings, and—''

''A decent man wouldn't be interested in such things!'' May snapped, and Addie quieted, understanding it would distress her mother to hear any more. There was silence between them, and then May spoke wearily. ''I guess you plan to marry him.''

''Yes.''

''I suppose you've taken time to figure out he's after the ranch as much as anything else.''

''He'd end up with Sunrise anyway. Daddy's planning to make him trustee in the new will.''

''I know. That would put him in charge of the ranch. But by marryin' you, he'll own the biggest piece of it.''

''He would marry me if I were a pauper.''

''Are you certain of that?''

''I've never been more certain of anything.''

May looked at her daughter's serious eyes and stubbornly set jaw, and her own face wrinkled with unhappiness. It was difficult for her to accept defeat in this, of all things. ''You've never looked so much like your father,'' she said, and left the room.

Addie sat alone, massaging her temples. An abnormal quiet reigned over the house and the ranch, the silence after the storm. She waited until she heard Russell's office door opening and the sound of subdued voices. Warily she crept out of the kitchen and stood in a shadow, watching as Russell went up the stairs to catch an hour of sleep before the beginning of a difficult day. Ben stood at the bottom step, rubbing the back of his neck as he turned to leave. He saw her but made no move as she walked toward him.

''Did he listen?'' she asked softly.

"Some." He sighed with a mixture of weariness and worry. "I don't know how much."

She reached up to him and smoothed back a lock of hair that had fallen over his forehead. "He always respects what you have to say."

As he felt her drawing closer to him and saw the tenderness in her face, Ben froze. He'd never turned to anyone for comfort before. He'd been raised to bear his burdens alone, and he'd always managed to get along just fine without anyone's help. The last thing he needed was a woman's solace. And yet . . . he had an irresistible urge to pull Addie close and pour out his frustrations to her. Here she was, confronting him, forcing him to include her in his private feelings.

Addie saw the indecision in his face and understood it more than he could have imagined. Until she'd met him, she'd fought to keep the same distance between herself and everything that threatened to come too close. But whether he admitted it or not, he needed her. She stood on her toes and wrapped her arms around his neck, her lips grazing his unshaven jaw.

"Try to keep me at a distance," she said huskily. "I won't let you."

He was still for a moment, and then he bent his head and kissed her, his hand fitting behind her neck and tilting it back. Addie sighed and gripped his shoulders tightly. Weariness and doubt scattered like leaves before the wind. When he buried his mouth in the curve between her neck and shoulder, she slid her arms around his back and felt the tenseness of his muscles.

"Me the first part of the night, then the fence-cutters," she whispered. "You haven't had any rest at all."

"You tired me out a hell of a lot more than the fence-cutters," he muttered, his hands wandering over her slim body.

"Will you be able to get a little sleep?"

"It's only an hour until dawn. Pretty soon I'll have to get the men started, make sure they know what they're supposed to be doing for the day. I might as well stay awake." Taking it for granted that she would stay with him, Ben picked her up and carried her into the dimly lit parlor. As he settled into a slick horsehair sofa, he pulled her into his lap and they shared another smoldering kiss.

"I was worried about you," Addie confessed, pushing past his shirt to lay her cheek against the bare skin of his chest.

"Me?" He strained his fingers through her hair and coiled a lock of it around his hand. "No reason to be, darlin'. The shooting was over long before I arrived on the scene."

"When I heard you were taking the body to town, I was afraid someone would take a shot at you."

Ben half-smiled for the first time, turning his face down until their noses touched. "I think I like having someone worry over me."

"You're not the only one I'm worried about."

He sobered instantly. "Russ."

"I don't like the position he's put himself in."

"I admit he'll have to be careful from now on, but I don't think there's as much cause for concern as you seem to—"

"I think it's more serious than that," she said earnestly. "It's obvious he'll fight until his last breath to keep the fence up. If you were the Johnsons, or any of the other people who are losing money and property because of it, wouldn't you think the only thing to do is get him out of the way permanently?"

Ben stared at her silently, denial hovering on his lips.

"He's in danger," she said. "I know it."

"I'll talk to him."

"He has to be protected." Though she tried to

sound matter-of-fact, her voice was strained. "Maybe I sound overdramatic, but I'm not certain he's safe in the house."

"Addie, don't start borrowing trouble when—"

"Would you think about having someone watch the house at night? Please."

"Are you serious?" Ben shook his head in bemusement. "Honey, no one would get past the line riders on the border of the property. And even if someone did manage that, do you actually think he'd have the balls to sneak into the house? And if he got that far, how's he supposed to find the room Russ sleeps in? And if—"

"What if it was someone who knew the ranch well?"

"If you're going to spend your time worrying, there are plenty of more likely things to worry about."

"Please." Unconsciously Addie clutched handfuls of his shirt. "Have someone watch the house every night." She searched for the right words to say, something that would make him agree. "Please . . . I'm afraid."

Her last words affected him visibly. "Addie," he said, cradling her face in his hands, his eyes searching, "have you seen or heard something?"

"Not exactly."

"I can't help unless you tell me."

Tell you what? That I lived in the future for twenty years and found out how my father was murdered? Oh, and not only that, but I helped plan it, although I don't happen to remember what the plan was. And by the way, if I hadn't fallen in love with you, I'd still consider you a suspect, and probably would anyway if I didn't know how much you care for Russell. Just how am I supposed to tell you all that?

"Just do as I ask," she begged. "And don't let

Daddy know, or he'll put a stop to it. He thinks he can protect himself.''

"Don't know why he'd think that. He's only lived thirty years on the range with hardly a scratch on him.''

"Are you going to post a man outside the house?'' She frowned until he nodded reluctantly. "Is that a promise? You aren't just telling me that to keep me quiet?''

Ben stared her down, his voice ominously soft. "I'd never lie to you, Adeline.''

"I didn't mean to imply that. I'm just—''

"Afraid,'' he murmured, stroking the side of her face with a fingertip. Despite the gentleness of his touch, she shivered with apprehension.

"You're angry.''

"I'd wring your little neck if I thought I'd find out what's happened to make you feel this way.''

"It's not important.''

"It is to me.''

"I'm just concerned about Daddy, that's all. And now that I know someone will watch the house, I feel much better.''

But Ben wasn't placated, and he continued to scowl, even as she decorated his face with invisible kisses.

"That's not helping, Adeline.''

Addie stopped and looked at him, aware that her attempt at playfulness had fallen flat. She was still afraid and they both knew it. Time was drawing nearer, bringing with it an unavoidable sense of doom. She was frightened for Russell, and for Ben. He'd been blamed for Russell's murder before: he'd fled Sunrise and wandered for fifty years. She'd seen him, a pathetic old man without a home. The opposite of everything he was now. The image was dim, but still it lingered in the back of her mind, haunting her.

"Hold me,'' she finally said, feeling wretchedly

guilty, and his arms drew around her. His voice was rough and caressing at the same time.

"Little fool. Do you think I'm going to let anything happen to you? Keep your secrets for now. But this is the last time I'll stand by and wring my hands over another of your little mysteries. There's going to come a time when I start asking questions, Addie, and I'll expect some answers. And God help you then if you try to sweet-talk me out of it. Understand?" Ben waited until he felt her nod against his chest. Then he pressed his lips against her hair. "Don't be afraid. Everything's going to be fine. You know I'll take care of you."

As she clung to him, the dread and guilt disappeared. Warmth stole through her with a penetrating glow. She luxuriated in the protection of his body, melting with pleasure as his hands moved over her back. As long as she was in his arms, he could keep her safe from anything. If only he would hold her forever. She longed to tell him what she was truly afraid of, but there was no way she could, unless it was indirectly.

"Ben? If you cared about a person and then found out he'd done some bad things in the past, would it change your feelings about him?"

"It depends," Ben said thoughtfully. His hands stopped in mid-motion, then resumed their stroking. "I suppose it would depend on what he did. If it was bad enough . . . yes, it would change how I felt about him."

"But what if he'd changed and was truly sorry about what he'd done?"

"I'm not one to judge. You're talking to a former mavericker, remember?"

"Is mavericking the worst thing you've ever done?"

Ben smiled slightly. "Oh, I'll admit to worse if I

have to. Anyone who knew me before I came to Texas would tell you I had a misspent youth.''

''Are you sorry now for the things you did back then?''

''I rarely bother thinking about the past. And no, I don't waste time regretting things. I've paid for my worst mistakes two or three times over.'' He noticed the hollow at the base of her throat, revealed by the parted edged of her robe, and ducked his head to nibble at the delicate spot.

''Why the sudden interest in sin and atonement?'' he asked, his voice muffled. ''Remembering some schoolroom prank you never got caught for? You hid the teacher's chalk, I'll bet. Or whispered with your friends in the middle of geography—''

''Never,'' she said, relieved at the change of subject. She let her head fall to his shoulder, enjoying the plundering of his mouth. ''I was always well-behaved.''

Deftly he unfastened the tiny buttons at the throat of her nightgown, one by one, moving down to her breasts. ''I've heard differently, Adeline.''

''Don't believe a word of it. And besides, you were probably no angel either.''

Ben grinned. ''I was always getting suspended.''

''Troublemaker.''

''Mmn-hmn. Once I hid a snake in Mary Ashburn's desk.'' He chuckled lazily. ''She pulled it out when she reached for her pencil.''

''How mean!''

''Just a little garden snake. Hardly worth all that screaming.''

''Why did you do it?''

''Because I liked her.''

''Your courting has improved.''

''Practice,'' he said, his hand slipping underneath

the folds of her nightgown, and she grabbed at it to stop his explorations.

"With many women?"

"Not as many as you seem to suspect. Haven't we talked about this before?"

"You said you'd tell me sometime about why you're so liberal in your ideas about women. About the one that had such an effect on you—"

"What makes you so sure it was one woman?"

"Intuition. Was it someone you were in love with?"

"In a way."

"Did you think about marrying her?"

Ben's face changed, and he looked uncomfortable, wary, perhaps a little bitter. "Addie, I'm not ready to talk about it."

"She hurt you, didn't she?"

Despite his irritation, Ben laughed ruefully at her persistence. And her accuracy. "Why is it so important?"

"I know hardly anything about your past. There's so much about you I don't understand, and it bothers me that you know so much more about me than I do about you. You're a puzzle. Why are you the way you are, and why—"

"Whoa. Before I explain anything. I'd like to point out I sure as hell don't understand everything about *you.*"

"Was she important to you?" Addie asked, ignoring his attempt to sidetrack her.

"At the time, I thought she was everything." Ben rested his head on the back of the sofa, looking up at the ceiling. "Have you ever wanted something so much you would have gone to hell and back to get it? And once you had it, the tighter you tried to hold on, the less of a grip you had? She was like that. I'd never met anyone so elusive. The more distant she was, the more I wanted her."

Addie was surprised to feel a stab of jealousy. Suddenly she wasn't certain she wanted to hear about his desire for another woman, but at the same time she burned to know about the mysterious past he talked so little about.

"Who was she?"

"The daughter of one of my professors at Harvard. Her father was one of the most brilliant men I'd ever met. Very New England—aloof, intelligent, dynamic. Sometimes when he spoke, his words just burned through your mind—God, the things he said were radical. Startling. There was a lot of that in his daughter, the same brilliance, the same intelligence. I'd never heard a woman talk like she did. He'd let her study the same things his students did, let her say and do anything she wanted. She was smarter than most of the men I knew—a woman with an education. Having been raised in a small town near Chicago where they'd barely heard of such a thing, I was fascinated."

"Was she beautiful?"

"Very."

Addie's jealousy doubled. Beautiful, intelligent, fascinating. "She sounds perfect," she said tonelessly.

"I thought so for a while. It was maddening, never knowing where I stood with her. One minute sugar wouldn't melt in her mouth, and the next she'd fly into a rage for no reason. Sometimes she was just plain crazy, taking chances, dragging me into wild adventures. I was either deliriously happy or miserable around her."

"Why was she so wild?"

Ben's gaze was distant, as if he were concentrating on elusive images. "There was no place for her. She'd been given the opportunity to become exotic . . . different . . . and then everyone kept trying to put her in a place she didn't belong. Including me. She was a bird in a cage, flying against the bars over and over again. I wondered why she couldn't act more like other women, why she wanted to talk about things that only men . . .'' He paused and looked at her, his eyes unreadable. "You should understand.''

Addie nodded imperceptibly.

"But she didn't have your strength,'' Ben continued. "She had no hope of finding a way to fit in. I watched her suffocating, and I didn't understand why. I thought the only way to help her was to try to change her. The tighter I held on, the worse it was. I loved her, and she felt the same about me. But everything I wanted from her—marriage, a child, a life together—all of that would have been a prison. She wanted no part of it.''

Ben took a deep breath and let it out slowly, amazed at the sudden lightness in his chest. It was the first time he'd ever talked about that part of his past. He hadn't planned to tell Addie, but now it made sense to unburden himself to her. Who else was capable of understanding? Who else could begin to know the kind of struggle it had been?

"How did it end?''

"She . . .'' Ben cleared his throat and stopped. He couldn't get the words out. Addie said nothing, waiting patiently, although inside she wanted to scream with the need to know. "She found out she was going to have a child,'' he muttered, his eyes flashing with guilt and remembered pain. "*My* child. I insisted we would get married. It was only a few weeks until graduation, and I already had plans to go back to Illinois and get a job at my father's bank. She was miserable, I was thrilled. I wanted the baby. I wanted her. And the day after she told me, she nearly killed herself having the child aborted. When I found out what she'd done, I wished she had died along with the baby. I never saw her again.''

Addie's heart was filled with compassion. "How did you manage to get through the rest of the semester?"

"Money in the right pockets. My father was determined to have his son graduate from Harvard. No price was too high to pay. I didn't care one way or the other. I was numb."

"I'm so sorry about what she did," Addie murmured. "About the baby."

"Part of it was my fault. I would have used the baby as a chain and manacle to keep her with me—"

"No. She should have talked to you about it. You would have helped her find a way to deal with it. She should have trusted you. You would have listened to her."

"No. I was different then."

"Not that different. Nothing will make me believe you would have ignored a plea for understanding. You wouldn't have made her life a prison."

"How can you be so sure?" he asked gruffly.

"Because I know you. Because my heart tells me so."

He turned his face away. Addie sat in his lap, trying to read his silence. Suddenly he drew his sleeve across his eyes, blotting an unfamiliar dampness, and she wound her arms around his neck, holding him fiercely. She had to convince him she wouldn't become like the other woman he'd loved, her spirit crushed by a disapproving world.

"I'm not like her, Ben."

"In some ways you are."

"Well, of course I hate not being able to say what I want, or do what I want, just because I'm a woman. But I'm not a bird in a cage. And I want to belong to you."

"I don't want to trap you—"

"I'm more afraid of being alone. Don't you see I have more freedom with you than without you?"

His hands bracketed her shoulders as he looked at her intently. The combination of innocence and experience in her face had never been so pronounced. He saw the eagerness of a child, the passionate love of a woman, and a depth of understanding that belonged to someone twice her age.

"God, I'll never let you go, Addie."

"I know that."

"And I won't try to change you."

"I wouldn't let you."

"No, you wouldn't," he said, and relaxed slightly. "You're quite a woman, Adeline Warner."

"Too much for you to handle?" she asked, her voice soft and teasing. Suddenly she found herself flat on her back, smiling as she stared up at him. His eyes warmed with desire.

"Not by a long shot," he said, proceeding to demonstrate in a way that left no doubt in her mind.

The agreements Ben and Russell had made in private about how to handle the crisis were never detailed to the family, but some things were very clear. Most important, the fence was going back up. Second, Russell had decided to restrain himself from riding roughshod over the ranch, the Warner family, and the cowboys, contrary to what they had expected. He stayed in the office and kept his distance from the ruins of his fence, while Ben supervised the construction of extra line shacks, doubled the number of riders who protected the Sunrise borders at night, and appointed men to hammer new fenceposts into the ground.

Barrels of precious water were used to soften the ground in order to dig holes for the posts, an outrage to those whose herds of cattle were parched and thirsty. May, Caroline, Addie, and even Leah were kept busy doctoring the gouges and scratches that the barbed wire left on the arms of the men who were engaged in constructing the new fence. After a few days Addie showed Ben ruefully that her fingers were permanently stained brownish-red from handling countless bottles of iodine.

The reactions of the town and neighboring ranches to the attack on Russell's property were mixed. Some cattlemen who had been entertaining the idea of closing in their own land with cheap, durable barbed-wire fencing were as outraged as if they had been victimized along with Russell. But some people said it was just what Russell deserved. Many cowboys hated the idea of fencing over the range they were accustomed to riding so freely. Small cowmen who often gleaned mavericks from the cattle drifting across the boundaries of their own properties resented the fence too.

As day after day passed by, Addie began to miss Ben acutely. She hardly ever saw him. He was busy dealing with all the problems that were brought to him, no matter how large or small. His work was unending as he supervised the building of the fence and coordinated the other chores done around the ranch. With the constant traffic in and around the house, there was no opportunity for him to come to Addie's room. A man had been appointed to watch over the house at night, the final guarantee that her trysts with Ben were over for a while.

Addie was consumed by frustration, emotional and physical, and it wouldn't be eased until she had Ben to herself again. She lay sprawled in her bed at night, arms and legs outflung as she thought moodily about the times he had visited her. How was it possible to want someone so much? The moments when she did see him weren't enough—there were always family members or ranch hands around, and no chance for any kind of privacy.

How long was she going to last without him? Her need of him grew stronger every minute, until she could hardly bear it when he was near. How strange it was to hunger and thirst for someone so badly, to resent everything that took him away from her. He had awakened needs in her, strong needs that must be assuaged. She'd had so few nights with him, but for the rest of her life, every night without him would be cold and empty. Looking around the table, she wondered if any of them would have understood how she felt. No, none of them, not even lonely, sensitive Caroline.

I'd go to any lengths to keep him. None of them have ever fought for each other. But they must have felt something once. They must have. Caroline and Peter acted like distant acquaintances, while May and Russell were wearily affectionate at best. *No passion, no tenderness. Not even anger. What do they talk about when they're alone? Or is there just silence?*

Addie missed the long, cozy talks with Ben the most. In the darkest hours of the night she had told him some of the scandalously intimate things that even wives weren't supposed to tell their husbands. Conversations with Ben had been a source of endless fascination, since there was almost no subject he was unwilling to discuss, and he never bothered to spare her modesty. He seemed to enjoy making her blush, and he could always tell when he'd succeeded, even in the dark.

After a week of being apart from him, she began to notice that Ben was changing in subtle ways. His easy manner had disappeared and his sense of humor was more biting than usual. He was always tense and short-tempered around her, and he made an effort to avoid her company. Why was he so brusque and abrupt? Why did it seem as if he were angry with her?

Every time she heard him walk into the house at dinnertime, saw him enter the room, watched him as he sat down at the table, there was an ache in the pit of her stomach. The extra time he spent in the sun was darkening his skin to a new swarthy shade, making his

LISA KLEYPAS

eyes glow like emeralds. He had never been so handsome, so unreachable. Why was it that as she looked at him across the expanse of the dining-room table, the distance seemed to turn into miles?

Addie poker her head around Caroline's door, her brow creasing with a frown as she saw the shades pulled down over the morning light and the small bulky figure huddled underneath the covers.

"Caro?" she said softly, and her sister stirred. "You don't feel like getting up yet?"

Caroline shook her head, looking annoyed. Her face was bloated from gaining a surprising amount of weight in a short time, and her eyes were underlined with puffy bags. "No. I feel sick. I'm tired."

"Has Dr. Haskin—"

"He says there's nothin' wrong with me."

"Well, that's wonderful—"

"Oh, don't sound so cheerful."

"Why don't I get you some tea? And I'll read you the story from yesterday's newspaper about—"

"No. Thank you, but I don't feel like drinkin' anything or listenin' to anything."

Slowly Addie walked over to the bed and sat down on the edge, covering Caro's limp hand with her own. "What's wrong?" she asked gently.

The sympathy seemed to be Caroline's undoing. Her eyes filled with tears. "I feel so fat and awful and mean-tempered. And I'm losing my hair. Can't you see how thin and stringy it is? I used to have such pretty hair."

"It's still pretty. If you have lost some, it's certainly not enough for anyone to notice, and it'll grow back just as soon as the baby's born."

"A-and Peter never wants to talk to me anymore, or hold me—"

"He doesn't know what you want from him. Tell him what you need."

"I want h-him to know without askin'."

"Men don't always understand what to do. Sometimes you have to tell them."

Caroline gave a watery sigh and wiped her eyes with a corner of the sheet. "This mornin' Leah came into my room and started bouncin' on the bed. I was sharp with her, and she doesn't understand why—"

"I'll see to her. Cade and I will take her to town. Yesterday she wanted some material to make her doll some dresses, and we don't have enough scraps here. We'll get her a length of cotton, and maybe some candy."

"Would you? Oh, she'll like that."

"What about you?" Addie asked, gently teasing. "Peppermint or licorice?"

"Nothing," Caro said, suddenly looking happier. Despite her pregnancy, she looked like a little girl with her tearstained face and plump cheeks. Addie felt a pang of love for her, wishing she knew how to make everything magically right for Caro.

"Tonight when I get back, we'll wash your hair. That'll make you feel better. And I'll tell Ben to play some music in the parlor after dinner, especially that song you always like to hear."

"But Ben is so busy—"

"He'll find the time," Addie assured her, and grinned impishly. "If I ask."

Caroline brightened, looking at her expectantly. "How are things between the two of you?"

Addie leaned closer, her brown eyes dancing with excitement. "He loves me," she whispered.

"Oh, Adeline—"

"I never dreamed I could be so happy. I'm so much in love it hurts."

"I'm so glad for you." Caroline gripped her hand.

LISA KLEYPAS

"Don't let him go. Don't let anything come between you."

"No, never." Addie flashed her a grin and squeezed Caro's hand before letting go and leaving the room. "Leah! Leah, where are you? You and I are going to town. Come help me look for Cade."

Leah's pigtails flew behind her as she raced down the stairs ahead of Addie, her voice shrill as she called for Cade. Addie followed her out to the front porch, where they found Cade reclining lazily on the steps with Diaz. Diaz was in the middle of one of his improbable adventure stories. He stopped his narrative and looked up as he saw them, his wizened face creasing with a smile.

Addie returned the smile hesitantly, suddenly aware of how many times she'd walked by him without a thought as he sat on this very porch. Accustomed to his presence there, she had given him as little notice as she gave the porch railing or the wooden boards under her feet. Every now and then they had exchanged a word, but she had never again sought out his company after the strange, almost nonsensical conversation they'd once had. It was rare that Addie let herself think about it, and everything she had once considered asking him or talking to him about had faded into the most distant part of her memory. He was just there, ever-present, contemplative.

"Cade, you have to take Adeline an' me to town," Leah burst out, reaching out to yank at his hand.

Cade smiled at her excitement, resisting her efforts to pull him to his feet. "Who says I have to?"

"Don't tease," Addie said, hooking her fingers into his shirt collar and tugging lightly. He made a gagging noise and stood up.

"Guess you'll have t' finish the story later," he said to Diaz, shoving his hands into his pockets and shrugging good-naturedly. "Otherwise Adeline'll strangu-

306

late me. You aren't gonna leave before tonight, are you?''

"Tomorrow mornin'," Diaz said, and Addie's eyes widened in astonishment.

"Leave? What do you mean? Where are you going? Why—"

"I never stay too long in one place, or with one outfit." Diaz smiled at her in a kindly way and lifted his stocky shoulders as if to indicate it was something beyond his control.

"But what will you do?"

"Lotta herds gonna be driven north soon. Always room for a good talespinner on the trail."

Addie was speechless. She didn't want him to leave. But she couldn't explain the feeling, not to him and not even to herself. There was no practical reason for wanting him to stay at Sunrise. She hardly knew him, hardly ever spoke to him. He was just as he described himself, a talespinner. He'd done nothing for her except throw out a few half-baked ideas one night that had struck her fancy. Some of the odd things he'd said about going back in time, about redemption, had frightened her with their accuracy. Maybe it had just been a lucky choice of words. And maybe not.

"There's something I must know," she said hesitantly. "Mr. Diaz—"

"Adeline," Cade interrupted, chuckling as Leah nearly sent him tumbling down the steps with her eagerness to leave, "he just said he'll be here tonight. If you want to go to town, quit talkin' and come on."

Addie scowled at her brother and then raised her eyes heavenward. "Later, Mr. Diaz?"

"Later," he agreed placidly, and she smiled at him before following Cade and Leah.

After they had reached town and Cade helped them down from the buggy, Addie and Leah headed for the General Store. Cade went further down the street to see if Ben was visiting with the sheriff as he had intended. Nowadays Ben made it a habit to keep the sheriff informed of every incident of friction that involved the Sunrise Ranch, doing what he could to keep him on their side. Not that the scanty forces that passed for law and order here could do much for them. In this part of Texas, you had to look after yourself and your own business, and you were in big trouble if you had to rely too much on someone else's protection. But Ben intended to maintain some appearance of respectability for the ranch, and having the sheriff's cautious support was better than his disapproval.

After buying a yard of checked gingham and a bulging parcel of candy, Addie walked Leah across the street toward the buggy. Leah's sugar-sticky hand caught at hers, and Addie grinned as they swung arms together companionably.

"Wanna lemon drop?" Leah asked with perfect politeness.

"No, thank you."

"Molasses cane?"

"Honey, if I'd wanted any, I would've gotten some for myself. But it's nice of you to want to share."

"Aunt Adeline?"

"What?"

"Why does Ben call you Addie? No one else does."

She nearly jumped at hearing *Addie* spoken in Leah's voice. It reminded her of the older Leah, and all the times she had heard her name spoken with just that inflection. "It's just a nickname," she said, trying to calm the thump-thump of her heart. "You can call me that if you want."

"Aunt Addie," Leah said experimentally, and giggled.

She couldn't help laughing. "So you think it sounds funny, do you?"

"Uh-huh." Leah pulled out a licorice strap and began chewing the end. "Aunt Addie, is Mama gonna have that baby soon?"

"Kind of soon. There's still about two months to go."

"Oh." Leah's face wrinkled in discontentment, and she bit clean through the licorice before chewing noisily.

Addie eyed her thoughtfully. Was that why Leah had been so cranky lately? Because she was jealous of the baby? Of course . . . Leah had always been the baby of the family, and she didn't want to give that place to someone else.

"Want to know something? You're ten years older than this baby, the same age your mother was when I was born." Leah looked at her silently, one cheek bulging with candy. "When I was little," Addie continued, "she had to show me so many things—why, I tried to do everything just like she did. I followed her everywhere. She would tell me stories, and brush my hair, and she even helped me get dressed in the morning. I thought she was the best older sister there ever was." Strictly speaking, Addie couldn't remember much about her relationship with Caroline. But Leah didn't have to know that.

Leah seemed fascinated. "Will I do things like that for the baby?"

"Well, I know she—or he—will probably depend on you like I did your mother."

Satisfied by the little girl's intrigued expression, Addie let the subject drop and smiled as they reached the other side of the street. Suddenly Leah's hand went lax in her grip, and Addie looked down at her. The child's face was pale, her eyes as round as saucers.

"What is it? What—"

"Adeline," a quiet voice interrupted, and she looked up into Jeff Johnson's intense blue eyes.

10

As she sensed Leah's uneasiness, Addie released her hand and bent down to the child. "Why don't you go and sit in the buggy?"

"The Johnsons are bad, Aunt Adeline—"

"Hush," Addie said swiftly. "Everything's just fine, Leah."

"I'll go get Cade—"

"No. Go wait in the buggy. I won't be long." Something in Addie's voice was hard, and her face had gone cold. Leah wasn't the cause of it, but she was too young to understand. She looked at Addie and Jeff with a touch of fear and went slowly to the buggy. Straightening up, Addie met Jeff's eyes and lifted her chin.

"The Johnsons are bad?" he repeated, amused.

"What would you say about someone who hired people to tear down another man's property and attack his employees?"

"That was just a warnin'. I guess Russell knows now what's gonna happen if he doesn't want to share his water rights. 'Specially when we offered to pay for the privilege—"

"He's let you share the water for years, at no charge. He finally had to stop when you started siphoning off his cattle and pushing your boundaries deeper into his property."

"I don't care to talk about him."

"Then say whatever you need to, and leave me as quickly as possible. I didn't come to town alone, and there'll be trouble if we're seen together."

He looked at her without blinking, puzzled by her sharpness. "How've you been, Adeline?"

She was in no mood for small talk. "What do you want?"

"You." Once it might have been a teasing suggestion. But there was no lightness in his voice, no smile in his eyes. "Won't be long, Adeline."

She understood immediately what he meant. He was going to carry out the plans they had made, and he would destroy everything she loved, everything she wanted. Everything she had once been indifferent to. She was terrified as she stood there and looked at him. How could she have thought she wanted him? How could she have helped him plan her own downfall?

The steadiness of her own voice surprised her. "Jeff, things have changed since I last saw you."

"What things?"

"Everything I felt for you. Everything I said to you was a lie. I never loved you."

"Adeline, what the hell . . ." He lifted a hand to touch her elbow, and she jerked away from him.

"Don't ever touch me. I don't want you. I don't want any part of you."

At first he was too stunned to be angry. "You don't mean that. What's happened. Is it what happened at the Fanins'? I was just a little drunk, honey. All men have a little too much once in a while—"

"No, it has nothing to do with that. Listen to what I'm saying. You and I won't ever be together. Forget about the plans you made about me and my father." She paused and tried to swallow back the lump in her throat. "I don't want him hurt. I swear, whatever you do to him will be done to you, only worse. I'll make sure of it."

"Jesus Christ! What are you sayin'? Have you told him anything?" Jeff took a step forward as if to shake her, then looked around and realized they were drawing a few stares. He flushed a dull red as he stared at her. "No, you haven't told anyone," he muttered. "You wouldn't risk him findin' out what you've done. And you won't say anything, 'cause you care too much for your own neck, and it's easier to sit back and let it happen. You know your father's diggin' his own grave anyway. He doesn't need much of a push. Why the last-minute change of mind? Jitters? It doesn't matter. I don't always understand you, Adeline, but I know what you really are. I know more about you than anyone, and I want you. And that's how you feel about me."

Her lips trembled as she held back the threats that flew through her mind. All of them sounded ridiculous, futile. If only she could remember the name of the man the Johnsons had hired. Whose name had she given them? *Remember,* she cried inside, and all she found was a thick wall, impossible to break through. *Remember!*

"I . . . I'll tell everything," she said, trying to hide her desperation. "I can ruin you and your family, and I will if you force me to."

"You won't," Jeff said with growing conviction, and the urge to swing out and strike him was nearly irresistible.

"I hate you," she whispered.

"Yeah. An' a few other things." He took her arm firmly, staring down at her with a half-formed smile.

"I told you not to touch me."

"Let's not talk about it in the middle of the street. I know a corner somewhere around here."

Addie wrenched her arm away and turned toward the buggy just in time to catch a glimpse of approaching disaster. Before she could make a sound, she felt the rush of air as Ben lunged past her and plowed into Jeff so hard they both tumbled into the street. They were like two young animals, fighting and snarling, rolling across the dusty ground. Stupefied, Addie watched as people came running from every direction, cussing and exclaiming, forming a loosely packed crowd around the two men. All of a sudden the noise was deafening. Taking a step backward, she spun around as someone bumped against her shoulder. Cade was right behind her, reaching out to steady her.

"Adeline, I couldn't stop him. He took one look at the two of you and went crazy."

"Leah," she gasped, looking wildly toward the buggy. It was empty.

"I'll find her. Stay here." Cade dashed off through the thickening crowd on the wooden sidewalk. Stumbling to the edge of the circle around Ben and Jeff, she fought to see them.

"Ben," she cried, but her voice was drowned in the cheers and shouts. "Ben!"

It didn't take long for the crowd to become violent. Since it was perceived as a fight between the Double Bar and Sunrise, sides were quickly chosen. You were either for or against Russell Warner, and there were very few undecideds. Retreating to the sidewalk, Addie was dumbstruck as the street erupted in a burst of flying fists and piercing yells.

"Bunch of idiots," Cade muttered in her ear, and she turned with a start to see him sidling up close to her with Leah tucked against his side. "They've all been itchin' for a chance to fight about the fence."

"It's not about that, it's about . . ."

"You?" Cade smiled a little. "Between Ben and Jeff, it's you. Between the rest of 'em, that damn fence."

"You feel like I do about it?"

"We need it," he said gravely. "We're too big and

clumsy an outfit to get along without it. But that doesn't keep me from hatin' it just as much as you do.''

Addie glanced down at Leah, who had twisted around to watch the fighting with wide eyes. "Did Leah go and get you?" she asked, and Cade shook his head.

"Ben and I just walked out of the sheriff's office, and there you were with Jeff." He grinned. "Ben said a coupla new swear words I'm still tryin' to figger out, and went after Jeff lickety-split."

"Where *is* the sheriff?" Addie demanded furiously, terrified that Ben would be hurt, might already be hurt, and then the sound of gunshots seemed to puncture her eardrums. Leah flinched and pressed close to her. The sound was repeated, and some of the men broke apart like scalded cats. Sam Dary, the sheriff, was a heavyset man with a definite swagger. He lowered his gun and walked through the crowd, hollering loudly. A small clearing formed in the middle of the street, where Ben and Jeff had been pried apart. It took several men to keep them separated, and they eyed each other with murderous intent, panting for breath.

"Easy, easy . . . simmer down. You two boys know better than to start somethin' like this when tempers are already runnin' high." Dary said weightily, his face red and perspiring. "An' it don't matter who started it, 'cause I happen to know you both been itchin' for this a mighty long time. Now it's over, an' you got it through with. Let's just go on, now, an' start thinkin' on better things to do than git everyone stirred up in sech a way. It's too damn hot to fight. Shake on it and make it a bygone, boys."

"Shake hands with *him?*" Jeff demanded in amazement, and Ben sneered.

"If you think I'm about to—"

"That's enough," the sheriff said. Slowly the restraining hands relaxed as everyone realized the fight was good and over. Dary braced his hands on his hips, seeming to feel the need to establish his authority. ''I'm still waitin' fer you t' shake.''

''We've stopped fighting,'' Ben said, breaking the frosty silence. ''Isn't that good enough?''

Addie was weak with relief as the sheriff nodded reluctantly and the men walked away from each other. Leaving Leah with Cade, she made her way to the street, needing to see for herself that Ben was all right. Anxiously she pushed past the people standing in her path, her eyes fastened on the tall figure several feet away. Moving through the crowd, ignoring the multitude of hands patting him on the back, Ben seemed not to notice her until she reached him.

She summoned a smile with difficulty. ''There was no need to start the whole town brawling, was there?''

He dragged a sleeve across his eyes to clear the sweat and dust from them. ''I told him once what would happen if he laid a finger on you.''

''Are you hurt?''

''No. Hell, he's as soft as the rest of the Johnsons.'' Disgust crossed his face. ''No wonder they have to hire someone else to do their fence-cutting. They don't have the spine or the strength to do it themselves.''

''Soft or not, he managed to do some damage,'' Addie said, looking at his bruised face. She ducked her head to hide a sudden wave of emotion. ''Come on. We'll take you home in the buggy.''

''Look at me.'' His tone was so commanding that she obeyed without thinking. Their eyes met, hers wide with bewilderment, his gleaming with a bright, hot light. Deliberately he held her jaw with one hand and bent his head to hers, kissing her lustily. Shocked gasps and a few whistles came from the crowd, but Addie was too surprised to pull away. Her nostrils were filled with the scent of sweat and dirt, and she tasted blood as her head was forced to his shoulder by the pressure of his kiss. Dizzily she leaned against him, her heart thundering.

She went weak all over, sinking into a well of fire. The only thing she was conscious of was his mouth on hers, his lips burning, demanding, sweet. When he lifted his head, she stared at him blankly, unable to make a sound. The whole town. He'd kissed her like *that* in front of the whole town.

"Consider that our engagement announcement," Ben said, and gestured for Cade, who was grinning widely, to follow them to the buggy.

May was livid when she heard what had happened, so angry that even Russell took care to walk softly around her.

"Do you understand the position he's put her in?" May demanded, striding back and forth across the parlor. Ben braced an elbow on the mantel over the fireplace and watched her expressionlessly, while Russell and Addie sat by each other on the sofa, not daring to make a peep. Russell was smoking like a chimney, occasionally glancing at Addie over the end of his cigar with a subdued twinkle in his eye.

"Fighting over her in the street," May continued, her voice raising in pitch, "as if she were some prize— and then . . . and then . . ."

They all knew the *and then* referred to the public kiss afterward, an incident fast becoming infamous as the town gossips chewed over the story. Ben lowered his head guiltily in a way that made Addie want to laugh. She knew very well it was an act for May's benefit. Ben didn't feel one ounce of remorse for what he'd done.

May pressed her palms to her temples as if to calm a raging headache. "My daughter's reputation is ruined. Ruined."

"Mama, no one took it seriously," Addie broke in.

"It was just an impulse. Everyone was all stirred up and emotional. It was just the heat of the moment." She ignored the sideways glance that Ben sent her, knowing there was a diabolic sparkle in his eyes. There had been ever since that afternoon. "I'm sure he didn't mean to do it. It just . . . happened."

"He should have controlled his impulse," May said, giving Ben a hard stare, and he nodded respectfully.

"Yes, ma'am."

"And I suspect, Ben Hunter, that you knew exactly what you were doing." She cut him off as he opened his mouth to reply. "Don't try to charm your way out of this. Everyone in this room knows you saw this afternoon as a convenient shortcut to having your way, and you didn't hesitate to take advantage of it. Well, I don't have to pretend I approve of your methods of getting what you want. It was ruthless and inconsiderate to gamble with Adeline's reputation as you did today, and I hope for her sake you don't make a habit of it."

"I don't intend to," Ben said evenly, and Addie realized that suddenly he was not amused anymore. He was taking May's words seriously, listening to her with a remarkable absence of mockery. He'd always been respectful to May, but Addie would never have guessed he would allow her mother to lecture him like this.

"I'm her mother," May continued. "I have a right to speak my piece, and it's your obligation to listen. There's nothing I can do to stand in your way, and I don't intend to fight the three of you any longer. The important thing is, Adeline thinks you're going to make her happy. I suppose you think that too. But you won't if you continue to treat her with so little consideration. She is not to be made a public spectacle, ever again. She is to be treated with gentleness and respect.

Her welfare should be considered first, above your own needs.''

As Addie heard May's admonition, she looked down at her hands, her cheeks burning. It was terribly disconcerting to hear herself being discussed as if she weren't even there. She wanted to interrupt, but there was nothing she could say on her own behalf, or Ben's. Only Ben could calm May's anxiety.

''Her happiness, not to mention her welfare, is my foremost concern,'' he said. As she saw his steely expression, not even May could doubt what he said. ''That's why I want her as my wife.''

''You know my objections to a marriage between the two of you,'' May snapped. ''You know I didn't approve of the idea. And so you put us all into an intolerable situation. It's impossible for me to refuse your marriage now. In fact I have to insist on it.''

Ben's eyes gleamed with satisfaction. ''I'll make her happy.''

''You haven't even bothered to apologize for your behavior.''

''I apologize for that. But with all due respect, not for the result.''

Sensing the grudging apology was all she was going to get from him, May switched her glare from Ben to Russell. ''You haven't said one word during all of this.''

Russell assumed an authoritative glower, standing up and motioning to Ben. ''I'm gonna have a man-to-man talk with him. Just because he's gonna marry my daughter doesn't mean he c'n get out of a good dressin'-down when he deserves one. C'mon, Ben—into my office.''

''Yes, for a drink and cigar and a good slap on the back,'' May said acidly.

Addie couldn't help snickering.

There was a definite tinge of whiskey on Ben's breath

when he came out of Russell's office. He smiled at Addie as he saw her outside the door, and followed her silently as she pulled him out to the front porch for a few minutes of privacy. His color was high from strong drink and a sense of well-being.

"Poor thing," she said. "I can tell he ran rough-shod over you."

Ben smiled, settling his worn felt hat on the porch rail. "He said it was the happiest day of his life."

"I'm glad someone feels that way," she said pertly. "I would've stayed in bed this morning if I'd known what today was going to be like."

He flexed his shoulders and winced. "I feel like I've been through a cattle stampede."

"How dare you complain? You're to blame for everything that happened. First the fight, then the kiss—"

"Please, darlin', I listened to a good hour of that from your mother."

"Than what should I say? You took your punishment like a man. Bravo."

"You're pretty feisty tonight," he observed, walking leisurely to the edge of the porch and bracing his hand on the railing. "Hey, Watts," he called into the darkness, and the cowboy who was patrolling the area answered softly.

"Yeah, Ben?"

"Why don't you do a little checking around back for a couple of minutes?"

There was the sound of a smothered chuckle. "I was just plannin' on doin' that."

"Get a move on."

Addie squinted through the shadows, her head turning to follow Watts's movement around the side of the house. She caught only a glimpse of his stocky shape. When the sound of his feet had died away, she looked at Ben with a mild frown, remembering the night when

Watts had cried drunkenly on Ben's shoulder after finding out his sister was a prostitute.

"Is his sister still working in that dance hall?" she asked, and Ben shrugged.

"Far as I know."

"You were going to offer him money to get her out of there."

"I couldn't get him to take it."

"Too proud?" she mused out loud. "What about offering him more work and paying him extra—"

"I've already tried that, and no, he doesn't want to work more. I think everyone's reconciled to what his sister is, honey. Now, stop trying to fix everyone else's problems and start worrying about me for a change."

"Worrying about you is all I've been doing lately!" Addie put her hands on her hips as Ben sauntered over to her. She'd been through a terrible day, all because of him, and a little accounting was in order. "Stop right there." He paused a few feet away, his eyebrow arched in inquiry. "I have no intention of letting you near me, Ben Hunter. You've been awful to me all week. Rude, bad-tempered . . . you've ignored and insulted me—"

"I've gone through hell. I've wanted you so damn badly I couldn't see straight, and I've had enough work and worry to make a saint cuss."

"And you think I've had it easier? How do you think I felt when I saw you and Jeff fighting in the middle of the street like a bear and a bull? It didn't accomplish anything except to make matters worse between us and the Johnsons."

Ben scowled, his playful mood vanishing. "I couldn't help it. When I saw him looking down at you like that—Jesus, you'd think you were the only woman in Texas, the way he looked at you—and when he touched you—"

"For heaven's sake, he wasn't exactly going to ravish me in the street! The whole town was there."

"He was acting as if he owned you," Ben said moodily, folding his arms across his chest and shifting his weight to one leg, the other propped out in a masculine stance. "He damn sure seems to feel he has a claim on you, Addie. Why is that?" There was a flicker of jealousy in his eyes.

"What are you asking?"

"Just how far did you go with him?"

She was amazed at his bluntness. "When he and I were courting?"

"Yes."

"Oh, for heaven's . . . you don't really expect me to answer that."

No reply. He stared at her obstinately.

"You do," she said slowly. "After all you and I . . . Oh, I'd never have expected this from you! How far do you *think* I went with him? You know you're the first and only man I've ever made love with. Isn't that enough to satisfy your precious ego? It's just too bad if it isn't, because I'm not about to tell you the intimate details of my relationships with any other men—not unless you're prepared to tell me what you've done with other women!"

"It's not the same."

"Not . . ." Addie started to repeat, and stopped in astonishment. Sometimes she forgot that although Ben was less chauvinistic than most men around here, he still had his moments. Suddenly she wanted to laugh. "Why isn't it the same?" she demanded. "If you have a right to know about my past experience, then I have a right to know about yours."

"We're not equally accountable for such things. A man is supposed to have experience. And a woman—"

"Is supposed to be ignorant? Pardon me—I forgot there was one set of rules for you and another for me."

"I'm not talking about rules—"

"Aren't you? You're supposed to be experienced and I'm not. Well, I was perfectly happy for you to be my first. But don't you think I would've liked to be your first too?"

Ben looked startled, as if the idea had never occurred to him before. "You have the damnedest way of twisting things around."

"Sometimes I have to. You're not always fair to me."

One corner of his mouth turned down, and he swore under his breath. "Look, I'm sorry I started this. I don't know why I asked you about that jackass. I just can't stand the thought of you being close to him."

"I can't change the fact that I used to care for him. But I never came close to feeling about him the way I do about you. You know that."

He shrugged, glaring at the floor.

Addie sighed. "Well, let me tell you something. I hate thinking of you with other women. I wish I could erase them from your memory. I wish you'd never been with anyone but me. But there's nothing I can do to change that, is there? Don't you see how pointless it is to fret about such things you have no control over?"

Ben looked up at her, his green eyes vivid in the darkness. He walked to her with measured paces, moving forward until she was forced to back up against the wall of the house. When there was no space left between her spine and the wall, he braced his arms on either side of her head. She turned her face away from his as she felt the crush of his body against hers, the touch of his breath against her cheek. God help her, she could never stay angry with him for long.

"I never said I'd be easy to get along with," he said.

"You didn't have to say it. I knew you wouldn't be."

He closed his eyes and kissed the wave of hair that had fallen over her temple, his mouth brushing against the soft skin just underneath her eye. Then his lips traced the line of her eyebrow, and she felt the touch of his tongue at the sleek point of it. She lifted her chin, seeking his mouth, and sighed a little as he kissed her with slow intensity. Silently they pressed closer to each other, clinging fiercely, hungering, prolonging the kiss until Ben made an uncomfortable sound and raised his head.

"I won't be able to stop," he said, breathing hard.

"Ben, when are we going to be able to—"

"I wish I knew." He looked pained. "I can't visit you tonight. No one's going to sleep well tonight after the trouble this afternoon."

"What's going to happen between us and the Johnsons?" she whispered, burrowing deeper into his embrace. "I hate it that things have gone this far."

"We'll have to take things as they come. I won't let my temper get out of hand again. It'll be easier now that our engagement is out in the open."

"You have so many responsibilities. I wish I could make things easier for you."

"I'll be fine." He groaned and rested his chin on the top of her head. "If only I didn't want you so much. I can't even look at you across the table without feeling *this* happen." He pulled her loins tighter into his, and she pressed her hot face into his neck, her heart racing.

"It's just as difficult for me."

"It's different for men, honey. Believe me."

"I'm sorry," she whispered with a smile.

"Addie!" came May's voice from inside the house, a signal they'd spent too much time alone on the porch.

"I'll be right in, Mama." Addie shifted away from Ben, knowing she had to leave him. She missed the warmth of his body as soon as they parted. In a sudden movement she reached out and pulled herself against him, her grip feverishly tight. "I can't let go of you."

"Addie," he muttered, crushing her against his chest. She clung to him and welcomed the pain of it, needing to know that the violence of his love matched hers. "I want you every minute. I miss being with you. I want to hold you for hours." He bit her earlobe carefully and then buried his face in her hair. "One more kiss. And then go in the house."

Shivering, she offered her lips to him, and though the kiss started out tender, it ended in rough eagerness.

"Now, go," he said, though his heart was hungry for a few more minutes with her.

"Don't be distant with me tomorrow," she whispered. "When other people are around, you never look at me as if you love me."

"You wouldn't let me before. Remember? It wasn't my idea to keep our relationship a secret."

"I was uncertain about how I felt," she admitted. "Weren't you?"

"Never. I've known for a long time how I feel about you."

She felt overwhelmed by the knowledge of his love for her. It wasn't difficult to remember the days when she'd had no one but Leah. She remembered the rainy night when even Leah had been taken away from her. Now she had more than she'd ever dreamed of.

But like a shadow, the memories of Adeline crept through her mind, dark and indistinct, inescapable. For the rest of her life she would have that part of herself to contend with, and deep in the back of her mind there would always be an awareness of what she had once been. What had happened to make her that way? How could a daughter plot against her own father?

Suddenly she heard the echo of something Caroline had once said to her. *"For a while I thought Daddy had finally done it—spoiled you rotten to the core."*

That's what I was, Addie thought with shame and despair. *Rotten to the core.* Oh, was there any way of making up for what she'd done? Guilt was a tangible pain in her chest.

"I don't deserve you," she said, and Ben's mouth twisted.

"Why in hell would you say that?"

"I've done terrible things in the past. Things I can never tell you about. I'm not half as good or kind as I should be, and—"

"I never expected you to be some plaster saint, Addie. And as for not deserving *me,* of all people . . ." He paused and grinned. "Let's just say it's more likely you do deserve me. It's possible I'm the punishment for your sins, and marriage to me will be your penance. Have you ever thought of that? Now, give me one more kiss and leave, or I won't be able to let you go."

Halfway irritated at his cavalier attitude toward her guilty conscience, she offered her cheek to him instead of her lips. Why, she'd been trying to unburden herself to him, and he was downright flippant about her worries!

Ben laughed softly as he lowered his mouth to her cheek and pressed a kiss there. "Why the sudden change in temperature? You were warm enough a minute ago."

"I was trying to tell you about my faults, and you just—"

"I don't care about your faults. The ones I already know about don't matter, and I'll discover the rest soon enough."

"I'm trying to warn you—"

"That you're not what you seem on the surface?" He smiled and settled his hands at her waist, pulling her closer. "I know that, and a few other things as well. You like to misbehave sometimes . . . ah, that may be a fault of yours, Addie, but I happen to like it very much. And another one—in bed you're one of the greediest women I've ever known—"

"Ben!" she exclaimed, color flooding her face.

"—but I happen to like that too. You have other faults which I enjoy equally. Should I continue or have I made my point?"

Addie pushed hard at his chest in an effort to break his hold on her. "You're being crude and—"

"Addie!" They heard May calling again, this time more insistent than before. "It's time to come in *right now.*"

"You heard her," Addie said impatiently. "Now, take your hands off me or we'll both get in trouble."

He grinned and kissed the tip of her nose. "That's a far cry from 'I can't let go of you.' " And he watched her with glowing eyes as she went into the house.

The next day Adeline discovered Diaz had left the ranch, despite his promise to talk to her before he went. No one could understand why she was so upset by his disappearance. When she started to complain to Ben as he strode out of Russell's office in the afternoon, he shrugged off Diaz's departure matter-of-factly.

"Most cowhands have to pick up and leave when they start to feel too settled-in. They're independent in a crazy way. They like to look out at the world from their saddles. The men out here can't stand any way of life that seems too civilized. They like things rough. They like their independence."

"What about you?" Addie demanded. "Are you

going to pick up and leave when you start to feel shackled by a string of fences and a wedding band?''

''No, ma'am,'' he assured her promptly, his eyes twinkling. ''I'm not your typical cowhand.''

Her eyes made a pointed survey of his dirt-encrusted boots, worn-out Levi's, and blue cotton shirt. ''You look pretty typical to me. How can I be sure you won't start to feel too settled-in and leave me?''

''Because I'm ready to belong somewhere. And I'd choose sleeping with you over bedding down on the trail any day of the week.''

''Are you certain having a wife and a family of your own isn't too civilized for your taste?''

''Oh, I've always had a secret hankering for respectability. And I won't mind being thought of as a family man. Hell, Russ doesn't mind it.''

''Yes, but he . . .'' Addie bit her lip before blurting out that Russell wasn't quite the family man he seemed. Russell didn't share a bedroom with May, and in all likelihood he had a woman on the side. Nervously she cast a glance at the closed office door.

Ben seemed to understand. Casually he hooked an arm around her neck and lowered his mouth to her ear. ''That won't happen to us,'' he murmured, and kissed her neck before letting his arm drop away from her.

Addie smiled uncertainly. ''Well, considering the way you were brought up and your fancy eastern education, I suppose I shouldn't be surprised to find a civilized streak in you.''

''We're all going to be civilized out here, and it won't take long, either. Not with the railroad spreading as fast as it is.''

''So you expect things to change around here?''

''Mmm-hmmmm. Everything, even the cattle we handle. Lately there's been a demand for better beef than what we're gathering in and trailing up to Kansas.

Longhorns are easy to take care of, but they're tough and stringy.''

"Weren't you and Daddy talking about breeding them with some better stock? Some shorthorns with more meat on them?"

"A lot of ranchers are talking about that. The problem is, shorthorns need more care and attention, and most of the boys don't want to fool with them. And breeding shorthorns means more fencing, which means soon there'll be so much wire around the district you'll have to cut your way to town. So . . .'' He cast a glance up and down the empty halls before leaning over and stealing a quick kiss from Addie. ''. . . the open range will keep getting smaller and smaller. And the East is going to keep spreading out here. And with all those changes going on, cowmen will have to change their way of doing things.''

"So you're going to become a new kind of rancher?"

"Yes, ma'am. And I'll be one of the best."

"To think of what you could do if you only had some confidence."

He grinned at her before heading out the door. Addie smiled wryly and shook her head, standing in the doorway as she watched him leave.

Fall roundup had begun. To everyone on the ranch it was a roundup like any other. Calves born since last spring were weaned from their mothers, branded, and marked as the property of the Sunrise Ranch. Bulls were gathered in so they could be fed and tended during winter, while the older, unproductive cows were destined for slaughter. Plans were made to drive a huge herd of cattle to market.

Those things came to everyone's mind when the word "roundup" was mentioned. But to Addie it meant Russell was in danger, and if anyone would try to kill him, it would be now. She lay awake at night listening for the slightest sound, occasionally getting up and looking out the window until she saw the cowboy whose duty it was to watch the house that evening. After discovering the nightly patrol outside the ranch house each night, Russell had demanded to know the reason for it. Ben had treated the matter casually, giving little explanation except to say he felt it was necessary.

Still fussing about it after dinner—"Whose damn ranch is this anyway?"—Russell went to his office and soothed his own temper with two fingers of whiskey. Addie crept in surreptitiously to see him. His back was to the door, but it was obvious he was pouring himself a drink. She grinned as he tossed a guilty look over his shoulder.

"It's just me," she said, and he relaxed with a grunt.

"Honey, don't tell your mama 'bout this. I promised her I'd cut down on this stuff."

"Are you going to?"

"Yeah. Sometime." He gestured her over and sighed with pleasure as the fire of the whiskey slid down his throat. "Whatcha in here for?"

"Oh, nothing. I just wanted to ask you about what you and Ben were arguing over—"

"Ben and his damn foolish notions," Russell said in disgust. "Havin' someone watch over the house at night . . . 'to protect the family,' he says, as if I can't protect my own family! And y' got Pete and Cade upstairs too! What does he think's gonna happen?"

"It might not be a bad idea. Everyone knows the Warners aren't too popular with the rest of the county." Addie hesitated before adding, "I wouldn't put it past the Johnsons to murder a man in his own bed. Daddy, don't laugh—I'm serious."

"The Johnsons can't touch me." Russell smiled

shrewdly. "My fence is goin' back up, an' there's nothin' they can do to stop it. And if they ever did get me outta the way, they still couldn't get their paws on my ranch, 'cause Ben's gonna be a part of the Warner family soon, and he'd tear it apart himself before lettin' Big George get hold of it."

But what if they made it look as if Ben is guilty of your murder? Addie wanted to cry out. That was what they'd done before. "All the same, there's reason to be extra careful," she said sharply. "And by the way, whenever you mention Ben marrying into the family, it sounds as if he's going to be Ben Warner. But I have a suspicion he likes his own last name and plans to keep it."

Russell laughed heartily. "The name don't matter to me, 's long as he marries my Adeline—"

"—and takes care of your ranch."

Russell chuckled and waved her out of the room before pouring himself another drink.

As several nights passed and nothing happened, Addie became less fearful. She started to let herself believe nothing would happen. There were many ways to rationalize things. Maybe Jeff had believed her warning and her threats. Maybe the Johnsons had decided it was too risky to send someone after Russell. Maybe the man they'd hired had already come and was frightened off by the sight of the cowboy watching over the house.

With roundup going on and May and Caroline making plans for her wedding, the ranch was overrun with activity. Addie missed Ben acutely, especially at night, but they had enough stolen moments together to take the edge off her hunger. Hardest of all were the hours when she lay in bed and knew that he was only a short distance away, alone in his small cabin near the main house.

Then finally the waiting became too much to bear

and caution lost to desire. Addie had planned to be patient and content herself with the odds and ends of time they had together until the wedding. But she needed him now. She wondered how she could find a way to be with him, when May's watchful eye was on them both. She would think of something, in spite of the risk of someone catching wind of it afterward. By now propriety meant little to her.

As she schemed on how to find time alone with Ben, Addie realized the answer was ridiculously simple. Why not just walk out of the house and go to his cabin? No complicated tiptoeing around the halls at midnight, no whispered plans of how or when they could meet. Just sneak out after dinner. As the family ate heartily, she picked at her food, unable to chew and swallow when her mind was preoccupied with the night to come. She could feel Ben's eyes on her often, and she knew he'd noticed the hint of tension in her face. She could feel the warm blood in her cheeks and wondered if her color was high. Before the meal was finished, she pushed back from the table.

"I'm a little tired," she said in response to May's questioning glance. "I believe I'll retire early tonight." Ben's gaze sought and found hers, and she saw the concern in his eyes. It was unusual behavior for her, and he suspected something was wrong.

"Addie—" he started, and she interrupted him gently.

"I'll see all of you tomorrow morning. Good night." As she left the room, she could feel Ben's eyes boring into her back. Pausing at the foot of the stairs, she waited until the sound of conversation resumed. Then she slipped out the front door. It was still too early for Robbie Keir, the boy who had been assigned to patrol around the house, to begin his watch.

Addie looked right and left before sneaking across the short distance to Ben's cabin, keeping to the shadows as much as possible. Triumphantly she reached the door and slipped inside, her heart thumping with excitement. She had no idea how she'd get back to her own room before morning without being discovered. Ben would have to figure it out.

Leisurely she moved around the cabin, finding it immaculate and sparsely furnished. The bed was narrow, with a hard, thin mattress, but it was covered with an intricately woven Indian blanket, and the sheets and pillowcase were snowy white. Since Ben did most of his paperwork in Russell's office, the small desk in here was bare except for a few books. She looked through them and discovered a thin volume of Shakespeare, a biography of Thomas Jefferson, a book on stock raising, and a report from a livestock journal about cattle transportation. How very boring, she thought, and smiled, reflecting that he probably didn't have that much time to read anyway. His guitar was propped up in one shadowy corner, a bootjack tucked into another. Wandering over to the bed, Addie settled down on the mattress and keeled over, burying her face in the pillow. It was scented of him, and she rubbed her cheek into it luxuriously, closing her eyes.

In spite of her anticipation, Addie fell into a shallow sleep until she was alerted by the sound of footsteps. The door was opened and she sat up, blinking as Ben entered the room.

To see Addie curled up kittenishly on his bed, sleepy-eyed and tousle-haired, was the last thing he expected. He stopped in his tracks as he looked at her, his green eyes widening as they moved from her tumbling honey-brown hair to her disheveled dress. Stunned, he could do nothing but stand there and stare.

"I don't believe you're here," he said, sounding bemused.

"I wanted you," she said, pushing a lock of hair

away from her eyes. "At least say you're glad I'm here."

"Glad?" he repeated thickly. In a fraction of a second he reached the bed and scooped her up, sitting down with her in his lap. He kissed her hungrily, stealing her breath away, and his lips moved down her throat. Clumsily he fumbled with the buttons of her dress. Reaching up to help him, Addie unfastened her bodice, and with each new inch of smooth skin revealed, his greedy kisses ventured lower.

"Was it a good idea for me to sneak over here?" she asked breathlessly, running her fingers through his hair.

His arms wrapped around her, and he engulfed her in a bone-crushing hug. "It was inspired," he said, burying his face in his throat. In a flurry of passion they talked at the same time, not bothering to take turns or even finish sentences.

"I've missed you so much—"

"Not half as much as I—"

"And every time I turn around, you're more beautiful than a minute ago—"

"All I can think about is you—"

"How do you get this off?" he demanded, searching for the hooks of her chemise, and before she could show him, he ripped the thin material straight down the front.

"Ben," she protested, torn between laughter and protest, and gasped as his lips moved over her breasts. His mouth fastened over an aching nipple, tugging gently. Moaning, she tilted her head back and arched up to him, her body on fire. There was a tremor in the arms that held her.

"It's been so long," she whispered.

"Forever."

Feverishly she worked at the buttons on his shirt while he reached under her skirts and stripped off her stockings. His hand ventured up to her knee, but her pantalets prevented him from exploring further.

"I've been going crazy," he muttered in the under-curve of her breast. "Wanting you, and seeing you every day, and not being able to have you—"

"Make love to me," she interrupted. "Quickly."

He half-laughed, half-groaned, lowering her to the mattress. In a few violent tugs he removed his boots and stripped off his shirt, then turned to help Addie wriggle out of her dress.

Impatiently he tossed the clothes to the floor and bent over her body. She pulled his head down to her breasts, purring as he kissed her, his tongue stroking lightly, sensitive to her every response. His warm palms brushed over her thighs, starting at the outsides, moving to the inner curves, and then his hand was between her legs. His breathing deepened as the wet sheath of her contracted around his fingers.

"So sweet . . . ah, I need you," he said against her lips, pushing deeper, and her nails dug into his back.

Brokenly she said his name. Her tongue thrust into his mouth, testing the even edge of his teeth. She writhed against him, her toes curling tightly as she felt the beginnings of a surging climax. Shocked that it was so quick, she reached for the fastenings of his jeans, wanting him inside her before the rising wave of pleasure broke.

Ben unfastened the stubborn buttons, his head spinning with the sound of her faint cry as he slid into the pulsing depths of her body. Addie's hands slipped downward and clenched over his flexing buttocks. Her body tightened around his as she was consumed by the white heat of fulfillment. He only had time for a few hard thrusts before the same ecstasy swept through him. They remained locked together, savoring the contractions of their joined flesh, tense until weakness flooded them both. Tenderly his mouth moved over hers, tasting and exploring. Everything before this moment had been flavored with desperation. Everything afterward was deliciously slow.

"I love you," he whispered, holding her body against his, resting his chin in the curve of her shoulder and neck. Sighing in contentment, Addie wrapped her legs around him possessively. They were both quiet for a long time, until the glow of splendor faded.

Addie was the first to stir, tugging at the waist of Ben's Levi's, and he smiled down at her, his expression lazy and relaxed for the first time in weeks.

"I had planned to take them off," he murmured.

"Are you going to?" she asked drowsily.

He was too exhausted to move. "In a minute."

She locked her arms around his back, loving the heaviness of his body over hers. "Don't move. Not yet."

"Don't worry."

His mouth found hers and they kissed languorously. Eventually Ben rolled to his side and stripped his jeans off. As soon as the garment was dropped to the floor, Addie snuggled close again, relishing the feel of his hair-roughened legs against hers. Her small hands wandered over his ribs and around to his back, and she marveled at how beautiful he was. "You're very strong," she said, walking her fingers up his spine.

"I wasn't always. Texas toughened me up a lot."

"What were you like when you were at Harvard?" she asked, tracing the indentations of his midriff. "All skinny and pale?"

Ben chuckled. "No, but I was in no shape to survive a trail drive, either."

"Texas must have been very different from what you'd been used to."

"I learned quickly." He smiled reminiscently. "At first I didn't even know how to rope a steer. I had to learn a lot of things the hard way."

"It must have been frightening."

"More lonely than anything else. The worst thing was never seeing any women. I ran a couple of long drives, and after several months of celibacy, those cattle towns were a taste of heaven. Whiskey that burned your guts out—they call it Kansas Sheep Dip—and women everywhere. God Almighty, those women . . . big, gaudy women with names like Hambone Kate and Dancing Annie. When the boys and I got to town, our eyes nearly dropped out of our heads at the sight of all those feathers and red dresses. The first night I spent in Dodge City, I went from saloon to saloon, and—"

"I hope you spent all your money and went back to Texas with a hangover."

Ben laughed. "I did."

"Feathers and red dresses . . ." Addie mused, wondering what Ben would say if he saw her in a skirt that barely covered her knees.

"Maybe I'll buy you a red dress someday," Ben said, his eyes twinkling. "Something different from all that pink you like to wear. And you can wear it for me in private, with your feet bare and your hair falling down your back."

"Buy me feathers too."

He grinned and rolled over, pulling her on top of him. "Lord, Addie, I'm never gonna get tired of you."

"Oh, I guarantee you won't," she replied, bracing her forearm across his chest. "I'll make sure of it."

He pulled her wrists out from underneath her, causing her to collapse on him, her breasts pressing into his chest. Before she could make a sound, his hands cupped the back of her head and exerted pressure to bring her mouth against his. Addie kissed him ardently, angling her head to the side. Her eyes slitted open as she felt a gentle light on her face. The moon was shining into the room, its beams reaching in through the window and touching everything with a silvery glow. Ben's face was thrown into relief, a study in light and darkness, and he was so starkly handsome that her heart missed a beat.

"I adore you, Ben Hunter," she said, touching his cheekbones with her fingertips. He drew her hand to his mouth and kissed her palm. Smiling with pure happiness, she laid her cheek on his chest and stared at the window with half-open eyes. A filament of light had fallen across the corner of the room, striking off the scuffed surface of the propped-up guitar. The sight of it caught her gaze for a reason she didn't understand, and she continued to stare, her smile disappearing.

There was a gap in the row of strings, like one tooth missing from a row of teeth. Addie blinked, wondering if her eyes were playing tricks on her. The gap remained. One of the strings was gone. The breath stopped in her throat. Panic stabbed her heart in a cold thrust.

"*No*," she gasped, suddenly springing into action, fighting to be free of Ben's arms. Stunned by the explosion of movement, he took hold of her flailing arms and tried to hold her still.

"Addie," he snapped. "What in the hell is wrong with you?"

"Let me go," she cried, turning white. "Please . . . Ben . . . go to the house. Russell . . . Oh, God, Daddy—"

"Nothing's happened to him. He's safe and sound. Addie, for God's sake, calm down."

"Please," she said, bursting into tears, feeling as if her heart would burst out of her chest. "We have to help him."

Reading the terror in her eyes, he swore and released her, reaching for his jeans and yanking them up to his waist. She scrambled for her dress, her hands shaking. Before she could pull on her clothes, Ben was already out the door.

A cloud drifted over the moon, dimming its light, but not before Ben saw the crumpled shape of a man near the steps of the porch. Suddenly he was gripped by the same fear that had taken hold of Addie, and he tore over to the house, sliding to his knees beside the body. Robbie Keir, the boy who was supposed to be watching over the area. He was unconscious. Someone had hit him on the side of the head with a blunt object.

Ben rose to his feet, the blood draining from his face. "Jesus Christ," he muttered, and took the stairs in two leaps, running across the porch and flinging open the front door. As soon as he stepped inside, pain burst inside his head like a brilliant light. He collapsed to the floor without a sound.

Buttoning her dress haphazardly, Addie left Ben's cabin and ran barefoot to the house, her hair flying out behind her. It seemed as if she had to run miles. *Don't let anything have happened,* she begged feverishly. She should have stayed in her room that night. She shouldn't have gone to be with Ben, not when there was still a chance Russell was in danger. But it couldn't have really happened . . . no, she was having a nightmare, just as she had so many times before. She felt small and terrified, like a child who faced a fear too great to comprehend, and now nothing would soothe her but the sight of Russell, safe and carefree and laughing at her worry.

Addie's steps slowed as she saw the boy on the ground, one arm outflung, the other curled limply around his head. Dread weighted her down like a heavy cloak. Without even pausing to look at the still figure, she went to the front door, which was ajar. She found Ben just inside, his dark-skinned torso blending with the somber color of the carpet. Sinking down beside him, she choked back tears and searched until she felt warm wetness at the base of his skull. He stirred and moaned as she touched the swelling wound, his eyelashes flickering.

There was a sound of clattering metal, seeming to come from the kitchen. Someone was leaving the house. Addie looked in the direction of the sound and stood up, hardly aware of what she was doing. Gasping for breath, she ran to the upstairs bedrooms, ignoring the sounds of the family waking and stirring in their rooms. Cade's door opened, and Caroline's, and sleepy voices were asking her what was the matter, what had happened, but she didn't speak or stop to look at them. She went to Russell's room and went inside, leaving the door half-open. Although the room was dark, she could see the gleam of his eyes as he lay on his side.

"Daddy?"

He didn't answer. The threat of tears passed as everything inside went cold. Moving to the dresser, Addie tried to light the lamp, but she was trembling too badly. Biting her lower lip until it hurt, she tried again, and the soft glow of a flame filled the room. As she turned back to the bed, she saw Russell's body frozen in a convulsion, his face tinted blue-white even in the golden light of the lamp. It was obvious without going any closer that it was too late to revive him. Something deeper than grief spread through her, more hurtful than any kind of pain she'd ever felt. She'd let it happen to him. Stumbling against the wall, she buried her face in her arms and clenched her fists.

"Adeline?" She heard Cade's voice near the door. The sound caused her to move quickly, blocking him before he got close enough to the doorway to see what had happened.

"Where's Mama?" she asked, her eyes as dark as coal.

"Seeing to Ben downstairs," he replied, bewildered. "He's just coming to. Someone knocked him out. What's happening, Adeline? Why do you look so funny? Why isn't Daddy—"

"Hush!" Thoughts swooped in and out of her mind, faster than she could catch hold of them. She had to force herself to concentrate. "Go to the bunkhouse and find someone to help you get the sheriff."

"I can go alone—"

"I don't want you going alone. Now, leave, and be quick. And tell Peter to keep Mama and Caro away from this room. And Robbie Keir is outside. He's been hurt. Tell Mama to see to him after she's through with Ben."

Cade nodded in a businesslike manner, but the tremble of his lower lip spoiled the effect. "Why isn't Daddy up? What's wrong? Something's happened to him, hasn't it?"

"Yes." She couldn't give him sympathy or tell him gently, or they would both fall apart. "He's dead."

His soft brown eyes went blank, then brimmed close to overflowing. "No. He can't be. Oh, Ad—"

"Don't," she said sharply, knowing that if he broke down, she'd fall into pieces. "Not now. Act like a man, Cade. I need you to help me." He shuddered and pressed his fists into his eye sockets, getting control of himself. "Hurry," Addie said, and went back into the room, closing the door. Drawing near the bed, she looked into Russell's staring eyes, reached out and closed them with her fingertips. Her face twisted as she saw the thin steel cord embedded in his neck. It was from Ben's guitar. She had to get it off him before May saw, before anyone saw. As she extended a hand to the bloodied string, she felt a shudder go through her insides, and she wrapped her arms around her middle, staring at Russell's body. *I can't . . . I can't touch him again.*

It was too grisly. But it had to be done. She took

hold of the cord and began to pry it away, breathing through her mouth to avoid the smell of death. It hurt more than she could have imagined to have him die this way. He hadn't deserved this, a death so ignominious for such a proud man. The circumstances, and her responsibility, made it more painful than when Leah had died. *I can't think about that yet,* she thought, her self-control faltering. She would have to break the news to Ben, and to Caro and Peter. But she didn't want to be the one to tell May. She couldn't look her mother in the face and tell her. Someone else could do it.

The doorknob turned, and May stood in the doorway without moving. An immaculate golden braid trailed over her shoulder, almost reaching the belt of her tiny-waisted robe. She looked incredibly fragile, her face chiseled out of ivory, her face etched with lines Addie had never noticed before. Cade must have told her. Addie let go of the cord and turned to keep her from coming any closer. Before anyone could see Russell, she had to clear the room of the evidence planted to frame Ben.

"Mama—"

"Leave me alone with him."

Addie moistened her dry lips. "Mama, I need a few minutes to . . ."

Like a sleepwalker, May went to the bed, not looking at her. Addie fell back a few steps. "He . . . he was murdered," she said helplessly.

May ignored her and knelt by Russell's body, her back perfectly straight.

Slowly Addie backed away and went out into the hallway, her mind spinning. There was no time to fix things now. She would have to let the guitar string remain where it was, and provide an alibi for Ben. It would have to be enough to protect him.

The house was quiet except for the muffled sounds

coming from Caro's bedroom. Ben was nowhere to be seen. Addie guessed he was outside with Robbie Keir. Walking to the stairs on trembling legs, she headed to Russell's office, where she was certain she'd find a bottle of whiskey. Maybe a drink would help to steady her nerves and stop her from shaking. She whirled around like a scalded cat as Caro's door burst open and Peter stepped out, his eyes wild.

"It's Caroline," he said in panic. "She's having pains. The baby—"

"Did her water break?" Addie asked, and he went scarlet, opening and closing his mouth like a fish. Either he didn't know or was too embarrassed to tell her. Irritation rose in her throat, and it was all she could do to keep from snapping at him. "You'd better go get Dr. Haskin," she said, brushing by him and going into Caro's room.

Caroline was curled up on her side, holding her stomach and biting her lip in agony.

"Caro?" At the sound of Addie's voice Caroline began to sob uncontrollably. "Caro, has there been any bleeding?" Addie took hold of her shoulders and repeated the question, her hands biting into Caroline's upper arms. The pain of Addie's grip seemed to break through her fear. She stared up at Addie, the flood of tears slowing a little. "Yes, some bleeding. And labor pains . . . but it's too soon . . . it's too soon for . . ." she broke off and gave a little moan, her face filmy with perspiration. "My water just broke," she whispered. "It's too soon."

She was having a miscarriage. Addie read the terror in her eyes and knew a moment of panic before an unnatural calm came over her. "I'm going to get some more pillows to prop you up," she said, "and a few other things. I'll be right back."

"I want Mama here. Get her . . . please."

"She'll be here in just a few minutes. And Peter's on his way to get the doctor right now."

Caroline closed her eyes, her eyelashes trembling against her cheeks. She writhed with a contraction. "Adeline . . ." she gasped. "Is he really dead?"

Something inside Addie twisted in anguish. "Yes, Caro," she said softly.

"Adeline, I don't want to die. I'm so afraid. I think . . . I think I'm going to die too."

It was hard for Addie to suppress a wave of helpless anger. All she wanted to do was find a private corner and cry. Hadn't enough happened tonight without this too? She didn't want to bear up under any more disaster. She didn't want to be strong for Caroline when she needed all her strength for herself.

Then she was horrified at her thoughts. How selfish she was. "You're not going to die," she said. "Don't waste your energy worrying about ridiculous things." Her voice was full of remorse, but it was doubtful Caroline heard her. Addie flew out of the room and ran to Russell's door, flinging it open madly. Startled, May looked up with her hands still clasped in prayer. "Caro's having her baby," Addie said hoarsely. "She needs you there."

May blinked and spoke as if in a dream. "She's upset because of Russ—"

"It's more than being upset. Her water broke, and she's bleeding. She's having labor pains. Stay with her while I find some things to clean up the bed with." She left without waiting for an answer, and nearly ran into Leah, who was standing in the middle of the hall- way.

"What's the matter with Mama?" the little girl asked, her eyes wide and her lips white.

"Leah, honey, go to bed." There was no use lying to her. "Your Mama's having the baby. You must stay in your room and keep out of the way."

Even at a tender age Leah had overheard enough conversations about childbirth to know it was often mentioned in the same breath as pain and death. To an observant child who'd heard the horror stories women liked to tell of their trials in labor, the mysterious condition of pregnancy was something dangerous and fearful.

"Is she going to—"

"She's going to be just fine," Addie said swiftly, giving her a push in the direction of her room. "Now, go, and don't get out of bed again."

11

THEY GAVE CAROLINE ENOUGH LAUDANUM TO TAKE the edge off the pain, but she still knew what was happening. The past months of discomfort, joy, and anticipation were coming to an abrupt end. Addie knew Caro's physical pain hardly compared to the emotional anguish of knowing she was losing the baby. It took Peter almost four hours to find Dr. Haskin, who was on another call, and bring him to the ranch. Addie suffered every minute of that time, silently cursing the doctor for not being there.

May sat by the bedside, calm but a little blank, slow to answer questions or to say anything at all. Instinctively Caroline turned to Addie for help, clutching her hand when in pain, asking her to talk when she needed distraction. Addie worked ceaselessly to keep her as comfortable as possible, bathing the sweat off her face, rearranging the mountain of pillows when Caroline's back hurt, changing the towels they had placed underneath her hips.

Addie was only dimly conscious of what was going on outside the small room. She was aware that long ago the sheriff had arrived and Ben had taken him up to Russell's room, that there were strangers' feet walking up and down the stairs, and men's voices outside as the ranch was awakened by the news of Russell Warner's murder.

Finally Cade knocked on the door to signal that the

doctor had arrived. Wearily Addie went downstairs to meet him, heedless of the blood on her dress or her straggling, hastily tied-back hair. She started in astonishment at the sight of Doc Haskin. She'd been expecting an old man with a shock of silver hair, crinkly eyes, and a weather-lined face. Slim shoulders, slightly stooped. A man who shuffled slightly when he walked. That was the Doc Haskin she had known all her life.

The man in front of her was young, well-built, and dark-haired, probably only a year or two older than Caroline. His face was strong, his gaze clear and direct. but he had the same shaggy eyebrows as the old Dr. Haskin she'd known, and the same comforting smile. She half-expected him to ask after Aunt Leah's health, before she remembered Leah wasn't her aunt anymore.

"D-Doc Haskin," she stammered, and he smiled briefly at her as they started up the stairs.

"It's been a long time since I've seen you, Miss Adeline. A year or two, at least."

Try fifty, she wanted to say, but held her tongue.

"Pete couldn't tell me much about your sister," he continued, and he was so blessedly calm she wanted to weep in relief at having someone there who knew what to do. "Has she gone into labor?"

"She's had the baby," Addie blurted out. "Stillborn. But no afterbirth."

"Has she retained all of it or just part?"

"I think all of it," she said, grasping the stair railing as she felt herself sway. Doc Haskin's steadying hand was on her shoulder.

"Why don't you go somewhere and rest?" he suggested gently. "I'll take care of her now."

Would it be deserting Caroline, not to go back to that room? Addie hesitated, her forehead creased with misery. She couldn't go back and face May's blank eyes any longer, or Caroline's suffering. She had to be somewhere quiet for a few minutes or go insane.

"Maybe I will rest a little while," she whispered. "Please see to Mama too. I'm worried about her."

"I will. And Miss Adeline . . . I'm sorry about your father."

Slowly Addie went down the steps, keeping hold of the railing. The sense of being small and ineffectual came over her, and she was too tired to fight it. A thirst welled up from inside, a desperate need to see Ben. He would hold her in his arms and let her lean on him as long as she needed. Only he could assure her that the world hadn't gone mad.

There was a murmur of voices from Russell's office. Silently Addie drew closer to the half-closed door, her ears pricking at the mention of Russell's name. The voices belonged to Ben and Sam Dary, the sheriff, and one or two others she couldn't identify.

". . . I agree," Ben was saying, his voice weary. "No horse was used. Whoever did it was on foot, and possibly still is—"

"We have a coupla men out lookin'. He couldna gotten far. If he ain't in the bunkhouse. Most likely we're lookin' for one of your own, Ben."

"The boys swear they didn't notice anyone coming or going out all night. And we've got a lot of light sleepers in there."

"Robbie Keir swears he didn't see who hit him. You got any idea?"

"No. I was hit from behind as I went in the house."

"That is a puzzle," Dary murmured. "Someone who knew his way around the ranch, even the main house."

"It's possible it was someone who—"

"Ben," Dary interrupted, and this time his voice was quieter, "it's time to git down to business. M' boys found some evidence in your cabin and in Mr. Warner's room. It's all pointin' in one direction."

"And what direction is that?" Ben asked softly.

"Seems t' me you're hidin' somethin', Ben."

"The hell I am. I've given you the go-ahead to search the whole goddamn ranch, including the bunkhouse and my cabin. You're welcome to make use of anything you find."

"Then what d' you have t' ay 'bout Russ bein' strangled with one of the strings from your guitar?"

"*What?*" Ben sounded stunned.

"Yessir, it was a guitar string, an' it matches up with one missin' from the one in your cabin."

Addie could stand it no longer. She strode into the room. Ben was facing a half-circle formed by the sheriff and two other men. In two steps she reached Ben's side.

"That proves nothing," she said hotly. "Anyone could have taken it from his room. People swarm all over this ranch from sunup to sundown."

Ben stared down at her with silent warning. His expression was implacable, but his face was pale under his tan, the only indication of how the news had affected him. None of the rest moved or spoke, astonished by her interruption, appalled by her audacity in interfering with men's business. Sam Dary gathered his wits and made an effort to smile at her.

"Miss Adeline, we're all real sorry 'bout what happened to your pa. But we're fixin' to git to the bottom of all this, soon as we can. Now, why don't you run along an' don't worry your little head 'bout—"

"My head isn't little, and neither is my mind. And I have a valid interest in all this, considering the fact that it was *my* father who was murdered, and *my* fiancé you're trying to—"

"Adeline," Ben said, his hand closing around her upper arm in a biting grip that belied his pleasant tone.

348

"The sheriff is only trying to get at the truth. We have no quarrel with that, do we?"

"But—" she started, and fell silent as his eyes flashed dangerously.

"Ben," Dary said, sounding almost apologetic, "she don't need to be here. Would you tell her to—"

"She won't be a problem." Ben gave Addie a meaningful glance. "In fact, you won't make another sound, will you, honey?"

"No," she said with sudden meekness, willing to promise anything as long as she was allowed to stay.

"Go on," Ben said calmly, turning to the sheriff. "Just pretend she isn't here."

"Well, ah . . . well . . . oh, yes . . ." Dary fished in his pocket and pulled out a small pouch, opened it, and shook the contents into his palm. Addie drew closer, peering at the small object that had rolled out. It was a small, distinctively shaped shirt button, dull gray and metallic. A tiny pattern of scrolls was engraved on the steel surface.

"It's a button from one of my shirts," Ben said quietly.

"You sure?" Dary asked.

"I'm sure. They come from a small place in Chicago, where I had some shirts made a couple of years ago."

"It was found on the floor, right by the . . ." Dary paused and looked at Addie before finishing. ". . . by the bed. One of the shirts in your cabin was missin' a button, and the rest of 'em were just this kind."

"He's being framed," Addie burst out. "Someone could have taken the button and put it by Russell to make it look like Ben—"

"Addie," Ben interrupted, and despite the seriousness of the situation, his mouth twitched with a faint smile. Although Addie had given a promise to keep quiet, there'd been no doubt in his mind she would break it.

"They know you're too smart to leave incriminating evidence behind," she persisted. "Especially your own guitar string! And how do they explain that lump on your head? Someone hit you pretty hard. They certainly can't think you did that to yourself. And besides, I heard someone leaving the house the moment I found Ben. Check around back—I know you'll find footprints there, and—"

"Possible he had a partner who turned on him," Dary commented laconically.

"That's absurd!" Addie exploded, and prepared to say more, but Ben interrupted her.

"One more word of your defense, darlin', and they'll probably take me out and hang me on the nearest tree. Why don't you go make some coffee?"

"I'm not leaving you," she said stubbornly.

"No need," Dary said, his forehead divided with a grave frown. "Only one more question, Ben. If the man who murdered Russ Warner was so quiet the folks in the house didn't wake up, how'd you know somethin' was wrong?"

Ben looked at him expressionlessly. "I had a feeling."

Addie trembled, wanting to cry out and defend him. *It was me. I told him!*

"Any way you c'n prove you were in your cabin at the time Russ was killed?"

"Yes," Addie said swiftly, knowing Ben would not implicate her even if it meant hanging for it. She was the only one who could provide him with an alibi. "Just ask me. I was in his cabin with him. All night."

Dary turned crimson, looking away from her. Addie kept her eyes steadily on him, ignoring Ben's hard stare. Dary seemed to be choking with embarrassment. Finally he looked at Ben. "That true, Ben?"

"Tell him the truth, Ben," Addie said.

Ben's green eyes snapped with anger. "Keep it under your hats, if at all possible," he said, his mouth twisting. "I don't want her reputation dragged through the mud."

But they all knew it was too late for that. The whole town would be delighted and scandalized by the story. Russell Warner, strangled in his own bed while his daughter slept with the foreman. There was no way anyone could keep that under his hat for long.

There wasn't reason for the sheriff and his men to stay after that. Ben saw them to the door and went back into the office, where Addie had found a bottle of whiskey and a glass.

"Don't stop pouring," Ben said, and she smiled wanly.

"There's only one glass." She took a swallow and handed the glass to Ben with a gasp as the whiskey seared the inside of her throat. He lifted it to his lips and followed suit. After a moment he sighed, closing his eyes.

"I could've used this a few hours ago."

"Is it going to help?" she asked dully, and took back the glass before he could answer.

"How's Caroline?"

She took a deeper swallow of the liquor this time. "I'm not sure."

"The baby?"

"Dead." Addie stared into the whiskey, her fingertips whitening. "The baby wasn't supposed to die," she said, more to herself than him. "She was supposed to live, and grow up to have a daughter of her own someday—"

"Addie, what are you talking about?"

"I should have saved him," she continued, the glass trembling in her hand. "That's why I came back. That's why I'm here. But what could I do to stop it? I tried to warn him. I tried to change things, and it all happened anyway, just like before—''

''Addie,'' Ben interrupted softly, taking the drink away and setting it down on the desk. He pulled her body against his warm, hard chest, her chatter muffled by his cotton shirt. ''Shhh. You're not making sense.''

She slumped against him in exhaustion. ''I'm so tired.'' Tears of grief rolled down her cheeks. ''I'm so tired, Ben . . .''

''I know you are,'' he murmured, smoothing down the wild locks of her hair, caressing her aching shoulders and back. ''I know what you've been through tonight. You need to sleep.''

''And your h-head . . . there's no bandage or—''

''I'm just fine,'' he reassured her swiftly. ''I didn't need one.''

''It can't have happened again,'' she choked, clutching at his shirt. ''I should've stopped it—''

''Again? What are you talking about?'' Ben asked, perplexed. ''Russ?''

''The Johnsons were behind it. You know that.''

His face changed, and he looked cold and thin-lipped—whether from anger or pain, she couldn't tell. ''There's no proof yet. But I'll find it.''

''They wanted you both gone, you and Daddy. But I saved you this time. They didn't count on that—''

''What do you mean, 'this time'?''

She ignored his question, her eyes fixed blankly on the window. ''They'll still be after you. Jeff hates you, and Big George wants the ranch as well as the water rights. You're the only thing standing in the way.''

Ben's gaze was sharp. ''What did Jeff say to you in town that day? You've been suspecting something like this would happen. How did you know what had happened tonight before anyone else did?''

Her lashes lowered as she sought to conceal her sudden leaping guilt ''I didn't know for certain. I've been worried about Daddy for so long, and I . . . just felt like something was wrong when we were in the cabin. I can't explain why. But it doesn't matter . . . I was too late.'' She didn't move a muscle as she leaned against him, some part of her mind waiting to feel him go tense with suspicion, waiting for him to hold himself away from her the smallest fraction of an inch. But he didn't move or betray his thoughts in any way. His fingers drifted through her hair, lightly stroking her scalp. She was lulled by the soothing touch. Her eyelids drooped heavily, eyelashes almost brushing her cheeks.

Feeling Addie's body begin to slacken, Ben sighed and brushed a tear off her cheek with his knuckle. "I'll walk you upstairs. You need to rest."

"I can't sleep—"

"Doc Haskin can give you a sedative. You're entitled to it."

"I don't want to go upstairs," she said, her voice cracking. "I don't want to go near that room where . . . Don't try to make me."

"I won't, I won't" he murmured, hunting for a handkerchief as she began to cry again. He located a crumpled wad of cotton in the back pocket of his jeans. "I'll sleep on the parlor sofa with the light on—"

"Whatever you want, darlin'."

"I'm sorry." She gulped, taking the handkerchief and wiping her nose. "I'll be strong tomorrow. I'll help you. Oh, God, there's so much to do."

"We'll get through it."

Her mind was jumping from one thought to another in a random pattern. "Ben, it was one of our own men who—"

"Yes. Most likely. But if I ever hear you say it again, I'll skin you alive. Rumors and accusations are going to fly fast enough as it is. We'll know more tomorrow, after the boys have been questioned."

"By the sheriff?"

"And me."

"What about the will?" she whispered. "Daddy never drew up the new one. That lawyer from the East didn't arrive in time. What's going to happen to the ranch and the family?"

"Russ did write a new one as soon as the fence-cutting trouble started, just in case something happened before the lawyer got here. He didn't want anyone to know. Pete and I were witnesses."

"He left . . . everything . . . in your hands?"

Ben nodded silently, his eyes locking with hers.

"Will it hold up?" she asked.

"It's not sewn up as neatly as the lawyer would have done it . . . but yes, I think it'll hold up."

A terrible sense of irony struck her. Then the old Adeline would never have won. The money would never have been hers anyway. It would still have been put in trust. And the Johnsons wouldn't win either, because Addie would stand fast by the alibi she'd provided for Ben. True, there were suspicions about Ben in the sheriff's mind, but suspicions wouldn't prove he had killed Russell. The only evidence that existed was circumstantial. The question was, would the Johnsons go to extra lengths to get Ben out of the way now?

"I'm afraid for you," she said in a low voice, and Ben gave her a humorless smile.

"Don't be. There's no need." But his confidence frightened her, as if he were thumbing his nose at the designs of fate.

Russell's funeral was short and efficient, the way he would have wanted it. He was buried on Warner land, in the family plot. The simple white marker would be replaced later by an elaborately carved marble one. Although only family members and ranch hands were allowed at the graveside service, there was an endless river of callers for days afterward, people pouring in from distant counties to pay their respects. Everyone had a story to tell about some favor Russell had done for him. It seemed he was owned thousands of favors.

Since Caro was bedridden and May grief-stricken, Addie was the only family member able to take visitors out to the grave site. Back and forth she trudged with the callers, wishing she could tell them how much easier everything would be for her if they'd just stayed at home and sent letters of condolence. It was a surprise when Ruthie and Harlan Johnson showed up as representatives of the Johnson clan, their faces strained with anxiety as Addie opened the door to let them in. They half-expected to be turned away. Big George or Jeff wouldn't have been let on the ranch at all.

Addie received the couple with as much graciousness as she could muster. Only one tense moment occurred, when Ben, who'd been informed of the callers, strode into the house, his manner deceptively relaxed. Harlan had asked diffidently about trying again to negotiate an agreement about the water rights, causing Ben's eyes to turn cold. "You tell Big George," he said softly, "that Russell's death won't make any difference in the way this ranch is run."

Finally the number of visitors slowed to a trickle, and Addie had more time to take care of the housework. May spent most of her time sleeping in her room or taking care of Caroline, leaving the running of the house to Addie, who had never suspected how difficult it was to oversee the cleaning and cooking, the washing and ironing, the hundreds of details that had to be taken care of. She also found time to help Ben with the overload of business correspondence. She wanted to know as much as possible about their circumstances now. Ben had been appointed executor of the will and would manage all the financial concerns of the Warners and the Sunrise Cattle Company. Upon his mar-

riage to Addie, he would jointly own Sunrise with the
rest of Russell's children.

It was the opinion of everyone in the country that
the marriage couldn't take place quickly enough. Addie was annoyed by the prudish streak in the towns-
people, who had such earthy ways it was difficult to
believe her affair with Ben was causing such a commotion. "You'd think we were the first couple ever to
sleep together before their wedding night," she had
complained to Ben, adding that their engagement
should have been enough to satisfy others' sense of
propriety. "For heaven's sake, after all Mama's been
through, people won't let her alone for asking about
when we're going to get married, and whether or not
she thinks we sneak off when no one's looking."

Ben was amused by Addie's self-righteous airs.
Nevertheless, he too insisted on having the wedding a
short time from now, in two weeks. That was nothing
even close to a decent interval of mourning for Russell, but Addie would be branded a scarlet woman if
they waited longer. As things were now, most people
preferred to think of her as an innocent girl who'd
been taken advantage of, which suited Ben just fine.
He'd rather be regarded as a debaucher of virtue by all
of Texas than have a single thing said against Addie.
As for sneaking off together, there was no question of
that. They each wrestled with private demons. Making
love was a pleasure neither of them felt entitled to,
and even if they'd had the inclination, there were eyes
upon the two of them at all times.

The routines around the ranch were the same as
they'd always been. Work on the fence continued, including repairs made to the new places that had been
cut. Cade and Leah went to school every day. Addie
found some comfort in the amount of work she had to
do. She liked the feeling of being useful and needed,
and was glad that May seemed to have little interest

in assuming her old responsibilities. To the rest of the family, life seemed curiously similar to what it had been before, and though they felt Russell's absence keenly, their world had not fallen apart with his death. Ben had taken the reins in hand, managing the ranch with apparent ease. His authority was well-established, and the support of the ranch hands was unfaltering, as it always was in times of trouble.

The family turned to Ben in the same ways they had turned to Russell, whether it concerned money, family, or personal matters. Although he'd refused to take Russell's place at the table, they all recognized him as the head of the family now. May mentioned to Ben that she wanted Russell's bed taken out of the house, and the next day it was gone, hacked to pieces and burned by the superstitious cowhands. Addie gave Ben lists of supplies needed for the kitchen, and a boy was dispatched immediately to the General Store. The porcelain face of Leah's doll cracked when she dropped it, and Ben gave her a dollar to buy a new one. They all relied on him without a second thought, casually adding their problems to the burdens he already carried. It seldom crossed anyone's mind that he might be mourning for Russell in his own way.

Only Addie understood the extent of Ben's grief and sense of loss. She'd been copying a letter in Russell's office the afternoon Ben had walked in with an absentminded look on his face. Suddenly he froze as he met her eyes, looking startled to see her there. He was the first to speak.

"I wasn't thinking," he said slowly. "I just walked into the house with a question for Russ. I forgot he wasn't here." And he stood looking at her silently, amazed at himself.

"I forget sometimes too," she said.

Ben swallowed hard, nodding briefly. Addie recognized his expression. It was the same one she'd worn as she'd looked into the mirror for the first time after waking up in another world, when she'd realized part of her life was gone forever. *That's one thing I'll never have to be afraid of again,* she thought grimly. *I know what it's like to lose everything, and I know that somehow I got through it. That must mean I'll get through all of this too.* Wordlessly she stood up and held out her arms to Ben, wanting to help ease his pain. He was not the kind to ask for comfort, but she would always offer, even if he decided to turn away from her.

Ben's face was strained. His mind was clouded with confusion. Long ago he had sworn never to rely on a woman he loved, never in this way. Enjoy her, pleasure her, take what she was willing to give, but never give her this power over him. And yet, hadn't he already taken that extra step, that one step too many? Addie's eyes were filled with knowledge of him, the secrets he had told her, the understanding he'd allowed her to have of him as a man. All of it he had given to her as if it had been her right. Now he was independent no longer. There were moments such as this when he realized the hold she had on him, and for a split second he wanted to break away from her.

"I know you're hurting," she said gently. "So am I. Don't turn away, Ben."

Before he could stop himself, he'd gone to her. He buried his face in her hair, his hands flexing convulsively in the loose material of her dress sleeves. The blessed, aching relief of it made his eyes and nose sting. His voice was hoarse as he sought to unburden his heart.

"I didn't know him for long. But he was more of a father to me than . . ." The rest of the sentence was choked off.

Addie stroked his dark head tenderly. "He loved you. He thought of you as a son."

"If only I'd known what was happening, I could have saved him. I should have—"

"All of us feel that way. His family was only a few doors away. Don't you think Cade blames himself for not having heard something? And me . . . oh, you can't imagine the things I wish I'd done." Addie felt much more responsible for Russell's death than Ben ever could. She'd known about it beforehand but still couldn't stop it. And that was a secret she would have to bear alone for the rest of her life.

Ben gave a shuddering sigh and squared his jaw, dragging a sleeve across his wet eyes.

"Don't blame yourself," Addie said, laying her cheek against his fast-beating heart, her arms wrapped around his waist. "He'd be mad if he knew you did."

And Ben allowed himself to hold her a few minutes more. In the back of his mind he knew he should have been overcome with shame, having given in to unmanly tears in front of a woman. But Addie was different from all others. There were no conditions to her love. He could trust her with his private thoughts, his deepest feelings. Finally he understood the real reason for wanting her as his wife. Not for the sake of propriety or passion, not for children, for the ranch, or even for a place to belong.

As a boy he had idealized love; as a man he had searched for it. And now that he'd found it, it was different from what he'd expected, more demanding, more vital, constantly changing. The bonds that tied him to her were stronger than steel chains, but within them there was perfect freedom. It was that way for both of them.

Caroline and Peter planned to leave with Leah after the wedding, as soon as Caroline was well enough to travel. May had decided to go with them to North Carolina, since most of her family and old friends were there. She'd made no mention of whether or not she intended to come back to Texas someday, but Addie suspected she would never return. Cade had opted to stay at the ranch for a while, until he was more certain of what he wanted.

The sheriff and his deputies finished questioning the ranch hands about what they might have seen or heard the night of Russell's murder, and they came up with no new information, no answers that threw any light on what had happened. Ben allowed his frustration to surface after they'd left, pacing around the ranch office and smoking cigarettes, crushing them out after only a few puffs. Addie's first inclination when she went in to talk to him was to sprawl comfortably in a chair, but the bothersome arrangement of skirts, small bustle, and petticoats forced her to sit upright in a stiff-backed, ladylike manner.

The air was stale with smoke. Leaning over, she struggled to open a window without getting up. Ben cursed under his breath and did it for her, and she made a face as she waved ineffectually at the air.

"Are you going to make a habit of this?" she asked. "I liked the smell of Daddy's cigars much better."

Ben stubbed out a cigarette and raked a hand through his dark hair. "I might not have enough time to develop a habit," he said curtly.

"Meaning?"

"Meaning that if I'm not dry-gulched by some well-meaning vigilante committee soon, I'll probably be taken out and hanged by the sheriff and a posse, nice and legal. I'm the most likely suspect. Everyone knows it."

"But I've provided your alibi. I said you were with me that night."

He shook his head, scowling morosely. "They think you're lying to protect me."

Addie sighed and pressed her palms to her temples,

desperate to remember the name she'd given to Jeff. Inside her mind somewhere was the truth. She closed her eyes and pressed harder, wishing she could squeeze out the memory. But her returning memories were infrequent and almost always incomplete.

"It's one of our own men," she said, curling her fingers into her hair as if she would tug it out, disheveling the perfectly coiffed braids. "Surely one of them knows something, or suspects something. Why isn't anyone saying anything? They wouldn't really protect one of their own even if he was a murderer, would they?"

"I don't know," Ben muttered, beginning to pace again. "I wouldn't have thought so."

Later that evening, as the family sat down to dinner in the main house, Ben strode in with a distracted expression. They all glanced up at him as he looked at Addie and spoke quietly.

"I've got some business to take care of. I might be gone until morning."

Addie's skin prickled with awareness. Something had happened. "Anything serious?" she asked with forced calm, and he shrugged.

"I won't know until later."

Slowly Addie took the napkin from her lap and put it on the table. "I'll walk you to the door," she said, darting a cautious glance at May, who offered no objection. As soon as they left the room, Addie clung to his arm. His muscles were taut. "What is it?" she whispered anxiously.

"One of the boys admitted to having seen one of the beds in the bunkhouse empty during the night of the murder."

"Whose?"

"Watts's."

"But . . . but he's taken me and Caro to town lots

of times, and you had him watch over the house so many nights while we were all asleep—"

"I can't prove he's the one. It's only a suspicion."

Addie took a deep breath and held on to his arm more tightly. "Where are you going now?" she whispered.

"To visit his sister."

"But . . . she's a prostitute."

"Hell, Addie, I'm not going to bed her. I'm just going to ask her some questions."

"She's not going to tell you anything to implicate her own brother, even if she knows something. Oh, Ben, I don't like this at all—"

"She's just a girl. A girl who likes money." He frowned as he looked down at her, prying his arm loose from her grasp. "And I don't have much to lose by visiting with her. In the meantime, don't worry about Watts. He's staying far away from the house in a line shack tonight, guarding the edge of the property."

"Ben," Addie said, her forehead furrowed, "she might try to get you to sleep with her. I know you and I haven't been together lately, but—"

"Oh, good Lord." Ben laughed suddenly. "If you think there's a danger of the two of us . . ." He continued to laugh, shaking his head as he went out the door. "For your sake, I'll do my best to control myself." She scowled as she watched him go, wondering what he thought was so funny.

In the cowboy's lingo, an especially dirty saloon or dance hall was called a dive. The place where Jennie Watts worked, the Do-Drop-In, deserved a new word all its own. It was filthy and noisy, the floors sticky, the customers raucous, the music boisterous. Ben ambled in and ordered a drink, discovering shortly thereafter that the cheap whiskey deserved its nickname of "rotgut." Ben drank sparingly, eyeing the fleshy girls and their skimpy clothes until he saw a bosomy dark-haired girl whose face reminded him of Watts. Lightly he caught her arm, and she automatically raised a hand to swing at him until she saw his face. Then she put the upraised hand to her hair, smoothing the stray wisps back as she smiled at him.

"Hey, han'some."

"Are you Jennie Watts?" It was unorthodox to ask someone's name. Part of the unwritten code was to wait until a stranger decided to identify himself—or herself. But this was a whore, and she couldn't afford to be offended too easily.

"Jennie's busy. But I'm not."

"Where is she?"

The girl frowned a little. "Upstairs. Don't know when she'll come down, neither."

He gave her a cajoling smile and slipped a few dollars into her hand. "Will this help you remember to tell me when she does?"

She smiled saucily, her palm closing around the money. "Maybe." She wiggled her backside enticingly as she walked off, causing Ben to submerge a grin in his drink. It was only a few minutes later that she returned to nudge him with her elbow while carrying a tray of empty glasses. He looked at the narrow stairs leading to the upstairs rooms and saw a girl just reaching the bottom step. She was young, thin and hard-faced, with exotic blue eyes set against strikingly pale skin. In a few strides he was at her side.

"Pardon me . . . Jennie Watts?"

She glanced up at him through adult eyes in a child's face, and the combination made him vaguely uneasy. "Why do you want to know?" she asked, surprisingly deep-voiced.

"If you are, I'd like a few minutes of your time."

"You want to dance first?"

"No, I—"

"Then come on." She turned and went upstairs, leaving him to follow. They went into a small, sparsely furnished room where the air reeked of sex and liquor. Ben glanced at the unmade bed and stained sheets, his eyes expressionless. The girl sat on the corner of the bed and began to unbutton the front of her dress.

"Wait," Ben said, and she paused, her eyes cold as they rested on him.

"You want it with my dress on?"

"I just want to talk."

Jennie swore under her breath and stood up, pointing to the door. "Get out."

He pulled out a few bills, holding them between his first two fingers. "I intend to pay for your time."

Leisurely she walked over to the small table by the bed and lit a cigarette, regarding him through a haze of smoke. She didn't ask who he was. It didn't matter as long as his money was green.

"What do you want to talk about?" she asked.

"Your brother."

She hesitated, then gave a short nod. "Yeah?"

"You seen him lately? Talked to him?"

"Maybe."

"Has he come into any money lately? Maybe even asked you to keep it for him?"

She looked at him silently, lifting the cigarette to her lips and taking a long drag. She had something worthwhile to tell.

"I have great respect for family loyalty," Ben continued, looking at her intently. "But it has been known to come with a price tag." He made a move to reach for his wallet again, then paused, waiting for her answer.

"Don't everything?" And she watched with an appraising gleam in her blue eyes as he tossed a wad of bills onto the bed.

GIVE ME TONIGHT

* * *

Addie curled up in the corner of the slickly uphol-
stered parlor sofa, feet tucked underneath her. The
house was hushed as the family slumbered upstairs,
the only sound the methodical ticking of the clock. An
unread book was spread open in her lap. Occasionally
she would turn a page, her hands compelled to do
something. She looked up as she heard quiet feet on
the stairs, and saw Cade enter the room, dressed in
his cotton nightshirt and a pair of worn-out breeches.
He looked tired and grumpy, his feet dragging as he
walked over to the sofa and flopped down at the other
end.

"What're you waitin' up for?" he asked, smothering a yawn. "He said he wouldn't be back till
mornin'."

"I don't feel like sleeping. Why aren't you in bed?"

"I keep wakin' up, thinkin' I heard a noise." He
closed his eyes, resting his head on the back of the
sofa.

"Cade?"

"Hmm?" he grunted, his eyes still closed.

"I'm glad you're not going to North Carolina with
the others. It's nice having you around."

His mouth turned down at the corners in a surly
expression, as was his habit whenever confronted by
sentiment. "I'm not gonna stay here forever."

Addie smiled slightly. "I know, Cade."

She closed her eyes too, lulled by the quiet and the
boy's presence, and gradually the book slid from her
lap onto the sofa as she let her head drop, too heavy
to support any longer. "Watts," she murmured to herself, her forehead aching as she pondered the name
and tried to remember, and slowly she was drifting,
drifting, her heartbeat slowing.

She was cuddled close to Jeff, caught up against the
side of his body, her slender fingers combing through

the mahogany hair on the back of his neck. Her mouth brushed close against the corner of his as she leaned closer. *"Help me with the name,"* he had urged.

Softly she whispered, her lips at his ear. *"Try George Watts. He'll do anything for money, anything. I'm sure of it."*

"And you're sure about the rest of it too?"

"Of course I am. We don't really have a choice, do we?" She kissed him sweetly, with a silent promise.

Addie moaned in her sleep, turning her head restlessly.

After leaving the saloon, Ben rode back to Sunrise, every coherent thought gone from his mind. Bloodlust burned in his stomach, dug into his sides like claws, driving him to push the horse to its limits. The ground raced beneath them, but the ride seemed too slow, sickeningly slow.

The wooden line shack was the only shape that broke the horizon, that and the ruins of the fence. Through the cracks between the boards came the light of a lamp turned low. Ben flung himself from the horse almost before it stopped. In a few steps he reached the door, bursting it open with the heel of his boot. A chair crashed to the floor as Watts snapped to his feet, a Colt .45 appearing in his hand. He started to lower it as he saw it was Ben, then instinctively checked the motion.

Ben was aware of the gun trained on him, but in his rage he hardly cared. "Why?" he demanded, breathing hard, his pulse drumming. "Was it just for the money? Did you bargain with them or take the first price they named? You bastard. Tell me why you did it!"

Watts met his eyes calmly. "Because they offered enough."

"And what other reason?"

surged through Ben, and he groped blindly as Watts strode past him to the door. He managed to catch hold of a booted heel, and clung with all his strength.

Stumbling, Watts landed on the floor with a thud. Ben rolled to avoid the swipe of Watts' free foot. The rickety building began to roar, roasting the two of them alive. They scrambled across the floor, grappling, grunting with pain. Watts tried to stagger to his feet and Ben hung on until they were both half-standing. For a split-second, Ben saw himself moving as if underwater. He tried to let go and stand on his own, but his reactions were too slow.

Raising his fist, Watts struck him on the jaw, sending him reeling to the doorway. The ceiling and walls folded in as if some giant foot had crushed the shack. Throwing an arm over his eyes, Ben stumbled outside and hit the ground, his body rolling once, twice before stopping.

It wasn't long before line riders and cowhands, alerted by the distant glow of fire, crowded on the scene with blankets, sacks and brooms, beating out grass fires. Left unchecked, a fire could race along miles of grazing land, covering entire counties, destroying property, killing men and livestock. Men came from both sides of the line to help, from Sunrise and the Double Bar. Ben regained consciousness slowly, watching with smoke-reddened eyes as the cowboys worked side by side, calling out warnings to each other. They succeeded in containing the fire to the shack, watching as it burned down to a pile of rubble and ashes.

The rest of the night passed in a haze. Although Ben had tended a number of gunshot wounds, he'd never experienced firsthand knowledge of them. As the bullet hole was pronounced clean and clumsily bandaged, it was all he could do to keep from snapping at the man who tended his shoulder to be more careful, the goddamn thing hurt worse than it looked. But complaining would have made him less of a man in their eyes, alienated their trust, so he kept his mouth shut except to down the whiskey they pressed on him. When they decided he'd had enough, he clambered up on his horse and slumped over the animal's neck as he was led back to the ranch house—an indignity, for someone else to have control of his reins, but better than being slung over the saddle like a sack of flour.

The entire Warner family was up by the time he was half-carried into the house. Addie's world had been suspended in motion from the moment she'd learned of the fire and knew Ben was probably in the middle of the commotion. She was frantic and relieved the moment she saw him. His clothes were bloody, his face haggard and soot-streaked. Every line of his body spoke of exhaustion and shock. She couldn't get words out of her mouth fast enough as she urged the men on either side of him to bring him into the parlor. As he slumped on the sofa, holding his head in his hands, she flew to the kitchen for a pair of scissors and the box of medical supplies, returning to find May fretting over the nicks the cowboys' spurs had left on the carpet and furniture legs.

Ben protested as Addie insisted on cutting away what was left of his shirt, cleaning his wound again and rebandaging it. Ignoring his muffled command to leave it alone, she tended his shoulder and washed his battered face. Eventually Ben went still under her hands, lulled by her gentle touch. Had May not been there, he would have pillowed his head in Addie's soft lap and gone to sleep. The idea was so tempting he considered using drunkenness as an excuse, but better judgment kept him from it.

"Addie," he said thickly, raising his hand to touch hers. "Watts . . ."

"I know." Her eyes were clear and serene as they

met his. He realized that somehow, the knowledge of Watts's death had lightened a burden on her shoulders. He wanted to tell her that it wasn't over yet, but the exhaustion was too strong to fight now.

"The rest . . . tomorrow."

Addie nodded in understanding. "Together," she said, and he shook his head wearily.

"No. No, Addie." Those were the last words he remembered before falling asleep, turning his face into the sofa cushion with a sigh.

Addie stayed with him for hours, ignoring May's remonstrances to go to bed. She knelt by him and stroked his black hair, her eyes wandering over him frequently to make sure he was really there. May dozed lightly in a large chair, waking to find Addie curled up close by Ben with a protective hand on his shoulder, her gaze fastened on his slumbering face.

"For goodness sake," May said, sounding annoyed, "you've been all over him ever since he was brought in. Let the poor man alone while he sleeps. Why do you have to watch over him as if he were a child?"

Addie looked up at her gravely. "He's been hurt," she said, leaving her hand where it was. "And he's mine."

Did she mean to imply Ben was actually in need of such outrageous pampering, or that the way she treated him was her own business? It was unclear to May. But she didn't offer another word of criticism, perhaps deciding Addie was as much an enigma as Russell had been, and there was no use trying to understand her. In the silence, an awareness came to the two women as they each thought over the short exchange.

Addie was no longer May's most dependent child, in need of spoiling and soothing and understanding. She was as much a woman as May, stronger in a perplexing way, more self-contained. It was not lost on the older woman that much of the difference had been made by the man sleeping on the sofa.

Ben was livid the next morning as he talked with the sheriff in Russell's office. "Dammit, Jennie told me straight out that Watts did it! He admitted it to her. He gave her the money to keep for him. I know she'd swear to it—"

"For nothin'?" Dary interrupted quietly, reading his answer in Ben's scowl. "No, I didn't think so. You'd have to pay her. Most folks will believe she'd say whatever she was paid to say. An' I'm not sure I wouldn't believe that too."

"The point is, she'll swear up and down Watts was paid by the Johnsons to murder Russell Warner."

"Anyone else hear his confession?"

"I did!"

"So . . ." Dary said, sighing and chewing on the end of a fat cigar, "We got your word and the word of a whore . . ." He paused and looked at Addie sheepishly. " 'Scuse me, ma'am. I meant—"

"I know what she is," Addie assured him dryly.

Dary turned again to Ben. "Your word and Jennie Watts's against the Johnsons'. An' no proof."

"I've already told you one of the hands saw his bunk empty the night of the murder."

"He mighta just gone out t' take a . . ." Dary paused and looked at Addie, clearing his throat. "T' relieve himself. 'Scuse me, ma'am."

"One look at Ben's shoulder is proof of what he claims," Addie said. "Why do you think Watts shot him? Because Ben found out the truth and confronted him with it."

"Or maybe it was just a cussin' match that got outta hand. Cowmen have been known to shoot each other with less reason."

"Dammit to hell. You're falling all over yourself to make excuses for him."

"Ben, I know how riled y'are. I know what you believe, an' I believe it too. But you can't convict a man without more evidence than we got. You know that."

Ben muttered something under his breath, staring out the window with hard green eyes.

"Tell you what I can do," Dary continued. "I'll take the Johnson boy t' my office in town and question him. And I'll have a talk with Big George, let him know the suspicions a whole lotta folks have 'bout him. The Johnsons are gonna lie for a long while, I c'n promise you that. It'll give y'all a chance to git back on your feet. They won't make trouble for you."

"We'd appreciate that," Addie said quickly, before Ben could reply.

"Alrighty," Dary replied, and picked up his hat. "Well, I'm gonna ride out to the shack an' take a look before goin' to the Double Bar. Ben—"

"I'll have one of the boys show you the way," Ben said, swallowing his frustration as best he could.

"I'd do more 'f I could, Ben."

"I know."

The two men shook hands, and Addie preceded them out of the office. She stood on the porch with Ben and watched the Sheriff ride off in the direction of the burned-down line shack. As she looked up at Ben's stiff-jawed profile, she understood how painful it was for him to have to sit back and do nothing, knowing the Johnsons would get a slap on the wrist.

"I know you feel helpless," she said quietly.

The words seemed to spur him into action. "Not for long." He settled his hat on his head and pulled the brim low over his eyes.

"Where are you going?"

"To pay the Johnsons a visit. Before Dary gets there."

"You mean you're going to settle the score," Addie

said in panic, following as he started to walk away. "Wait. I'm going with you." He wouldn't do anything rash or dangerous if she was with him.

Ben stopped and faced her. "No."

"You can't keep me from going. I'll follow you."

"You'll stay here if I have to tie you to a tree."

"Why not lock me in my room? I'll be less trouble to you that way. Or don't you remember what you told me that night about giving me freedom?"

"No. You're not going to win that way. This has nothing to do with that."

"I believed you when you said you wouldn't hold me back."

"*Dammit*, Addie—"

"I have a right to go. He was my father. And I was practically engaged to Jeff."

"I have to keep you safe—"

"What's the danger in this visit? What are you planning to do, brandish your guns and start shooting?"

He looked at her without saying anything, his face set with anger.

"Take me with you," she urged. "I won't say anything. But I have to be there. You're not the only one who has ghosts to put to rest. How can I face the future, always looking over my shoulder?" She went over and touched his hand, her eyes locked with his. "Don't leave me behind. My place is by your side."

For a moment she thought he would refuse her. But then his fingers closed around hers.

They weren't stopped by the Double Bar men as they rode over the property line and up to the Johnsons' main house. The sleeves of Addie's black dress fluttered in the breeze like banners. Respectfully the cowboys touched the brims of their hats as she rode by, and she wondered how many of them might have suspected the Johnsons were behind her father's murder.

When they reached the house, Ben helped Addie down from Jessie, his hands tightening around her waist. She threw him a quick, nervous smile. They walked up the steps and were met at the front door by Harlan, who was trying to conceal his anxiety.

"Mornin', Ben, Miss Adeline—"

"We're here to see Big George," Ben interrupted.

"Ben, I'm sorry t' tell you he's in the middle of somethin', some business stuff, but if I can help you with somethin'—"

"I'm sure he wouldn't mind sparing a minute or two for a neighborly visit."

"No, but—" Harlan was cut off as Ben shouldered him aside.

"I didn't think so." Solicitously Ben took Addie's elbow and drew her to his side. "George in his office, Harlan?"

"Yes, but—"

"Thank you."

Addie swallowed hard as they entered the cluttered office, unprepared for the tide of hate that swept over her as she saw Big George and Jeff sitting at a mahogany table. They rose to their feet as she walked in, Big George grunting with the effort of raising himself out of the chair. Jeff stared at her with unblinking blue eyes. How could they look her in the face after what they had done?

"Looks like we got visitors," Big George said, turning and indicating his chair with a meaty hand. "Have a seat, Miss Adeline?"

She shook her head, falling back a step closer to Ben.

"Seems you had quite a night, Ben," George continued, his mouth crinkling with the hint of a smile. "Lotta folks glad to see you still in one piece."

"Some more than others."

Big George chuckled. "You're a lucky man."

"Watts wasn't," Ben said, and let the silence draw out until the other man's smile had died away. "From what I saw, you can pour what's left of him into a teacup."

"What's that got to do with us?" Jeff burst out, and Ben smiled grimly.

"Please. Save the show for Sam Dary."

"Dary?" Big George repeated, his eyes narrowing. "Yeah, I'd 'spected he'd be over here this mornin'." He noticed his son's worried expression. "Don't fret, boy. Just a little lecturin' . . . that's all Dary can do."

"But I can do more than that," Ben said. "I can make life very uncomfortable for the Johnsons. And I intend to."

"You have no proof of anyth—"

"Proof would make it easier. But I can manage without it."

Big George's face reddened. "If you're talkin' about dirtyin' up the Johnson name, I'll land on you so hard—"

"You do a fine job of it on your own. The Johnson name's beginning to leave a bad taste in peoples' mouths, and I sure as hell don't expect it to improve."

"Worry about your own name," Jeff said fiercely. "Adeline sure as hell ain't gonna do well by it."

"Boy!" George snapped, but Jeff ignored him.

"Didn't she tell you how we settled on Watts as our man? She told me he'd do it. She named her own father's killer, all 'cause of his new will. Didn't you know that? No. You just don't know what kind of woman you're fixin' to marry, do you?"

Addie felt faint as she heard the words. "No," she gasped, turning away, and Ben caught her by the elbows. Addie quivered, her knees weak, and she gripped his arms for support.

Ben stared at Jeff over her head, his eyes chilling.

"Mention her name again and I'll spread you all over this ranch."

"Don't you believe me?" Jeff taunted. "She said Watts would do anything for money. She told him when and where to meet me, helped arrange it all. How did you think we got him so easy? Am I makin' this up, Adeline? Go on, tell him it's not true. I want to hear how easy it is for you to lie."

Addie couldn't make a sound. She knew she should deny the accusation to save her skin, but she couldn't.

"Addie?" Ben said, and she lifted her head slowly, frightened of the suspicion she would see in his face, knowing she couldn't deny him the truth if he asked it of her. Time seemed to stand still, and she was faced with two different pasts, wondering which one would claim her future. An eternal judgment was about to be pronounced, and although she was terrified to face it, there was no other choice.

Trembling, she looked up into Ben's eyes. She saw no suspicion, no condemnation, no questions. Only concern for her, and a flicker of tenderness. "I should have left you at home," he said quietly. "You shouldn't be exposed to this."

She nodded mutely, overwhelmed with relief. It was alright. He loved her enough not to believe it. He'd dismissed Jeff's words as so much trash. Ben slid his arm around her waist and looked at Big George, his mouth twisting sardonically.

"Eventually you'll do yourselves in. I just want you to know I'll do my best to make it as easy as possible for you." He paused casually, as if just remembering something. "And if you have any questions about the Sunrise Ranch and its policies now that Russ Warner is gone, be assured it will follow in the same traditions. Only you'll find I'm not as good-natured or forgiving as Russ was. I won't rest until the debt has been paid and you're on your knees. It might take some time, but I'll do it. The fence is going back up, this time for good, and I'm going to bleed every last drop from you until your ranch is bone dry and the cattle worn to skeletons. I'm going to ruin you, and one day you'll wish to God you hadn't taken Russ out and left me in charge.''

After that visit Ben seemed more at peace in his own mind about Russell's murder. He was not, as Addie had feared, consumed with the idea of revenge, although there was a certain gleam in his eyes whenever the Johnsons were mentioned. He walked with a lighter step now, as self-assured as ever, slower to anger, quicker to smile. The ranch seemed to be infused with new life, as if the sun had come out from behind a cloud. Addie was still the only one who dared argue with Ben or challenge him, and she did so as much as she pleased. In return he was remarkably possessive of her, claiming her time and attention with the matchless arrogance she scolded him for and secretly loved.

No part of his life was closed to her, including his work. Having elicited his promise to take her with him to Kansas City when he bought new shorthorn stock for Sunrise, she pored over his books on cattle breeding and transportation. When May overheard one of their business discussions and tried to upbraid Ben for it, he smiled and said he expected Addie to come up with ideas that would make the ranch a pile of money. The entire family, as well as most outsiders, shook their heads over Ben and Addie, who seemed to be developing one of the most extraordinary relationships the town had ever seen.

As for the two of them, they knew there was still much to find out about each other, more than could be discovered in a lifetime. Addie never failed to surprise Ben, even on their wedding night, when she began to cry as soon as he carried her over the threshold of her refurbished room. He sat down on the new double bed and cradled her in his arms, earnestly entreating her to tell him what was wrong.

"We're finally married," she said, mopping her face with his handkerchief. "I'm so happy and relieved . . . and overwhelmed."

Ben held her for a long time, his head bent down to hers as he pressed lingering kisses on her face, whispering his love to her. As she twined her arms around his neck, her body soft and warm against his, they were both shaken. They kissed hungrily, desperately aware of how long they had gone without making love. With fumbling haste they stripped their clothes off, and it was different from the gentle reunion they had expected, so savagely sweet to feel their naked bodies clasped together. Slowly Addie felt herself dissolve in an ocean of darkness in which there was nothing but his body, his hands, his mouth on hers. She matched his boldness, equally fierce, equally tender, until pleasure shuddered through her in a torrent that seemed to reshape her very soul.

In the aftermath she lay contentedly in his arms as he twirled a lock of her hair around his finger and brought it to his lips. "I used to dream about you making love to me," she whispered, and felt his soft laugh against her temple.

"Before we actually did?"

"Before I even met you. I didn't know your name, or even what you looked like."

Ben smiled lazily. "How do you know it was me?"

"Don't be silly. How could I mix you up with someone else?" She slid a hand over his chest to show him he was hers to touch whenever she wanted. Ben leaned over her, dark hair falling on his forehead as he lowered his mouth to her throat.

"Why don't you show me some of the things we did

in those dreams, Mrs. Hunter?'' he whispered, his lips wandering over her skin.

"It might take all night,'' Addie warned.

"I insist.''

And she laughed, wrapping her arms around him and kissing him passionately.

The train had come rumbling into the depot with a hiss of steam and a deafening whistle, exciting Leah to the point of speechlessness. Since no one in the family believed in long good-byes, they all tried to be brisk and cheerful. May was the first to move, kissing Cade and admonishing him to behave himself. She turned to Addie with glassy eyes, and hugged her.

"I'll miss you, Mama.'' Addie said, her throat aching. She breathed in the scent of vanilla and ducked her head against May's shoulder, not wanting to let her go.

"I'll be happier in North Carolina,'' May whispered. "I belong there, just like you belong here.''

Then May let go of her and turned to Ben, who took her hand and raised it to his lips in an odd and strangely appropriate gesture. She pressed his hand, the most affection she could bring herself to show him. "Take care of them,'' she said, and turned away, assisted by the conductor as she boarded the train.

Addie and Caroline held on to each other, both of them searching for something to say. Addie knew if she tried to make a sound, she would start bawling and wouldn't be able to stop. She would miss Caroline more than anyone, even May. Caroline finally cleared her throat and spoke in a tremulous voice.

"Be happy, Adeline. I will.''

Addie nodded, swallowing painfully as they let go of each other. She returned Peter's perfunctory hug, then looked down at Leah, whose solemn eyes seemed to read her thoughts. Addie picked up one of the little girl's perfect braids and smoothed an imaginary wisp of hair in place. She stared at the small face and wise gray eyes, and in a flash she was lost in a memory . . . curled up with Aunt Leah by the radio, shrieking with laughter at a comedy show. And then, striding into Leah's bedroom, making the older woman laugh by singing . . . *you're the cream in my coffee* . . . Strange, that what they'd once been to each other, they now would never. But Addie had memories. Maybe that was why it was so hard to let this Leah go, because of her memories of the other one. She knelt down and put her arms around the girl. "I love you, Leah," she said, and although she spoke to the child, she was remembering the woman. "You have a good trip."

All the good-byes were said and they boarded the train, leaving Addie, Cade, and Ben standing in the depot. Suddenly Addie knew she didn't want to watch the train pull away, and she turned to Ben with tears in her eyes and a question hovering on her lips. He smiled before she had to say a word, putting one arm around her and clapping a hand on Cade's shoulder.

"I've had a sudden inspiration," he said, breaking the solemn mood. "Let's go have lunch somewhere. And ice cream for dessert."

"Strawberry," Addie said immediately.

"Vanilla," Cade said at the same time, and they wasted no time in leaving the depot.

When they returned to the ranch it was late afternoon, and Addie flew into the kitchen to start dinner. She was elbow-deep in flour when Cade came whooping into the house to find her.

"Adeline! Adeline! Guess who I've been talkin' to. Guess who came back!"

"Who?"

"Diaz! He's out on the front porch right now, settin' there like always, gettin' ready to tell a few tall ones."

Distractedly she picked up a rag and wiped her hands on it. "Have you done your homework for tomorrow?"

"You're soundin' like Ma already," Cade said, immediately disgusted.

"Well, have you?"

He grinned crookedly. "Okay, okay, I'm gettin' to it."

As he disappeared upstairs, Addie walked out to the front porch. Just as Cade had said, Diaz was out there, half-reclining on the steps in his usual position.

"Mr. Diaz," she said, and as he started to move, she gestured for him to stay still. "No, please don't get up. I was thinking of joining you." He made a show of dusting off a step with his bandanna, and she sat down. "It's nice to see you here again, Mr. Diaz."

"I'm an old drifter, ma'am. No use fightin' against it."

"How long are you planning to stay?"

When he didn't reply, she smiled, realizing he never knew how long he would stay somewhere or when he would leave. Folding her hands in her lap, she looked out at the sky, which was streaked with pink and gold. "Nice sunset," she remarked, and he nodded. They were companionably silent for a few minutes, watching the sun dip closer to the horizon.

Diaz was the first to speak. "Damn shame about Mr. Warner."

Addie sighed and stared at the ground. "It's hard to forgive myself. I feel . . . responsible."

"How's that?"

"Remember that discussion we had once, about someone having a second chance? About miracles and being able to . . . go back and change things?"

Diaz nodded slowly.

"I had a second chance," she said, watching cautiously for his reaction. He didn't seem surprised or shocked. "You know, don't you? I don't know how or why, but you understand what happened to me the day I disappeared and came back."

"Yes, ma'am."

Was he a crazy old man for believing her? She wasn't sure. No one in his right mind should accept that she'd been transferred to the future and back. Certainly it was a secret she would always have to keep from Ben, who would think she'd gone out of her mind if she tried to tell him. But she knew Diaz understood, whether it was because of his age, his superstitious nature, innate wisdom or maybe even senility.

"I'm responsible for not having saved Russell," she said, unburdening herself further. "I knew about it beforehand. I should have been able to stop it."

"Maybe you weren't supposed to," Diaz said matter-of-factly. "Maybe you were just supposed to save yourself." He looked out to the open range and gestured to a ride in the distance. They could tell by the way he sat the horse that it was Ben. "Or him. Who's to say?"

Addie frowned thoughtfully. "It's something to think about." It was possible Diaz was right. She had changed Ben's destiny as well as her own. Her second chance had given them both a future. Maybe Russell's death had been inevitable, and *his* second chance would come in another time and place. Who was to say?

All at once she felt light, as if a burden had been lifted from her shoulders. Perhaps she should try to let go of the old Adeline Warner. She couldn't change what she'd been, but she could make the most of what she had now. Shading her eyes, she watched Ben's approaching figure, her heart beating faster. Nothing was as important as his love. Together they had made a new beginning, and life promised to be good for them.

Heedless of the old man watching, she stood up and ran to meet Ben.

He reined in the horse and dismounted, catching Addie around the waist and lifting her a few inches off the ground. Warm green eyes traveled over her face. "What's got you in such a hurry?" he asked, and kissed her before she could answer.

Addie laughed breathlessly as soon as her toes touched the ground. She looped her arms around his neck. "Dinner's going to be late. I hope you're not hungry."

"Of course I am," Ben said, lowering his head to kiss her again. "But only for you, darlin'."

table when all she wanted to do was throw herself at him and snuggle into his arms. Her throat loosened in relief. It seemed as if she had been holding her breath for hours. Her eyes moved over him as she tried to assure herself that he was all right, and she focused on the bloodstains on his shirt. She was shaken by sudden panic.

"Ben, there's blood—"

"One of the fence-cutters was killed," he interrupted, downing half a mug of coffee in one swallow. "Pete and I took the body to town. The sheriff seems to have taken our side in all of this, but the rest of the county is going to be hopping mad—"

"What the hell for?" Russell exploded. "You mean a man can't defend himself and his own property when he's bein' attacked?"

Ben shrugged as he regarded the other man. "You know what the general opinion about your fence is, Russ. On top of that, the first rule of the code is never shoot a man in the back, whether he's law-abiding or a damn horse thief. It just doesn't smell good."

"The rest of the county had better take a good whiff of it anyway," Russell fired back. "It'll help 'em understand what happens to anyone who lays a goddamn finger on my fence."

"Daddy," Addie broke in, "I know your pride is involved, but there are times when—"

"I'll be damned if I need to start takin' advice from my own daughter," Russell roared.

Addie closed her mouth, sensing the surprise that had flickered through the room, not at Russell's reaction but at her attempt to state an opinion. Disapproval was etched in every face but Ben's, and he was looking at Russell steadily.

"Russ, you know I'll back you no matter what you decide," Ben said, his face inscrutable. "But it's my position to make you aware of all your options." He slid a glance in the direction of the office and looked back at Russell with an arched brow. "Let's go have a drink, hmmn?"

Ben's persuasive tone and the welcome suggestion caused Russell's anger to fade magically. Without hesitation he nodded and preceded Ben out of the room. Ben gave Addie a reassuring glance before following. She felt better immediately, certain that he would prevent Russell from doing anything drastic.

"Peter, aren't you going with them?" Caroline prodded. "You're a member of the family, and—"

"They don't need me," her husband replied, yawning and standing up. "I'm going to bed."

Caro fell silent and followed him, leaving May and Addie alone in the kitchen.

Addie fidgeted with the sleeves of her robe before making a move to stand up. May stopped her with a single observation.

"Ben's treated more like a member of the family than Pete, isn't he?"

Addie wasn't sure what May was really asking. "I don't know what you mean. Peter's your son-in-law, while Ben's only—"

"Your father couldn't care less about what Pete has to say. He relies on Ben."

"Everyone does, to a certain extent."

"But especially your father. And you."

She was stunned by May's bluntness. "What do you—"

"Is Ben going to be my other son-in-law?" May asked, surprisingly resigned. "I saw the way he looked at you just now. You're two of a kind. I couldn't bear to admit it until now."

"Mama, maybe we should talk about this when you're not so tired."

"I want to hear it from you. It's worse suspectin'

288